CW00347481

'Suppose I cannot do what you want?'
'Then we'll do a smear job on you.'

The Smear Job was an intelligence coup which had been a year in the planning by Hunter. It revolved around a West German minister, an impoverished English Earl and an American Congressman and along the way involved card-sharps, drug-dealers and London gangsters. And the catalyst needed to make it all work was Callan, the Section's most efficient killer. But Callan was no longer with the Section – he was in business (mostly legitimate) with his only real friend, Lonely. Hunter had need of them both and when Hunter needs something he usually gets it, and so Callan embarks on a mission which takes him from Sicily to North America and then to an ambush on the deserted Suffolk coast, with violence stalking him at every stage.

James William Mitchell (1926–2002) was born in County Durham into what he described as "cheerful poverty" in the year of the General Strike, the son of a trade union activist father who went on to became Mayor of South Shields. After graduating from Oxford and qualifying as a teacher, he sampled a number of careers before finding his true vocation as a writer. His first novel was published in 1957 and over 30 more followed under his own name and the pen-names James Munro and Patrick O'McGuire. His greatest success though, came as a writer for television. After contributing scripts to The Avengers *and* The Troubleshooters, *he created the legendary anti-hero Callan in the television play* A Magnum for Schneider, *a character which went on to feature in the eponymous television series and film starring Edward Woodward. Writing as James Munro, Mitchell had already established a reputation for super-tough secret agents in his novels featuring John Craig, who was tipped as credible replacement for James Bond following the death of Ian Fleming in 1964. He was also to be responsible for another iconic figure in television drama, Jack Ford, the rogue hero of the BBC series* When the Boat Comes In.

**Also available from Ostara Publishing
By James Mitchell**

Callan

A Magnum for Schneider

Russian Roulette

Death and Bright Water

Bonfire Night

Callan Uncovered

Callan Uncovered 2

John Craig

The Innocent Bystanders

The Ron Hogget Mysteries

Sometimes You Could Die

Dead Ernest

Dying Day

SMEAR JOB

A CALLAN NOVEL

JAMES MITCHELL

Ostara Publishing

First published in 1975

Ostara Publishing Edition 2016

Copyright © James Mitchell 1975

ISBN 9781909619333

A CIP reference is available from the British Library

Printed and Bound in the United Kingdom

Ostara Publishing
13 King Coel Road
Colchester
CO3 9AG
www.ostarapublishing.co.uk

The Series Editor for Top Notch Thrillers is Mike Ripley, author of the award-winning 'Angel' comic thrillers, co-editor of the three *Fresh Blood* anthologies promoting new British crime writing and, for ten years, the crime fiction critic of the *Daily Telegraph*. He currently writes the 'Getting Away With Murder' column for the e-zine *Shots* on www.shotsmag.co.uk.

1

The dogs were not so dangerous as the panther, but they were more disgusting. Besides, she loved the panther, loved and feared, but the panther was not there, not this time; only the dogs: yellow-toothed, mangy, obscene with the obscenity of mediaeval demons: incubi that rubbed and touched her even as she ran across the harshness of the desert, seeking the panther that she loved and feared, calling out to him even: but there were only the dogs, mangy and obscene: touching—

The desert was hard to her feet, the heat hurt her body like a physical thing, pressing in on her, aching, so that she called out again to the panther, loving, fearing, begging him to make an end. But he would not come. Only the dogs tormented, the desert light hurt her eyes even though they were tight-shut. Brighter than a thousand suns she said aloud, but they were only words, and meaningless: not even true. The light on her eyelids was a small light, but it was cruel, too.

A man's voice said, 'Baby, baby,' and the dogs fell back, the desert landscape misted.

'Baby, come *on*,' the man's voice said, and she opened her eyes at last, and at once raised her arm to shield them from the room's one light bulb.

'Bad trip, baby?' the man's voice said, and she turned to look at him, knew him to be Wino.

'The light,' she said. 'Oh please, the light,' and he tilted the light bulb, left her face in shadow, then picked up the jug of wine beside him, poured wine into a jelly-glass, drank.

'There were demons,' she said.

'You should lay off that stuff,' Wino said.

'You can see them in the great cathedrals of France,' she said. 'Rouen and Chartres. Like incubi—but not like men. Like dogs.'

'You're killing yourself, baby,' he said, and drank.

'You too.'

'We've all got to go sometime.' There was satisfaction in his voice, even smugness. 'I better get you cleaned up.'

'I'm tired,' she said. 'Please let me rest a while.'

1

He sighed, and reached for the sheet that covered her, pulled it away, and the last of the desert-ache left her body.

'Oh that's good,' she said, and lay back, naked, not caring that his gaze showed only compassion as he looked at her, saw how thin she was: ribs and pelvic bones showing, noting too that the sweat had dried on her, that her body stank.

'Time for a shower,' he said.

'Please,' she said. 'Not yet.'

'You got a customer coming,' he said.

'I can't.'

He picked her up with impersonal gentleness; carried her to the shower.

'Baby, you must,' he said. 'This one's a *cash* customer.'

'I truly *can't*,' she said.

He bent to look at her, and she could smell the sourness of the wine on his breath.

'Baby, you must,' he said again. 'The trips you take—there ain't no free tickets. No way.'

As he propped her up in the shower, she was crying. He was used to that, too. It happened every time.

2

Mr Musgrave said, 'You'll take a drop of something?'

'Thank you,' said Callan, and Mr Musgrave unlocked a cabinet, poured whisky, replaced the bottle, and locked the cabinet again. Callan looked round at the office: nice, very nice. Axminster carpet and mahogany desk and chairs, and a half-size reproduction of Turner's 'Fighting Temeraire' on the wall. And his Scotch in a crystal glass. Very nice indeed.... But then, Mr Musgrave could afford it. He owned the biggest jeweller's shop in a ten-mile radius.... Callan asked for water with it, and looked again at the Axminster. A tiny strip of white paper protruded from one corner.... So Lonely hadn't been idle either.... He took the glass that Musgrave offered, raised it, and drank.

'Well now,' said Musgrave, 'I've examined your proposition very carefully, Mr Callan. Very carefully indeed.'

Callan thought: He's going to turn me down.

'The thing is,' said Musgrave, 'that so far I've found my existing security system effective—very effective.'

Callan said nothing. People who bought security usually wanted the hard, silent type, but Musgrave, it seemed, was anti-silence. It made him nervous.

'And you're not exactly cheap, are you?'

'Cheap?' Callan considered the word as if its meaning had momentarily escaped him. 'Oh, cheap. No, Mr Musgrave. We're not cheap. We can't be. We're the best.'

According to the salesman's manual, that handed it back to Musgrave. No prospect, the manual said, likes the inference that he can't afford the best. Musgrave apparently had not read the manual.

'Maybe,' he said, 'but so far as I'm concerned the best is what works. My present system works extremely well.' He watched as Callan sipped his whisky. Callan was certain Musgrave had regretted the measure he'd poured. Waste....

'I'm afraid,' said Musgrave, 'that under the circumstances—'

'You did agree to a demonstration,' said Callan.

'That won't be necessary,' said Musgrave. 'Of course I shall

3

pay your expenses—but I really haven't time for a demonstration.'
'You've already had one,' said Callan.
'That sales-talk of yours?' Musgrave said. 'I hardly think that—'
Callan said, 'You've been done, Mr Musgrave.'
Musgrave's eyes went at once to the picture.
'Nonsense,' he said.
'Why don't you open your safe and check?' Musgrave made no
move. 'If I'm wrong,' said Callan, 'I'll look a fool. I'm willing to
risk that.'
Musgrave liked that. He walked to the safe, and as he did so,
Callan picked up the scrap of white paper, and dropped it into
Musgrave's waste-paper basket. He had no doubt that the paper,
tiny as it was, would smell.... Musgrave pulled back the picture
to reveal a wall-safe: latest pattern, combination lock; wired for
alarms. The whole thing just as it should be. He looked
suspiciously at Callan, who obligingly turned his back while
Musgrave opened up.
'I'm afraid,' said Musgrave, 'that you do look a fool.'
Callan looked at the safe: rings, watches, necklaces, neatly
stacked.
'All there, Mr Musgrave?'
'Every item,' said Musgrave.
'Everything just like it was before?' Callan asked.
'Exactly,' said Musgrave, rummaging happily.
'Sure you haven't got something extra?'
But Musgrave had already found it, under a tray of rings. It was
a neat square of white pasteboard, and on it was written, in
italic, With Compliments. Callan's. Specialists in Security. Callan
was quite sure that the card would niff too—when Lonely did a
job everything he touched was niffy—but Musgrave was too dazed
to notice.
'We at Callan's,' Callan said, 'pride ourselves that our
demonstrations are unique.' He finished his whisky. 'Good day,
Mr Musgrave,' he said. 'There will be no bill for expenses.'
But Musgrave was already back at the liquor cabinet, fumbling
with the keys.
'Oh please, Mr Callan,' he said, 'stay and have another drink. I
believe I do need you after all.'
'We really are the best,' said Callan.
'My God,' said Mr Musgrave.

*

There he was, his silent partner, sitting in a corner of the bar,
watching the door and picking out dogs for White City at the

4

same time. Callan bought him a light and bitter and a small Scotch for himself, then went over to join him.

'Oh,' said Lonely. 'Cheers, Mr Callan. Went off all right, did it?'

'After you'd done your stuff,' said Callan.

'So long as you keep them bosses out of the way,' said Lonely, 'there isn't any problem.'

'Don't I always keep the bosses out of the way?' said Callan.

But Lonely was brooding.

'I could have got five grand for the stuff in that safe,' he said.

'You could have got five years an' all,' said Callan. 'This way you get five per cent of a contract that's worth three thousand quid—that's a hundred and fifty nicker your cut—and I've got another prospect lined up for tomorrow.'

'But I got to pay tax on it,' said Lonely.

'Well, of course you do,' said Callan. 'You've left the baddies and joined the goodies. Goodies always pay their taxes.'

Lonely sighed.

'Monotonous, innit?' he said. 'You set up the mugs and I do their gaffs—over and over—and I never thieve nothing.'

'The worst week we had,' said Callan, 'you made a hundred and twenty quid.'

'I know,' said Lonely, 'and I'm not ungrateful, Mr Callan.... Honest. It's just that I miss—well—the glamour.'

'The glamour?'

Callan sat back to look at him. Natty raincoat, pork pie hat, suit, shirt and tie all bought up West. Lonely had never had it so easy in his life—and he missed the glamour.

'Oh dear, oh dear,' said Callan. 'Glamour he wants. Did you like getting nicked then?'

Lonely said, 'There was good times an' all, Mr Callan. With you for a minder I couldn't go wrong.'

Good times, Callan thought. The feel of bone breaking under your hand, a Magnum 357 in your fist: the certain knowledge that you were the best there was until somewhere, sometime, you would meet somebody better, and when that happened you would die....

'We'll go on like we are,' he said, and Lonely knew that voice. The discussion was over.

'Just as you say, Mr Callan,' he said. 'We're doing all right.'

'Very nicely thank you,' said Callan.

'Going public are we?' said Lonely.

Callan looked at him again. Two surprises in one day.

'You what?' he said.

Lonely opened the paper. 'It's what you do when you make a lot of money,' he said kindly. 'Go public. Issue shares and that.

5

Nice that would be. Could I go on the board?'

Callan thought he'd better find more things for Lonely to do. He had far too much time for reading.

'You?' he said. 'And just what name would you use? Blimey, you've had enough aliases.'

'I been thinking about that,' said Lonely. 'I need a new one. How about Roger de Vere Bullivant?'

'Again?' said Callan.

'Roger de Vere Bullivant,' said Lonely. 'Classy that is.'

Callan gave in. 'All right,' he said. 'As soon as we make our first million.' He picked up his glass, and looked towards the door. The man in the doorway was smiling, but that smile had never reached his eyes. The handsome head made an abrupt, beckoning gesture, then the man walked out. Callan finished his drink and looked again at Lonely, once more pondering the imponderable: bleeding greyhounds never ran to form.

'I better be off,' said Callan.

'Can't I buy you one?' said Lonely.

'Paper-work,' said Callan. 'Never have a board to put you on, if I don't do the paper-work.'

'You won't forget, will you, Mr Callan?' said Lonely. 'Roger de Vere Bullivant. Want to write it down?'

Callan crushed down his laughter. Why hurt the little man's feelings?

'Don't worry, old son,' he said. 'I think I'll remember.'

The car at the kerbside was an Aston-Martin, and its nearside door opened as soon as Callan appeared.

'Get in,' said Meres, 'Charlie wants to see you.' He looked at the pub Callan had left. 'What dreadful places you drink in.'

There was nothing in that for Callan, and he let it lie. After all he could quarrel with Meres any time he wanted to. All they had to do was meet.... The car eased its way into a part of London Callan would never forget. Long streets of dark, decaying houses, garishly lit shops, dingy pubs, where the accent was as likely to be Irish or West Indian as cockney: and at the top of one street a school without pupils, half its windows boarded up, its yard strewn with clapped-out bangers, smashed lorries, worked-out vans, and on the wall a sign that read: C. Hunter Ltd. Dealer in Scrap Metal. Hunter. Charlie. His old boss. The head of Hunter's Section of British Intelligence.... The man at the entrance door had seen Callan hundreds of times, but even so he searched him, and the search was thorough—and therefore humiliating.

'He's clean,' the man said, but even so Meres gestured to Callan to precede him. When you worked for Charlie the only risks you took were unavoidable—if you wanted to survive. And Meres would

6

infinitely sooner be at Callan's back than have Callan at his—every time.

They walked up the stairs and along a corridor between deserted classrooms where men now worked on weapons, bugging devices, high-speed transmitters, to an ante-room where Liz sat, the perfect English rose, with every possible attribute of beauty except passion. It was a Section axiom that Liz owned two deep-freezes. She used the other one for sleeping in. She watched Callan walk towards her, looked at her watch and logged him in.

'Mr Hunter's expecting you,' she said.

Not even a hello, thought Callan. And certainly not: 'I've missed you.'

He kept on going—and Liz at once resumed her typing—and he reached the door labelled 'Headmaster', the only joke Hunter had ever made, knocked and went in, Meres still behind him.

And there Hunter was, in the only setting he could call home: Sheraton sofa-table for a desk, Aubusson carpet on the floor, and on one wall a little Degas of a dancer tying her slipper. He sat at the desk in a position that Callan remembered as typical, hands clasped lightly in front of him, an inch of glistening white cuff round each wrist, old, dark suit from Savile Row still exquisitely neat, the face long, aristocratic, clever, with eyes that told you nothing, nothing at all. But the clasped hands rested on a red file, and the red file meant that somebody was going to die.

'Wotcher, Charlie,' said Callan.

Hunter spoke to Meres. 'Thank you, Toby,' he said. 'You needn't wait.'

Callan turned fast enough to see the look of chagrin appear on Meres' face. He wiped it off quick enough, but it had been there. Callan was about to be in on something that he wasn't, and Meres couldn't stand it: he never could. He left.

'Sit down, David,' said Hunter. 'You're looking well.'

'Mustn't grumble,' said Callan, and Hunter winced. Callan being aggressively working-class had always upset him. It seemed that nothing had changed.

'You're doing quite well, I hear,' he said. 'Selling security. Rather neat, that. The poacher turned gamekeeper.'

'It has the charm of novelty too,' said Callan. 'It's legal.'

'Really?' said Hunter. 'I heard your sales methods were a little unorthodox.'

'The client always signs an indemnity first,' said Callan. 'Mind you, he doesn't know what he's signing for.'

'Cautious as ever,' said Hunter. 'I'm glad about that.'

He rose and poured drinks, dry sherry for himself, whisky for

7

Callan. That makes four in one day, thought Callan. I'm turning into a lush. But Hunter was pouring Chivas Regal, and he wasn't missing that.

'You've done rather well,' said Hunter. 'Supermarkets, jewellers, furriers. Even a merchant bank. Your odoriferous friend must have quite a talent.'

'You know he has,' said Callan. 'You've got a file on him.'

'But only, I think, when he works with you,' said Hunter. 'You have the happy knack of making him feel secure.'

Suddenly Callan could stand it no longer. Cat and mouse was a good enough game in its way, but these days even the mice learned karate.

'Why did you send for me, Hunter?' he said.

'Why do I ever send for you?' said Hunter. 'I have a job for you.'

Callan looked at the file on Hunter's desk.

'You want me to kill somebody?' he said. 'For God's sake, Hunter, I haven't even handled a gun for a year. Let Meres do it. He'll enjoy it.'

'My dear David,' said Hunter. 'Who said anything about a killing?'

'That's a red file on your desk.'

'I'm quite aware of it,' Hunter said. 'It's yours.'

Callan willed himself to sit still, show nothing.

'You left me,' Hunter said. 'There was an awkwardness, and I let you go. But you knew—I told you—that you were in a red file, and that the file would remain open as long as you lived.'

'You also told me that I'd be all right so long as I kept my nose clean.'

'Agreed,' said Hunter. 'But I don't think you have kept your nose clean. You've gone into partnership with a habitual criminal.'

'What, Lonely?' said Callan. 'Come off it, Hunter. He doesn't even know you exist.'

'But he might,' said Hunter, 'if you told him. He might even inform his criminal friends.'

'Lonely's criminal friends,' said Callan, 'are lucky if they make fifty quid for a hard night's thieving, and you know it. If they knew about you they'd have heart attacks.'

'And take their knowledge of me to the hospitals,' said Hunter. 'I'm sorry, David, but it just won't do.'

He moved the red file across the desk. Beneath it was a yellow file—surveillance only.

'This file,' said Hunter, 'is Lonely's. I'm rather worried about the colour. I want you to advise me whether he should be in a red file or not.'

'Well, of course he shouldn't,' said Callan. 'You know he—' Callan paused, then added: 'All right. Let's have it.'

8

'One of the many things that makes you so useful,' Hunter said, 'is that you think realistically. I want you and Lonely to do a job for me, David.'

'Why us?' said Callan.

'Because the two of you can do it better than anybody else. I wasn't exaggerating. With you beside him, Lonely is a thief of extraordinary ability. Almost a minor genius.'

Roger de Vere Bullivant, thought Callan. Minor genius.

'Bit of larceny, is it?' he said.

'In the main, yes,' said Hunter. 'I also want you to make a man lose money at cards. Rather a lot of money.'

'I'm no card player,' said Callan.

'Doubtless Lonely will find you somebody who is.'

'Yeah,' said Callan. 'He could do that.' He put down his glass and looked at Hunter. 'And if he doesn't he goes into a red file, I suppose?'

'He does,' said Hunter. 'A red file just like yours.'

Callan sighed, wearily. 'I knew it was too good to last,' he said. 'All right. Who do we rob?'

'The Earl of Hexham,' said Hunter.

'Well at least we'll be mixing with the cream,' said Callan.

'He has an estate in Sicily,' said Hunter. 'One of his ancestors was ambassador there—two centuries ago, when Sicily was virtually an independent state. Its king gave him rather a splendid house. I want you to burgle it.'

'And steal what?' said Callan.

'A book,' Hunter said.

'First folio Shakespeare? Gutenberg bible?'

Hunter looked at him in surprise. 'Where did you learn of such things?' he asked.

'Prison library,' said Callan. 'The poor man's university.'

'Of course,' said Hunter. 'No, it's nothing like that. What I'm after is a paper-back edition of *Das Kapital* in German. It was published in Dresden last year.'

'Along with about a hundred thousand others,' said Callan.

'A quarter of a million actually.'

'But you just happen to want this particular one.'

'Precisely,' said Hunter.

'And to get it I have to go all the way to Sicily and nick it from an English earl.'

'You and Lonely,' said Hunter.

Callan sighed. 'I suppose it would be a waste of breath to ask you why?' he said.

'It would indeed,' said Hunter. 'But I can give you an incentive.'

'That's nice,' said Callan. 'I could use an incentive.'

'If you and Lonely do this job for me, I'll pay you twenty thousand pounds—and Lonely will get ten thousand. If you can arrange the gambling loss I mentioned, you personally will receive another five thousand—all paid into a Swiss bank. And of course the Section will pay all your expenses. On top of that, both your files will be made inactive for a year from the day you finish the job.'

And if I don't, thought Callan, you'll have us both knocked off—and you'll let it be known—what was the French phrase?— *pour encourager les autres.*

'You're too good to me,' he said.

'No,' said Hunter. 'I'm not. I pay for value received, and only for that. And you know very well, David, in my contracts there is always a penalty clause. Fail me and you'll suffer for it. I promise you.'

'I've never failed you,' said Callan.

Hunter sipped his sherry. 'You've punished those who have,' he said.

'This geezer I'm going to take at cards,' said Callan. 'Is he in Sicily too?'

'In Taormina,' said Hunter. 'Near Hexham's place. His name is Gunther Kleist.'

'A German?' said Callan. 'What is this? An SSD operation?'

'So far as I know,' said Hunter, 'the East Germans are not involved.'

'Thank God for that,' said Callan, and meant it. The SSD, East Germany's security service, played very, very rough indeed. The less involved they were the better. All the same, that edition of *Das Kapital* had been printed in East Germany, even if it did belong to an earl.

'You're not in training,' said Hunter, 'and you haven't used a gun for a year. I think you'd better come back to us for a while, David. You need practice.'

'Why should I need a gun to go thieving?' said Callan.

'I think,' said Hunter, 'that with a gun you'll feel more secure. Come in tomorrow.'

'I see,' said Callan.

'Yes,' said Hunter. 'I rather think you do.'

10

3

Roger de Vere Bullivant was surprised to see him, and said so.
'I thought you had paper-work to do,' said Lonely.

Callan hung up his coat and looked around Lonely's gaff. In a changing world, this was immutable. Junk all over the place: World War One German helmets, fake art-nouveau inkstands, flags of all nations on the walls, Noddy clocks and naked lady lampstands and a stag's head. In the old days he would have thieved it: now he paid cash. But his passion for junk never varied.

'I've done it,' he said, and sniffed appreciatively. 'What's for supper?'

'Jugged hare,' said Lonely. 'Me Uncle Lenny was down in Sussex.'

Not only jugged, but poached as well, thought Callan. It wouldn't spoil the flavour.

He put a carrier-bag on the table, and Lonely delved inside, produced light ale and wine.

'Oh ta, Mr Callan,' he said. 'One thing I will say—you never come here empty-handed.'

And that's not all I've brought, thought Callan.

Aloud he said, 'You know I've been thinking—we've been grafting pretty hard lately.'

'Oh, I wouldn't say that,' said Lonely. 'I've been opening up one drum a week—two at the most.' He poured light ale. 'Why, I can remember the time I used to do three a night.'

'All the same,' said Callan, 'there's a lot of nervous strain.'

'Nah!' For once Lonely sounded almost contemptuous. 'No strain at all, Mr Callan. What we're doing's legal.'

'You and me,' said Callan, 'are executives. Right?'

'Right, Mr Callan.'

'And when we go public I'll be managing director, and you'll be a member of the board. Right?'

'Right,' said Lonely. 'And thanks very much, Mr Callan.'

11

'And what happens to executives?' said Callan.

Lonely concentrated. 'They get rich?' he said.

'Certainly,' said Callan, 'but getting rich is a strain. They overwork, they worry, they spend so much time making the gelt they forget how to enjoy themselves.'

'Blimey,' said Lonely. 'Do they?'

'Ulcers,' said Callan inexorably, 'heart-attacks, nervous breakdowns, premature death.'

'Oh my Gawd,' said Lonely.

'You want to end up like that?'

'No,' said Lonely. 'I don't. While I've got it I want to enjoy it.'

'Exactly,' said Callan, 'and that's just what we're going to do. You and me, old son, are going to have ourselves a holiday.'

At once the smell came: real, vintage Lonely.

'Oh gorblimey,' said Callan. 'What did you want to do that for?'

'You know I can't help it, Mr Callan,' said Lonely. 'And anyway, you know what happened last time we had a holiday. We ended up kidnapping a bird and you were duffing geezers and that.'

'And you made five thousand quid,' said Callan.

'Certainly I did,' said Lonely, 'and I'm not saying I'm not grateful. But if it's all the same to you, Mr Callan, I'd just as soon go on being an executive and take my chance on a heart-attack.'

Callan looked at him, the old, hard look that Lonely had almost forgotten.

'Mr Callan,' he said, and this time his voice was a wail, 'I'm no good when it comes to the physicals. You know I'm not.'

'Who wants you to be?' said Callan. 'All I said was we could do with a holiday.'

'This isn't a proper holiday,' Lonely said.

'Isn't it?'

For once in his life the little man achieved dignity.

'No,' he said. 'It's not. If you was going on a proper holiday, Mr Callan, you wouldn't take me.'

There was no way round that one.

'Sorry, old son,' said Callan. 'All right. It's a job.'

'Kidnapping a bird?'

'No,' said Callan. 'Thieving.'

'Big job?'

'Big place,' said Callan. 'But all we're after is a book.'

'Doing a library?'

Lonely sounded incredulous: he often did when Callan outlined the jobs Hunter wanted done.

'No. It's a house,' said Callan. 'A lord's house.'

Nobody was more English than Lonely. He dearly loved a lord.

12

Be a treat for him to go over a lord's house—even on an informal basis. And for a moment it was.

'Mayfair?' he asked, and his eyes lit up.

'No,' said Callan. 'Sicily.' The happiness died.

'But that's foreign,' said Lonely, and recalled an even greater enormity. 'And it's Mafia an' all.'

'What's taking a book off a lord got to do with the Mafia?'

'How do I know?' said Lonely. 'But them Mafia knows all the nobs these days. Film stars and that. You go annoying their mates and you get done.'

'Sea air,' said Callan, 'sunshine, Italian food. All expenses paid—and just one easy tickle. Not even a night's work. And I'll be your minder.'

'Mr Callan,' said Lonely, 'that Mafia'll kill you. They'll kill you *dead.*'

'There won't be any bloody Mafia,' said Callan, and wondered at once if he lied.

'And there won't be any danger either, I suppose?' said Lonely. 'Not much there won't. Not with you bossing the job. You never set up a job yet and somebody didn't get done.'

'It's never been you,' said Callan.

'Not so far,' said Lonely. 'And I'm not risking no first times. The answer's no, Mr Callan.'

He waited in terror for Callan to react, but all Callan did was pour him another beer.

'Got any whisky?' Callan asked. He'd had his quota for the day, but this was serious....

Lonely fetched the bottle and poured.

'Look,' said Callan. 'We been mates for years now, right?'

'Ever since the Scrubs,' said Lonely.

'And you've helped me and I've helped you,' said Callan. 'When the screws duffed me for fighting you patched me up, and when I got out I took care of the bloke who was going to carve you.'

'That git Rinty,' said Lonely. 'You been good to me, Mr Callan. I don't deny it. All I'm saying—'

'Don't say anything,' said Callan. 'Just let me finish. You helped me, old son, and I've helped you. That's the way it's been. Now I'm asking you to help me again. The geezer who set this up—' Callan searched for a suitable name—'he's known as Mr Big.'

'There you are,' said Lonely. 'What did I tell you? It's the Mafia.'

Callan's hand slammed on the table.

'It is not the bloody Mafia,' he said, and fought his way back to calm. 'Sorry, old son. Drink your beer.'

Lonely sucked at a tankard that had been cast in the shape of a skull. Alas, poor Yorick....

13

'He's English,' said Callan. 'And he's big. My God he's big. And he's got things on me, old son. I'm in no position to refuse him a favour.' And that at least was true. 'He wants this book. I don't know why and there's no point in asking. But I know what'll happen if I don't get it for him.'

'You'll get duffed?' said Lonely.

'If I'm lucky.'

Lonely shuddered. 'You couldn't, like, scarper?'

'Not from him,' said Callan. 'Nobody can hide from him.' And that also was true. 'I got to do it, old son, but I can't do it alone. I need help. Your help. Because when it comes to thieving you're a minor genius. But if you turn me down I'm done for.'

'This Mr Big,' said Lonely. 'Does he know about me?'

Callan lied, frankly and openly. 'No,' he said. 'Not a chance. He just told me to get myself a team. And you're the only one who can do it.' Lonely was softening. 'And after we've done it,' Callan added, 'there's ten thousand quid in it for you.'

'Ten thousand quid,' said Lonely, 'just for thieving a book?' He was appalled. 'Mr Callan—it *has* to be dangerous.'

'Maybe it will be,' said Callan. 'But I'll handle that end. Don't I always? But you turn me down and it's got to be dangerous. For me. Lonely, I'm begging you.'

'No!' The little man's voice was a yell. 'You mustn't do that, Mr Callan.'

Let Callan beg of him, just once, and Lonely knew that their whole relationship, the one permanent thing in his life, would be destroyed. He couldn't stand it.

'I'll do anything you want, Mr Callan,' he said.

'Thanks, old son,' said Callan. 'And don't worry. Nobody's going to hurt you.' And that was a promise.

Over dinner he told Lonely that he was going away for a while, and Lonely panicked again. Who was going to take care of the business?

'There's only Musgrave,' said Callan. 'The electrician'll put in the new alarm system.'

'But who'll be in charge?' said Lonely.

'You will,' said Callan. 'You're the executive.'

Lonely smiled. 'Roger de Vere Bullivant,' he said.

'Maybe not yet,' said Callan. 'But with ten thousand quid you're a damn sight nearer.'

He began to ask about card-players while Lonely, riding the crest of his euphoria, served the jugged hare. Card-players didn't make sense, but then nothing in Mr Callan's jobs made sense.

'I'll ask around,' he said. 'Most of the good ones is pricey.'

'Money no object,' said Callan. Lonely loved it. And the jugged

14

hare was delicious too, but when they got down to it, neither of them was hungry, though Callan finished the bottle of wine, and Lonely mopped up all the beer in the flat.

*

[ii]

'Craziest broad I ever met,' said Caulfield. 'Crazy like you wouldn't believe.'

His companion forced back a yawn and signalled for two more bourbon and water. Harry Caulfield on the subject of the women he had was the biggest bore in the city of New York—and you could throw in the state as well—but he was big in the automobile business—very big—and if you had accessories to push you just sat back and listened, and kept the drinks coming.

'Crazy how?' he asked.

'You name it,' Caulfield said. 'First off she's skinny—and usually that doesn't bother me because I don't like broads with too much meat on them—but this one's really skinny. She says food makes her sick. Can you beat that? And next she's an acid-head.'

For once his companion was impressed. 'While you were with her?'

'No,' said Caulfield. 'While I was there she just smoked a couple of joints. But she's an acid-head all right. Hell, my own son was on that stuff before he even went to UCLA. But, boy, could she perform! I was with her two days and I was exhausted, man. Exhausted.'

'She was a nymphomaniac?'

Caulfield pondered the question. It pleased him.

'Yeah,' he said. 'I guess she was. Hell, I never thought of that. What do you know?' He shook his head in self-congratulation. 'Old Harry Caulfield and a nympho. But that wasn't all.' He paused impressively. 'She talked.'

Oh sweet suffering Jesus, the other man thought. What do you think you're doing right now? 'Talked, Harry?'

'Yeah. You know. Like culture. French cathedrals and German poets and some painter called Kandinsky. The reason I remember I know a guy in Detroit he's got one of his. It was very educational.'

'You mean she talked while you were doing it?'

'All the time,' said Caulfield. 'This broad was wild.' He thought for a moment. There had been more, so much more, but it wasn't easy to find the words. 'Even her name,' he said.

'What about her name?'

'"You can call me Trudi," she said. "Trudi von Nichts. The von

15

is very important." You wouldn't believe what she did after that.'

The other man had just worked out that von Nichts meant of nothing.

'What did she do?' he asked.

'She burst out laughing,' said Caulfield. 'Right in the middle of what we were doing. And then this guy knocked at the door.'

The other man was now genuinely bewildered. Caulfield loved it.

'What guy?' he asked.

'The guy who looked after her, I guess. Looked like a drunk, but he had a lot of muscle. Are you all right? he says, and she says, Has he paid? And the drunk says sure. In that case, she says, we are both ecstatic—and believe me, Charlie, she sets out to prove it with the guy right there. There's no place like Vegas, believe me.'

'Vegas? Is that where it was?'

'Yeah,' said Caulfield. 'Downtown. One of those new developments in back of Fremont Street. Vegas. Oh boy, oh boy, oh boy.' He finished off his bourbon, and the other man signalled for refills.

'Now,' said Caulfield. 'About those prices you quoted me on air-conditioning units.'

He began to talk money, and he was fast, accurate, precise. He was also trying to rob Charlie blind, and both men knew it. Suddenly there was no more bourbon, no more locker-room camaraderie. When Caulfield left, Charlie had just, and only just, got his percentage. He sat in the dark, cool bar, sipping at the melted ice in his glass, listening to a looped tape of vintage Sinatra. 'Mean to me,' sang Francis Albert. 'Why must you be mean to me?'

'Good question,' said Charlie, and walked out on to 42nd Street: go-go bars, porn shops, blue movies, and a rising tide of garbage and trash. After what he'd just heard, it felt like sanity.

4

Lonely pondered the problem of where to stay while Mr Callan was away. No sense living in his own gaff on his tod: it would only make him nervous. The aunt who loved him was dead, and the aunt who didn't was just out of the nick, and by no means full of peace and goodwill towards Lonely. Cousin Alfred was all right in his way, but thick with it, and his kids were awful. Suddenly he remembered the hare. Maybe the best was his Uncle Lennie, if he was still in the right mood. Nice place Uncle Lennie had, and the grub was smashing. He considered taking a mini-cab to his uncle's place, but vetoed the idea at once. Uncle Lennie was all right, but it wouldn't do to let him get the idea his nephew had money.

He lived on the outskirts of North London, in a suburb that ten years ago had been a village, and still retained a hard core of village attitudes: general shop cum post-office, parish hall, and one surviving village pub, all restricted to the use of those who could remember when the village was a village. The good old days. Uncle Lennie lived in a house bang in the middle of the village that was, a mid-Victorian house that had been built as a rectory, and was overlooked by a hill with a ruined mill on its summit. The house was old and rambling and falling to pieces, but Uncle Lennie didn't mind. There were enough rooms still water-tight, and anyway he lived by himself: his wife had died years ago, and his son was a chartered accountant in Wolverhampton, his daughter had married a doctor in Westmorland. A big disappointment to him, Uncle Lennie's children. But he had his garden, four acres of it, with its fruit trees and currant-bushes, and inside the house were his seventeen deep-freezes. Doing all right, Uncle Lennie was.

Lonely walked from the Green Line, carrying his suitcase, then looked at his watch as he passed the Bird In Hand. Nearly four o'clock. Been shut for ages. Uncle Lennie never went anywhere except the Bird In Hand, unless he was off on one of his shooting

17

trips. Silly old git, thought Lonely. Why doesn't he get hisself a telephone? But he knew the answer to that one. Uncle Lennie didn't need a telephone. Everybody he wanted to talk to was in the Bird In Hand.... He looked at the house: a few more tiles off the roof, three more windows boarded up, but the brass door-knob was like yellow-gold in the summer sunshine, the path was weedless, the front garden neat. Lonely noted with relief that Uncle Lennie's car, a vast, elderly Rolls, was parked in the driveway: so Uncle Lennie was at home. As Lonely walked up the path he took another look at the car, parked in front of outbuildings that had once been stables. Old it was, no question, but the paintwork gleamed, the metal shone like it was ex-works. Lonely tugged at the antique bell-push and, as always, listened hard. But he'd never yet heard Uncle Lennie's footsteps, and he didn't now. Suddenly the massive door swung open, and there was Uncle Lennie, as small as Lonely, and as slight, but pushing sixty, brown all over, and hard as a nut.

'You got yours,' he said at once. 'I sent it to you Thursday.'

Lonely groped for, found enlightenment.

'Oh, the hare,' he said. 'Smashing it was. I just popped in to say thank you.'

Uncle Lennie's gaze shifted to Lonely's side.

'That must be some vote of thanks you've prepared,' he said, 'if you had to bring your bleeding suitcase with you.' He savoured the dismay on Lonely's face, then relented. 'All right,' he said. 'Find yourself a room.'

Gawd knows there's enough to choose from, thought Lonely, but he hefted his suitcase up the stairs, explored the rambling corridors. The first three rooms were all deep-freezes, but the fourth held a vast, brass-knobbed bed with a patchwork quilt and sheets that smelled of lavender. On the wall was an embroidered text that proclaimed 'God is not mocked', a relic of the days when the vicarage really was the vicarage. Lonely unpacked and went downstairs to the kitchen, the only downstairs room Uncle Lenny used: a vast, stone-flagged, low-ceilinged room that held seven deep-freezes, a fridge, a telly, and Uncle Lennie's hi-fi, and still seemed half-empty. He walked through the door and found himself looking down the barrel of a Mannlicher rifle. Uncle Lennie was cleaning his arsenal. Uncle Lennie took one look at Lonely's face and put the rifle down.

'Now, don't start,' he said hastily. 'I was only giving them a bit of a rub up.'

Beside the Mannlicher were two custom-made shotguns, Purdeys, and a Spanish job that had been sawn-off, stock and barrel, to eighteen inches in length.

18

'Have a drop o' wine,' Uncle Lennie said. 'Do you good.'

He poured two tots from a bottle labelled 'Saxby's Best Malt Vinegar', and handed one to Lonely. Cowslip, damson, gooseberry, dandelion, Uncle Lennie made them all. This one was parsnip, smooth and sweet and with a kick like a mule. Lonely sipped and felt better, and Uncle Lennie sniffed the air approvingly.

'That's it,' he said. 'Now tell me what the trouble is.'

'Trouble?' said Lonely, indignant. 'I'm going straight.'

Uncle Lennie regarded him with amazement not untinged by horror.

'You're never,' he said.

'Well, more or less,' said Lonely. 'I got one job on. Out foreign that is. Sicily.'

Uncle Lennie regarded his globe-trotting nephew.

'I got a letter from your Aunty Gertie just before she had her accident,' he said, 'and I took your Cousin Alfred his hare personal. They told me you was going mates with a heavy. Name of Callan. Alfred says you did a job out foreign for him last year. Over in Crete that was.' He paused, and Lonely knew he was remembering. Been everywhere, Uncle Lennie had: done everything: and he liked to remember.

'You been there then?' Lonely asked.

'Yeah,' said Uncle Lennie. 'In the Commandos. 1943 would it be? Rough it was. Didn't sound like your sort of place at all.'

'It wasn't,' said Lonely. 'Mind you, they have good beer for foreign.'

'I been to Sicily too,' said Uncle Lennie. 'Blew up an airfield. It went up a treat. Terrible beer in Sicily them days. You're better off at home, my son.'

'I can't,' said Lonely. 'Mr Callan's my mate.'

The hard little eyes looked into his, appraising, and Lonely willed himself to look back.

'Well well,' Uncle Lennie said. 'Well well well. Big stuff is he?'

Lonely's chest swelled. 'The biggest,' he said.

'And hard?'

'Hard all over,' said Lonely.

'And he's your mate?'

Uncle Lennie was not the first to be incredulous at this information, and Lonely had long since ceased to be offended.

'Sometimes I can't believe it neither.'

'So what you come here for?' Uncle Lennie asked. 'Bit of company?'

'That's it,' Lonely said.

Uncle Lennie rose and rummaged in the fridge, produced the two biggest T-bones Lonely had ever seen.

'Steak and chips for supper?' he said.
'Smashing,' said Lonely.

[ii]

Retrieving the hard, arrogant fitness he had once taken for granted was more difficult each time. Too much whisky, too many expense-account meals and last-minute taxis, and not nearly enough training. And he'd lost the desire for it too: the deliberate fashioning of body and mind into precision instruments whose only function was killing. The desire was dead, and once he thought the need was dead, too: but Hunter had resurrected the need: told him as plain as day that if Callan didn't do what he wanted, then Callan would be at risk, and so would Lonely.... Callan sweated it out in the gym, worked with the weights and medicine ball, showered, and went to face the unarmed combat instructor.

Hunter switched on the television monitor as Callan went into the shower. Beside Hunter sat Snell, the Section doctor and psychiatrist. The two men looked at Callan's naked body like two butchers assessing the marketing potential of a side of beef.

'He looks a little flabby,' said Hunter.

Snell said, 'Not grossly so. He could lose four pounds. A week should do it.'

'You saw him shoot this morning?'

'I did,' said Snell. 'Once he'd found his rhythm he was as good as ever.'

'Like riding a bicycle,' said Hunter. 'Once you've learned you never lose the knack.'

Callan dried himself, then put on a track suit and went into the unarmed combat gym. The camera monitors followed.

'But I'm still worried about his attitude to combat,' said Hunter.

The instructor threw Callan with a hip throw, and Callan's break fall was slow and clumsy, his retaliatory strike far too late.

'You have reason to be,' said Snell, and asked, 'Callan's going into danger?'

'Almost certainly,' said Hunter. 'Can you do something about this?'

Snell watched as the instructor threw Callan again. This time his fall was a disaster.

'Match him against Meres,' he said at last.

'Will it work, do you think?' Hunter asked.

'If it doesn't,' said Snell, 'nothing will.'

20

[iii]

The steaks were smashing, and there was beetroot wine to wash them down. Bit like port, Lonely thought, but with more body to it. Gooseberry fool to follow.

Over it, Lonely said, 'D'you ever know anybody who was good at cards, Uncle Lennie?'

'Fortune telling?'

'No,' said Lonely. 'Taking mugs.'

'In the circus you meet all sorts,' Uncle Lennie said. 'Three-card trick, pea and thimbles, all that lot. Educational in a way. Mind you, there was no sense getting into a game with them. Good times at the circus. I was a roustabout. Used to do a cowboy in the Wild West bit.' He drank more beetroot. 'What were we on about?'

'Blokes good with the cards,' said Lonely.

'Ah,' Uncle Lennie said. 'Would this be for your mate Callan?'

'That's right,' said Lonely.

'I'm sixty,' Uncle Lennie said. 'Sixty-one if I'm spared till November.'

Spared, thought Lonely. If they was all like you they'd need a machine-gun to start a cemetery.

'I've got a nice little business,' Uncle Lennie said, and added cautiously: 'Enough to keep me going, anyway. What I don't want is trouble.'

'No trouble for you,' Lonely said. 'Honest. All I want to know is if you know a good card player.'

'Well, you just make sure there's no trouble for me,' Uncle Lennie said.

'See this wet, see this dry, cross my heart and hope to die,' said Lonely, gesturing appropriately.

'You really want to help this mate of yours?' Lonely nodded, and Uncle Lennie sighed. 'The bloke you want is Bulky Berkeley,' he said. 'If this mate of yours is as good as you say he is—he'll know where to find him.' He finished off his wine. 'Let's go down the Bird In Hand.'

Uncle Lennie knew how to give you a nice evening, all right, Lonely thought. Steak and wine, and a few pints to top it off. Nice boozer, too: old and roomy, with beer still pulled from the wood, and a barmaid of mature charm with an ill-concealed passion for Uncle Lennie. Nice class of customer too. Farmers and haulage contractors and that, all with wallets stuffed to busting. Lonely calculated he could have lifted a hundred quid in ten minutes. But Uncle Lennie had told him ... told him straight. They were all his mates. Thought the world of him, they did. And

21

Uncle Lennie had a nice way of introducing him. 'This is my nephew. He's a business executive up west.' Went down well. The only thing was, he didn't like the darky drinking by hisself in the corner of the bar. Nothing against darkies—he'd known some could thieve as good as white men—but he shouldn't have worn a donkey-jacket in a pub like that. No class....

The bloke who took Uncle Lennie to one side was class all over: Mr Fish suit and a Longines watch and a dirty great Scotch on the rocks in his hand. Done bird, thought Lonely, and he didn't get that scar on his face tripping over no daffodils, but class.

'Let me buy you a drink,' he said.

'I'm with my nephew,' said Uncle Lennie, and the classy one bought two pints.

'I want to talk with you,' the classy one said.

'Talk then,' said Uncle Lennie.

'Your nephew is with you, is he?'

'Knows all about it,' Uncle Lennie said.

The classy one looked at Lonely, a hard, appraising look that would once have reduced him to terror, but all he thought was: Mr Callan could break you in two.

Uncle Lennie said, 'Spanner, this is Lonely, my nephew.'

'Bent, are you?' said Spanner.

'Yeah,' said Lonely. 'Same as you.'

It came out a croak, but it came out. Spanner chuckled. To Lonely it sounded like a sandpaper on cobble-stones.

'It takes one to know one,' he said, and turned to Uncle Lennie. 'I could do with some more steaks,' he said. 'Fillet, rump and porterhouse. Fifty-six pound of each. And pheasant soon as you can get them. Say fifty brace. Same price as last time?'

'Spanner,' Uncle Lennie said, 'where you been this last two months? Don't you know we got an economic crisis? Ten p. a pound on the steaks, twenty p. a brace on pheasant.'

'You bloody are the economic crisis,' said Spanner. 'I'll give you three on the steaks and ten on the pheasants.'

They settled at five and fifteen, as both had known from the beginning that they would. No handshakes, and to expect a contract would have been naive, but Lonely knew a deal had been made, and would be honoured. Uncle Lennie bought a round.

'By the way,' he said, 'you ever see Bulky Berkeley these days?'

'He's barred,' said Spanner. 'I won't let him in. Can't afford him.'

'You ever see him?'

'Sometimes,' said Spanner. 'What for?'

'I owe him a Christmas card.'

'In August?'

Uncle Lennie said, 'I'm a slow writer. Where is he, Spanner?'

'Chelsea Mansions,' said Spanner. 'Flat 5—if he's not working Nice or the QE2. What *is* this, Len?'

'What's what?' Uncle Lennie said. 'I never asked you nothing.'

'Oh,' said Spanner. 'Like that, is it?'

'Exactly like that,' said Uncle Lennie.

Spanner left them, and Lonely found that the negro had already gone. After that Lonely could enjoy the evening, even if he'd promised faithful he wouldn't lift no wallets. At least he didn't have to buy any drinks....

On the way home Lonely said, 'What's he do, that Spanner? Run a restaurant?'

'Clubs,' Uncle Lennie said. 'That's why I asked him about Bulky.'

'I'm very grateful, Uncle Lennie,' Lonely said. 'You think he'll keep his mouth shut?'

'Yeah,' said Uncle Lennie.

'Looked a hard geezer to me,' Lonely said.

'We got a business arrangement,' Uncle Lennie said. 'He'll stay stum.' He turned to Lonely. 'That coon looked a hard one an' all.'

'Too true,' said Lonely.

'I wonder,' said Uncle Lennie. 'D'you think he could have been following Spanner?' He stopped then, sniffed, and looked indignantly at his nephew.

'If you're going to start that game,' he said, 'the sooner you get back to your mate the better.'

*

Spencer Perceval FitzMaurice enjoyed sitting in a car at night, being driven, and enjoyed it even more when the driver was Meres. Meres never had, never could, overcome his repugnance at having a negro for a partner, and the big Barbadian loved it.

'Looked to me like a white folks' pub,' he said. 'Too rich for the coloured people's blood.'

'I should have gone in,' said Meres.

'That unfortunate little man with the personal freshness problem just might have seen you,' said FitzMaurice. 'Besides: I tossed. You lost. It wasn't even my coin.'

Meres concentrated on the Merc they were tailing. No sense in losing his temper now. The over-dressed lout had a driver who was both fast and accurate.

'Name of Spanner, the gentleman in the Mercedes,' said FitzMaurice. 'The BO king had another little runt with him. He called him Uncle Lennie.' He eased his massive body in the Aston-Martin's passenger seat.

'Amazing how puny the white folk are,' he said. 'And to think they call us the under-developed people.'

'Shut up, will you?' said Meres. 'Just shut up.'

The Merc made a left turn without signalling, and Meres only just held on, only just saw it make the next turn right.

'It is my opinion,' FitzMaurice said, 'that they're on to you, white boy. They are pros.'

Meres thought so too, but he held on anyway, and the Merc gave up at last, led them sedately to a street in North-West London that was mostly shops and bingo-halls and a one-storey neon-lit building with a neon-lit sign that said: Club Flamingo. The Merc turned into its car-park, and Meres kept on going, made a couple of turns, then pulled up by a telephone-box. For once both handset and directories were intact. He dialled. A voice said, 'Club Flamingo.'

'Put Spanner on,' he said.

'Who wants him?'

Meres hung up. As he went back to the car he was smiling. True, he had to drive FitzMaurice back to the Section, but tomorrow he was down to fight Callan, and Callan, so Hunter had thought, was past it. Meres thought so too.

5

Charlie Berman was doing all right: nice apartment, nice wife—
the one and only—and a son who'd got straight A's in physics
ever since the fifth-grade. Motor accessories wasn't a bad game
to be in either, even with the present price of oil, not if you'd got
in early with the kind of accessory that conserves gas. And as for
Harry Caulfield, every occupation has its hazards. You had to
learn to put up with them. What he couldn't put up with was his
wife's brother.... Dick Uhlmann taught sociology at NYC, and once
a month Sally Berman thought it would be a good idea to have
Dick and Dorothy over to dinner. Charlie Berman thought it was
a terrible idea, but he gave in to it. There were hazards in marriage,
as well as in occupations.

The trouble with Dick was he knew it all. He could put the US
right in an hour; any other country took twenty minutes. And
when he came to Charlie's house he drank Black Label, fast and
frequent. When you went to his place you got one jigger of bourbon
in an hour and a half. Mind you, he explained why ... Dick
explained everything.... Teachers' salaries, that was the reason.
Only capitalists like Charlie could afford Black Label. And roast
beef, Charlie thought, sniffing the smell from the kitchen. And
Christian Brothers Burgundy. He pulled the cork so viciously it
broke. Charlie Berman swore, and at once Sally came in from the
kitchen. It was like rubbing a magic lamp.

'Anything wrong, hon?' she asked.

'I bust the cork,' he said. 'Half of it's still in the bottle-neck.'

'Push it down and decant it.'

'Yeah,' said Charlie. 'The last time I did that I got a lecture on
something called oenophilia. Hell, I thought it was a blood disease.'

'Love of wine,' she said at once. 'Dick explained....'

'Yeah,' Charlie said dully. 'Dick always explains.'

'Honey,' she said, 'it's only once a month.'

'I know,' he said, and she kissed him, his arms came round
her. Marriage has its hazards, too.

She eased her hip into him. 'If you'd just do one thing for me, Charlie.'

'Any time,' he said, meaning it.

'Oh, you,' she said. 'Still they might leave early.'

'Not a chance,' said Charlie. 'I opened two bottles.'

'Just don't talk politics.'

'Me?' said Charlie. 'Talk politics? With him here? Once he comes through that door, I don't talk period.'

And it was true. Dick's wife, Dorothy, was dark and pretty, and the most silent woman Charlie had ever known. Never once did she interrupt her husband: never once. She'd been like that for years. Charlie had a private theory that she didn't even *listen* any more, didn't even hear him for Chrissake. A total defeat till you thought about it. Then maybe in its way it turned into a kind of victory....

Dick Uhlmann said, 'Charlie? I don't think you're listening.'

Charlie hated him most when his voice was roguish, but he sent up a barrage of apologies and excuses: tough day at the office, oil crisis, big decisions.

'I just made a big decision too,' said Uhlmann. 'I'll take another drink.'

Charlie got up and fixed him one, and Dick went on talking as he did so, but he kept his eye on Charlie as he tipped the bottle.

'You really should listen, Charlie,' he said. 'That way you might even begin to accept the one essential fact I've been telling you all these years.'

Charlie handed him his drink in silence. This sounded like it could turn into politics.

It was his wife who asked: 'What fact?'

'You see?' Uhlmann said. 'You don't listen either, sis. Charlie's problems are out-moded. Things of the past. Historical relics. Dinosaurs. This is the nineteen-seventies—don't you know that? And you're still consumer-orientated.'

And so are you, thought Charlie, when it comes to Black Label; oh boy, are you! Aloud he said, 'There's millions like me.'

'The dinosaur in its day was prolific too,' Uhlmann said. 'Then the environment changed—and goodbye, dinosaur. Now what you really want to worry about—'

And here it all comes again, thought Charlie. The changing needs of society: do your own thing; legalise abortion; legalise pot. He watched in awful fascination as his brother-in-law's mouth opened and shut, the voice droned on and on and on. Hell, he thought, the guy's even handsome. And he was too: big shoulders, frank blue eyes, big, white, even teeth.... Women's Lib, said Dick, and too much fuzz. The incipient threat of a Fascist state. The

26

happiness of the group: the uninhibited aspiration of the liberated soul. And then, inevitably, if only we were all twenty years younger. Anyone over the age of twenty could aspire to be no more than an Old Testament prophet: the new Messiahs were all in their teens.... Charlie fell from grace.

'Sex and drugs hunh?' he said. 'Is that the new religion?'

'Liberation,' said Uhlmann, and gulped at his drink.

'Well, I'll tell you,' said Charlie. 'If my son ever starts getting liberated, I'll de-liberate him with a whip.'

Sally Berman said, 'I think we'd better go into dinner.'

The thing was he still went on talking: the mobile lips sucked in soup, the big teeth bit into beef and potatoes, the wine in his glass disappeared, and he still went on and on and on. Charlie was well-meaning, sure, but he was a reactionary. If he didn't watch his step he'd wind up a Fascist, and it would be *too late*. There was such a thing, said Uhlmann the childless, as responsible parenthood. And what had Charlie to say about that? Uhlmann gulped at his wine, and Charlie waited, then filled his glass to the brim. This time he was really good and mad, and even Sally's warning glance couldn't stop him.

'You asked me,' he said, 'and I'm going to tell you. So you just drink your wine and listen. I met a guy the other day, and he told me about a girl. I don't know if she'll ever make a female Messiah— from what I hear she's three or four years too old to qualify—but she's sure as hell young enough to have parents living. And if she was mine and I knew about her I'd be breaking my heart. But she's liberated, Dick. Oh boy is she liberated.'

He told them about Trudi von Nichts. He told it well, and in detail, and maybe it was compassion that had given him such complete recall. By the time he had finished even Dorothy Uhlmann was listening: Sally was appalled.

'So that's why I won't buy it, Dick,' he said at last. 'If that's liberation I'm not ready for it. I hope to God I never will be.'

He'd finished, and Uhlmann knew it.

'A casualty,' he said at once. 'In any great movement there are always casualties. But that doesn't affect the movement's essential truths.'

Charlie's reply was monosyllabic: it was a word he'd rarely used since his service, and never before in front of his wife.

The party broke up, and the Bermans went to bed early, and were happy. Sally, it seemed, had at last learned certain truths about her brother, and her husband.... Next morning Dick Uhlmann phoned him at the office. That story Charlie had told last night, though in many respects a banal cliché of our times, might nevertheless be of interest to a class he'd recently taken over. He wondered if Charlie could let him have some notes....

[ii]

Even when you know you're a loser, it doesn't help when you're losing. Callan went to the mat with Meres and took the hiding of a life-time. Twice the instructor was moved to intervene, but Hunter's orders had been explicit: he just sat where he was and watched, as Callan was beaten, thrown, kicked about the gym, each throw, each blow, delivered with an exact precision. Meres had no desire to knock Callan unconscious: always he left him with enough strength, just enough, to get up again and take more punishment. Only towards the end did things get better: when Callan worked with the last tattered sheds of his strength, evaded Meres' fist strike and threw him, followed it up with a kick that sent him sprawling, waited till he got up and threw him again. But after each throw Meres got up grinning. There was all the time in the world.... Callan gathered himself again.

In Hunter's office, Hunter and Snell watched the fight on the monitor, and when Callan scored at last Hunter gave a grunt of satisfaction. It was Snell whose hand reached out, touched the bell push that signalled in the gym that the fight was over. They watched as Callan dived in again, the sound of the bell a meaningless noise, and knocked Meres flat with a fist-strike. This time the instructor did intervene, and immobilised Callan. It took quite a time....

'Weren't you a little premature, Snell?' Hunter asked.

'I don't think so.' Snell thought back to what he had just seen. 'There was a possibility—a very slight possibility that Callan might win.'

'But I want him to win,' said Hunter.

'Of course,' Snell said, 'but not against Meres, surely?'

'When *do* you want them to fight again?'

'I don't,' said Snell. 'Callan is hungry. I suggest you keep him that way. Every opponent he meets will be no more than a preparation for Meres. The "return bout", I believe it's called.' He rose. 'If I were you I shouldn't let it happen. One of them could quite easily die.'

'What an ingenious chap you are, to be sure,' said Hunter. 'I'm obliged to you, Snell.'

Snell ducked a bow, and left, and Hunter pressed his intercom buzzer. 'I'll see FitzMaurice now, Liz,' he said.

*

Callan showered again, and this time he made it a long one. Hot at first, to soothe the aches in his body, then cold enough to put some life back into him. But it would take time for the bruises Meres had inflicted to heal.... Meres had enjoyed himself all right. Had himself a ball. And he'd only given him two good ones back.... Callan winced as he reached out for the towel, began, cautiously, to dry his body. Meres had given him a right belting, and enjoyed every minute of it. Berk, Callan told himself, to let yourself get soft like that. Before he tackled Meres again he'd be as hard as he'd ever been. And then he remembered. Only the day before he'd been thinking that the desire for that hardness had gone, and the only need for it was Hunter's orders. But now it was different. Now he had Meres to think about. The need, the desire, were all his own.

He dressed, wincing at the pain he felt, and left the shower-room. In the corridor he met Meres, also showered and dressed. Meres wasn't limping, like Callan, but the bruise on his chin would be a cracker by evening. They met, and faced each other, the hate between them almost tangible.

'Well, old man,' said Meres, 'so you're past it at last?'

'I got you twice,' said Callan.

I'm talking like a kid he thought: Bang bang. I shot you dead.

'You cheated,' said Meres.

Callan said, 'It's the only way I win.'

Meres lunged at him again, and the instructor erupted from his office, smashed his way between them.

'Knock it off, gentlemen,' he said, and grabbed Meres' fist as he threw another punch, his fingers pressing between Meres' knuckles till he gasped with the pain.

'I've orders to put you both out if you don't,' he said. He was perhaps the one man in England who could do it. Meres pulled his fist free and walked out. The instructor turned to Callan.

'I'm ashamed of you, Mr Callan,' he said. 'Really I am. There was times I didn't know where to look.'

'I got soft,' said Callan. 'It won't happen again.'

'That's right, sir,' the instructor said and looked at his watch. 'You go off and get yourself a cup of tea. Work out in the gym in half an hour....'

[iii]

They'd meant to go down the pub next evening, but what with one thing and another they didn't bother. Uncle Lennie had made boiled silverside and Norfolk dumplings, and opened a bottle of the damson with it. Then they got to talking, and Uncle Lennie

29

was a treat to listen to: been everywhere, Uncle Lennie had, done everything. Deckhand on a banana boat, ghillie in Scotland, cowboy in Montana. All that and the circus and the Commandos and a spell as a welter-weight that hadn't lasted too long. Uncle Lennie had combined great promise with a total incomprehension of the Marquess of Queensberry's rules. But he'd done all right, Lonely thought. No question. And Lonely was going to do all right too, if he ever got back from bleeding Sicily ... Uncle Lennie topped up their glasses.

'Great days all of them,' Uncle Lennie said, 'but taking it by and large, my son, I reckon I'm better off as I am. You can't beat being your own man.'

And that's exactly what you are, thought Lonely. Making Spanner tell you what you want to know: copping sheep's eyes from that barmaid. Bristols like footballs she had, *and* hard blown.

'Your own man,' said Lonely wistfully. 'Sounds great, Uncle Lennie.'

'You can't beat it,' Uncle Lennie said. 'Now you sound more like you're that Callan's man.'

'Me and Mr Callan are mates,' Lonely said. 'You know—like partners.'

He broke off as Uncle Lennie walked to the cupboard, opened it, took out the sawn-off shot-gun and the rifle, and pushed the shot-gun at Lonely.

'Someone's breaking in,' he said softly, and the sound was less than a whisper. 'Take it, you twit. You don't suppose I'd give you one that's loaded.' But the Mannlicher was, and Lonely knew it.

Aloud, Uncle Lennie said, 'Your own man, my son, that's the way to be, but never take no hanky-panky from nobody.' He reached over and pulled back the shot-gun's hammers, then moved to the door.

'Say something,' the soft voice said.

'Yeah—well—yeah, I do see what you mean,' said Lonely, 'but somehow it isn't always that easy. The hanky-panky lark, I mean.'

He moved soundlessly across the stone-flagged floor, and stood in the angle that the door would make when it opened.

'You niff,' Uncle Lennie said softly, 'and I'll kill you.'

But the door was already opening: Lonely already niffing, and Spanner and the heavy he'd brought with him looked at the Mannlicher's barrel as it moved from one to the other.

'Come for your order, have you, Spanner?' Uncle Lennie said. 'Why didn't you try the door? I can still hear it—if you knock hard.'

The heavy grabbed for Uncle Lennie's rifle, and Uncle Lennie lunged, the barrel rammed into the heavy's stomach, and he doubled over, retching, as the rifle swung back on Spanner.

'Lucky I didn't have a bayonet on the end,' said Uncle Lennie genially. 'What can I do for you, Spanner?'

'Bit of a talk,' said Spanner.

'We'll have that all right,' said Uncle Lennie. 'Keep them covered, Lonely.'

Lonely stepped forward, his face twisted into a grimace of terror that Spanner mistook for blood-lust: the niff was indescribable, but Spanner mistook that, too, for a need to kill. He took a step backwards.

'Keep him off me,' he gasped. Uncle Lennie risked one look at Lonely.

'That's all right,' he said. 'Lonely won't hurt you—till I tell him to.'

Carefully he went over Spanner and his heavy, and produced nothing more lethal than the heavy's cosh.

'Now,' said Uncle Lennie, 'we'll all sit down and have a drink.'

The heavy, still groaning, uttered something crude.

Equably, Uncle Lennie said, 'I'll tell you something, son. For your own good. I'll tell you why my nephew's called Lonely. Over in Detroit, Michigan that was. When he ran with the mobs there. Put a sawn-off shot-gun in his hands and he behaved so disgusting even his own mates didn't want to know him.... And when he starts stinking like that it's because he needs to behave disgusting.... Sure you won't sit down?'

Spanner and the heavy seemed to find chairs by a process of levitation, and Lonely realised that these two large, strong men were afraid of him. It wouldn't last—nothing in Lonely's life lasted—but it had happened.

'You can put the gun down now,' Uncle Lennie said.

'No,' said Lonely. His voice came out a croak that Spanner and his mate once more took for blood-lust just, and only just, throttled back. 'I like it handy.'

He sat across the table from Spanner and the heavy, holding the gun in the manner approved in all the gangster pictures Lonely loved so much. Uncle Lennie opened a bottle of cowslip, and Lonely drank one-handed.

'I'm surprised at you, Spanner,' Uncle Lennie said. 'Busting in on us like that.'

'If it comes to that,' said Spanner, indignant, 'I'm surprised at you.'

Lonely put his glass down. 'Watch it,' he said.

Spanner said hastily, 'No offence meant, I'm sure. But what did you want to have me followed for last night?'

'Who followed you?' Uncle Lennie asked.

'You saying you don't know?'

Lonely and his sawn-off leaned forward. 'Uncle Lennie isn't saying anything,' he said, in that same, appalling croak. 'He's asking.'

'I didn't mean no harm,' said Spanner, and his voice was so exactly the voice that Lonely used in similar situations the whole thing tasted even better than the cowslip.

'It was a darky,' said Spanner. 'Big geezer. Hard. Six foot two. Thirteen-fourteen stone. He was in the pub. Left before we did. Him and his mate followed us in an Aston-Martin.'

'What mate?' said Uncle Lennie.

'White man,' said Spanner. 'I only saw him when we parked our car at the club. Looked a toff, but hard with it. Not a mug. Dark and good-looking, and a hell of a good driver, wouldn't you say, George?'

The heavy again uttered something uncouth, was made aware of Lonely's shot-gun and apologised immediately.

'And you say I hired these two to tail you back to your club?' Uncle Lennie said.

'Looks like it,' Spanner said.

'You great steaming berk,' said Uncle Lennie. 'Where would be the point in that? I know where your bloody club is.'

'I don't know what the point is,' said Spanner, 'but,' he glanced at the shot-gun, 'with respect, it seemed to me you were up to something.'

'All I'm up to,' said Uncle Lennie, 'is selling you steak and pheasant as and when available. Now, do you believe me or don't you?'

Lonely once again put down his glass.

'Oh we do, we do,' said Spanner. 'The only thing is, who else could have done it? I mean nobody else even knew we was meeting at the pub.'

'You're sure?' Uncle Lennie asked.

'Dead sure,' Spanner said. 'In my business I got to be.'

'I think you better go, Spanner,' Uncle Lennie said. 'Looks like you've got troubles I don't need.'

'Oh come on, Len,' said Spanner. 'Can't you think of anybody—'

Lonely said, 'Beat it,' and the two men rose at once, went to the door, and Lonely followed, saw them into their Mercedes, and went back to Uncle Lennie.

'If you're going to go on like that,' Uncle Lennie said, 'I'd better teach you how to use that thing. Now give it here.'

Reluctantly, Lonely yielded up the sawn-off.

'You—you think I could, Uncle Lennie?' he said. 'Use it I mean.'

'You may have to,' Uncle Lennie said. 'I don't like the sound of those two geezers tailing Spanner. I thought George was the best driver going.... You sure you never met that coon?'

'Positive,' said Lonely.

'How about that mate of yours?'

'Mr Callan knows all sorts of people I never heard of,' said Lonely.

Uncle Lennie sighed and picked up the sawn-off.

'Now listen carefully, Lonely,' he said. 'This here's the butt and these here are the barrels. You pull back the hammers like this, and load it in here....'

*

Spanner drove back to the club—George's stomach was too sore.

'I don't like it, George,' he said.

'Who would?' said George. 'If I ever catch that niffy geezer without his gun—'

'You never will,' said Spanner. 'That kind wears them in bed. Anyway I didn't mean that.... Sure we're not being tailed now?'

George looked round, and grunted as his stomach hurt.

'No,' he said at last. 'We're clean.'

Spanner drove on, thinking hard. 'Bulky Berkeley,' he said. 'I wonder.'

6

The week wasn't interminable, but it felt like it. Work-outs in the gym, unarmed combat instruction, session after session in the armoury, and a high protein diet as boring as it was nutritious. And no chance of another fight with Meres: not even a sight of him.... But the unarmed combat instructor reported that Callan was becoming a bit of a handful, the armourer that Callan was as good as ever he had been. At the end of the week Hunter consulted with Snell, and both men were satisfied. Hunter sent for Callan, and blinked in surprise when he came in. For a week Callan had been no more than a shadow on a TV monitor: to see him in the flesh was a surprise indeed. He'd lost weight, but all that was left was lethal, and the eyes had regained that quality he'd almost forgotten: that look of remorseless patience that had made Callan the best he'd ever had.

'Our health farm suits you,' said Hunter.

Callan said, 'When do I fight Meres again?'

'Be reasonable,' said Hunter. 'Meres is valuable. I can't afford to have him damaged.'

Callan grinned. 'Compliments?' he said. 'From you?'

'I *could* arrange for you to have a session with FitzMaurice,' said Hunter.

Callan remembered Spencer Perceval FitzMaurice. Jesus, he would never forget him. The Barbadian had given him a beating it was impossible to forget: a beating that was no more than a reminder that when Hunter gave you instructions you never, never forgot to carry them out.... To the letter.

'No,' said Callan. 'I don't think I'm ready for him yet.'

'FitzMaurice *is* available,' said Hunter, 'if he should be needed.'

'He's not,' said Callan, 'and you know he's not. I said we'd do the job.'

'Jolly good,' said Hunter. 'Now, about your briefing.'

He began to talk, and Callan sat back and listened. Yellow file stuff, surveillance only, all of it, and the Earl of Hexham was in a yellow file only because there was a book in his house: a book he mightn't even know was there. And even Kleist was only under

34

observation because he might have information to sell if he was skint. What kind of information, Callan gathered, was none of Callan's business. There were maps of the district, plans of Hexham's house, a plan of the hotel where Kleist was staying. Breakdown on Hexham: Eton, Christ Church, spell in the Coldstream, spell as a painter.... He'd been a very bad painter. Now he was in antiques. Thirty-four. Unmarried. Breakdown on Gunther Kleist. Dresden Gymnasium, star pupil—till 1943. Then a spell at Berlin Gymnasium. Star pupil again. Then the Wehrmacht. Six terrified months as a sixteen-year-old dodging the Ruskis. And after that he was a star pupil again, at what was left of Heidelberg University. Kunsthistorische, whatever that was. And after *that* he was an archivist Grade One for the German Civil Service. Age forty-seven. Widower. (Wife died of cancer, 1965.) No known children.... Callan put the files back on the desk.

'I lift the book and get this Kleist into a card game, and that's all?'

'That's all,' said Hunter.

'How much does he have to lose?'

'Ten thousand pounds should do it,' Hunter said. 'He's not a rich man.'

'Bad loser, is he?' Hunter looked puzzled. 'Nasty with it?'

'Oh,' said Hunter. 'No need to be nervous, David. You could break him with one hand.'

'I see,' said Callan. 'Let's talk about his lordship then. Bit of a tearaway, is he?'

'Certainly not.' From Hunter, this was outrage.

'Guard dogs round the house? Heavies with machine pistols?'

'It's adequately protected, no more,' said Hunter, 'and it's all in his file.' He looked hard at Callan. 'What is troubling you?'

'You are,' said Callan. 'Like always. Kleist's a pushover, right?' Hunter nodded. 'And the Hexham house is a nice, easy tickle for a couple of experts like Lonely and me?'

'With any luck, yes,' said Hunter. 'What *is* the matter, David?'

'All that unarmed combat's what's the matter,' said Callan. 'All that time in the armoury an' all. Why d'you have to resurrect a killer to play cards and thieve a book?'

'There is a possibility,' said Hunter, 'a very remote possibility ... that there will be ... complications.'

'Like the SSD?'

'I've already told you that the East Germans are not involved—to the best of my knowledge.'

'And how good's your knowledge?' Hunter shrugged. 'Who is involved then, the Mafia?'

'My dear David,' said Hunter, 'have you turned into a Romantic?'

35

'No,' said Callan, 'and neither have they. We're talking about Sicily. Who else is there?'

'Greed takes many forms,' Hunter said, 'and most of us succumb to it in one way or another. My own particular craving is for knowledge—no, that isn't so. Knowledge is a respectable word. What I crave is information, and I'm not alone in that craving. All my counterparts suffer from it too. I want that man ruined, and I want that book. It's your business to bring it to me—whatever the obstacles in your path. I trust I make myself clear?'

'Transparent,' said Callan. 'It looks like I'll be earning my money.'

'Now that you're fit,' said Hunter, 'you'll have every chance of collecting it.... By the by, you *are* leaving today?'

'You said tomorrow lunch-time,' said Callan.

'We're desperately over-crowded, David,' said Hunter. 'There'll be a desk for you here tomorrow if you wish to go through the files again, but if you wouldn't mind leaving us now—'

Callan shrugged. 'Of course,' he said.

'Just two things,' said Hunter. 'Snell is of the opinion that you drink too much. You will not do so while this job lasts.' Callan made no answer. It had been said, and that was enough. 'The other concerns Lonely. I take it you'll want to look him up?'

'Too true,' said Callan. 'He's going to find me a card-player.'

'I think you'll find he's at this address until tomorrow,' said Hunter, and handed Callan a sheet of paper. 'Curious how nervous he is. He always seeks company when you're not there.'

Callan looked at the paper.

'Oh,' he said. 'Uncle Lennie.' He rose. 'Right. See you tomorrow then.'

Hunter nodded. 'And set off as soon as possible. I'm in rather a hurry, David.'

Callan left, and Hunter pressed the inter-com buzzer.

'Mr Meres is in his room?' he asked.

'Yes, sir.'

'Make sure he stays there,' said Hunter, 'until Callan has gone.'

*

Callan used the company car, a 4.2 Daimler automatic. Lonely would have preferred a Bentley, but then Lonely was a snob, and anyway they hadn't gone public yet.... The fact that Hunter knew where Lonely was didn't bother Callan. Before a job like this, Hunter made sure he knew where everybody was.... A job like what? he wondered. Steal a book, cheat some poor geezer at cards.... 'I'm in rather a hurry, David.' We'll see about that, Callan

36

thought. Rush jobs can be murder. Your own, more likely than not. He'd seen it happen. Too often he'd seen it. Slow and easy was the way, and make sure you know who your enemy are, and where they are.... Uncle Lennie, he thought, and eased his way through the traffic. Bloke who hands out hares like cigarettes. Tough old geezer, according to Lonely, but like all the enormous clan of Lonely's relatives, determined that the little man should be protected. Must be nice to have relatives, thought Callan, and dismissed the idea at once. Relatives like that meant love, and love meant vulnerability.... He reached the vicarage at last and thought, Blimey, the House of Usher, then prised up a knocker that was a half-scale replica of the one on Durham Cathedral. He let it fall, and the massive door shuddered, but nobody answered, and Callan waited in the car, until at last an elderly Rolls waddled into the vicarage driveway, and a tough little runt got out carrying a shotgun, then Lonely got out of the passenger side. Incredibly, he was carrying a shotgun too, and even more incredibly, he was carrying it correctly.

*

Uncle Lennie handed him a glass of the beetroot, and Callan sipped, cautiously. It had a kick to it like an old Lee-Enfield.

'So you're this mate Lonely's always on about,' Uncle Lennie said.

'That's right.'

Callan looked at Lonely; he was cleaning his shotgun.

'I hit a rabbit,' Lonely said. 'Third shot I ever fired and I hit it.'

Callan said, 'You go on like this and you won't need a minder.'

Lonely looked up then, alarmed, wary, but Mr Callan was grinning. Uncle Lennie wasn't.

'You could be right,' he said. 'We had a bloke with a minder come round to see us last night. Name of Spanner. Ever heard of him?' Callan shook his head. 'Came round to be nasty, the pair of them, but Lonely frightened them off.'

'Lonely?' The incredulity in Callan's voice was obvious, but Lonely was too busy smirking to notice. Uncle Lennie rummaged in the cupboard, produced the sawn-off.

'Frightened them with this,' Uncle Lennie said. 'Mind you, it wasn't loaded.'

'Nasty,' said Callan. 'Very nasty.'

For once Uncle Lennie looked defensive.

'It's not for using on people,' he said. 'There's nothing like it for pheasant if you can get up close enough. See for yourself.'

He threw the gun to Callan, his beady little eyes watched as

Callan caught it, broke it open, checked the action of hammers and triggers, one, two, three, smooth and sure, then snapped it together again. He thought: Lonely wasn't kidding. This geezer's good. Callan looked back with a stare as hard and unwinking as his own, then nodded at Lonely, jerked his head in a dismissive gesture.

'Lonely,' Uncle Lennie said, 'slip upstairs and fetch me another bottle of beetroot. And don't come back without it. Jump, my son.' Lonely jumped.

'Why do I worry you?' said Callan.

'Who says you—'

'Don't waste time,' said Callan. 'He'll be back any minute.'

'He'll have a job,' Uncle Lennie said. 'All the beetroot's down here.' He refilled his glass. 'All right. You worry me. On account of Lonely. He's told me a bit about you. His Aunty Gertie wrote me about you an' all. You're not for him, mister. Leave him alone.'

One thing about Lonely's relatives: they all sang the same tune.

'He took care of this Spanner for you.'

'No,' Uncle Lennie said. 'I did that. With a Mannlicher.'

Callan looked at the little man, perky as a sparrow, and twice as cocky. I believe you, he thought. And I bet the Mannlicher *was* loaded.

'Lonely was just a bit of a giggle,' Uncle Lennie said. 'Good for his morale an' all. Spanner read him wrong, see?' He smiled. 'It did Spanner good—taking liberties like that. But you won't do Lonely good.'

'I need him,' said Callan.

Uncle Lennie looked at the Mannlicher on its brackets above the fireplace. 'I could stop you,' he said.

'No,' said Callan. 'You couldn't. You'd never reach the rifle.'

'Hard stuff,' Uncle Lennie said. 'The second time in twenty-four hours. And in me own house. Drinking my wine, too.'

'It's good wine,' said Callan.

'Have some more.'

'Not when I'm working.' Uncle Lennie sighed, and Callan said: 'He can't go on as he is. Nobody lives for ever—not even you. He'll have to learn to stand on his own feet some time.'

'You're talking like a probation officer,' Uncle Lennie said. 'But you're taking him into danger.'

'Who told you?'

'He did,' Uncle Lennie said. 'And don't ask me how he knows. He just does.'

'I do big jobs,' said Callan.

'I believe you.'

'With big jobs there's always danger—but I don't let him get hurt.'

'I believe that an' all,' Uncle Lennie said, 'but one day it'll happen and you won't be able to do a thing about it.'

Callan said again, 'I need him,' and heard himself adding, 'I'm sorry.'

'You need him,' Uncle Lennie said. 'You say it like it was a magic spell—and it bloody is. It works. Take him then. I'm too old to stop you.'

'This Spanner,' said Callan. 'A hard boy?'

'Average,' Uncle Lennie said. 'Not like you. Runs a few gaming-clubs. I do a bit of business with him.'

'Gaming?' said Callan, and Uncle Lennie chuckled maliciously.

'That's right. You're after a card player, aren't you? Lonely asked me if I knew one, and I recommended Bulky Berkeley. Best there is, old Bulk. Only I didn't have his address and I asked Spanner, see? In the Bird In Hand that was, two nights back. And Spanner reckons he was followed by a bloody great coon and a hard-looking toff in an Aston-Martin.'

Callan's face told him nothing at all, but Uncle Lennie knew he'd scored.

'Bothers you, does it?' he said.

'No,' said Callan. 'They sound like mates of mine.'

Uncle Lennie said, 'Poor old Lonely.'

From the top of the stairs Lonely yelled, 'Will parsnip do?'

'No, it bloody won't,' said Uncle Lennie. 'Come down here. Your mate's waiting—I'll find it meself.'

Lonely came in with the scuttling motion that was all his own.

'We off then, Mr Callan?' he asked.

Callan rose. 'Work to do, old son,' he said, and Lonely seemed to shrink.

'Your mate's going to make a man of you,' said Uncle Lennie. 'I wish I could stop him, my son, but I can't. I'm passed it.'

7

Chelsea Mansions was locked, but Lonely obliged with a strip of thick plastic, and Callan sent him back to wait in the Daimler, then stepped into the elderly but thickly-carpeted lift. Chelsea Mansions, Lonely had told him, was class, and Lonely knew. He'd done a couple of flats there three or four years back. And Callan could see what he meant. Warm corridors, mahogany doors, crystal lamp-shades: only the cream lived in Chelsea Mansions, and that applied to Bulky Berkeley too. When it came to manipulating cards, Bulky *was* the cream. Callan knocked at his door: no answer. Callan knocked again, the sustained, inexorable knock that only one profession ever dares to use.... And Bulky opened up.

At least, thought Callan, it looks like Berkeley, the way Uncle Lennie described him. Nothing was said about twin brothers. A fat and comfortable man, with a round and innocent face that would have made Mr Pickwick's look shifty. Round blue eyes, slightly protuberant, a little button of a nose, small, smiling mouth—and a round head, its dome bald as an egg, but with curling tufts of silver hair at the sides. The body too was rounded, the paunch ample, the pudgy hands well-manicured, scrubbed clean. But the guileless blue eyes were sharp enough: the well-padded body mightn't all be fat.

'Yes?' Berkeley said. 'What is it?' The voice was a rich, soft baritone: mellifluous as an archbishop's performing a royal wedding.

'Mr Berkeley?' said Callan. 'Might I have a word with you, sir?'

'I don't think so,' Berkeley said. 'I don't know you.'

Callan sighed the patient, professional sigh of the man who's played the same scene a thousand times.

'All right,' he said loudly. 'If you really want your neighbours to hear—' His hand moved inside his coat. It was a gesture Berkeley knew only too well.... 'I am Detective Inspector Thing and this is my warrant card. Bertram Alphonso Berkeley, alias Alistair Innes-

40

Moncrieff, alias Sir Albert Ramsbothome, I have reason to believe....'

'All right,' said Berkeley, 'you can come in. But please wipe your feet.'

Callan released the butt of the 357 Magnum under his coat, wiped his feet, and walked into Berkeley's flat. Nice it was. Very nice. English brown furniture in the hall, 1770-1830 most of it, including a couple of Hepplewhite chairs even Hunter would have welcomed; then on through to a study: heavy Edwardian desk, rose-wood bookshelves, and a set of stuffed leather chairs that reminded Callan of Hunter's club.

'I really can't think why you come badgering me at this time of night,' Berkeley said. 'Really, Inspector—' he paused. 'It is Inspector, isn't it?'

'No,' said Callan.

'I realise the force is undermanned these days,' said Berkeley, 'but I should doubt of your being a superintendent.' His voice became indignant. 'You're not a sergeant, are you?'

'Now did I say I was Old Bill?' said Callan.

'Old Bill? Oh, the constabulary, I believe. No, you didn't.' Berkeley sat in the chair behind the desk. 'Do sit down and tell me *who* you are then.' Callan sat, and Berkeley stretched out his legs, wriggling into comfort.

Callan said, 'Let me show you my card,' and reached again inside his jacket, and this time produced the 357 Magnum. The barrel's unwinking eye stared at the centre of Berkeley's forehead.

'You pressed an alarm, didn't you, Mr Berkeley?' Callan said. 'Now that's not nice, really it isn't. It shows a lack of trust.'

'My dear sir,' said Berkeley, 'I assure you in all sincerity—'

Callan got up and crossed to the desk, let the Magnum's muzzle rest on Berkeley's forehead.

'There's a geezer at the door,' he said softly. 'If he starts anything you'll die. If I was you, Bulky, I'd tell him to go away.'

'Fred,' Berkeley called, and considering everything his voice was remarkably well controlled. 'Is that you?'

'Yeah,' a hoarse voice answered. 'I was having me bath. You said I could have me bath. Then you went and rang.'

'I'm entertaining a friend,' said Berkeley. 'We would like some coffee.'

'Awright,' the hoarse voice said. 'Me bath'll be cold, anyway.'

'Really,' Berkeley said. 'The service one gets nowadays.'

'Why the coffee?' said Callan.

'I had to ask for something,' Berkeley said. 'Fred's very suspicious.'

Callan tilted the Magnum's barrel, let it fall lightly back on Berkeley's forehead.

'I can understand that,' he said. 'So am I.'

'I don't keep my money here, you know,' said Berkeley.

'Pity,' said Callan. 'But your furniture's worth a few bob.'

'Are you asking me to believe you brought a pantechnicon?'

That from a man with a gun-barrel between his eyes, thought Callan. I've come to the right shop. He put the gun back, and the movement was so sure, so quick, that Berkeley blinked.

'When the coffee comes,' Callan said, 'you take it at the door. I'm the shy type.'

'Very well,' said Berkeley. 'But I wish you'd tell me what this is all about.'

'You're going to do a job for me,' said Callan.

'I,' said Berkeley, 'am self-employed.'

'Not while you're working for me,' said Callan. 'We're going to take a trip; then we're going to fleece a mug. Shouldn't take more than a week—and you're on five thousand quid.'

'What do you mean—fleece a mug?'

'Hand of cards,' said Callan. 'Poker's his game. He *thinks* he's good. You know you're good.'

'I don't know you,' Berkeley said. 'Don't know you from Adam.'

'That's your good luck,' said Callan, and for the first time the baby-pink cheeks turned pale.

'Then why should I do it?'

'Because if you don't,' Callan said, 'you'll die.'

There was a tap at the door, and Callan's Magnum was once more in his hand. Bulky got up, and came back with a coffee tray: two cups of Sèvres china, very nice, a Georgian silver cream jug and sugar basin. Berkeley put the tray on the desk, picked up the nearest cup and said, 'I like mine black but help yourself.' He sipped.

Callan said, 'I'll let mine cool a little.... You know, Bulky, I'm finding this a bit difficult. I came here to scare you, and you're acting like a man who won't be scared.'

'Who told you my name?' Bulky asked.

'You see?' said Callan. 'Rule One is never ask questions. You just broke it.'

Berkeley drank his coffee, put down the empty cup, and Callan put cream and sugar into his.

'Maybe you have to be shown,' he said. 'I hope not for your sake; but maybe you're that kind. Try not to be, Bulky. It'll hurt you more than it'll hurt me.'

Berkeley said, 'I never work with people I don't know.'

'Yeah,' said Callan. 'But I'm the exception. Have another cup of coffee.' He rose.

'That's yours,' said Bulky.

'I know,' said Callan. 'But I'm feeling generous tonight. You have it.'

This time the Magnum's muzzle came down hard enough to hurt. Berkeley reached for the cup.

'Down the hatch,' said Callan. 'Bottoms up,' and Bulky swallowed.

Whatever it was, it worked fast. In seconds Bulky's eyes had the glazed look of a three-day drunk's.

'Pity,' said Callan. 'I did give you a choice. It's like my old sergeant-major used to say. There's two ways to do a thing—the hard way and the easy way. The easy way ain't easy and the hard way's ruddy hard. Now then.' But Bulky wasn't listening: he was asleep. Callan put his weight on the chair, tilted and pulled, and Bulky fell with a soft thud into the thick-pile carpet, as Callan moved to the angle of the door.

Outside the hoarse voice said, 'Mr Berkeley? ... Mr Berkeley?' then the door opened and hoarse-voice came in, moved at once to where Bulky lay. Let that be a lesson to you, Bulky, thought Callan. Never buy a minder on the cheap: and clipped hoarse-voice behind the ear....

Outside Lonely waited in the Daimler, and wondered how Mr Callan was getting on with that Berkeley. Not that he was worried. When Mr Callan got that look in his eye, most geezers fell over themselves to get on with him.... Nice it was, sitting in a Daimler. One executive waiting for another. Only trouble was he'd run out of snout. Maybe he'd left a packet of ciggies in the glove-box.

In the Merc parked farther back, two men watched Lonely lean forward.

George said, 'I think he's on to us, Spanner.'

Spanner said, 'Don't talk wet. How could he be?'

George said, 'He's opening up the glove box. Those Daimlers have big ones.'

'Big enough for—?'

From where George sat he could see the long, thin strip of metal in Lonely's hands.

'Yes,' he said. 'Oh my Gawd yes.'

He turned the key and the Merc shot off, screaming down the street and not a light showing. Barmy, Lonely thought. Stone barmy. Come to that a glove compartment was a bloody silly place for Mr Callan to put a tyre lever.

[ii]

Wino said, 'A good one, hunh?'

'The best,' she said.

He began to sponge her down, and the water was cool, relaxing: carried with it a memory of the trip she had made. Bartok's violin concerto, she remembered, a cascading torrent of music that was in her eyes as well as in her ears: shapes and sounds inextricably co-mingled, perfect shape, absolute sound, and in the centre of it, black on crimson, the panther waited, velvet-pawed, and in the slow movement he—the darling—breath honey-sweet, great eyes not glittering for once, but cool, serene—found her at last. That was freedom. That was fulfilment. Nothing but the panther, the cool, untroubled eyes. Even the music had faded....

'You talked a lot,' said Wino.

'What about?'

He shrugged. 'You didn't talk English,' he said. 'My guess is it was Kraut. Sounded good. Like you were happy.'

'I was happy,' she said. 'So happy.'

He didn't tell her he'd taped it. Any kind of bugging device made her nervous, even a tape-recorder. But he'd enjoyed the sweetness, the sensual content in her voice. That was music if you like: not like the crazy sounds she'd got from the hi-fi.

'I wish you could remember *some* of it,' she said.

He drank from the jelly-glass.

'There was one word,' he said. *'Kunst* something. Over and over.'

'Kunsthistorische?'

'Hey,' he said. 'That's it. What's it mean?'

'Nothing,' she said. 'Not any more. But it used to be fun.'

He got up and pulled open the drapes from the windows, and as always she winced.

He looked across the patio with the little fountain he'd been going to fix for how long? Six months, was it? A year? Across the street two kids were playing astronauts. By the sounds they were making they'd just blown up the world. And down below Las Vegas was still at it, the way it always was; cars hustling in down town from the airport, neon signs gleaming. If you listened real hard, he thought, maybe you could hear the rivet-hammer crash of a hundred thousand fruit machines.

'We ought to leave this place,' he said.

'Why should we?' she asked. 'It's warm.'

And that was the only part of reality that could still get through to her: the cold.

'It's killing you,' he said.

In the last vestiges of the trip, the panther stirred.

'No,' she said. 'I'm doing that.'

He emptied his glass; put it down.

'I better get cleaned up,' he said.

'You're going out?'

'I got to hustle for you, baby,' he said. 'Acid costs money.'

'I like talking with you,' she said. 'Honestly I do. Even if our conversations always end the same way.'

[iii]

Bulky too came back to reality. His head hurt, and the light was far too strong.

'Bad trip?' said Callan.

'Fred,' Bulky said. 'Fred.'

'Fred left,' said Callan. 'He doesn't like it here.'

He altered the position of a standard lamp, and the light burned in Bulky's eyes.

'If I were you I'd get up,' Callan said. 'You're the wrong shape for lying on rugs.'

'Help me,' said Bulky.

'No,' said Callan. 'A man has to do what a man has to do.'

Somehow Bulky got himself to his feet, righted his chair, and sat. For a fat man he moved with a neatness that was almost elegant, even then. Automatically he straightened his tie, smoothed the flying wings of hair on the sides of his head.

'Fancy a cup of coffee?' Callan asked.

Bulky groaned again. 'One day,' he said. 'One day.'

'You're being foolish,' said Callan. 'Aren't you being foolish?'

Bulky closed his eyes, and the Magnum barrel tapped at his forehead.

'Answer your old mate,' said Callan.

'I'm being foolish,' said Bulky.

'Why? And look at me when I'm talking.'

Bulky opened his eyes: looked into Callan's. Beyond compassion, beyond pity, he thought. Perhaps beyond even fear.

'I tried to beat you,' he said, 'and I can't.'

'There's another reason too,' Callan said. 'Think, Bulky.'

But Bulky couldn't think, not till the Magnum moved in Callan's hand: then it came out a yell. 'Five thousand pounds,' he said.

'Tax free,' said Callan. 'Now.... Here's what you have to do to earn it.' He began to explain.

'Sounds easy,' Bulky said at last.

'It is easy.'

'Only there has to be a catch.'

'Has there?'

'Yes,' said Bulky. 'There does,' and Callan made a discovery. The fat man's courage was lean and hard. 'Why are you doing it?' Bulky asked.

45

'Why?' Callan chuckled. 'Oh dear oh dear. You and me—we're errand boys, Bulky. The likes of us aren't ever allowed to ask why.'

'That's the catch,' said Bulky.

Callan said, 'People say that the worst fear of the lot is fear of the unknown. Don't you believe it.'

Bulky said, 'Any kind of fear is bad for what I do,' and watched in relief as the Magnum disappeared inside Callan's coat.

'When I get scared my hands don't work,' he said.

'Mine do,' said Callan. His right hand made a short, abrupt arc, and there the Magnum was. Bulky looked down its barrel.

'You're going to do me this little favour,' said Callan.

'What choice have I got?' said Bulky.

'None. We start on Sunday.... And till then you stay here in your flat, Bulky. You don't move till I tell you. And you don't make phone-calls.'

'As if I would,' Bulky said.

'You can't,' said Callan. 'Your phone's out of order.'

Bulky looked at the telephone table: telephone wires ripped out, handset smashed.

'You're thorough,' he said. 'I'll give you that.'

'That's just the start,' said Callan. 'Now: what don't you do?'

'Leave my flat.'

'You see?' Callan sounded delighted. 'You're not really foolish at all.'

'I've got more sense than to cross you,' Bulky said.

'Course you have,' said Callan. 'Not that it matters, because like you say—I'm thorough. You're being watched, Bulky boy. Watched round the clock. And compared with the geezers who're doing the watching, I'm the Queen of the Fairies.'

Bulky's head-ache got worse.

8

Spanner had been a gambler all his life. He'd made money out of it, and he didn't deny it, but when good luck happened you didn't fight it, didn't try to channel it even, not if you knew about gambling. You just lay back and enjoyed it. And maybe now was the time to lie back and enjoy.

'Go on, Fred,' he said.

Fred looked round Spanner's office. Now this is real class, he thought. Leather, chrome and glass. Not like those old museum pieces Mr Berkeley spends all his time fussing over. All that polishing.... That wasn't proper work for a minder. Demeaning, that's what it was....

'Well, like I say,' he said, 'I knew that you and Mr Berkeley was mates.'

'Oh we were, Fred,' Spanner said. 'We were indeed.'

'Only—I think Mr Berkeley's in a bit of trouble.' Fred leaned forward as he spoke, and Spanner caught a glimpse, no more, of the purple blossom behind his right ear.

'I think you're in a bit of trouble too,' he said.

'No,' said Fred. 'Not me. He let me scarper.'

'Who let you scarper?'

'This hard geezer,' said Fred. 'Took me from behind. Knocked me cold. Took Mr Berkeley as well. Made him drink the coffee with the knock-out drops.'

'What coffee with the knock-out drops?'

Fred sensed the impatience in Spanner's voice.

'It's the system,' he explained. 'Mr Berkeley's system. Two rings on the buzzer and I put the drops in the cream-jug. Only this geezer made Mr Berkeley drink it.'

'What did he look like?' Spanner asked.

'Hard,' Fred told him. 'Hard like you wouldn't believe.'

'Didn't niff, did he?' Spanner said. 'No.... He couldn't have done. That was the other one.'

Fred looked bewildered. It suited him. Spanner remembered

47

the man who'd gone into Chelsea Mansions, leaving Lonely in the car.

'About five foot nine?' he said. 'Twelve stone?—maybe a bit more? Looked like he wore barbed wire underwear to stop hisself itching? Would that be him?'

Fred said, 'You seen him.'

'Never mind what I've seen,' said Spanner. 'Why did you come to me?'

'I thought,' Fred said, 'I thought you and Mr Berkeley being mates—'

'We're not mates,' Spanner said. 'You know we're not. Not any more. He's barred.'

'Yeah, well, all the same,' said Fred, 'I thought what I seen, I mean, it could be useful to you, Spanner.'

Spanner looked bored.

'I don't see how,' he said. 'All the same, I appreciate it, Fred. I really do. Nice to know your mates are on the look-out.'

He reached for his wallet, and extracted ten tens. Fred thought: it still looks as thick as the bible in Wandsworth prison chapel.

'Here you are, old son,' said Spanner, and passed over the hundred. 'If I were you I'd keep away from old Bulky. No point in going back if that heavy's still there.'

'Gawd no,' said Fred.

[ii]

Hunter said, 'It's a pity that criminals should be involved.'

'Yeah, I know,' said Callan. 'Banal.'

'I beg your pardon?'

'That's a word you taught me,' said Callan. 'Establishment word. Means trivial, or commonplace. I looked it up.' He grinned. 'I look up everything you tell me.'

'I trust you are about to make a point,' Hunter said.

'Sorry,' said Callan. 'I digress. Criminals, you said. Thieves, blackmailers, murderers. And they're only in it for the money. Like I said: banal.'

'The money is what worries me,' said Hunter. 'If one of them should be on to you—Uncle Lennie say—'

'A job is a job,' said Callan. 'So far as Uncle Lennie's concerned, Lonely's looking after his old age. The one that worries me is Spanner.'

'The Club Flamingo gentleman?'

'That's right,' said Callan. 'FitzMaurice and Meres tailed them. They were spotted.'

'I've had a word with them about that,' said Hunter.

48

'So they changed their trousers,' said Callan, 'but why tail them at all?'

'This job is important,' said Hunter. 'Very important. I concede that without Lonely you couldn't do it. But I do need to know who his associates are.'

'Let's hope,' said Callan, 'they don't find out who we are.'

'What the devil do you mean?'

'Uncle Lennie asked Spanner where Berkeley was living,' Callan said. 'As a favour to Lonely. He told me that and I believe him. Then you had Spanner followed. Don't you think he might get interested in Berkeley?'

'Go on,' said Hunter. 'Tell me why.'

'Because Meres and FitzMaurice tailed him in an Aston-Martin, and that smells like money. And Berkeley smells like money as well. Big money. And being just banal criminals, money's what they're after, and they want in.'

'You could have a point,' said Hunter.

'Who's watching Berkeley?' Callan asked.

'Neither FitzMaurice nor Meres.'

'That's something,' said Callan.

'My dear David,' said Hunter. 'You go on like this and you'll end up sitting in my chair.'

'Not me,' said Callan. 'I'll never make a daddy bear.'

Hunter said: 'You're not a bad Goldilocks.'

Give up, Callan told himself. You're never going to win. Not ever: then killed the thought at once because he couldn't stand its truth.

[iii]

After Spanner had got the unobtainable signal from Bulky's number for the seventh time, he believed that for once the GPO was telling the truth. After that the only solution to the problem was to go to the firm he bought protection from. The snag with that was, the firm cost money. Big money. On the other hand Spanner couldn't help believing he was sniffing round the edges of very big money indeed. Heavies like the one who'd cooled off Fred never took on a job for less than five figures, and when he'd told Bulky he was barred from his clubs all Bulky had said was he could get just as good practice at home. Hell, even the little niffy feller had carried a gun in Detroit. This was a big operation, and Spanner knew all about the big time. He'd been waiting for it all his life. If you wanted in, you had to pay. He called up the firm.

A grand a day that cost him, but when you were a gambler, you expected to put your money up front. It stood to reason.... The

49

men he hired were experts. They had to be, the prices they charged. The only trouble was, the geezers watching Bulky's gaff were experts' experts. Not that the firm put them through any interviews. They just looked at them and they knew. One look and they phoned Spanner, and told him that the grand had gone up to fifteen hundred—not including the physical. For the physical they wouldn't even give him a quote.... When you lose you either increase your stakes or get out of the game, and Spanner was a gambler. He paid. Then he and George picked up a couple of birds and went off to Bournemouth. They didn't take the Merc....

Meres and FitzMaurice missed them by ten minutes. Meres got in because he was full of boyish charm, and FitzMaurice because Meres said he had money, and the blonde on the door liked both. By the end of the night Meres had lost two hundred, and FitzMaurice had won three, but there was no sight, no smell, of Spanner or George.

'Oh God,' said Meres. 'I suppose I'd better take the blonde.'

'Yassuh,' said FitzMaurice.

'And just what is that supposed to mean?'

'It means,' said FitzMaurice, 'that I have no wish to be involved with the sexual mores of the Caucasian race. For myself I propose to further my acquaintance with the cute little trick from Saint Lucia who was dealing blackjack. Excuse me, massah. See you back at the plantation. First one home's a cissy.'

9

Big man, thought Callan. Big hero.... So you managed to frighten a fat man. So what? Intimidation was one of the dirtiest jobs he had to do, and he hated it. The trouble was the hate spilled over into the intimidating, made him even more terrifying....

Liz said again: 'You've to go in.'

'Pardon?' said Callan.

'Mr Hunter's waiting for you,' she said. 'And please don't scowl at me.'

'I wasn't,' said Callan. 'I was scowling at me. It's just that I forgot my mirror.' He went in.

'You've arranged for that man Berkeley, I take it?' Hunter said.

'Yeah,' said Callan. 'I've arranged it.'

Hunter ignored the bitterness in his voice.

'Splendid,' Hunter said. 'Now.... Just one or two final details....'

*

Lonely got on with the packing. Light-weights, Mr Callan had said. Nice, that was. Lonely liked it hot, and anyway they made them in all kinds of colours nowadays. Reds and yellows and blues.... Compared with Lonely, Gauguin worked in monochrome. All the same he packed a black linen sweater, black jeans and sports-shoes, and tucked a pair of thin, black gloves into a pocket of his suitcase. Tools, he thought, and remembered Mr Callan had said he wasn't to bother about tools. They would be provided. And they'd be the best, he knew that. On Mr Callan's jobs, everything was the best. He wondered if Mr Callan would be provided with tools an' all. But that was barmy. Of course he would. Revolver it would be, like always, and Mr Callan would break it open, check it, slip in the ammo round by round, his hands sure, steady, almost loving.... Now, Lonely, he thought. You get on with your packing, old son. No sense getting into a state. Just think of all the lovely lolly you're going to make.... All the same, he wished Uncle Lennie hadn't said the beer was awful. When you did a job with Mr Callan you could do with a drop of proper beer.

When Callan came for him he was all ready: matching, light-weight suitcases, airline bag for his duty frees, and smart with it: canary yellow shirt, orange tie, light-weight suit the colour of milky coffee, jaunty straw snap-brim hat the same colour as the suit.

'Well well,' said Callan. 'We do look smart.' Lonely smirked. 'I brought you a present, old son.' He handed Lonely a cine-camera case.

'I don't know how to use it,' said Lonely.

'You'll learn,' said Callan. 'You're a tourist, old son. All tourists carry cameras, otherwise they look conspicuous. Now you don't want to look conspicuous, do you?'

It was the last of Lonely's desires.

Taxi to the Cromwell Road Terminal, then on to Heathrow by the airport bus. Demeaning, that was, thought Lonely, they should have had a car, but maybe that would have been conspicuous too. Then he brightened. At least they'd come to Heathrow, and a scheduled flight, and not Gatwick. Dead common, Gatwick was. Nothing but charters. No class at all.... They reached the departure lounge and Callan bought Lonely a pint, and himself a whisky, sipping slowly, making it last.

'Mr Callan,' said Lonely, and Callan looked up. The little man was worried.

'That Berkeley geezer,' Lonely said. 'Is he here yet?'

'He will be,' said Callan, then added: 'Don't worry, old son. He's not travelling with us.'

'How d'you mean?' said Lonely.

'He's travelling first,' said Callan.

'First?' said Lonely. 'A ruddy card-sharp? It's us should be travelling first, Mr Callan. We're the pros. Let him do his ruddy card-tricks in the steerage.' He was indignant, and indignation made his voice shrill. That would never do.

'I think,' said Callan, 'you'd better belt up.'

Lonely glowered, and went to buy himself another pint.

The hired Daimler arrived for Bulky bang on time, and the peak-capped chauffeur busied himself appropriately, stowing away luggage, making sure that Bulky was comfortably seated. Bulky's dark suit was tussore silk, his shirt hand-made, his watch by Boucheron. Everything about Bulky reeked of money, including, so the chauffeur hoped, his tipping habits. All the same he wished the fat man didn't have that sour look on his face.... No way to start a holiday, looking like that.

The firm that was doing the tailing did a neat, smooth job: a man and a woman in a Scimitar, two blokes in a Merc 250, another bloke on a 500 c.c. motor-bike. Hunter's two men didn't even

52

spot them. Nothing had been said about tails anyway. Their business was to see Bulky went to the airport, checked in, and made the flight. When they reached the motorway and got into the fast lane, it was no business of theirs that a Merc was ahead of Bulky's Daimler and a Scimitar behind them. The fast lane was full, anyway. There was nowhere else the cars could go. When they reached the turn-off for the airport, the Merc kept straight on, a motor-bike pulled out ahead of the Daimler and led the procession. Nothing funny about that, either. The bloke on the motor-bike wore a security service uniform. Blokes in that rig were ten a penny at airports.

Bulky got out, the chauffeur did some more fussing, and copped a quid, and Bulky checked in at the Alitalia desk, went up the escalator. Behind him rode one of Hunter's men, and behind him the bird from the Scimitar. They saw Bulky into the departure lounge, and settled down to wait, the woman looking round as if waiting for someone, moving restlessly, Hunter's man just sitting. If Bulky got aboard the Rome flight, their jobs were over.

Bulky went into the departure lounge, ordered a large brandy, and had no doubt he would catch the Rome flight. Callan was sitting at a table near the bar, sipping whisky, and with him was the little man he'd been told about, dressed like a Van Gogh cornfield. Callan's gaze had flicked by him once, but Bulky had no doubt that he'd been seen. The trip was on.

The metallic, accented voice said, 'Alitalia announce the departure of flight 259 to Rome.'

'That's us, old son,' said Callan.

'I thought we was Catania,' said Lonely.

'That's right,' said Callan. 'Change at Rome.'

This somehow mollified the little man. Changing aircraft at Rome. Class that was. He began filling up the airline bag with practised speed: whisky, cologne, two cartons of ciggies—his whack *and* Mr Callan's—and Bulky knew at once he was a tea-leaf the way his hands worked, and reminded himself that *his* hands must never give him away. Callan and his mate took off, but Bulky finished his brandy at leisure. Let the peasants jostle each other for seats: Bulky was travelling first, his place assured.

Lonely enjoyed the flight, the third one he'd made in his entire lifetime, and Callan thanked God that all three had been smooth. But then, given the absence of terror, Lonely could enjoy anything that included beer and food—even airline food, and proceeded to do justice to both. And more than justice, thought Callan, and gave Lonely his sweet, a soggy cake soaked in something that tasted like saccharin glue. He even ate that. Still, anything was better than having him niff.... He even behaved well at Leonardo

53

da Vinci airport. True, he didn't like the colour scheme, or the lack of seats on the transfer bus, or the fact that everybody spoke Italian, but at least he was broadminded about it. As he explained to Mr Callan, you could say what you liked but foreign was foreign.

The only trouble about the Caravelle to Catania was they didn't serve beer, and he had to make do with a free lemonade. But the hostess was pretty, the flight quick, and Mr Callan seemed relaxed, so why shouldn't he be?

'My Uncle Lennie was in Sicily once, Mr Callan,' he said. 'Said the beer was awful. I must say the beer seems to have got better since his day.'

'When was he there then?' Callan asked.

'The war,' said Lonely. 'Commando he was.'

Callan looked at Uncle Lennie in his mind's eye: remembered the way he'd thrown him the sawn-off shotgun; remembered how Lonely had described his handling of the Mannlicher. Yeah. Uncle Lennie had been in the Commandos all right, and he hadn't forgotten what he'd been taught.

'Tell me, old son,' he said. 'What exactly does your Uncle Lennie *do*?'

Lonely looked at the two nuns sitting opposite. Jabbering away in foreign they were, but you never knew. He lowered his voice.

'Uncle Lennie's a rustler,' he said with pride.

'You what?'

'Honest,' said Lonely. 'Beef and venison. And he does a bit of poaching an' all.'

'Good for him,' said Callan, 'the open air life.'

'That's what he says,' said Lonely. 'I never reckoned it meself. Mind you, there is the glamour.'

The plane screamed high over the Straits of Messina, and below them the sea was a rich, unsullied blue, lustrous and deep in shade. Before them the mountains, range after range, savage and beautiful. Real Uncle Lennie country, thought Callan, but no place for his nephew. From what he'd deduced from the map, Lonely was going to need a bit of handling. This place was as bad as Crete.... They landed at last, and Lonely looked about him as they moved through passports and customs. First class passengers out first, he thought bitterly. Always the way. Real pros standing about in the heat while a Find The Lady twister takes it easy. He looked about him, but the only first class lot he could see were two old birds, a posh geezer and a bishop. They picked up their suitcases at last, and moved out to the car-park. The posh geezer was watching a chauffeur shoving his suitcase into a dirty great Mercedes. Callan walked up to the chauffeur.

'Hotel Isola Bella?' he asked.

'*Si, signore.*'

'Oh, are you staying there too?' the posh geezer said. 'How do you do? My name is Berkeley.'

Callan said, 'Mine's Callan. My friend answers to L—'

'Roger de Vere Bullivant,' Lonely said.

The drive to the hotel was like driving always is these days, Lonely thought. Suburbs and motorway. Still it was nice to see they *had* towns: caffs and shops and the pictures and that. And the motorway was just like home an' all, except they all drove on the wrong side of the road.... Mr Callan had copped a back seat next to that git Berkeley. Getting on like a house on fire they were, and there he was stuck next to the driver, and all the driver spoke was foreign. Suddenly there were no more houses: just fields baked hard by summer, interspersed with orange and lemon groves. Pretty they were: like ads on the telly. It was their background he didn't like. All them mountains. It reminded him of Crete.... Suddenly the driver pointed.

'Taormina,' he said.

They were climbing up a winding road, and on Lonely's side the sea was below them, mildly, gently heaving. Nothing wrong with that sea. And after that was tunnels, and then more sea, and houses, shops, hotels. The Mercedes slowed as they passed a small and beautiful islet, wooded, exquisite.

'Isola Bella,' the driver said.

'Blimey,' said Lonely, and twisted in his seat. 'We're not staying there are we, Mr Callan?' But the car had already turned through wide-flung wrought-iron gates, its tyres scraped on a gravel path as they descended towards an old and rambling house, haphazard yet cared for. It was built into the cliffs, and around it like a frame were terraced gardens: pines and cactus, jasmine and bougainvillaea. And roses, thought Lonely. There must be a million roses. Porters in striped waistcoats came running, and Berkeley hauled out a massive crocodile skin wallet.

'I'll do this,' he said, and tipped the driver, as the porters carried their luggage inside.

Class, thought Lonely, real class, and even more class when they got inside, to public rooms, shuttered and cool, and Mr Callan registered to the manner born. Nice bar, Lonely noticed, big, comfortable chairs and not hot at all. Open too, even if it was four in the afternoon. You had to admit it. Out foreign they did some things even better than in England.... They followed the porters to their room, and Lonely thought he'd died and gone to heaven. Biggest bath he'd ever seen, and a shower, all in white tiles with blue squiggles on them. And a smashing big bedroom all done up white and blue, and twin beds with white lace

55

coverlets, fitted wardrobes that lit up when you opened the doors, and vases and bowls of roses everywhere you looked. And beyond that a balcony about the size of that gaff he'd once had in Notting Hill, before Mr Callan got him into the security lark, with tables and deck chairs and a padded-like bed for sunbathing. And beyond that a strip of sand and then the sea, whispering yet calm, the great arms of the bay folding round it, the hillsides a glowing green of vineyards and pine.

Lonely went out on to the balcony, and the heat struck at once. But even the sunshine here was the posh kind, he thought. At the airport you just had to stand there and take it, no shade, no nothing: here there was beach umbrellas and geezers in white coats fetching drinks with ice in them, and even a breeze, a cooling, tender breeze that, Lonely was sure, would never get above itself and turn into a wind....

Callan came out and joined him.

'Like it, old son?' he said.

'Cor,' said Lonely. 'Cor.'

'Got everything you want?'

'I thought places like this was only on the pictures,' said Lonely. 'Could I go down and get a beer, Mr Callan?'

'Have it up here,' said Callan. 'We haven't unpacked yet.'

He demonstrated the miracle called room service, and Lonely's Paradise was complete. Unpacking was no problem to Lonely. His hands moved with the same deft speed that Bulky Berkeley had noticed at once, and Callan's clothes and his own were stored neatly, precisely away.

'You know, old son,' said Callan, 'if you weren't going to be a company director I'd take you on as a valet.'

Greatly daring, Lonely said, 'You didn't bring no gun with you.'

'Use your common,' said Callan. 'You saw how we were searched at the airport.'

'Does that mean you won't need one then?'

'I'll get one here,' said Callan, and Lonely, like Adam before him, discovered that Paradise had to be paid for.

'Now don't start getting upset,' said Callan. 'You know I said I'd look after you properly.'

'Ah, and that's another thing,' said Lonely. 'I haven't got no tools.'

'Yes you have,' said Callan. 'Look in your camera.'

Lonely opened up the case. Inside there was the most complicated looking cine-camera he'd ever seen. He'd never handled anything like it in his life, but he took it out and had it opened up in seconds. The camera had been lined with cloth, and nestling on the cloth was a zip-bag of heavy plastic. Lonely eased it out and unzipped. Inside was the best set of tools he'd ever seen, better even than the one Mr Callan had got for him in Crete: twirls, probes, keys, the lot. All scaled down a bit, but all heavy duty stuff. Tools for a craftsman.

'All right?' said Callan.

'*All right?*' Lonely's hands explored the zip-bag. 'Mr Callan, with this lot I could open up the Bank of England.'

'That's all right then,' said Callan.

'Yeah,' said Lonely, 'but I was looking forward to taking pictures.'

'Listen, Goldwyn,' said Callan. 'You came here to do a job of work.'

'And that's another thing,' said Lonely. 'If I'd got nicked with this lot they'd have put me down for years—and you let me carry it all the way here. That's not nice, Mr Callan.'

'If I had told you,' said Callan, 'you'd have stunk the plane out, now wouldn't you?'

'All the same,' said Lonely. 'I do know now, and I've got to carry them back.'

'No you don't,' said Callan. 'We'll ditch them.'

'Ditch them?' Lonely was appalled. 'These are the best I've ever seen.'

'Phone down and order yourself another beer,' said Callan. 'Put your trunks on and get some sun. Relax.'

Lonely looked suspicious. 'What you going to do?' he asked.

'Take a look at the town,' Callan said.

'I'll come with you.'

'Better not,' said Callan.

'You working, then?' said Lonely.

'You got your tools,' said Callan. 'I better pick up mine.'

There were no clouds to cover the sun, but Lonely shivered.

10

To get to the old town it was best to take the funicular, Hunter had said, and he was right. The silent, elegant gondola slid smoothly up the steel cables, climbing the steep hillside in a whisper, and as it climbed revealing a panorama of a beauty quite incredible: sea and mountain and sky: their colour and masses in perfect proportion, and, for all that he could see, unchanged since first the Greeks had settled there, almost two and a half millennia ago. But he hadn't come there to look at beauty. Souvenirs, that's what you bought in Taormina. All right, he would get himself a souvenir.

There were plenty to be had. The long, sloping street was lined with souvenir shops, from the piazza at the top to the cathedral at the foot: and what wasn't souvenir shops was restaurants, cafés, jewellers, perfumers, modistes. This was a holiday town, and a rich one. Callan dawdled his way down the street, looking at windows loaded with lace-work, silk, Sicilian puppets, antique furniture, with all the spaces between filled up with every conceivable kind of trash. The one he wanted looked much like the others, but it had a tie in the window exotic enough to measure up to even Lonely's exacting standards: three different kinds of pattern, and no colour more muted than purple. He went inside.

The woman in the shop was elegant and old, with the remains of what must have been a wild and hawk-like beauty. She wore the traditional black of the widow, but her clothes too were elegant and old: exquisitely hand-embroidered dress, a lace cap on her head that made her white hair gleam like polished silver. Her eyes were a brown as dark as cream sherry, shrewd and alert.

'Signora Lunari?' he said.

'Yes, sir?'

'I wish to buy a tie,' said Callan. 'A special one. A gift for a friend.'

'Please look about you, sir,' she said. 'As you can see, there are many.'

Her accent was harshly Sicilian, but lurking in it too was a hint of the North Country she had picked up from the soldiers who'd taught her thirty years ago.

'You were recommended to me by a friend,' said Callan. 'Mr William Robinson of Pimlico. He sends you his regards.'

'And I send mine,' she said. 'Please tell him I wish him well.'

Callan handed her the tie he'd picked out for Lonely: all the formulae had been spoken. As she took it a party of Swedes came in.

'One moment,' she said, 'and I will get your parcels.'

She disappeared into the back of the shop, and came back with two gaily wrapped parcels that Callan stowed away in his airline bag. Callan paid.

'Come back and see me again, sir,' she said.

'I should like that very much,' said Callan.

As he left she embarked on a long haggle about the price of a tablecloth. Her Swedish too had a Sicilian accent....

Callan walked back up the street to a car-hire agency that Hunter had said would do him an Alfa-Romeo Sud. The price per day shook him, but Hunter was in a hurry, and speed had to be paid for, and the Alfa was the ideal car for mountain roads, holding on well, and nippy too. And it was a four-seater: if one of the passengers was Bulky they'd need plenty of room....

Lonely loved his tie: loved it so much that he put it on at once. Callan gathered that his taste was impeccable. While Lonely worked at a double Windsor, Callan opened up his own present, to reveal a shoe-box, and inside it a Smith and Wesson 357 Magnum, the kind of webbing harness he preferred as being lighter than leather, and easier in the heat, and twelve rounds of ammo. So Hunter hadn't anticipated a war at all: just one battle and out. He strapped on the harness, eased the gun into the holster, drew, the quick, abrupt pull that was one continuous movement so that the gun became at once an accusing finger pointed at its victim. Lonely turned, peacock-proud from the mirror, and saw what Callan was doing.

'So you're all tooled up an' all,' he said.

Callan broke the gun open and began to load, his fingers sure and precise in the way that Lonely remembered.

'That's right, old son,' he said. 'Now we've got nothing to worry about.'

Lonely said, 'You have to be joking.'

*

Bulky took a nap. Admittedly first class travel is the best there

59

is, but when it came to aircraft that isn't saying much, he thought, and remembered with regret the good old days: first class on the *QE2*, suite on the *France*, before the bastards had got on to him and warned him off. Really good old days they had been. Good food, good wine, and the richest mugs in the world. Bridge or poker, they couldn't wait to lose. There were times he'd almost had to ask them to form a queue.... And his own boss, all the time. No interference. And no heavy stuff either. Not like this job. Do it and I'll pay you. Don't do it and I'll kill you. What kind of a choice was that? Unbidden the thought came into his mind. What was Callan up to? If he thought about it, worked at it, Bulky was sure he could find an answer.

He said aloud, 'No no, Bulk, old sport. Don't do it. That way madness lies.'

Better to practise his Yoga exercises: lie supine, relax, breathe through the diaphragm.... Bulky slept. But in his dreams, Callan was waiting.

[ii]

The cute little trick from Saint Lucia said, 'You're ever so nosey.'

'Curious,' said Spencer Perceval FitzMaurice. 'We writers are invariably curious.'

He poured more burgundy, and waited as the plates were cleared. Just as well he hadn't tried to fob this one off with soul-food, he thought. She ate even more of the chateaubriand than I did.

'You see my dear,' he said. 'To us man is always an enigma and woman even more so. Particularly a young and beautiful woman such as yourself.'

She smiled. Her teeth *were* beautiful: even, and dazzling white. They'd gone through the chateaubriand like a waste-disposal unit.

'Let us consider,' he said, 'yourself. A young lady fighting for survival in the big city. A young lady who is black and very beautiful.'

'I am black, aren't I?' she said. 'Just about as black as you.'

For that moment he loved her; there was nothing but pride in her voice. Then the moment passed and he poured on more molasses.

'A lovely young black lady working for Whitey,' he said. 'Why should that be?'

'Don't you work for Whitey?' she said.

'My chains were struck off long ago,' he said.

'Hey,' she said. 'You're not from *Ebony*, are you?'

The waiter came back then, and brought fruit salad. She poured on enough cream to drown a corgi.

'I,' said FitzMaurice, 'am working on a book. And I want to put you in it.'

'Oh I don't know,' she said. 'I wouldn't want to be named.'

'The case of Miss B,' he said. 'No names. Just the black and beautiful Miss B, and how Whitey exploits her. I take it you are exploited, my dear?'

'Oh boy,' she said. 'The things I could tell you.'

'It is my intention to listen,' he said, 'but not here. Here we can be overheard, the aura of white exploitation is all around us. My place, baby. I have cognac there. VSOP.'

'Oh I don't know,' she said.

But she did know, and when she saw the Bentley she was certain. Loved his place too, and at a hundred a week it sure is lovable, he thought, even if it's my first and last night here. The cognac, it seemed, was lovable too, and so was Spencer Perceval FitzMaurice. Together they moved from satisfaction to happiness, and FitzMaurice had to remind himself that when he joined the Section they gave him an operation that removed his sense of shame.

'It grieves me,' he said, 'that all this should be exploited by Whitey.'

'It grieves me too,' she said, 'but we all got to live, Spencer baby.'

'We're living,' he said, and she began to cry, very softly. 'My dear, what's wrong?'

'When I think of this,' she said, 'and that bunch of crooks I work for.'

'Crooks?' said FitzMaurice, horrified. 'You mean really *criminals*?'

'You just listen,' she said, and he gathered her in his arms.

'Go right ahead,' he said. 'I'll do just that.'

*

Dinner, thought Lonely, was an ordeal, and there was no use pretending it wasn't. The only good thing about it was you could have beer with it: how Mr Callan could cope with that wine he couldn't imagine. Course after course an' all. Spoons and knives and forks all laid out on each side: that was all very well, but what were you supposed to use when they gave you a plateful of that wriggly-stuff? Fair wore-out, he was. Callan, having watched Lonely knit together a plate of spaghetti, agreed that it wouldn't hurt Lonely to have an early night.

'I mean it's not as if I didn't know how to behave meself in public,' said Lonely. 'I did all right on the plane, now didn't I, Mr Callan?'

Callan remembered Lonely's first triumphant stab into egg-mayonnaise. Half the aircraft had got a piece. Gravely he agreed that Lonely was crême de la crême.

'All the same I don't see how anybody could cope with that like wool,' said Lonely, then added fair-mindedly: 'Mind you it was tasty. Drop of tomato-sauce and it would have gone down a treat.'

Callan went to the bar, where Berkeley was drinking coffee. More chat, more formulae: 'Let me buy you a drink?' and 'I was thinking of having one in town,' and in the end Bulky accepted a lift in Callan's Alfa, and they walked out into the warm, scented darkness of the car-park. Callan opened up the car, and Bulky moved forward, tripping against Callan as he did so, clinging to him for support. Callan reached out and held him, and Bulky was sure it took no effort at all. It was too dark to see, but he'd be ready to swear that Callan was laughing in silence.

'No, Bulk,' he said. 'I'm not wearing it tonight. I don't have to.'

They took the spiralling road up to town, climbing on past the Greek amphitheatre to the brand-new, sparkling, luxury hotel, the Villa Rosa. A hell of a villa, thought Callan. It must be nine storeys at least. But the air was conditioned, they had Westinghouse's word for it, the lighting discreet, the furniture as plump and luxurious as Bulky himself. And in that atmosphere, Callan noticed, he revived like a watered flower: voice steadier, walk firmer, glance more self-assured. Make no mistake about it, Bulky was home.

They went to the bar, and Bulky ordered cognac, French cognac, and the barman at once began warming balloon glasses with a sort of frantic deference. Bulky pulled out a cigar-case, clipped the end of a Romeo y Julieta, and made his triumph complete.

'To the manner born,' said Callan.

'I beg your pardon?'

'Just an expression a friend of mine uses,' Callan said. 'You do it very well.'

'Habit,' said Bulky, and smiled. 'Preference too. As that profound American said, "It's no crime to be poor, but it might as well be."'

He struck a match, and worked at lighting his cigar with a fat man's massive concentration. By the time he'd finished he'd seen everybody in the bar.

'Our mug here?' he asked.

'Not yet,' said Callan.

Bulky accepted his cognac from the barman, sipped, and nodded acceptance.

'Make it poker if you can,' he said.

'Why?' said Callan.

'It's the quickest,' Bulky said.

'You mean you don't like it here?'

'A cradle of civilisation,' said Bulky. 'Greek, Roman, Byzantine, Arab, Norman, Spanish—and the indigenous Sicilians of course. It must be marvellous for a holiday, but somehow I don't want to work here.'

'That's me,' said Callan.

'How very perceptive you are.'

But Callan was watching the door, and the man who had just come in: blonde and bronzed, with a face like a kindly fox's. With him was a girl: a tall, black-haired girl with a very white skin and an insolent grace of movement. Foxy-face led her to a table, and at once began to fuss with her chair, the table, her wrap, looking round as he did so to summon a waiter.

'Our mug's just come in,' Callan said.

Bulky studied the end of his cigar, and was satisfied at last that it burned evenly.

'It would seem,' he said, 'that he has more vices than one.'

'At least it proves he's human,' said Callan.

Bulky sighed.

'There is something heart-rending about mugs,' he said, and sipped his cognac. 'I wonder if wolves feel the same way about lambs? And a lamb in love.... Our only problem will be to detach him from that truly delectable piece of crackling. How do you propose to play it?'

'By ear,' said Callan.

Foxy-face was giving the waiter far too many instructions for two gin and tonics, and Bulky picked up his glass and cigar.

'Ah well,' he said. 'Here we go. Into battle.'

11

'Did you get much?' Meres asked.

'That would depend on what was to be had,' said FitzMaurice.

'Your Uncle Tom act's bad enough,' said Meres, 'but this pedantic bit's even worse.'

'You is very touchy today, massah.'

'So are you,' said Meres. 'Your girl was awful, I take it?'

In no way had the cute little trick from Saint Lucia been awful, but FitzMaurice had learned long ago not to tell Meres the truth about such matters.

'She was,' he said.

'The blonde was unbelievable,' said Meres. 'The refined ones always are. Still she did talk.'

'Mine too.'

They began to fit the pieces together. There was more than enough to take to Hunter, who listened with patient concentration to statement, conjecture, justification.

'It amounts to this,' he said at last. 'The Spanner creature is aware of something, but he is by no means sure of what that something is, apart from the fact that it involves Berkeley and hence money in large quantities. To further his investigations he has hired this group called a firm, but you are not yet aware of the identity of its members. I think it is time to discourage Spanner. Attend to it, will you?'

'He's in Bournemouth,' said Meres.

'I had assumed you could reach Bournemouth unaided.'

Meres flushed. 'I merely wondered if we should wait till he came back to town,' he said.

'I don't wish to wait at all.' Hunter reached for a file, and the two men rose to leave. 'On your way one of you had better call on Lonely's Uncle Lennie,' said Hunter. 'FitzMaurice, I think. The old man is in no sense a gentleman.'

'Yes sir. I'll call on him,' FitzMaurice said. 'What would you like me to tell him?'

'To go away,' said Hunter, 'before this so-called firm reaches him. Get on with it.'

[ii]

The lady's name was Nivelle: Jeanne-Marie Nivelle. Her nationality, so she claimed, was French, though there were times when Bulky doubted it. All those trips on the *France* had given him an ear for the French language spoken by Frenchmen, and he did not always detect it in her voice. On the other hand her French-accented English was perfect. Alsace? he wondered. Somewhere like Metz? And what was she up to anyway? Again the unbidden thought, and again its instant suppression. All Bulky wanted was to do his job and get out. The rest of the script was no business of his.... It was apparent, however, that Gunther Kleist was besotted. For a middle-aged man he was behaving like a schoolboy: but *au fond*, thought Bulky, he is a lamb, as I spotted from the first. A real, woolly baa-lamb.

Getting next to them had been dead-easy. All it needed was to move over to the table next to Kleist's and talk about gambling, and Bulky could do that all right: reminisce about Monte Carlo and the Casanova Club and a poker game in Texas that hadn't stopped in years. Every time somebody left the table somebody else took his place. The turnover was well into seven figures. He spoke softly, but his voice was powerful and deep, and he could pitch it just as far as he wanted it to go, and Kleist was eating it up. The trouble was that the girl was eating him up, thought Callan. He was like a gourmet who couldn't make up his mind between the lobster and the tournedos, but at last, like a true gourmet, he opted for both.... He discovered he'd run out of matches and asked Bulky for a light, just as the girl picked up a book of matches from the table.

'How stupid of me,' Kleist said. 'I did not see they were there.'

He's terrible, Callan thought, and watched him labour away at asking Bulky and him to join them, at the same time sweating with terror because his girl didn't fancy the idea at all. Bulky, on the other hand, played it like a master: gentlemanly, correct, anxious not to impose, and yet gradually overpowered by the woman's beauty, the man's insistent charm.

'You're very kind,' he said at last. 'But I insist that we buy the drinks.' He signalled, and the waiter came over like a greyhound out of a trap: more brandy, more gin and tonic.

'You are on holiday here?' Kleist said.

'Yes,' said Bulky. 'Mr Callan and I are at the Isola Bella. We met this evening.'

'So,' said Kleist. 'Two strangers?' For some reason this pleased him, but it didn't make his bird any happier. 'You like it here?'

'Very much,' said Callan. 'And you?'

'Miss Nivelle and I are very happy here,' said Kleist.

Baa-lamb, baa-lamb, how cold you'll be when you're sheared, thought Bulky.

And then they talked professions. Callan claimed to be in electronics, Bulky announced that he'd left the Stock Exchange years ago, Kleist that he was a civil-servant. Miss Nivelle remained Miss Nivelle, pale and uncommunicative and beautiful. Bulky complimented Kleist on his English.

'I have had to practise to speak with Miss Nivelle,' Kleist said. 'She speaks no German and my French is terrible.' He grinned at her, and at once she smiled back. We do not need these people, the smile said. We have each other. But a baa-lamb must fulfil a baa-lamb's destiny.

'Forgive me,' Kleist said. 'I could not help overhearing. You spoke of gambling, I think.'

'Did we?' said Bulky. 'Oh yes. The subject did come up. My friend here owns a couple of horses, you know.'

Let's hope the Nivelle bird doesn't, thought Callan. I don't know a bloody thing about it.

'You also mentioned, I think, cards.'

Miss Nivelle's smile clicked off.

'Oh yes,' Bulky said. 'I saw quite a few games in Monte Carlo last year.'

'Saw?' Kleist's disappointment was manifest.

'Oh—and played as well. Of *course*,' said Bulky.

'You were telling me about that game in Texas,' Callan said.

'So I was,' said Bulky. 'Now that *was* a game. I was there on business, you know. Representing some oil interests. Dallas. A curious city. Do you know they all carry guns there?'

Watch it, Bulky boy, thought Callan. Don't go whimsical on me.

Aloud he said, 'This game had been going on for years, you said.'

'That's right,' said Bulky. 'Thousands of dollars in every pot. Some of the best poker I've ever seen.'

'You play poker?' said Kleist.

'Occasionally,' Bulky said. 'Among friends at the golf club.'

'And you, Mr Callan?'

'Now and then,' said Callan. 'After a day's racing.'

'Would you like to play here?'

'Here?' said Callan. 'You mean they have casinos and things? That isn't really my style.'

66

'No, no,' said Kleist. 'I meant a game among friends.'

Miss Nivelle emptied her glass, put it down hard enough to be heard.

'Really that's awfully kind of you,' said Bulky, 'but I don't think—'

'You gentlemen have a compatriot here,' said Kleist. 'Lord Hexham. Perhaps you know him?'

'I don't think I have that pleasure,' Bulky said.

'He also plays poker,' said Kleist. 'Unfortunately it is not always possible to find enough—congenial spirits? Do I have that right?'

'Darling,' Miss Nivelle said, 'I am very, very tired.'

'Of course,' said Kleist. 'You gentlemen are at the Isola Bella? Perhaps I may call you?'

'Please do,' said Callan, and watched them walk away, the woman cool and graceful, Kleist still frantically fussing.

'Baa,' Bulky said, softly. 'Baa.'

Callan finished his brandy.

'It looks easy and it should be easy,' he said, 'but somehow, Bulky, I doubt it.'

[iii]

Uncle Lennie opened the front door, and the black man seemed to fill the frame; Uncle Lennie thought wistfully of the hunting rifle and three shotguns in his kitchen, but that was madness. The guns might as well be in Siberia.

'I'm sorry,' Uncle Lennie said, 'I'm not buying,' and swung the door to. The black man's arm moved in a blur of speed that was faster than a punch. One moment his hand was in his pocket, the next it was pushing open the door that Uncle Lennie was trying, failing, to close.

'I'm not selling,' he said. 'I'm not even bringing you trouble. Just talk, man.'

Uncle Lennie, a strategist for fifty years, gave in.

'You better come in,' he said.

'I thank you, sir.'

Spencer Perceval FitzMaurice walked across the threshold, waited unimpressed while Uncle Lennie closed the door, then raised his hands.

'I surrender,' he said. 'I am your prisoner, sir. If you want to frisk me, you go right ahead.'

'Beg pardon?' said Uncle Lennie.

'Sir,' FitzMaurice said, 'in your possession are three shotguns and a hunting rifle. I just want you to know that I'm unarmed.'

Uncle Lennie went over him, and did a thorough job.

At one point FitzMaurice said, 'Sir—I also want you to know that there are those among my race—and yours—who would resent what you've just done—but I'm not among their number. A pro, my friend, is a pro.'

Uncle Lennie's head tilted up, his small, glittering eyes looked into the negro's.

'We'll go in the kitchen,' he said. 'There's some gooseberry ready.'

FitzMaurice loved the kitchen. It was a place designed for work, where work was pleasure. One lazy glance around the room and he'd seen the Mannlicher above the fireplace, the cupboard that was the shotguns' home. Uncle Lennie poured out the gooseberry.

FitzMaurice said, 'I am obliged to you for such a peaceful reception.'

'You got a mate, ain't you?' Uncle Lennie said. 'A mate who's maybe the mate of a relative of mine.'

'If you would elucidate further, sir...?'

'Three shotguns, you said. And a hunting rifle. You got it right,' said Uncle Lennie. 'There's only one way you could know. Now then.'

Whitey, FitzMaurice thought. Oh my dear lord. How can you do this to me? Just when I'm set to hate you all, one of you has to act like this. Small and old and unafraid, and he is his size and I am mine. And he knows it. He watched as Uncle Lennie poured out two measures of gooseberry, took the one he was handed, and sipped. It had a kick like home-made rum, but somehow he didn't cough. He took another sip instead. Uncle Lennie looked approving.

'I said we both know a geezer,' he said. 'Would you like to give him a name?'

FitzMaurice made a decision. 'Callan,' he said.

'Ah,' said Uncle Lennie. 'Doing a job with my nephew. Nothing wrong with that. We all got to grow up some time.'

'Just so long as we all know it,' FitzMaurice said. 'This one is definitely adults only.' He told Uncle Lennie about Spanner and the firm. 'So what we thought was,' he said at last, 'maybe you shouldn't be here for a while.'

'Who's "we"?' Uncle Lennie said.

FitzMaurice said, 'You should know better than to ask me that.'

'Hard lot,' Uncle Lennie said. 'Real hard.'

'What makes you think so?'

'I've seen Callan,' said Uncle Lennie. 'And now I've seen you. You ever go fishing, Mister FitzMaurice?'

'Sometimes.'

'Millponds,' said Uncle Lennie. 'That's where it happens. One

68

chub in the middle of a school full of pike.' He sighed. 'That's my nephew Lonely.'

FitzMaurice said, 'I think he's ready to tell us,' but Meres' man myself.'

'But a job is a job,' said Uncle Lennie.

'That's right.' The negro waited.

'I'll leave you,' said Uncle Lennie. 'I've got orders to fill anyway.'

'Can you be traced?'

Uncle Lennie chuckled. 'If I can I'm out of business,' he said. 'How long do you want me away?'

'A week should do it.'

'I'll need a week anyway.'

Uncle Lennie reached up and lifted the Mannlicher from its rack. Placidly FitzMaurice sipped at his gooseberry wine.

'You're all right,' Uncle Lennie said.

'And you, sir.' FitzMaurice lifted his glass. 'I wish you success in your business.'

Uncle Lennie took off in the elderly Rolls, and FitzMaurice walked to the car-park of the Bird In Hand where Meres sat waiting behind the wheel of a Jensen Interceptor. It was time to go to Bournemouth.

[iv]

Callan took Lonely for a drive. Since his rise to riches Lonely had made a study of cars—even if he didn't drive he had his dignity to consider—and the name Alfa-Romeo was meaningful. He approved. Plenty of room, and real leather on the seats, and the stereo worked a treat. It could move an' all, but that didn't bother him, not when Mr Callan was driving. What did bother him was the scenery. All mountains and that, and vineyards and fruit trees, and villages so small you were through them before you even knew you'd arrived. Then on and up to where there was only scrubland and rocky outcrop and maybe a few sheep: no people at all. Lonely hated it when there were no people. It wasn't natural. He sat huddled in misery as Callan drove on, turned off at last on to a spur of shale, stopped and braked.

'Here we are, old son,' said Callan. 'Shangri-La.'

'Beg pardon?' said Lonely.

Callan pointed, 'There's the drum we've got to turn over.'

Lonely looked where Callan had indicated. Down in the valley that was, with all like trees and that. Big, it was. More like enormous, with all pillars round it and a courtyard you could have used for a third division football ground. Stone, all of it, no brick at all, and some of it was black and some of it was goldy

69

colour. And all clean. Mr Callan had said the place was over two hundred years old and it was all clean: clean; black and gold; vast.

'You mean just one geezer lives in *that*?' said Lonely.

'That's right.'

Callan reached into the pocket in the door of the car, took out the zoom lens from Lonely's camera. 'Take a good look.'

Lonely twiddled, and the great house leaped to his eyes: portico, pilasters, columns, colonnades: flower-beds set in circles of raked gravel, statuary and fountains. From the roof of the house a flag was flying that was a blue-like dragon set on yellow. Make a nice design for a tie, that would.

'All that for one man?' Lonely said again.

'Those days they did things in style,' said Callan.

'Yeah,' said Lonely. 'Even the chairman of the board wouldn't rate a house like that. Not nowadays.' Then a new terror assailed him: 'They got dogs?' he said. 'I mean with all that space and they let the dogs out what chance you got?'

'Not guard dogs,' said Callan. 'Just hunting dogs.'

'*Hunting dogs*?' Lonely was horrified. 'That's worse.'

'No it's not,' said Callan. 'They're kept locked up.'

'Honest?'

'Cross my heart,' said Callan.

Lonely relaxed, but not much.

'Yeah but even so, Mr Callan—just look at the place,' he said.

'I am looking,' said Callan.

'What I mean—look at the size of it.'

'All right,' said Callan. 'It's big.'

'*Big*? It's bloody enormous. You telling me we're going to bust in there and find one book?'

'That's what we're here for.'

'They got libraries in places like that,' said Lonely. 'Thousands and thousands of books. And in the bedrooms an' all. Shelf of books in every room in case one of the guests can't sleep and fancies a read.'

'How do you know?'

'It's on the telly,' said Lonely. 'Them historicals. Nice, they are. Class. All the same—how we going to find one book?'

'I know where it is,' said Callan.

'Oh,' said Lonely. 'That's all right then.' He adjusted the zoom lens. 'Which room is it, Mr Callan?'

Carefully Callan said, 'I don't know which room exactly....'

'Oh you don't,' said Lonely, and added with withering scorn, 'well, don't let that worry you, Mr Callan. I mean there can't be more than a couple of hundred rooms in the whole place. Mind

you we might have to break in nine or ten times—'
'Now listen,' said Callan.
'Still I mean that's nothing to a couple of pros like us. I mean we actually *like* breaking into dirty great gaffs and looking for needles in haystacks.'

Callan's hands shot out to the lapels of Lonely's brand-new pink safari jacket, the fists turned and pressed, and Lonely felt pain scald into the muscles of his neck.

'You're being cheeky,' Callan said. 'I don't like it when you're cheeky.' His fists pressed harder. 'Now—are you going to be a good boy?'

Lonely nodded.

'Say it,' said Callan.

'I'll be a good boy,' Lonely croaked. 'Honest, Mr Callan.'

Callan let him go. Suddenly it was necessary to get out of the car, and not just because of Lonely's niff. He crossed the narrow road, scrambled up a shelving slope, and sat with his back to an outcrop of rock. Around him cicadas shrilled, birds looped and swerved in the clear mountain air, below him was one of the finest architectural gems in Europe, the view was incomparable, the sun shone, and he hated himself. It was bad enough terrorising that Berkeley—if he didn't watch himself he'd get to like old Bulky enough to apologise—but to get physical with Lonely, after all these years. His mate, he thought. The mate who relies on me and I rely on him. No good blaming it on his nerves either; the way he wanted a drink and couldn't have a drink. That was effect, not cause. The cause was Hunter, who had set up a job that needed discipline, so that when that discipline had to be applied, he'd applied it in the only way Lonely understood.

'I hate you, Hunter,' he said to himself. 'Jesus, I hate you.'

Suddenly Lonely was beside him. Even after what Callan had just done to him, the little man moved with no sound at all.

'I'm sorry, Mr Callan,' he said. 'I got a bit above meself.'

Follow it through, Callan thought. Don't let up now.

'Yeah,' he said. 'You did. Don't let it happen again.'

'Oh I won't,' said Lonely. 'Straight I won't.'

'There's beer and sandwiches in the car,' said Callan. 'Get them.'

Lonely scuttled off and set up a picnic. Even when his neck muscles hurt he could still drink beer.

'What I was saying when I was so rudely interrupted—' said Callan.

'Mr Callan, I said I'm sorry,' said Lonely.

'See?' said Callan. 'You're at it again.' Lonely quailed. 'I know where the book's hidden,' said Callan. 'All I've got to do is get in there and look around.'

71

'Get in there?' said Lonely. 'Like do a recce?'

'That's right.'

'On your tod?' said Lonely. 'With all due respect Mr Callan, I don't think you'd get in there without me.'

'I know I wouldn't,' said Callan. 'Thank God I don't have to. I've been invited, old son.'

'Invited?' said Lonely. 'Who by?'

'The owner,' said Callan.

Lonely looked at him, awed. There was nothing Mr Callan couldn't do. Nothing.

He said reverently, 'You mean you've been invited by a lord?'

12

Spanner's place was laughable. He had, it was true, gone to some trouble. The bungalow was only fifteen yards from its neighbours on either side for example, and his locks were the kind that created problems. Meres and FitzMaurice were also of the opinion that he would have the equivalent of a supertanker's anchor chain on his front door: but even so.... FitzMaurice went through the gate and into the back of the house. From the drawing-room window he could hear soul music, the kind he quite liked when he was feeling lazy. It wasn't Handel, or Pergolesi, but even so not bad, not bad. He went past the flower-beds to the kitchen garden, and looked at the back door. Plywood, most of it. The right kick, and it would fall apart. And Spanner called himself a professional. What was he going to do? Call the police? He moved back to where Meres could see him, and waved an O.K.

Meres began a virtuoso performance on the front door knocker, the inexorable yet deferential tattoo that means the law is here and they aren't going to stop till you open up no matter what. On and on and on and on, and the Spanners of this world always crumple first. And so it was. First the laughter from the drawing-room died, then there was no more soul music, and then the door opened as far as the chain allowed.

'Yes?' said Spanner.

'Could I have a word with you, sir?' said Meres.

'Got a warrant?' Spanner asked.

Now that, thought Meres, was clumsy. Who said I was the fuzz?

'Nothing like that, sir,' he said. 'Just a few questions about your club.'

Spanner, thought Meres, was greedy but naive. Why the hell should the Bournemouth fuzz come asking about a club in London? He should have slammed the door, but he hesitated instead, and while he did so FitzMaurice eased his weight into the back door at the points experts had shown him, reached

73

through a shattered panel to draw a bolt, and walked into the drawing-room brandishing a Colt 45 Wyatt Earp might have coveted. George the chauffeur had until then been reassuring a blonde and a redhead that all was well. One look at the negro and he knew he lied.

'Oh my Gawd,' he said, and turned green. FitzMaurice aimed the Colt at a point between his eyes. It looked like the entrance to the Mersey tunnel.

'You stay hushed,' FitzMaurice said, then shut the door on them, went into the hallway, and met Spanner's rush head-on, picked him up one-handed, shook him, struck him playfully with the barrel of the Colt.

'Massa Spanner,' he said, 'that ain't no way to act. You got visitors.'

Spanner crumpled, and FitzMaurice let him fall, took the chain off the front door. Meres came in.

'Having fun?' he said.

'We didn't come here for fun,' said FitzMaurice. 'Now you remember that.'

He reached down for Spanner, tucked him under his arm like a messy parcel, and carried him into the drawing-room. George, the blonde and the redhead looked at his Colt as if it were the only reality they'd seen in years.

'Well now,' said Meres. 'Where shall we begin?'

George the chauffeur said, 'I might have known. The geezers in the Aston-Martin.'

Casually, scarcely looking at what he was doing, Meres hit him, and George fell.

'Get up,' said Meres, and George began the long, slow journey from the horizontal to the vertical. As he did so Meres pulled on a pair of thin leather gloves.

'It seems,' said Meres, 'that I must teach you that a rhetorical question requires no answer. It also seems that you're a slow learner.' He turned to the women, huddled together on a sofa.

'I don't think I know you,' he said.

'I'm Barbara,' said the redhead. 'And this is Marilyn.'

Meres looked from one to the other, taking his time. Neither woman had ever been more afraid. When he spoke the soft, upper-class voice contained a hint of breathlessness, yet he was utterly relaxed.

'It may be,' he said, 'that you know nothing about the reasons why we are here.'

'Oh we don't,' said Marilyn. 'Honestly we—' Her voice faded. Meres was smiling at her.

'I hope so, ladies,' he said. 'I honestly do. Two such lovely creatures—it would be a pity, don't you think?'

He turned to FitzMaurice, and FitzMaurice also smiled. The two women felt sick.

'Lock them up,' said Meres. 'If they've lied to us we can rebuke them later.'

'This way, ladies,' FitzMaurice said, and they got up at once. He took them to the master bedroom, and tied each of them up in a sheet. It was demeaning to them both, but that was part of the treatment.

In the drawing-room Meres looked at the two men, Spanner still sprawled in the armchair where FitzMaurice had dropped him, George swaying on his feet.

'If you want to take me,' said Meres, 'now's your chance.'

George kept on swaying: Spanner groaned.

'Well well well,' said Meres. 'And they told me you were tough.'

'We get by,' said Spanner. '*And* we've got friends.'

FitzMaurice came back in.

'I've just had lovely news,' said Meres. 'They've got friends.'

'Oh how super,' FitzMaurice said.

'Tell us about them,' said Meres.

Neither George nor Spanner spoke.

FitzMaurice said, 'Maybe you think when you start screaming the neighbours will call the fuzz. But we thought of that. We'll play your record-player loud. Now, what's your favourite tune?'

George said, 'What is this anyway? We've done nothing to you.'

Again Meres knocked him sprawling.

'We speak,' he said, 'only when we are spoken to,' then turned to Spanner. 'You were about to tell us things about your friends.'

FitzMaurice said, 'This is a good one, I like it,' and turned on the record-player. A rock-group blared.

'I've got protection,' Spanner said. 'Good protection. The best. They'll find out who you are and—'

Meres' hand moved, and Spanner stopped speaking, began to scream. FitzMaurice turned up the volume on the record-player. At last, at merciful last, Meres' hands were still: the rock-group pounded on.

'Not like that,' Meres said at last. 'Politely. Respectfully.'

Spanner began to talk about the firm. He was all politeness and respect, and Meres listened, then asked questions that Spanner answered at once. The record finished, and FitzMaurice played the flip-side. Meres said: 'Now tell us about Bulky Berkeley.'

'Bulky Berkeley?' Spanner's politeness and respect hadn't slipped a bit: it was just that the switch of questions bewildered him. Meres' hands moved again: again he screamed.

75

FitzMaurice said, 'I understand your feelings. I'm a family hands still moved.

FitzMaurice moved up beside him. 'I mean it,' he said, and Meres' hands were still.

He looked up at FitzMaurice. 'You old spoil-sport,' he said. He was panting.

'Tell us about Bulky Berkeley,' FitzMaurice said.

'Yes, sir,' said Spanner, and told them. Bulky and Fred, his minder, and Uncle Lennie, and the hard geezer who'd crashed in on Bulky and the trip to Sicily and how there might be money in it. FitzMaurice and Meres got the lot.

'Well,' Meres said at last, 'we're getting on very nicely.'

He turned to George, who had hauled himself up on to a chair. 'Have you anything to add?' he asked.

'No, sir,' said George; respectful, polite.

'He's your minder I take it?' Meres said to Spanner.

'Yes, sir.'

Meres turned to FitzMaurice. 'What do we know about minders?' he asked.

'Minders are tough,' FitzMaurice said. 'They have to be. It is the nature of the breed.'

'I wonder,' said Meres, 'if I might ask you to put on another record? I'm a little tired of those repetitive young men.'

FitzMaurice did so, and George also screamed until Meres let him go.

'Did I refresh your memory?' he asked.

They got the dregs: the address of Fred's bird, the pub Uncle Lennie used. Everything else was repetition of what Spanner had already told them. Still, it was nice to have it all confirmed. The record ended, and George continued to talk until there was no more he could say. When he was silent at last, neither FitzMaurice nor Meres spoke. On and on went the silence, until Spanner couldn't bear it.

'Please, sir,' he said at last.

'You sound as if you were still in the third form,' said Meres. 'You should put your hand up.' He smiled. 'Let's try it like that.'

At once Spanner's hand went up. 'Please, sir?' he said.

'Well, Spanner,' said Meres, 'what is it? Speak up, boy. Speak up. And sit up straight.'

Spanner sat up straight.

'Please, sir,' he said, 'what do you want us to do?'

'I want you to keep quiet,' said Meres. 'As quiet as teeny weeny mice.'

'Yes, sir,' said Spanner.

'No running to this firm of yours,' said Meres. 'That wouldn't do at all.'

'No, sir,' said Spanner.

Meres looked at George.

'No, sir,' said George.

'Because if you do, we'll know,' said Meres, 'and we'll call on you again. And next time we'll have such jolly romps you wouldn't believe.'

'Not a word,' said Spanner.

'Honest,' said George.

'I believe you,' said Meres, and sighed. 'It's rather disappointing.' He turned to FitzMaurice. 'Shall we go?'

'I'll just put them out first,' said FitzMaurice, and his hand moved twice, the force of it accurately controlled, and Spanner and George found the oblivion they had longed for.

'Shall we join the ladies?' said Meres.

'No,' FitzMaurice said. 'We got the lot. It's time to go.'

'What a soft-hearted fellow you are,' said Meres.

[ii]

'Nice of you to drop in,' said Hexham.

Callan said, 'Nice of you to invite us.'

They stood in the great hall that was two storeys high and twenty feet to a storey. Above them a wrought-iron chandelier hung from a massive chain, its electric bulbs giving out enough light for your local cinema. Around them was marble, and below them too, walls and floor of a delicate pink picked out with gold. The ceiling was stucco, heavy and ornate, flowers and fruit that served as a frame to circular paintings: Venus and Mars, Helen and Paris, Cressida and Troilus. On each side of the hall was a wrought-iron staircase painted gilt, delicate, fragile-looking, yet designed to last for centuries. Scattered on the floor were Persian and Chinese rugs: the furniture of the hall alone would be worth a fortune, thought Callan. Hell, in this place even old Bulk doesn't look quite so well off.

'Gunther hasn't arrived yet,' said Hexham. 'I thought we might wait for him in the library.'

'By all means,' Bulky said, and looked about him. 'This place is enchanting. Really enchanting.'

'It's not much—but it's home,' said Hexham. 'This way.'

Callan followed him up the stairs, so many stairs, and worried as he climbed. Hexham was all wrong. A member of the aristocracy who'd resigned from the brigade, failed as a painter, turned to antiques and remained a bachelor should have been some sort

77

of lightweight, and Hexham was no sort of lightweight. At thirty-four he was in hard condition, with the long slabs of muscle that belonged to a horseman or a hunter. He wore his hair long, his face was handsome and the pale blue silk suit he wore would have caused Lonely an agony of envy, but he wasn't a queer: he had in fact that peculiarly relaxed air of the man who knows that his need of women is all taken care of....

The library was vast: big enough to supply the needs of an Oxford college, it ran the whole breadth of the house. More painted, stuccoed ceilings, but this time the figures were philosophers: Pythagoras, Socrates, Hippocrates. From the floor to ten feet up the walls were bookshelves painted white and gold, except for where the windows stretched across either end of the room. Before the windows, at either end, were great globes mounted in oak-frames.... Callan preserved his rôle of stolid business man. Bulky gasped aloud, and not all of it, Callan thought, was acting.

'My dear sir,' he said.

The earl looked around the book-lined walls; morocco and calf glowed in the light.

'Yes,' he said. 'Some of my ancestors were great readers.'

Bulky moved over to the great ranks of books, and selected one, not at random. 'But you have treasures here,' he said.

'So I'm told,' said Hexham. 'It's a great bore, you know.'

'Indeed?' said Bulky.

'There are the books,' said Hexham, 'and a large quantity of pictures: a Titian, a Claude, a Mantegna, and a dubious, a very dubious Tintoretto. There are tapestries and statuary and a salt cellar by Cellini. They are not in themselves boring—far from it—but consider the insurance.'

'Yeah,' said Callan, 'I know what you mean. In my factory we—'

'It must cost a fortune,' said Bulky.

'Not so much as in England,' said Hexham, 'but enough. When you add to that the cost of burglar precautions and servants one is perhaps a little self-indulgent in choosing to follow this way of life.'

'I can't agree with you,' said Bulky. 'As an exercise in nostalgia I find it enchanting. How much I should like to see your pictures.'

The earl looked at his watch.

'Later, perhaps,' he said. 'Gunther should be with us at any moment.' He went over to a drinks table. 'Brandy, gentlemen, or whisky? I have a rather decent single malt here.' Callan opted for brandy. It looked like being a long night.... Together the three men strolled to the window, and looked out at the mountains of Sicily by moonlight.

78

'Even the view,' Bulky said.

'Sooner or later,' said Hexham, 'one gets tired of views, just as one gets tired of electronic devices to deter burglars. Don't you find that, Mr Callan?'

Now what is this? Callan wondered. Just what in hell is this? 'Well, no,' he said. 'With me it's different. If there weren't any electronic devices I wouldn't be in business.'

And that at least is true, he thought, and worried again as the earl nodded with the air of a man who acknowledges a point scored. Callan looked again at the view of the mountains, taking note as he did so of the burglar alarms set in the windows. The earl was cautious, he thought. You had to give him that. The library must be all of twenty feet above ground level.... From below, very faintly, came the rasp of tyres on gravel.

'Good,' said Hexham. 'That must be Gunther,' and led the way to the other window. Callan followed, and looked at another series of alarms. Nothing there Lonely couldn't handle, if he hadn't lost his head for heights.... He looked down to where a Volkswagen Beetle had parked next to the Alfa. As it stopped Gunther Kleist shot out of it, then hared round to open the door for Jeanne-Marie Nivelle.

'It would seem,' said the earl, 'that we are not to spend a bachelor evening after all.' He moved away from the window: Berkeley and Callan stayed where they were.

Callan said softly: 'Well?'

Bulky's answer was only just audible.

'I don't like it,' he said. 'It's nice when the customers are happy, but this geezer's delirious and it bothers me.'

The library door opened, and an elderly butler came in.

'*Il Signore* Kleist,' he said. '*La Signorina* Nivelle.'

Hexham bustled forward.

'But this is charming,' he said. 'Really delightful. Jeanne-Marie, how nice of you to drop in.'

It sounds sincere, Callan thought, and it looks sincere, but something's wrong.

'Gunther insisted,' she said, 'and you know how much I love this place.'

Callan and Berkeley moved forward, and she bowed to them, and smiled. 'Mr Callan,' she said. 'Mr Berkeley.'

The smile came right out of the deep-freeze.

'You've actually come to play poker?' Hexham asked.

'Oh no,' she said. 'You know I can't play. But I should very much like to watch. I promise you I shan't be in the way.'

'You could never be that,' said the earl.

The card table he led them to was eighteenth-century English,

79

the chairs by Hepplewhite. Even the chips looked antique.

Cautiously Bulky sat on his, but it gave no sound of protest.

'Thank God,' he said. 'I'd hate to break it.'

'My dear sir, don't worry,' said Hexham. 'One of this set once supported the Prince Regent. Now—how shall we play?'

Callan had learned his lines from Bulky.

'Just ordinary straight poker if you don't mind,' he said. 'And no wild cards.'

There were no objectors.

'Now—what about stakes?' said the earl.

Bulky said, 'What do you usually play?'

'Ten pounds in the pot,' said Hexham. 'Five pounds to bet. Raise to a twenty pound limit.'

Bulky whistled.

'I can see you take your poker seriously,' he said.

'A friendly game,' the earl said. 'The money is a safeguard against frivolity.'

'Talking of money,' said Kleist, and the earl looked pained, 'how do we arrange payment?'

'I shall be happy to cash a cheque on a London bank,' said Hexham.

'No need,' said Berkeley. 'I just happen to have a large sum on me.'

'And I've got traveller's cheques on a Swiss bank,' said Callan. 'I take it you do trust Swiss banks?'

The earl looked again at Kleist.

'Really, Gunther, that was inept. You've managed to upset both my guests.'

Jeanne-Marie said, 'I do not understand these insults. Surely if one wins one wishes to be paid.'

'Precisely,' said Bulky.

There was an ungainly pause.

'I think,' said Hexham, 'that we'd better have another drink.'

The ones that Bulky and Callan got were immense....

They played under a chandelier with enormous glass lustres, and the heat it gave off was tremendous: the brandy didn't help either. Cut back on your drinking, Hunter had said, but Hunter hadn't allowed for belted bleeding earls who poured out brandy as if it were bottled stout.... Jeanne-Marie wasn't much help either. She perched on a library ladder between Bulky and Callan, and fidgeted incessantly, with her glass, her ash-tray, her cigarettes, her matches. Callan thought, I know you don't like gambling, darling, but there's no need to make it so obvious.

His hands were terrible, particularly when Bulky dealt, but that had been part of the arrangement. Bulky, a conservative by nature, believed firmly that mugs should always win the first time. It made them greedy. Watching Bulky deal was a treat. The plump, short-fingered hands were only just short of clumsy: he put the cards down with a steady deliberation that contrasted nicely with Kleist's easy flow. Even his shuffling was perfect: nervous and heavy-handed. As the brandy went round again he even boxed the cards.

Losing to Bulky all the time was all right: in the script as you might say. Losing to Kleist and Hexham was a bit harder to bear. His hands were terrible, all right, but he should have won one pot. He didn't. At quarter to three Bulky started to yawn; by quarter past he was almost asleep. When at last he dropped his cards Callan said: 'I think we'd better pack it in.'

Jeanne-Marie jumped up at once.

'Eh?' said Bulky. 'I'm sorry. I must have dropped off.'

'We'd better settle up,' said Callan.

Bulky was out two hundred pounds, and Callan over five hundred. When the time came to do sums with Swiss francs, Kleist was right there with his conversion tables, his kindly fox's face showing nothing but concern.

'Such terrible luck,' he said. 'Really appalling.'

'I've had worse,' said Callan, and the German's eyes glittered. 'I've had better an' all.'

'One ought perhaps to discuss the possibility of revenge,' said Hexham.

'Suits me,' said Callan. Jeanne-Marie scowled.

'Really I'm not sure,' Bulky said. 'At my age these late nights don't agree with me.'

Jeanne-Marie brightened visibly.

'We could start earlier,' Kleist said.

'I don't honestly think—'

'I tell you what,' said Hexham. 'Why don't we dine here—let me show you over the house? You said there were things you'd like to see—and then we can have an early game?'

It took them ten minutes, but in the end Bulky gave in. They would play again in two days' time.

They left then, all four of them, and the earl walked with them to the courtyard where their cars were parked, waited politely as first the Volkswagen then the Alfa-Romeo drove off. As Callan drove past him he could see that he was smiling: a frank, ingenuous smile: no irony in it at all.... As they drove down the mountain road Bulky said, 'If you don't mind we'll talk later. I don't want to put you off your driving.' And then he slept, as neat and contained as a cat. When they reached the autostrada he was awake at once, as alert and sure as he'd been when the evening began. Callan thought: I like you, Bulk. I really do. You're a treat to work with.

Aloud he said, 'Let's have it.'

'The most extraordinary thing,' said Bulky. 'Really in all my experience, which I may say is considerable and varied, I've never come across anything quite like it.'

'Look, Bulk,' said Callan, 'it's been a long day and I'm just about knackered. Just tell me. That's all I ask.'

'He cheats,' Berkeley said. 'He's a peer of the realm and he cheats.'

'Hexham?' said Callan, and he too sounded incredulous.

'Kleist too, of course,' said Bulky, 'and the *soi-disant* French girl. One expects *that* of course—or at least allows for it. But Hexham. Eton and Christ Church and the Coldstream and a card-sharp. It ought not to be possible.'

'How?' said Callan.

'You mean you didn't see?'

'You stick to your scene, Bulk, and I'll stick to mine. How?'

'The girl,' said Bulky. 'She fidgeted all the time. Right?'

'I thought she was bored.'

'She never took her eyes off your hand, or mine. That's why she perched on that damned uncomfortable library ladder. So she could look down. And she fidgeted with four things—cigarettes, ash-tray, matches, drink. Spades, hearts, diamonds, clubs. She was telling them our hands, my boy. A German amateur and a peer of the realm. That I should live to see the day.'

'Don't get too upset,' said Callan. 'We'll win next time. I mean you can still take them, can't you?'

'Certainly,' said Bulky. He sounded insulted. 'They're woefully inept.'

'That's all right then,' said Callan. 'All you've done is add to your knowledge of human nature.' He drove on. '*Soi-disant*,' he said. 'That means so-called, doesn't it?'

'It does.'

'Why is Jeanne-Marie Nivelle so-called?' said Callan.

Bulky told him.

13

House Representative Manette had a hard day, but that was no novelty: all his days were hard. Politics was like that. If you wanted to make it big you had to work for it. Congressman Manette, of French-Canadian extraction, reared in New England, knew all about hard work. He wasn't crazy about it, but it was the only tool he knew how to use.... Letters to supporters in the morning, then a plane from Washington to Boston, plastic food on plastic trays, and nothing to drink except a coke, because even though you didn't know anybody in the first-class section, you could never be quite sure they didn't know you. More work for dessert, a whole briefcase full of it, then the ride to his sister's house in Boston, where his mother was visiting, and on the way he was still working on the briefcase as he rode.

'Go and see your mother every chance you can,' his PR man had told him. 'She's old and she's tetchy and her English is terrible, but for whatever crazy reason people like your mother.'

For the one and only time in his life, Edouard Philippe Manette, now known as Edward Philip, nearly struck a PR man: even though Manette was running for public office. Reason prevailed, but only just. He loved his mother. When he'd told her about it she'd laughed, but he hadn't. He should have swung at the PR man. The fact that he hadn't was somehow tied in with What Was Wrong With America Today.

She was glad to see him, which was more than he could say for his sister, but then his sister didn't see things his way. Before she'd moved to Boston she'd even voted against him, but at least she had the decency to leave him and maman alone, and maman served him cherry gâteau she'd made, and coffee that tasted as no other coffee would ever taste.

'You look tired,' she said.

He shrugged. His gestures, like his French, became fluent only when he was with maman. 'We're all tired,' he said.

'It is worth it?'

'Not yet,' he said. 'It will be.'

She sighed. Her eyes moved as they always did to the bulging briefcase.

'What is it this time?' she asked.

'Oh,' he said, 'trail-walking, new roads for ski-resorts, farm prices. Stuff like that.'

'You are not bored?'

He shook his head, then smiled.

'Some of it's exciting,' he said.

'What is exciting?'

'I can't tell you, maman.'

'Secrets?' He nodded. 'You must take care of that briefcase.'

He promised he would, finished his coffee and kissed her goodbye, then his sister drove him to the garage where he'd left his car, and they quarrelled all the way about CIA intervention in Chile. As if she knew a damn thing about it, he thought. Why, he had documents in his briefcase that very minute—he bit off the thought. Maman was right: he should take good care of that briefcase. He gave in and let his sister enjoy her triumph. At least it left her euphoric enough to cope with the down-town Boston traffic. God it got worse, he thought. The Prudential Centre and the campus and those shopping precincts. All that glass where once there had been stone. Every time it got worse.

He left her and they kissed and there was no contact at all: flesh touched flesh and not even friendship was exchanged: forget about love. And after that it was his turn to fight the traffic, and think about nothing but survival till he made the freeway. After that House Representative Manette, not one drop of alcohol in his veins, never exceeding fifty-five miles per hour, was free to think once more of his problems. First the trail-walkers. Back-packers were nuts, always had been, always would be. Anybody who wanted to walk twenty, thirty miles a day and sleep in a lean-to shelter was, by Manette's definition, a nut. In his youth he'd slept rough often enough and walked miles often enough because he had to. On the other hand back-packers liked Manette: his French-Canadian background carried an aura of limitless pine forests, of tough men in plaid shirts striding out, trusty axe on shoulder. And he looked the part: grizzled, in his fifties, but with a flat stomach and a healthy tan. The stomach stayed flat because of diet, the tan he got from a lamp, and he'd get his car out to drive two blocks, but he looked right. There'd be no trouble with the back-packers.

Ski-resorts now: there you had to be careful. There you had local interests to consider: townships and realtors and contractors. The pie was a juicy one, but there were a lot of

84

fingers in it. Even NAACP, for Christ's sake. Suddenly negroes had discovered ski-ing, and they wanted in. Hundreds of them, maybe thousands. Jesus, he could remember when there weren't more than a hundred negroes in the whole state.... He called himself to order. Nostalgia wouldn't solve anything. Cautiously he began to pick his way between conflicting interests. Enthusiasm, he told himself. That's the way to play it. Be enthusiastic by all means, but for Christ's sake don't get involved.

That brought him to farm prices. Well, when you got right down to it, farm prices was just figures, complex, and dull. And he'd done his homework. He could handle the figures. When he made his speech in the House that would be complex and dull too, and maybe he'd take some joshing from the boys in the wash-room. That didn't worry him. The local farm papers would report him in full, and for him the farmers' vote was vital.... Near home, he thought. Just time to think about what maman called secrets. And boy, did he have secrets. That CIA committee. The thought delighted Manette. Hard work was what he lived by: it had brought him a long way to a nice home, nice cars, an office in Washington; but every two years it was at risk, and every time he thought about it Edward Philip Manette worked harder. But even a hard-working congressman could daydream, and Manette dreamed about espionage: agents, live-drops, safe-houses, controllers. And then one wonderful day he'd been elected to that CIA committee. He was under no illusions: he'd got there because he was safe, dependable, dull, and smart with figures. Old Eddie wouldn't fall for wildcat schemes: old Eddie wouldn't let them squander public funds. Nor did he; but he got to know things: fascinating, incredible things. A girl went missing and suddenly a man was at risk: maybe even a government. And good old Eddie had it all in his briefcase....

He turned off the highway and drove carefully through the town, carefully waved back to everyone who waved to him. His street looked—nice: old, shingled houses, each with its picket fence: the trees still green. The fall was weeks away. Manette drove into his driveway and carried his briefcase into the house. His wife Louise was undemonstrative, but delighted to see him. Everything about their current way of life delighted Louise, and he loved her for it. She fixed him a bourbon on the rocks the way he liked it, and that was fine too. When he went to the back-packers' meeting she'd go along, and she would drive.... She fixed him a sandwich as he went through his notes; and his daughter Elizabeth came in.

'Hi,' she said.

'Hi,' he said, and went on reading. This didn't bother Elizabeth.

85

At twenty she had developed an enormous tolerance towards her father: the tolerance, she thought, of the polar bear for the gorilla. Each had its own way of life, its own behaviour patterns, and if they both got away from the zoo their paths didn't cross. But they were in the zoo, and it was feeding time. Louise, head-keeper, made her daughter a sandwich, and talked softly to her, as Manette read up on shelters, blazes, freeze-dried concentrates and wished to hell he knew what freeze-dried concentrates were. The only thing he knew about it for sure was that he wouldn't like it.

'Trudi von Nichts,' his daughter said. 'Did you ever hear such a crazy name?'

Manette put down his notes.

'You've met a girl called Trudi von Nichts?' he said.

'No, dad,' his daughter said. 'I just heard about her. We had a party by Vicki's pool and this boy from New York—he was doing sociology somewhere—he was talking about her. Sort of a case-history.'

'Honey,' said her father, 'I want you to tell me all about it.'

He smiled at his daughter. The warm, compassionate, politician's smile, thought Elizabeth. The old vote for me because I love you. Really there was no point in gorillas trying to make contact with polar bears, even in the zoo. But she told him anyway.

[ii]

The first step was to have the firm bugged, and that was easy. They had a garage out Newington way that did very nicely and was strictly legit, except when they used it to provide cars and lorries for their other operations. Crime like everything else these days depends on transport, and to the firm the garage was vital. That made putting a bug on them dead easy. Hunter made certain arrangements, and suddenly the firm's telephone no longer worked. Arthur Nichols, occasionally known as Loopy because of a tendency to unnecessary violence, went to a phone-booth and called the GPO engineers. His voice was vibrant with indignation and why not? He'd paid his bills.

'My name is Nichols,' he said. 'I'm general manager of Super Cars. Now look here—'

'One moment, sir,' the voice said, and the call was transferred.

'Engineers,' said Meres. 'Who's calling, please?'

'It's still Nichols,' Loopy said, more indignant than ever, 'and I'm still manager of Super Cars—but I won't be if you keep me hanging about much longer. Listen....'

The engineers arrived in half an hour, and they did a smooth, efficient job. They should have done: they both held degrees in electronic engineering. It seemed that one of the handsets was responsible, and they replaced it with a new one, checked it, and left. Grudgingly Loopy admitted that for a nationalised outfit they hadn't done so bad. Loopy was a passionate advocate of private enterprise. Out in the yard two mechanics were tuning up an E type Jaguar 2 + 2 and a Rover 3500, ready for a spot of work. Loopy and his partners had to raise their voices to make themselves heard. For the two men from the GPO that was an unnecessary bonus. They were in the back of an old van parked behind the garage, and the bug in the handset picked up everything. It went on to the tape a treat.

The target was a security van out in Slough that picked up wages from the bank and delivered at a radio components firm: over five hundred employees—say twenty thousand quid and nothing bigger than a tenner. Nice, easy tickle: make sure the van got a slow puncture on a quiet stretch of road, two of you drive up as AA men just when they've changed the tyre and knock off whoever's out of the van. Then on to the peace and quiet of the countryside and open up: do the rest of the guards, stick the loot in the Rover and have it away. And if the Rover gets a puncture there's the E type in reserve. The senior maintenance man changed tapes.

'And they say crime doesn't pay,' he said. 'Twenty thousand quid in less than two hours. And all tax free.' He handed over the used tape. 'You'd better get this back to the Section.'

His junior wheeled a Honda 250 from the parked van, and set off....

Hunter liked what he heard. All good planning was a pleasure to him, and this planning was meticulous. If the personnel were as able as the planning.... 'Will they bring it off, do you think?' he asked.

'Oh yes, sir,' said Meres. 'I've checked with Special Branch. They are regarded as very competent.'

'Four men, I think you said?'

'Yes sir. Arthur "Loopy" Nichols, Norman Burt, Patrick Higgins and Lewis "Boston" Smith.'

'Boston?'

'He's an ex-wrestler, sir,' said Meres. 'His speciality was the Boston crab.'

'Indeed,' said Hunter, not understanding a word. 'They will be formidable?'

'Yes, sir.'

'Armed?'

'Crowbars and coshes,' said Meres. 'Almost certainly sawn-off

87

shot-guns. It is possible that Nichols will carry a revolver.'

'How many men to overpower them?'

'Four of us should be adequate, sir.'

'I don't want adequacy,' said Hunter. 'I want a show of force.' He brooded for a moment. 'These four represent the hard core of the—er—firm?'

'They *are* the firm, sir,' said Meres. 'Anyone else they use is contracted. Quite often without knowing what the whole job is. That way if they're caught they can't talk.... Even if they dared.'

Hunter looked approving. 'Excellent,' he said. 'Really quite excellent. Now.... This is what you will do.'

[iii]

Lonely's sun tan was coming along nicely, and Callan had even coaxed him to get his bikini briefs wet in the pool. They'd taken a drive to Messina an' all: even found a place where they did chips. Smashing holiday, if you looked at it like that, but you couldn't look at it like that, not properly. This wasn't supposed to *be* a holiday.... He sat outside this caff with Mr Callan—funny the way you always sat outside when you went foreign—and drank his beer and brooded. Callan put down his coffee-cup.

'All right,' he said. 'Let's have it.'

'It's the job,' said Lonely. 'It's getting me down.'

'Getting you down?' said Callan. 'You haven't even started yet.'

'That's what's getting me down,' said Lonely. 'It's the waiting, Mr Callan. I never could stand the waiting.'

'Not many of us can,' said Callan. 'All the same we have to, haven't we?'

Lonely went back to his brooding, and Callan ordered him another beer.

'Did you find where the book was?' Lonely asked.

'Not yet.'

'But you went there last night,' said Lonely. 'You went there special.'

'I'm here to do two jobs,' said Callan. 'Last night one job got in the way of the other.'

'You and that fatty,' said Lonely. 'If you put him at the North Pole he couldn't nick snow.'

As if I didn't have enough problems, thought Callan, now I've got jealousy as well.

'He isn't here to nick things,' he said. 'That's your department. You're the expert.' He waited, but Lonely wasn't in the mood for smirking. 'Anyway I'm going back to the palazzo tomorrow night. I'll suss the book out then.'

88

'Going back where, Mr Callan?'

'The earl's gaff,' said Callan.

'And that's another thing,' said Lonely. 'You going skiving off with that fatty all the time—I thought *I* was your mate.'

Oh dear oh dear, thought Callan. This is worse than being married.

'So you are,' he said. 'You're in the firm, aren't you? When we go public you'll be on the board.'

'Roger de Vere Bullivant,' said Lonely, but his heart wasn't in it.

The waiter brought him his beer. Lonely had half a mind not to drink it.

When they got back to the hotel he threw another tantrum. Callan had to go into conference with Berkeley and he wasn't invited. It upset him, and he said so.

Callan said, 'I'm making every allowance for the artistic temperament—' and Lonely went on muttering. Callan's voice hardened. 'Look at me when I'm talking to you,' he said.

At once Lonely was silent: his eyes looked up to Callan's face.

'Yes, Mr Callan?'

'Now you've got a choice,' said Callan. 'It's up to you. Either you belt up or I'll get physical. Now.... Which is it to be?'

'Oh, I'll belt up,' said Lonely. 'You can rely on me.'

'That's all right then.'

'Not a word,' said Lonely. 'You know I always do what you say. I'll stay stum, Mr Callan. Not a peep.'

'For Gawd's sake,' said Callan. 'Don't keep saying it. Just do it.'

He fled to Bulky's room. Bulky, master craftsman, was practising his trade. As Callan watched he dealt out two poker hands. Callan had a full-house, jacks and tens; Bulky had a full-house: kings and eights. Next time Callan had four kings and Bulky had four aces. The time after that he had a running flush to the ten: Bulky's was to the queen. On and on it went, till Bulky asked Callan what hand he'd like to have. Callan asked for four aces and Bulky obliged.... And always Callan's eyes watched Bulky's hands and always Bulky dealt in the same methodical, not quite clumsy manner, and always, Callan was ready to swear, the cards came off the top.

'You like the cards?' Bulky asked.

'Yeah. A nice pack,' said Callan.

Bulky chuckled comfortably.

'I wish you really were a rich business man,' Bulky said. 'I'd clean you in a week. These are the same cards Hexham uses. I bought them in Catania this morning.'

'You're going to switch packs?'

The heavy shoulders shrugged.

'I may not have to,' he said. 'We'll see.'

'Do whatever you like,' said Callan. 'So long as we take them tomorrow night.'

'The whole lot?'

'The whole lot.'

'Ten thousand nicker,' said Bulky. 'Besides what Hexham drops.'

'Hexham doesn't have to drop anything,' said Callan.

'Oh yes he does,' said Bulky. 'Earls shouldn't cheat. All the same, old man, it's a bit of a tall order.'

Callan said, 'I know, and I'm sorry I have to rush you, but my other cohort's getting nervous.'

'Tea-leaves,' said Bulky, more in sorrow than in anger. 'Prima donnas to a man. Still, if we must, we must.' He thought for a moment. 'I suggest we play it like this.'

14

Manette was a romantic who didn't take chances. A more thorough-going romantic would have got the car out and driven over to Vicki's place: an utter realist would have put in a call to Langley, Virginia. Manette compromised: his whole political life had been based on compromise, and he made the decision automatically. He would do the thing himself, but he would do it right: the agent in place, fulfilling his destiny. And having done it right he would be a hero, and heroes got more votes. So it was that he briefed his daughter carefully. She could get more information out of Vicki Davies in one phone call than he could in a two-hour interrogation, and besides, nobody would wonder if she talked to Vicki, but if *he* did—that was no way to be a spy.

'What are you up to, dad?' she asked. 'A *cause célèbre*?'

Her French accent was as good as maman's. He loved to hear it.

'I don't think I'd put it like that,' he said.

'I don't think you could,' said Elizabeth. 'What's one more junky nowadays?'

My daughter, he thought, my beloved daughter, even nowadays this junky is special.

'Just call Vicki,' he said. 'If I can tell you the story one day—then I will.'

Gorillas should stay out of the polar-bears' pool. They shouldn't try to eat fish either. It could never work. But this gorilla had such pleading eyes.

'O.K.,' she said. 'I'll call her. But not from here, dad.'

'What's wrong with here?'

'You put me off,' she said.

She called from her bedroom. From its walls the poets looked down on her: Rimbaud and Baudelaire, Rilke, Keats, Chatterton on his death-bed. She looked at them.

To Keats and Chatterton she said, 'This is bananas.'

To Rimbaud and Baudelaire: 'C'est de bananes.'

91

In fairness to Rilke she added: 'Diese sind bananen.'

She called Vicki. Now there was an act of filial solicitude if you like. Vicki was permanently bananas. And maybe it was just as well—the dumb questions she had to ask.

'Mrs Davies? This is Elizabeth Manette. Could I speak to Vicki please?' Let's hope the dumb-bell is home just once in her life, she thought, then heard the extension lifted. 'Vicki?'

'Elizabeth?' Vicki said.

Oh you idiot. You *stupid* idiot, didn't your mother tell you it was me?

'I just phoned up to say thank you for the party,' she said. The silence at the other end denoted only incomprehension. 'You know—by the pool?'

'Oh *that* party,' said Vicki. 'Fun, humh?'

'Just the greatest. And all those *fabulous* people.'

'You really enjoyed meeting them?'

Oh God, Elizabeth thought. Now I'm on her party list till the end of time.

'Did I? Where did you find them all?'

She heard in turn about Chuck from Florida, Emily from Nassau, Charley from Harvard. It took for ever, but it had to be endured.

'They were all just fantastic,' she said at last. 'And that tall boy too. The one from New York.'

'What tall boy from New York?'

'You know—long dark hair. Sort of good-looking. He was studying sociology some place.'

'Sociology?'

Vicki was getting bewildered again. Time to get back to basics.

'He wore blue swimming trunks and brought a couple of joints,' she said.

'Oh *him*. He was pretty all right. But sort of clever. You know? Marcie Ambruster brought him.'

This is just great, Elizabeth thought. On top of everything else I've got to call Marcie Ambruster—a girl who can't even dig Camus. But she was her father's daughter. Work was what got results. Patiently she waited while Vicki ran out of steam, and utilised the time by looking up Marcie's number.

[ii]

The job was a breeze. True, the security van driver wet himself, and Loopy bust one of his mates out of sheer exuberance. All the same a breeze. They didn't even have to change vehicles: went straight back to Super Cars for the carve up. A four way split, just like always. Equal pay for equal work as those mugs on the

92

soapboxes said. Not that you could call it work. Just a nice quiet drive in the country and a little gentle exercise. Boston got the whisky out, and Loopy lit a cigar with a five-pound note. It was the one ritual gesture they indulged in, and they always enjoyed it, and it came out of Loopy's cut anyway. The only flaw to their happiness was the sound of the pneumatic drills outside, but what was a bit of noise when you were rich?

Meres put down the headphones, and looked at the other men in the van. Hunter's army, he thought. If they weren't on my side they'd even frighten me.

'Sounds like quite a party,' he said. 'Pity to interrupt it really. Nevertheless I suppose we'd better. Everybody ready? Good.'

He rapped on the driving cab panel, and FitzMaurice drove off. FitzMaurice was sweating slightly, but the sweat was that of anticipation, not fear. With the goon-squad that Hunter had loaned them they could take on a tank. He drove round the block and on to the main road and the men behind the Gas Board tarpaulins opened up again with the drills as he drove into the garage's forecourt. Nobody about. He braked, knocked twice on the panel, and a couple of the goon-squad got out of the van, swung the doors of the garage to, as the rest of the goon-squad leaped out, silent and deadly as cats, and Meres last of all, his eyes glittering with excitement, a machine-pistol in his hands. Like a little boy at Christmas, FitzMaurice thought. Oh daddy.... It's what I always wanted.... And after the briefing Hunter had given them this really was Christmas.

Meres and the goon-squad went round to the back of the office, and FitzMaurice left the van, walked to the front door. The drills were going off like .5 machine guns and FitzMaurice sweated more freely. If he was going to get it, it would be in the next half minute. He raised one massive fist and pounded on the door. It made good competition for the drills.... Norman Burt answered the knock. He had a glass of whisky in his hand, but he was displeased.

'Fuck off, Sambo,' he said. 'We're closed.'

Behind him there came the splashing tinkle of glass breaking, and FitzMaurice hit him rather harder than he'd intended, Burt shot back like a champagne cork leaving a bottle, FitzMaurice reached inside his donkey jacket, pulled out the Colt .45 mini-cannon, then picked up Burt, closed the door with his foot, and walked into the office. The goon-squad was in place exactly the way it should be, and Higgins, Nichols and Smith sat absolutely motionless, like a freeze-frame shot in a movie. But they weren't looking at the goon-squad: they weren't even looking at Meres. They were looking at the machine-pistol. FitzMaurice dumped the unconscious Burt on the floor and Higgins's eyes swivelled to the negro.

93

'Jesus,' he said. 'Jesus.'

'You seem to have hit him rather hard,' said Meres.

'Yassuh. He insulted mah race.'

Meres sighed petulantly.

'I do wish you wouldn't be so touchy,' he said. 'You know they all have to be conscious when we start.'

'What the hell is this?' Nichols said, and FitzMaurice tapped him with the Colt's barrel, hard enough for the foresight to break the skin.

'You bloody bastard,' he said, and lunged forward. FitzMaurice hit him again, this time hard enough to daze him.

'That's much better,' said Meres. 'Do what you like so long as they don't faint. You'd better bring the other one round.'

FitzMaurice emptied a jug of water over Burt, who groaned, but his eyes stayed closed, until FitzMaurice began to kick him in the ribs, controlled, even kicks always on the same spot. Burt groaned again, and this time his eyes opened.

'What—?' he said. The kicking went on.

'On your feet, boss,' said FitzMaurice.

It was the only way to stop being kicked, and Burt knew it. He got up, swaying like a drunk.

'That's better,' said Meres, and looked from one to the other of the four, the machine-pistol following his gaze.

'I think they're conscious,' he said to FitzMaurice. 'Though with them it's hard to tell.'

'They're as conscious as they'll ever be,' FitzMaurice said.

Meres looked about him as if waiting for silence: there wasn't a sound. 'Well,' he said, in his best platoon-commander's voice, 'I expect you chaps are all wondering why we're here. Let me tell you. You've been naughty.'

The machine-pistol motioned briefly to the table on which the money was stacked, then came back to the firm.

'You really are the most dreadful people,' he said. 'You *steal*.... You stole twenty-two thousand eight hundred and thirty-four pounds seventy-two pence this very afternoon.' He paused as if pondering the enormity of such conduct.

'Twenty-two thousand eight hundred and thirty-four pounds seventy-two pence,' he said again. There was a pause. Like every pause that Meres arranged, it soon became unbearable. It was Higgins who broke it.

'How in hell did you know?' he said.

At once FitzMaurice hit him with the Colt, and Higgins swayed. FitzMaurice put the gun away then, but his hands were even more menacing.

'You must learn to ask the right questions,' said Meres. Nobody

94

spoke. 'Come along, chaps,' said Meres. 'Surely somebody has a question. You're not in the picture yet.'

At last, Boston Smith said: 'You want in?'

'No,' said Meres. FitzMaurice hit Smith, and still the drills roared on.

'Now you,' said Meres, and the machine-pistol pointed at Higgins.

'You're cutting in?' said Higgins.

'Better,' said Meres. 'Really, much better. Rather good in fact.'

One of the goon-squad stepped forward, and with gloved hands began stowing the money into a plastic bag.

'Here,' said Nichols. 'Hold on.'

Meres turned to him. His face showed nothing but polite concern, but his eyes still glittered. 'You are no doubt about to tell us,' he said, 'that we can't get away with it.'

'Yes,' said Nichols. 'I am.'

Higgins made a deprecatory gesture that Nichols didn't even see.

'Look,' he said. 'You're not talking to amateurs, you know.'

Meres waited in silence, and Nichols continued: 'We run this patch, mate. Always have and always will.' Neither Meres nor FitzMaurice moved. 'What I mean, you bust in and you've got a fancy gun. All right. But don't you go getting greedy, mate. Not with us. Fifty per cent—all right. But you nick the lot and we'll find you, Mr La-di-da. And when we do you'll wish we hadn't.'

As he spoke he stood up, and FitzMaurice sweated harder. Snell and Hunter between them had figured Nichols just right. Let him counter-attack, they said, and see what happens. That particular kind of psychotic personality will take every step forward as an indication of victory to come. He stood upright now, weight balanced evenly on the balls of his feet. I bet you even think we've forgotten something, thought FitzMaurice. If you weren't so awful I'd be sorry for you. But who needs my sorrow?

'Fifty per cent?' said Meres. He sounded as if he liked the idea.

'It's that,' said Nichols, 'or it's war. You take your choice.'

Again Higgins made the deprecatory gesture: again Nichols failed to see. Meres looked away to where the goon-squad man still stowed the money into a plastic bag. At once Nichols went for the gun in his pants' waistband, and as he did so, Meres swung back, the machine-pistol chattered, and Nichols was smashed, hurled across the room, the row of bullet holes in his chest neatly, evenly spaced. The noise in that confined space was appalling. The machine-pistol swung back to the firm's survivors.

'And then there were three,' said Meres.

They sat in silence.

'How very foolish he was, to be sure,' said Meres. 'Did he actually think we'd forgotten to search him?'

'You take the lot,' said Higgins. 'We won't give you any trouble.'

'Indeed you won't,' said Meres. 'You see, chaps, you're in my power. Oh I know you're all big and strong and daring. But so was that idiot Loopy—and look where it got him.' He looked from one to the other of the three faces: Burt was still in agony, Higgins shrewd enough to know terror: only Boston Smith remained impassive.

'I just killed your partner,' said Meres. 'Doesn't that make you feel anything?'

'Yes,' said Higgins. 'It makes me feel afraid. Isn't that what you came for?'

Higgins and Burt were taken care of by that one sentence, but the ex-wrestler was still silent. FitzMaurice stood over him, yanked him to his feet.

'Why don't you take me, boss?' he said. 'It can't be no worse than waiting to be shot.'

Boston Smith swung. There was anger in the blow, and fear, and outrage that a king should be treated as a serf, but there was accumulated skill, too. He missed by a mile. Methodically, frowning in concentration, FitzMaurice hammered him into submission, using skills the white man didn't know existed, then, after he had defeated him, administered the same systematic beating he'd once given to Callan: careful, methodical, slow.

At last Meres said, 'Careful. He still has to hear what I say.'

FitzMaurice pushed Smith flat-handed into a chair, and Meres put the machine-pistol on the table next to the bag full of money.

'Be honest, chaps,' he said. 'We've got you. We've got you like that.' He held up his hands, palms touching, fingers interlaced. 'Now haven't we?'

Higgins agreed at once: Burt nodded: Smith groaned.

'And we can do it any time we choose,' said Meres. 'Beat you, I mean, or have you killed. We can also have you arrested.' He looked at the money-bag. 'All your fingerprints are on it, and you've recorded the most fascinating tapes. You'd go down for years and years and years—Would you like that? It's up to you. I could have you beaten and then shot. I could even have you beaten and sent to prison and then shot. And I'd enjoy it. Do you believe that?'

'Jesus yes,' said Higgins.

Meres looked at him approvingly. 'You are not altogether stupid,' he said. 'It's up to you to keep the others in order—and see that you do. Now—listen carefully.'

He never had a better audience. Never again would they ever

96

see, telephone or even think of Spanner, Berkeley, Callan or Fred, nor hire anybody else to do so. If they did—he looked from Smith's battered face to Nichols' splayed-out body.

'I trust I've made myself clear,' he said. 'I think that's all.' He picked up the machine-pistol. 'Come along, chaps.'

'Mister?' said Higgins.

'Yes?'

'What about—' Higgins gestured at the body. 'What about Nichols?'

'If I were you,' said Meres, 'I'd get rid of him. If the police were to drop in and find him it wouldn't make a good impression.'

They went out, and the goon-squad climbed into the van, Meres rode in the cab with FitzMaurice.

'The things one does for one's country,' he said.

'Yeah,' said FitzMaurice. 'I'm glad it's not my country.'

As they drove down the road the gas-board men were packing it in for the day.

15

Callan watched Lonely finish his beer, empty out the last crumbs from his bag of crisps.

'That's the lot,' he said. 'No more beer till we've done the job.'

'No beer?'

'Take it easy,' said Callan. 'We're doing the job tonight.'

Lonely looked at Callan's blue light-weight suit, white shirt, figured tie. 'You can't do no jobs wearing that clobber,' he said.

'I can change, can't I?' said Callan. Then Bulky appeared.

That evening his silk suit was of dark grey. He looked like a bishop in mufti. 'All ready?' he said.

For once Callan was dithering. He went to the mirror, looked at his coat and took off the jacket, then unlocked his suitcase, took out the gun harness and put it on.

'Oh lord,' said Lonely.

Callan checked the Magnum, put it into the webbing holster, and drew the gun, put his coat on and drew again. Bulky smiled placid approval, an expert admiring another's expertise.

'Is it going to be like that?' said Lonely.

'I don't know,' said Callan, 'but if it is and I go in there undressed I'll look a right Charley, won't I?'....

The palazzo was magnificent. Most of the furniture was under what Callan dimly remembered as being called holland covers, but what was exposed was superb. Over-ornate for Callan's taste, but nonetheless magnificent: chairs, console-tables, sofas, commodes, all lacquer and gilt to the point where the original woodwork was almost invisible. Eighteenth-century baroque verging on the rococo, and worth a fortune.... Room after room full of elaborate elegance, until Hexham led them at last to the long gallery where the pictures hung, among them the Titian, the Claude, the Mantegna and the dubious Tintoretto. Bulky cooed happily, very much the knowledgeable dilettante, and Callan wandered away from pictures to look at the bureau-cabinet that stood at one end of the gallery. It was a tall piece, walnut veneered, with elaborately worked brass fittings, and panelled with mirror-glass. Compared with some of the stuff

Callan had just seen it was almost reticent.

'Like it?' Hexham asked.

'It looks—different,' said Callan.

'That's because it is different. Made by Martin Schnell of Dresden in 1734. Rather splendid in its way, don't you think?'

Dresden, thought Callan. Hunter hadn't said anything about Dresden: just a looking-glass cabinet. Dresden was SSD country—and Hunter knew it.

'Very nice,' said Callan.

They went back to looking at pictures, till the butler announced the arrival of Jeanne-Marie Nivelle and Kleist, then went to a drawing-room and more elaborate furnishing and pictures. Say fifty thousand quid's worth, thought Callan. And this is the smallest room I've seen so far. Why would this geezer want to cheat? ... Hexham went forward to greet Jeanne-Marie and Kleist, and Kleist was innocent and kind, Jeanne-Marie sulky, just like before. They really worked hard at their act.

Drinks, and then dinner, and on the table the salt-cellar by Cellini. It was solid silver, ornamented with a design of nymphs and satyrs, and weighing, Callan guessed, seven or eight pounds. Bulky cooed again.

'A bit clumsy if all one happens to want is salt,' the earl said, and picked it up by two convenient nymphs: 'but rather fun to handle.'

The dinner was excellent, and the wines superb. Somehow the butler managed to fill up Callan's and Bulky's glasses far more frequently than the others, till Callan left a brimful glass beside him throughout an entire course. Bulky, unconcerned, ate and drank everything that was offered.

After dinner, the library, and brandy, any amount of brandy, then they moved to the table and Jeanne-Marie perched on the library ladder, arranged her matches, cigarettes, ash-tray and drink.

Then Bulky got whimsical.

'You don't look at all comfortable there, Miss Nivelle,' he said. 'Do let me get you another chair.' He moved towards an elaborate structure of gilt and carving with a very low seat.

Naughty old Bulk, thought Callan, that wasn't in the script. He looked from one to other of the three. Jeanne-Marie sulked more than ever, for once the earl looked less than calm, and Kleist was close to panic.

'Please don't bother,' Jeanne-Marie said.

'It's no bother,' said Bulky, and grasped the chair. 'Dear me, how heavy it is.'

Callan thought he might as well have fun too.

'I'll give you a hand,' he said, and stood up.

'If you don't mind, old boy,' Hexham said, 'I'd rather leave that chair where it is. It's a Corradine—the Venetian sculptor, you know. 1730 or thereabouts. *Rather* expensive, and I'm inclined to suspect woodworm.'

Bulky desisted.

'After all Miss Nivelle assures us she is comfortable,' the earl said, 'so why don't we just play poker?'

After all, his smile said, if Miss Nivelle chooses to be both a bore and a nuisance, what possible concern is it of ours?

The four men played, Jeanne-Marie fidgeted, and once again Bulky and Callan lost steadily, until, it seemed, Bulky became rather the worse for drink. It was his deal, and the cards came out clumsily, he looked at his hand once and put it down. Jeanne-Marie looked outraged: she only had Callan's hand to look at. Bulky bet high, and Callan and the others followed, round after round.

At last Bulky said, 'It seems silly to have such small stakes. Why don't we raise them?'

'You have a good hand, Mr Berkeley?' Kleist said, and smiled. The earl looked pained.

'What sort of limit did you have in mind?' said Callan.

'Fifty pounds.'

'Now hold on a minute,' said Callan.

'Sportsmen,' Bulky said thickly. 'I thought we were sportsmen.'

'Never let it be said that I am not a sportsman,' said the earl. 'I accept.'

At once, Kleist said, 'I also.... And you, Mr Callan?'

'Oh very well,' said Callan. He sounded as if he didn't like the idea at all.

Bulky at once raised the bet to fifty, and first Callan dropped out, then the earl. Kleist was perceptibly sweating. He called at once.

'Four kings,' said Bulky, and reached for his cards.

Kleist for once looked less than kindly.

'Four queens,' he said, and showed them. Bulky spread out his cards in a clumsy fan and reached for the pot. The earl coughed delicately, but it was Callan who spoke.

'Hold on, old man,' he said. 'One of those kings is a jack.'

Bulky picked up his cards, held them close to his face, and peered.

'I really am most awfully sorry,' he said. 'I do hope you don't think I was trying to cheat.'

Callan found that trying not to laugh can hurt. One more ad lib from Bulky and his ribs would go.

Kleist took it like a gentleman. 'Of course not,' he said, and raked in the pot.

'That's all right then,' Bulky said, and leaned back heavily.

'Maybe if you're not feeling well we should postpone the game,' said Callan.

'But I am feeling well,' said Bulky. 'I'm feeling perfectly well.'

Callan looked helplessly at the other two men: his whole demeanour that of a sportsman unwilling to take advantage of a drunk. The earl shrugged, Kleist looked away.

'It's only my eyes,' Bulky said. 'I'm getting on, you know. Eyes always have given me trouble. I wonder if we could have a bit more light?'

The earl got up at once to fetch a standard lamp, Kleist fussed with a switch, and Jeanne-Marie went to pour herself another drink. Except for Callan, Bulky was unmarked, but afterwards Callan was never quite sure how Bulky switched packs: all he knew was that Bulky's hands were as fast as his own. When Hexham came back to the table he brought refills for Berkeley and Callan, and had no trouble in avoiding Callan's reproachful look.

They went on playing, and for a couple of hands Jeanne-Marie had no trouble in sending out her signals: Berkeley and Callan still lost. Then it was Callan's deal, and Berkeley leaned forward to push the pack over to him. He pressed too hard at one end, and the pack spluttered open, then his pudgy hands struggled to put it together.

'Sorry,' he said. 'This damn light.'

He reached up and tilted the lamp as Callan dealt. By the time Callan had finished dealing the light shone full in Jeanne-Marie's eyes.

'That's better,' said Bulky.

Callan noted without surprise that he held four aces, put his cards down and looked about him. Neither Kleist nor Hexham seemed particularly worried. After all, so far as they knew they were playing with their own cards.

It was Kleist who called him. Until that moment his four kings had looked good. He went down for fifteen hundred pounds.

'It would seem that your luck is changing, Mr Callan,' Kleist said.

'Not before time,' said Callan, and slid the cards over to Bulky.

'If you don't mind,' Jeanne-Marie said, 'the light is shining in my eyes.'

'My dear,' said Bulky, 'I'm most awfully sorry.' He reached up and fiddled. 'There. Is that better?'

'Thank you.'

101

Laboriously, Bulky dealt, and Jeanne-Marie sent out her signals. Callan was beginning to know them well. A full house, jacks and tens, for himself, and for Bulky a full house kings and eights. The betting began. After two hundred pounds worth he stacked, and it was up to Bulky. The fat man looked at his hand again, pushed it together, then reached for his handkerchief to mop his eyes.

'It is your bet, Mr Berkeley,' said Kleist.

'Eh? Oh, I'm sorry,' said Bulky. 'These eyes of mine.' He tossed another chip into the pot. 'I'm in,' he said.

Again the pot was fifteen hundred pounds: again Hexham stacked and Kleist called.

'Three aces,' said Bulky, and Callan relished the disbelief on Jeanne-Marie's face. It took a lot out of Kleist, too.

'I'm sorry,' he said at last. 'I have four threes.'

He reached for the pot, and as he did so Bulky showed his hand.

'Hey, wait a minute,' Callan said. 'You made a mistake, Mr Berkeley.'

'Nonsense,' said Bulky.

'But you did,' said Callan. 'You've got four aces.'

Bulky peered down, delighted.

'So I have,' he said. 'Much obliged to you. You know I really must change my optician.'

Kleist and Hexham were looking at Jeanne-Marie. Even Kleist's kindliness was reproachful, and the earl had lost his aloofness. The woman herself had a dazed, unbelieving look, as if a chair had backed off when she tried to sit on it. Bulky let them win a few hands. They didn't make much, because Callan and he stacked early, but even so, a win is a win, and the mug turned sharp has never quite shaken off the mugs' disease, which is called euphoria. It was Hexham who suggested they raise the limit to a hundred pounds. It took all his charm to overcome Berkeley's and Callan's resistance, and it was only after Kleist had pointed out that it was the only way they would get their money back that Berkeley at last agreed and talked Callan round.

Berkeley and Callan lost again, and again; small pots, but every little helps. The looks of reproach at Jeanne-Marie faded and almost died. Once more it was Bulky's deal. Callan picked up the nine, ten and king of hearts, Jeanne-Marie fiddled, and Bulky had a terrible fit of coughing.

'I wonder, my dear,' he said, 'if you would fetch me a glass of water?'

Jeanne-Marie scowled, and did so, and Bulky fumbled out the rest of the cards.

'Thank you, my dear,' said Bulky. 'I'm most grateful.'

Hexham and Kleist weren't unduly worried. The odds against filling an inside straight are phenomenal, and a flush was no hand at all.

'Why don't we double the limit again?' Hexham said.

'Now look,' said Callan. 'What is this exactly?'

Hexham's eyebrows rose. 'Sportsmen?' he said. 'Didn't I hear the word used? Or are you afraid?'

'All right,' said Callan. 'Two hundred. But that's as far as I go.'

It cost Kleist and Hexham three thousand pounds.

After that, Bulky decided to speed things up. They'd said they'd finish at eleven, and there wasn't much time. Kleist won once, and Hexham twice, but after that Bulky wiped his eyes, dropped his cards in his lap and fiddled with the lamp, and their opponents went down three times, each crash bigger than the last. After the third disaster, the earl's air of relaxation was as thin as cigarette paper. Kleist looked appalled.

Bulky wriggled in his chair, yawned, looked at his watch, and stacked the cards together, clumsy to the last.

'Eleven o'clock,' he said. 'Time for beddy-byes. What's the damage?'

Callan, electronics tycoon, did sums. What it amounted to was that the earl had lost seven thousand pounds, and Kleist eleven thousand. Both men looked dazed—and Jeanne-Marie looked worse. To Callan it was as if she had died, then been put into the hands of a competent taxidermist.

At last Kleist managed to say, 'If you gentlemen would care to come to my hotel, I shall settle with you there.' His voice was a croak.

Genial, Pickwickian Uncle Bulky smiled and said, 'Of course,' then looked at Hexham, but Hexham's eyes were on Callan.

'I'm afraid,' he said, 'I must ask for a little time, unless you would care to accept a book instead.'

Callan was standing: his eyes watching the earl, hands open by his sides.

'A book?' he said. 'Are you kidding?'

'I'm perfectly serious. It's a book I think you'll find you very much want to have.'

Callan's right hand moved up, loosed the top button of his jacket.

'What you trying to flog me?' he said. 'Porn?'

'I'm trying to flog you the aspirations of the human spirit,' said Hexham.

And for all Callan knew, that could be Hexham's definition of Marx's *Kapital*.

103

'John Florio's translation of the Essays of Montaigne,' said the earl. 'The 1583 edition. At current prices it should be worth more than seven thousand.'

Bulky said, 'You're asking us to share this book?'

'I am.'

'I should prefer money,' said Bulky. 'Cash.'

'No doubt,' said the earl. 'Unfortunately I haven't got any.'

Callan looked around the ornate library.

'Looks,' said Hexham, 'can be deceptive.'

He walked over to the bookshelves, took out a leather-bound book and offered it to Callan, who took it left-handed, and passed it on to Bulky.

'The Essays of Montaigne,' said Bulky. 'The Florio translation, just as you said. And by the look of it a first edition.'

'But you would prefer money.'

'In my experience,' said Bulky, 'everybody does.'

'I'll think about it,' said Callan. 'Let you know tomorrow.'

'There really is no other way,' said the earl, then shrugged. 'Very well. Tomorrow. I think I should warn you—my telephone has been cut off.'

'We know our way,' said Callan, and turned to Kleist. 'Shall we go?'

Kleist's hotel room was a small one on the first floor, the balcony a concrete strip just big enough for a table and two chairs. He ushered them in, but Callan and Bulky waited to let Jeanne-Marie go in first, and Callan took care never to give his back to Kleist, not totally. The German had moved on from shock to a state of febrile movement, hands restlessly touching: his face, his suit, his girl. It was as if he had to keep moving them, because if he let them be still he would see how much they trembled. He went over to the table he used as a bar: three bottles, whisky, gin and brandy, all half full.

'It was brandy, wasn't it?' he said.

'Thank you, no,' said Bulky. 'I've drunk too much already.'

But Callan wanted to see if he was right.

'Just a small one,' he said, 'with water.'

Kleist tried: he even managed to lift the bottle, but he couldn't hit the glass. Jeanne-Marie had to do it, add water from the carafe on the table.

'I'm sorry,' said Kleist. 'As you can see I've had rather a shock.'

Jeanne-Marie handed Callan his glass, and he turned a little towards her, took it left-handed, still watching Kleist. The German's eyes were glittering with what might be madness, or fear.

'Eleven thousand pounds,' he said.

104

'Three thousand to me,' said Bulky, 'the rest to Callan here.'
'Quite so,' said Kleist. 'I am afraid I have no book to offer you in lieu.'
'We'd prefer money,' said Callan.
'I'm afraid,' said Kleist, 'I have no money either.'
His hands went up to his face, and he wept, his sobs clearly audible. Jeanne-Marie watched him, her face showing nothing at all. Bulky waited placidly. Callan just waited. At last Kleist lowered his hands and Jeanne-Marie gave him a drink he needed both hands to hold. His face was sticky with tears, but he had to gulp his drink before he could handle a really tricky job, like taking out his handkerchief.
'I'm at your mercy, gentlemen,' he said.
'I'm not at all familiar with Italian law,' said Bulky, 'but it may well be that debts of—honour are not legally recoverable in Italy.'
'But that's just the point,' said Kleist. 'Even the phrase you used—debts of honour. My honour is involved.'
'If you have no money,' said Callan, 'I don't see how you can have any honour, either.'
'Now now,' said Bulky, placidly kind. 'I'm sure we want to avoid unpleasantness if we can.'
Kleist looked at him gratefully. The old interrogation technique, thought Callan: the one that never fails, even when you're the victim and you know it's being used. Mr Nice Guy and Mr Cruel.
'Perhaps you'd like to tell us a little more,' said Nice Guy Bulky.
Cruel Callan snorted.
'Gambling isn't just a hobby with me,' said Kleist, and for once even Bulky's placidity flickered. In his scheme of things cheating at cards could never be a hobby. 'To me gambling is a compulsion—almost a disease.'
'Is Hexham like that?' Bulky asked.
'No, no. He enjoys winning of course—and usually he does win—but if the necessity arose he could put his packs of cards away and never miss them. I could not. I *must* play. Jeanne-Marie says I should go to see a psychiatrist.' He turned to the woman, but the barriers were still down: she made no answering move. 'I am like an alcoholic,' he said, 'and, like so many alcoholics, so far I have refused to seek treatment.'
'It looks to me,' said Callan, 'as if you just ran out of bottles.'
Kleist flinched.
'Now now,' said Bulky. 'Now now now.' Then to Kleist: 'You really have no money at all?'
'Perhaps two thousand deutschmarks,' Kleist said. 'No more.'
'Then perhaps we can work out some arrangement,' said Bulky.
'No,' said Callan.

Bulky said, 'But, my dear fellow, if he really has no—'

'Balls,' said Callan, and Bulky winced. 'What would have happened if you and I had lost? It was him and his mate that conned us into raising the stakes, remember.'

'Conned?' said Bulky, enjoying it. 'I hardly think—'

'You know what I mean,' said Callan. 'You suggested it first and they liked the idea so much that they suggested it twice. And when I didn't fancy it they said we weren't sportsmen. This geezer even told us it was our only chance to get our money back. Well, we did get our money back, and a bit more, and now he says he's very sorry but he can't pay. Balls.'

'But if he really can't—'

'What proof have we got?' said Callan. 'His word? I've a damn good idea what that's worth.'

Bulky withdrew from Kleist very slightly.

'Mm, yes,' he said, and waited.

'Very well,' said Kleist. 'I have a property in Bonn. Apart from my salary, it is the only thing I do have.'

'That's more like it,' said Callan.

Jeanne-Marie said, 'You can't mean what you are saying.'

'He hasn't said anything yet,' said Callan.

'I'm saying that I will pay you.'

'Well, isn't that nice?' said Callan. 'When? When you win the football pools?'

'When I have sold my property,' said Kleist.

Bulky beamed. 'Splendid,' he said.

'Splendid?' said Callan. 'What's to stop him reneging?'

'How can I?' said Kleist. 'If I did that and you made it known—I could never gamble again. You would see to that. You and Lord Hexham.'

'Hexham?' This time, even Bulky seemed surprised.

'He is an English lord,' said Kleist, with the air of a man explaining a sociological complexity. 'He is very correct.'

Callan thought: He means it. The poor mad bastard means it.

Aloud he said, 'All the same, I think I'll take an IOU.'

It took some argument, but in the end he got it. Very reluctantly, Bulky accepted one as well....

They left the hotel room, and Callan gave Bulky the car keys, raced out of the hotel and round to where he could stand beneath the balcony of Kleist's room. The doors to it were still open. They should have been quarrelling, yelling at each other, but instead he had to strain to hear.

'You are a fool,' Jeanne-Marie said, but there was no anger in her voice, not even accusation. She merely stated a fact.

'I am aware.'

'You really will sell up to pay this debt?'

'My darling, I must,' said Kleist. 'You heard the old Englishman. This is a debt of honour.'

'Honour?' She spoke the word as if savouring its strangeness, and there followed the small, harsh rustling sounds of a woman undressing.

'And where is this famous property?'

'In Bonn. On the Schiller Strasse.'

'Schiller Strasse?'

As she repeated the words it occurred to Callan that Bulky could be right. The rustling continued, then there was the sound of a drink being poured.

'Here,' she said.

'If you knew,' said Kleist, 'what a joy it is for you to pour me a drink when you are naked.'

'I do know,' she said.

I bet you do, thought Callan, and listened as Kleist swallowed.

'Does this mean that you are not leaving me?' he said.

'Of course I'm not leaving you.'

'*Ah, liebchen, du*—'

'In English, please,' said Jeanne-Marie.

'My darling,' said Kleist, 'if I didn't have you I really would have nothing.'

'Come to bed,' she said.

Other sounds succeeded, but there were no words. Callan left.

16

Lonely said, 'You ain't half late.'

'You know,' said Callan, 'you're getting to sound more and more like my aunty. The one who brought me up.'

'I get worried,' said Lonely.

You and me both, mate, thought Callan. But it would never do to say it aloud.

'Piece of cake,' Callan said.

'Won, did you?' Callan nodded and reached for the telephone. 'That fatty all right?'

'Lay off him, will you?' said Callan. 'In his own way he's almost as good as you are.'

It was almost too subtle for him, but in the end Lonely smirked.

'Pronto,' said the night operator, and Callan asked for a London number. For once the lines were easy. He got through at once.

'937-7162,' said a refined, Kensingtonian voice.

'Mrs Dinsdale?'

'Speaking. I don't know you, do I? It's extremely late to make phone calls.'

'My name is Callan.'

She dropped the protest at once.

'I take it you want to speak with Charlie?'

'You take it correctly.'

'I'll get on to him at once.'

Callan hung up.

'Funny time to call a bird,' said Lonely.

'I'm like that,' said Callan. 'Impulsive. You know. A creature of mood.'

He looked at Lonely. Bottle green lightweight suit: pale green shirt.

'Better get your overalls on, old son,' he said. 'Time to go to work.'

Lonely sighed but made no protest. He'd known it was coming. He went to the wardrobe.

108

'If I were you I'd change in the bathroom,' Callan said. 'I've got another call coming.'

'Another bird?'

'Even worse,' said Callan. 'It's a feller.'

Lonely looked bewildered, but then he often did....

'You have news for me,' said Hunter.

'Yeah,' said Callan. 'The figure is eleven.'

'Satisfactory.'

'Unfortunately our subject can't reach the figure. But he has a property in—'

'I know about the property. A poet's name is involved.'

'That's the one.'

'He'll sell?'

'Yes.'

'Excellent,' said Hunter.

'You don't think he'll renege?' said Callan.

'No,' said Hunter. There was a world of certainty in that 'no'. 'Now, when will I get the book?'

'Blimey,' said Callan. 'You don't believe in giving me any rest, do you?'

'Certainly not.'

'How about later tonight? Would that be all right?'

'It'll have to do,' said Hunter, and hung up.

Callan changed into a black shirt and jeans, black work-coat, then tapped on the bathroom door. 'Come on out, water nymph,' he said. 'The night shift's just started.'

Once more they parked the Alfa on the spur of shale, and looked down at the palazzo. Seen by moonlight it had a quality of lightness, of flowing grace, like a palace built of frozen clouds: something out of a fairy tale. But they hadn't come to rescue a sleeping princess: they'd come for a book.

'All right,' said Callan. 'Let's go.'

Lonely sighed. 'And I said the waiting was the worst part,' he said.

Callan led off down the sloping hillside: Commando instructors had trained him how to move in rough country years ago, and he'd been improving on their instructions ever since, but even so Lonely kept up with him, moving always in the same ungainly shuffle, but silently, and as sure-footed as a goat. And just about as niffy, thought Callan, but with Lonely you expected that. It was the price you had to pay. They reached the foot of the valley, and watched from cover. The palazzo had a wall round it, but here and there the wall was crumbling. Lonely reached a decision at last, nudged Callan, and pointed. Callan looked, and nodded agreement, motioned Lonely to go first.

The little man moved like mercury, a smooth, effortless flow that took him across the road and up the wall in total silence. At the top of the wall he paused for a moment, head and hands making questing movements—looking for burglar alarms, Callan thought—then he was gone. It was Callan's turn. Lonely had made it all look so easy, but it wasn't easy at all, thought Callan, it was bloody difficult, and concentrated on moving equally silently, equally swiftly. It would never do for Lonely to get the idea that he was slipping....

Lonely was waiting in the shadows of a tree, and Callan joined him. Before them the great house waited, not a light showing.

'Mr Callan,' said Lonely, in a voice that could only just be heard.

'Yeah?'

'When I do a job I always go round the back,' Lonely said. 'Where would round the back be?' It was a fair question. As they moved forward the palazzo seemed to expand in front of them, till at last they could see nothing but its vastness: the great flight of stairs covered by a portico, and flanked on either side by row upon row of windows.

'We could get lost in there,' said Lonely. 'Lost for days.'

'No we couldn't,' said Callan. 'I told you I've done a recce. Come on.'

He moved across the parkland to where a wing jutted, and even the wing was bigger than the school he'd gone to, all those innocent years ago.

'Blimey,' said Lonely. 'This place is bigger than a nick.'

And maybe that was a more realistic assessment. But at least if it wasn't round the back it was round the side. It even had a side-door. Callan and Lonely checked, their heads moving from side to side, until at last they were sure, and darted for the side-door. Even across gravel they made no sound at all. Lonely moved up to the door and examined it with the easy speed of a surgeon seeking familiar symptoms.

'Better try a window,' he said at last. 'The lock's dead easy, but there's a bolt an' all.'

No use ever asking Lonely how he knew, thought Callan. He just did. And he was always right.

The windows had little balustrades of wrought iron in front of them, designed both for elegance and the discouragement of burglars. They depressed Lonely, but they didn't discourage him. Callan crouched, linked his hands to make a stirrup, and lifted as Lonely stood in it. The little man swung his legs, elegant as a premier danseur, and stood inside the balustrade, feet spread wide like Charlie Chaplin because there was no other way he could stand: the balustrade was too narrow, yet he moved like an actor with a whole stage to himself; all the room in the world. Deftly, surely his hands explored the window, and all the time he niffed. You just wait till we get inside, Callan told himself. You'll be looking back to this with nostalgia.

There was a soft, plopping sound—suction cup, thought Callan—and then the scrape of a diamond on glass. Lonely gestured, and Callan moved beneath the balustrade, caught the circle of window-glass in his gloved hands, removed and pocketed the suction cup, laid the glass on the ground. By the time he'd done it Lonely had located the burglar-alarm, and severed it with cutters: then his body squirmed, his hand reached through the hole he had made, and even Callan didn't hear the window unlatched. Slowly, carefully Lonely eased up the window, and wriggled his way inside. As soon as he was in the window closed again. That's my little minor genius, thought Callan. Always leave the place the way you found it. That way the mugs take longer to find out they've been done.

A minute passed, two, and Callan began to sweat, but the door opened at last, just enough, and Callan slipped inside. At once Lonely closed the door.

'You took your time,' said Callan.

'Mr Callan!' Lonely was indignant. 'I had to oil the bolts.'

'Sorry, old son,' said Callan. 'You're the expert.'

He took out a pencil-torch—no sense in getting lost—and led the way to the gallery, past pictures, furniture, and objets d'art. Lonely's mouth, Callan knew, would be watering.

'Nick anything and I'll kill you,' he said.

'Yeah, I know,' said Lonely. 'A book. One bleeding book.'

Barmy, it was. Stone barmy.... They reached the gallery.

Lonely didn't go much on pictures. A good tickle, true, but then you had to flog the bleeding things to a bent collector, or else start negotiating with insurance companies, and either way he was out of his depth.... A nice snuff-box now, that was different. Slip it in your pocket, hop on a bus and fence it, and it was worth twenty quid minimum, every time. Besides, they were pretty. All that fine work. Just look at the hinges. A geezer who could make hinges like that could open up this drum almost as fast as he could himself. He looked, unimpressed, at the Claude landscapes, the Mantegna Mother and Child, that Callan examined by the light of the pencil-torch. This wasn't no time for art-appreciation lectures. He'd had enough of that in the nick.

'Mr Callan,' he said, 'I thought we came here for a book.'

Like a blooming library, he thought. Break in and borrow. Thieve yourself a read.

Callan led the way to the bureau-cabinet with mirror-glass

panels by Martin Schnell of Dresden: 1734.

'It's in there,' he said.

Bureau and cabinet were locked, but neither presented much of a problem to Lonely. He didn't even scratch the brass fittings.... Bureau and cabinet were empty. Carefully Lonely checked, shelf by shelf, and drawer by drawer.

'Looks like your geezer got it wrong,' he said.

'My geezer never gets it wrong,' said Callan.

He looked again at the tall, elaborate piece of furniture: so much inlay, so much glass. 'Could you take this apart?' he said.

'I *could*,' said Lonely, 'but it'd take hours.'

'Have you got anything better to do?'

'Of course I have,' said Lonely. 'Scarper.'

'After you've taken this apart,' said Callan.

Lonely sighed but submitted. When Mr Callan talked like that you did what he said, but he had his revenge. The niff was appalling, and Callan couldn't move out of range: he had to hold the torch....

Lonely set to work, and almost at once began to like the job. Lovely piece it was; beautiful. Like a bleeding great snuff box. All dovetail and that. Hardly a nail in it, and not much glue neither. It all fitted, and it all worked. Screws counter-sunk, and all the wood solid: the back as thick as the front. Craftsmanship. In them days they had jobs worth doing. If he'd been born then even he might have gone straight.... He worked on steadily, and the bureau-cabinet became a very large 3D jigsaw, each piece lovingly removed, carefully placed on the carpet to avoid damage. Callan inspected each piece of wood as Lonely removed it: solid stuff, the only join the walnut veneer, and that had been there since the piece was made. He looked at the skeletal frame which was all Lonely had left.

'No book,' said Lonely. 'We might as well scarper, Mr Callan.'

Callan looked again at the cabinet doors. In 1734 they made mirror-glass to last.

'Get the mirrors off that,' he said.

'Gorblimey,' said Lonely, then looked into Callan's eyes and got to work.

It wasn't easy. You had to go at it from the back, and even then you had to saw a bit loose to get a chisel in, and when you got the chisel in and levered the wood cracked. Well, it stood to reason didn't it? It was good enough wood, but it was hundreds of years old. Lonely hated what he was doing, but he did it, and the glass was so heavy Mr Callan had to help him lift it.... Nothing. Not a thing. The mirror was just a mirror and the door-frame a door-frame; and that was it.

'Now the other one,' said Callan.

Lonely sighed and obeyed, working gently, kindly with wood that was just too old to withstand even the loving strength he gave it. Two more cracks, loud even in that vast gallery, and Callan held up a hand in warning, sped to the door, listened, looked out. Beyond the gallery the great house brooded in silence: no light shone. He went back to Lonely and helped him lift out the massive piece of mirror-glass. The door-frame was just a door-frame.

'There you are,' said Lonely. 'What did I tell you?'

He looked lovingly at the dismembered bureau-cabinet.

'I wouldn't half like to put it back together,' he said.

But Callan wasn't interested. He'd turned the mirror-glass over. Cut into the thickness of the glass was a rectangular pocket about seven inches by four and a half, and stuck into the pocket, two thirds of its thickness protruding, was a rectangular package wrapped in opaque plastic. He took out a knife, cut the tapes that held it in place, and eased out the package. Lonely wasn't interested. He crouched down beside the sheet of mirror-glass, and looked at the carefully made cavity that had been backed so that the mirror in front of it still reflected.

'Vandalism that is,' he said. 'Bleeding vandalism.'

Callan stripped away the plastic. Beneath it was the paperback edition of Marx, just as Hunter had forecast. But then Hunter only forecast certainties....

Suddenly the gallery was ablaze with light.

'Ah,' said Hexham. 'I see you decided on a book after all.' His voice was jovial enough: the BSA Monarch rifle he held was not. 30-06, thought Callan, or maybe 308. Big enough to blow a hole in you whatever it was, and Hexham handled it as if he knew what he was doing. Callan stayed motionless: Lonely could have spent the last three months in the deep-freeze. The earl moved further into the room.

'Do tell me how you knew it was there,' Hexham said. The rifle barrel indicated the cabinet-bureau, swung back on Callan.

'Information received,' said Callan. Hexham chuckled, moved a step further, sniffed, and looked accusingly at Lonely.

'You smell dreadfully,' he said. 'Don't you ever bathe?'

'You make him nervous,' said Callan.

The earl stepped back a little.

'I should,' he said. 'I find burglars in my house, I risk my life to confront them, they attack me—and I kill two of them. The rest of the gang escapes.'

'No,' said Callan.

'Why not?'

113

'Because of Berkeley,' said Callan. 'He knows I'm not a burglar.'

'Does he?' Hexham said. 'He knows you're a card-sharp, and so is he.'

'You should know,' said Callan. 'You cheat too.'

'But not awfully well,' said Hexham. 'Not nearly so well as you.'

The hands on the rifle tightened.

'You will now tell me why you are here,' he said. 'Otherwise I will shoot your friend.'

The rifle-barrel turned on Lonely, who made yet another useful contribution to the evening by pitching forward in a dead faint.

Hexham was thrown. He thought he'd been prepared for every possible reaction, but he hadn't been ready for that one. The BSA jerked in his hands, boomed, and a mirror-glass panel shattered to fragments. As it did so Callan fell into a crouch, his right hand described the same short, abrupt arc, the Magnum filled it and he fired in one continuous flow of movement. Hexham cursed and dropped the rifle, looked in disbelief at the neat, circular hole in his shoulder. Callan crunched his way to him over broken glass.

'Seven years bad luck,' he said, and pulled the BSA away left-handed.

'They started ages ago,' said the earl.

Callan backed off, and crouched by Lonely. The little man was unharmed. Being unconscious he'd even stopped niffing.... Callan looked back up at Hexham.

'You'd better sit down,' he said. 'You've had a bit of a shock.'

The earl found that his legs were trembling, but somehow he walked to a chair and sat.

'You shot me,' he said.

'That's right,' said Callan. 'You were going to shoot my mate.'

'I was bluffing,' said Hexham. 'Surely you realise that?'

He sounded horrified.

'You're new to this lark, aren't you?' said Callan. 'Pros never bluff with guns. Didn't they tell you that?' Still no answer. Callan aimed the Magnum between Hexham's eyes. 'Your servants are a bit slow, aren't they?'

'Servants? Oh, you mean the ones at dinner. They don't live in,' said Hexham. 'Nobody lives in, except me.' His head sagged.

'Don't go to sleep on me,' said Callan. 'A big strong boy like you shouldn't be bothered by a hole in the shoulder.'

The earl's head jerked upright.

'That's a Magnum revolver,' he said.

'That's right.'

'I thought nowadays one used dum dum bullets in a Magnum.'

114

'Only when one is feeling really nasty,' said Callan. 'Take your coat off.'

Somehow Hexham did so. He lacks many things, Callan thought, but not courage.

'The bullet went right through you,' Callan said. 'If you feel behind your shoulder you'll find the exit hole. It'll be no bigger than the one in front.'

The earl did so, then looked at the blood streaks on his left hand.

'You're quite right,' he said. 'There isn't even very much blood. I realise I'm fussing unduly, but I should like a drink.'

No, thought Callan, you don't lack courage. That means you might even try again, and if you do I'll kill you.

'In a minute,' he said, and backed off, dumped flowers from a vase, slopped water from the vase over Lonely. The little man sat up spluttering.

'Mr Callan, what happened?' he said.

'I just shot an earl,' said Callan.

'You never.'

Callan nodded at Hexham, and Lonely scrambled to his feet, and remembered. Reproachfully he said, 'You were going to shoot me. That's no way for a lord to act.'

Hexham said, 'I'm beginning to realise that. I wonder—could I have that drink?'

They went to the library, and Callan sent Lonely to pour, made pads of handkerchiefs, and covered up Hexham's wounds with them, used his tie to hold them in place. The little man never could stand the sight of blood.

Lonely said, 'There isn't any beer.'

'I really am most awfully sorry,' said the earl.

There's the aristocracy for you, thought Callan. The bastard means it—and told Lonely to have brandy instead.

'But I don't like brandy,' said Lonely.

'You're not supposed to like it,' said Callan. 'Brandy's medicine. Get it down you. It'll do you good.'

The little man poured and sipped distastefully, then poured whisky for Callan and Hexham. They were large whiskys, but Callan offered no criticisms. He reckoned he'd earned his. He turned to Lonely.

'You ever been over a lord's house before?' he asked.

'No, Mr Callan.'

'Go and take a look round,' Callan said. 'There's nobody else here. Bit of an education for you.' He threw Lonely the torch, and the little man headed for the door.

'Oh ta,' he said.

115

Callan said, 'And what is it we don't do?'

'We don't nick anything,' said Lonely, and scowled at the earl. 'It's not bleeding fair.'

He left, and Callan walked over to where Hexham sat, sipped his whisky, and looked down.

'Now,' he said, 'you're going to tell me things. It may take a bit of time, but that doesn't bother me. I'm not in any hurry.'

The earl drank his Scotch.

'I'm not really awfully good at talking,' he said.

'You'll learn,' said Callan. 'Believe me, son, you'll learn.'

At first it was merely brutal and degrading, and Hexham could cope with that: but very soon it became appalling, reached the outermost limits of what he could bear. Callan sensed it and let him go, even allowed him to gulp at his Scotch.

'I don't enjoy this,' Callan said.

'I know,' said Hexham.

'But you have to tell me things,' said Callan, 'and I'll go on till you do.... Look, son. You're human—just like the rest of us—and you haven't been trained for this. Sooner or later you'll have to tell me. There's no other way.'

He waited, but Hexham stayed silent. Callan took his glass from him.

'Whenever you're ready,' he said.

Three minutes later Hexham told him, and Callan listened with the concentration he'd been taught, then began asking questions. Once or twice Hexham jibbed, but in the end he always answered. What had been done to him was too much. At last Callan was satisfied.

'All right,' he said. 'I think I've got all I need.'

'You've got the lot,' said Hexham, 'and you know it.' He lay back in his chair, looked up at Callan. 'One day,' he said. 'One day....'

'You'll kill me? It's possible, son. It's possible. But there's a hell of a long queue.'

But Hexham didn't hear him: he'd passed out. Callan poured himself another Scotch and waited for Roger de Vere Bullivant, company-director and connoisseur. He didn't have to wait long: Lonely couldn't stand being on his own. There was a gentle tap on the door.

'Enter,' said Callan, and Lonely entered: awkward, scuttling, and about as noisy as a falling leaf. He looked at Hexham.

'Bit tired, is he?' he asked.

'A bit,' said Callan.

'I thought I heard noises,' said Lonely. 'Like shouting and that.'

'Singing,' said Callan, and gulped at his whisky. 'He was singing.'

'Oh,' said Lonely. 'Pop?'

'In a way,' said Callan. 'This was stuff I'd never heard before.'

'How was it?' said Lonely.

'Interesting,' said Callan. 'Very very interesting.'

He poured more whisky, added water, and Lonely looked at the mixture. Dark it was, and that meant strong.

'Something bothering you?' said Callan.

'You got your book, Mr Callan,' Lonely said. 'Don't you think we ought to go?'

'In a minute.'

'Only—no offence, Mr Callan—but you'll have to do the driving because I can't.'

The terror in his voice reached Callan at once. He took the glass from his lips and put it down. 'Sorry, old son,' he said. 'It's been one of those days.'

He picked up the BSA, worked the action and the shells spilled out. Callan gathered them up and put them in his pockets, propped the BSA by Hexham's chair.

'Funny way for a lord to act,' said Lonely. It sounded like an epitaph.

They left by the side-door, and Callan deliberately smashed the window Lonely had opened, broke the circle of glass and added it to the shards.

'What you do that for?' said Lonely.

'There wasn't a burglary,' said Callan. 'We were never here.'

'Oh,' said Lonely, and pondered. 'But Mr Callan you shot him—we bust up his like chest of drawers.'

'No we didn't,' said Callan. 'He did. He got drunk and smashed some furniture and fooled around with a gun and shot himself.'

'Nice if we could work it,' said Lonely. 'But he saw us, Mr Callan.'

'I have worked it,' said Callan. 'If nobody asks he'll stay stum. If the coppers should come, he'll tell them exactly what I told you.'

'You're sure, Mr Callan?'

'It was one of the things he was singing about,' said Callan, and Lonely shivered.

They went back the way they had come, but this time Lonely led all the way, scuttling up hill as fast as he'd scuttled down. Callan slogged on behind him, slowed down by whisky, far too much whisky. He needed that walk if he was going to drive.... Lonely reached the road, dropped flat, and waited as Callan moved up beside him. Together they looked at the car. Nothing had changed.

'No harm in making sure, Mr Callan,' Lonely said.

You're right, mate. You are so right. And your drunken minder

117

was going to walk straight up to the car, and even if it is empty, your drunken minder is wrong. They got into the car and Callan backed and turned, then coasted down the winding, twisting road. On either side of him the mountains towered, but for once the beauties of nature held no terrors for Lonely. He was asleep.

The road levelled and Callan switched on the engine, Lonely rhythmically snored. Home tomorrow, thought Callan, me and Lonely and old Bulk. Hand over the book and collect our payoff, then back to flogging security and roll on the day when we go public. A cloud obscured the moon and he switched on his headlights. Should have done it ages ago. Berk, he thought. Stupid, drunken berk. Suppose he'd met a police-car? They do exist, even in these bloody mountains. Drive carefully, he told himself. Watch what you're doing. The object of this exercise is an early retirement.

The bullet spanged into the handle of the passenger door, then ricocheted wailing to crease the bonnet. Later Callan was unable to remember the sound of a shot: the only sounds he was sure of were the throaty roar of the Alfa as he put his foot down, and Lonely using language. He braked for the bend, straightened, and switched off the lights. Police cars now were the least of his troubles. They roared on in darkness.

'Oh my Gawd,' Lonely yelled, 'the moon's gone off an' all.'

More bends, more twists and turns, more frantic braking and acceleration, and Lonely yelling about the dark, till at last the moon broke out of the clouds, and Callan was sure they were out of the sniper's range. He switched on his lights again, and Lonely whimpered in terror. Mr Callan had finally lost his marbles. Callan made soothing noises.

'But, Mr Callan,' Lonely said, 'you should have put your lights on when it was *dark*.'

'Sorry, old son,' said Callan. 'I forgot.'

Lonely sighed. 'It's just like what they tell you on the telly,' said Lonely. 'You should never drink and drive,' then remembered a previous terror. 'There was a bang,' he said. 'Did we hit something?'

'A stone,' said Callan. 'We ran over a stone.'

'Then what was all the Stirling Moss bit for?'

'I'm tired,' Callan said. 'I want to go home.'

Lonely snorted. He wanted to go home an' all. In one piece.

They reached the hotel at last, and Callan parked, then Lonely found he couldn't open his door. Callan stowed the book in his pocket, and let Lonely out at his side. At once the little man ran round the car and looked at the door-handle. It was smashed flat. He looked from the handle to the car's bonnet. The paintwork was gouged: the chrome of one headlight gashed.

'Hit a stone, did we?' he said.

'That's right.'

It was the voice that haunted his nightmares: the voice that was a prelude to fear and pain. Lonely sighed. 'Whatever you say, Mr Callan,' he said.

[ii]

The tall boy with the blue swimming trunks was called Harry—or was it Charlie? Robson, Thomson, something like that, and Maisie rather thought he was studying in New York somewhere.... Elizabeth thought, just great. That narrows the field to about twenty-five thousand, but she was her father's daughter. Work was what got results.

'Where d'you meet him?' she asked.

Marcie Armbruster stopped fiddling with her collection of Bach records.... Les Swingles. It would be.

'You gone on him?' she asked.

'He had some back copies of *L'Arche*,' said Elizabeth. 'He said he would lend them to me only we were both smoking and I forgot to ask his name.'

'*L'Arche?*'

Oh daddy, darling daddy, you banana-happy gorilla. Why do you have to set me down among the dumb-dumbs?

'It was a French literary magazine,' Elizabeth said. 'Published a lot of early Camus and Sartre.'

'Intellectual stuff,' said Marcie. 'He was an intellectual boy. You'll get along just fine.'

'It might even be peachy,' Elizabeth said. 'But how can I tell if I don't know where he is?'

'Any Simone de Beauvoir?' said Marcie.

'Hunh?'

'In that *L'Arche* magazine. Would there be any Simone de Beauvoir in it? What I mean—I got this vacation assignment on Beauvoir. I'm not into her at all.'

'Oh heaps,' said Elizabeth. 'Nice, short pieces. Stuff that isn't in the books.'

'Would you help me, Elizabeth? I don't read French too well.'

You sure understand trading, thought Elizabeth, and waited.

'He's a friend of Bill Yerkes,' said Marcie. 'We met at a barbecue at Bill's place. I think he was sort of travelling around. You know. Bed roll—all that stuff.'

'Thanks,' said Elizabeth, and rose.

119

'You didn't say you'd help me with Beauvoir.'

'Just let me find the guy first. I'll help you.'

'Thanks, Elizabeth,' said Marcie. 'You're a sweet person.' She smiled, but there was only malice in her smile. 'I don't think you'll like him very much,' she said. 'He's a very physical-type boy.'

Elizabeth drove on to the Yerkes place. So now my fair body is at risk, she thought. A very physical-type boy. Well, any friend of Yerkes' would have to be physical. And abrupt. Much much too abrupt. No luxe, calme et volupté at the Yerkes house. To hell with gorillas anyway. You tried to help them and look where you were headed. To the Yerkes place. But she drove on.

The Yerkes place was beautiful. It should have been, she thought, the money they'd spent on it. But that wasn't fair. She'd been to places where even more money had been spent, and each one of them had been a mess.... But the Yerkes place was beautiful. Stone built, single-storey, framed by trees that were framed by mountains, with flowers all around it and a pool and a barbecue pit that could have supplied half the town. Old Man Yerkes had made his money in farm-machinery, and he'd made it in quantities so vast as to be embarrassing, except that Old Man Yerkes was never embarrassed. He'd quit when he was fifty, and gone in for marriage instead. Four, was it? Five? And that didn't embarrass him either, even if he was seventy-four. He was in Europe some place now with the current one, and Bill, his only child, had the place to himself. She parked her Dodge Coronet alongside a red Ferrari that was the only other car visible. Well, she thought, the crown prince is home, and all by himself for once.

She walked towards the house, but a voice from the pool hailed her. She went to it. At least he was wearing trunks, what there was of them. A big guy, with a good build, even features, a toothpaste smile, and grey, needle-bright eyes that never missed a thing. He'd gone to Cornell, she remembered, and everybody said he was brilliant. He could have done anything—if he hadn't preferred to do nothing at all.

'Hi,' he said.

'Hi.'

'Want a swim?'

'No thanks,' she said. 'I didn't bring a swimsuit.'

'Don't let that bother you.'

'Suppose it bothers you?'

He laughed. It was, she thought, a hunter's laugh.

'Drink maybe?'

'D'you have a coke?'

'My old man,' he said, 'has everything.'

But he takes no pride in the fact, she thought. He lifted up the covers of a long cabinet by the poolside, and the cabinet became a wet bar. A wet bar. Right there by the pool.

'In the can?' he asked. She nodded and he brought it to her. It was exactly the way she liked it, cold but not stinging.

'Sit down,' he said. 'Tell me your troubles.'

She sat on a lounging chair, and he took the one next to her. They looked through the fretted green of the trees to mountains and sky.

'Do I have to have troubles?' she said.

'Unless you are unique—and I use the word in its literal sense—yes.'

'I'm not unique.'

He looked quickly at her, then back at the trees.

'You're a very pretty girl,' he said.

'Thank you.'

'And a very clever one. All the other pretty girls I know are dumb. You've come to ask me for something.'

'What makes you say that?'

'Because I also am pretty and clever. You want something, girl. But it isn't me.'

'No,' she said. 'It isn't you.'

He laughed again, but this time he wasn't hunting. Just amused.

'What is it?' he asked. 'A magazine subscription?'

'I'm looking for someone,' she said. 'Someone you know,' and told him the story of *L'Arche* magazine. The second time round it sounded even better, except that this time she didn't bother with Camus and de Beauvoir and Sartre: she talked of philosophy, and used Ayer, Teilhard de Chardin and Wittgenstein instead. He listened gravely.

When she had finished he said, 'I thought you were majoring in French?'

'I am.'

'So what's with the philosophy?'

'I'm just interested,' she said.

'And *Barry* was interested?'

'That's what he told me,' she said. 'But he was smoking at the time, so maybe he—'

'One joint,' said Yerkes. 'That's as far as Barry ever goes. Just enough for satisfaction, never enough for fulfilment. One joint. Two drinks. There's a guy if he could find a way to do it, he'd ration his prick. Don't tell me you're like that.'

'How could I be?' she said.

121

This time the laughter was hunter and amusement both.

'You're sure you don't like me?' he said. 'I mean really sure?'

To say 'Not in that way', would be an insult. 'I'm sure,' she said.

'I just don't figure why you have to come here and tell me such bright, imaginative lies,' he said. She willed herself to stay silent. 'Somebody's turning you on, sweetness. Now who could turn you on?'

She watched him as he sat motionless, absorbed in concentration. There was power in him, my God there was, but it was a flawed power.

'Big Daddy Congressman?' he said at last. 'Is he the one?'

'My father never even heard of Wittgenstein,' she said.

'But he turns you on, baby,' he said. 'From where I sit he's the only one who ever has. Could it be you dig the more mature male?'

He put his hand in her lap, and pressed. For once he was strong but careful, not abrupt at all. 'Nice, huh?' he said.

'I doubt if Teilhard de Chardin would agree with you,' she said, but this time he didn't laugh; went on pressing.

A car-horn hooted, and a battered E-type Jaguar, the 2 + 2, pulled into the car-port next to Elizabeth Manette's Dodge. A man and two women got out.

'Fuck,' said Yerkes.

She looked at the girls. 'I expect so,' she said.

'Barry Johnson,' he said. 'Lives in New York with his parents. He would.'

'You live with your parents.'

'I live in their house,' he said. 'But only when they're away. Barry Johnson. Brooklyn Heights. New York City,' He took his hand away. 'I was doing all right,' he said.

'You were travelling hopefully,' she said. 'I doubt that you'd arrive.'

She stood up, and he walked with her to the car-port. The man and girls had gone.

'What on earth—?' she said.

'They're in the house,' said Yerkes. 'My father and stepmother's lovely home. This time of year you can't have an orgy without air-conditioning. Sure you won't join us?'

'I'm sure.'

'O.K.,' he said. 'Come back when you're less inhibited. See you around, Daddy's girl.'

She drove off faster than she'd intended. Harry or Charlie, Marcie had said. Robson or Thomson. And it turned out to be Barry Johnson. One thing about Marcie, she was reliable. Never got a name right in her life. She continued to try to drum up indignation, but it wouldn't work. Bill Yerkes had touched her, and she'd neither yelled nor flinched. But then he'd been entitled to touch her: he'd guessed her secret. She was Daddy's girl, all right, and what kind of career was that for a sweet, wholesome twenty-year-old? Looking for bananas to feed a gorilla....

17

Callan woke late, and even after a shower his head ached. After breakfast he announced that he was going to see Bulky, and expected his head to ache even more: but Lonely took it well. He was still in a state of shock after last night's activities—armed earls getting themselves shot and geezers sniping at him—and when Lonely was in a state of shock he needed beer. Callan gave him money—there was no need to tell him where the bar was— and went to call on Bulky.

The fat man—shaved, hair brushed—was dressed in cream-coloured pyjamas and a dressing gown of scarlet silk. Both quantity and quality were impressive. As Callan entered he put down a book: it was Burke's *Reflections on the French Revolution*.

'Read it?' he said. Callan nodded.

'A thousand swords leaped from their scabbards,' said Bulky. 'Do you believe that?'

'Not for a bird,' said Callan. 'Not even Marie-Antoinette.'

'I'm not a Romantic either,' said Bulky, 'though I wish I could be. Somehow it doesn't go with card-sharping. Is our—er—mission completed?'

'Yeah,' said Callan. 'We go back on the first flight we can get.'

Bulky asked no more questions.

'Suits me,' he said. 'It's pretty enough, I suppose, but a little too rural for my taste. It beats me what Nelson saw in the place.'

'Emma Hamilton,' said Callan.

Bulky chuckled, went over to a table and poured two drinks, handed one to Callan, who looked at it and hesitated.

'I take it you go back to report success?' Bulky said.

Callan thought of Hexham and took the drink.

'Yes,' he said. 'You'll get paid.'

'My dear fellow,' said Bulky, and waved his hand. It was a very graceful gesture. 'May I ask—did you decide to take Hexham's book?'

Callan put down his glass. 'Book?' he said.

Bulky said patiently: 'The Florio edition of Montaigne.'

'Don't worry,' Callan said again. 'You'll get paid.'

They conferred about flights, then Callan left. He liked Bulky, but he didn't want to talk to him, didn't want to talk to Lonely either. He went back to his room: the chambermaid had been in and made the bed. He lay on it, and wished for the thousandth time that he could smoke, then got up and poured himself a drink instead. The reason he couldn't smoke was that it was bad for his shooting.... He lay back on the bed and drank. In the middle of the next drink somebody knocked on the door and he yelled, 'Come in.' The Magnum was in his suitcase and the suitcase was locked and he was too fed up to bother. To yell 'Come in' might be to get it over with.

It was Jeanne-Marie Nivelle. She wore a thigh-length robe of sapphire blue towelling over a very small bikini of sapphire blue, and she had the kind of body that could get away with a very small bikini. She carried a beach-bag, and for once she wasn't scowling.

'A thousand swords leaped from their scabbards,' said Callan.

'I beg your pardon?' she said, and the scowl came at once, but it was bewilderment, no more.

'I was just quoting,' said Callan. 'I'm like that sometimes. Come in and sit down and I'll get you a drink.' He swung his feet from the bed, and looked her up and down. 'You know, without your gun you look quite undressed.'

In the corridor a chambermaid got to work with a vacuum-cleaner. Jeanne-Marie Nivelle sat on a chair, stretched out her legs.

'I do not have a gun,' she said.

Callan poured two drinks, and handed her one. She reached for it, and the robe slid apart.

'You're a very pretty woman,' he said, 'perhaps even a beautiful one.'

'Thank you,' she said, and sipped her drink.

Even half-way drunk Callan's hands could still move accurately and fast. He scooped up the beach-bag from beside her chair, and rummaged inside. Lipstick, cigarettes, matches spilled on the floor, then a beach towel. Beneath the beach towel was an Armi Galesi 22 automatic: a six shot, four and a half inches long, twelve ounces in weight. Not much of a gun, but if she got up close, enough.

'What a shame that a very pretty, perhaps even beautiful woman should tell lies,' he said.

She took it well, just went on sipping.

'I had hoped not to use it,' she said.

125

Callan eased out the magazine, counted out the shells. She'd fed in all six. He put them in his pocket. 'You just realised your hope,' he said, and went back to his drink. 'And anyway you wouldn't have used it while that maid's around.'

He gulped at the whisky, put the glass down and lay back on the bed. He was tired, getting drunk, and fed up. To the back teeth.

Jeanne-Marie stood up, put down her glass, then slid out of her robe. 'You have the look of a man who is fond of women,' she said.

'My looks do not belie me,' said Callan.

'I want you to forgive Gunther his debt.' Callan said nothing. 'After all,' she said, 'you won back what you lost. You are a rich man. What pleasure can there be for you in ruining that sad little man?' She moved a little closer. 'There are other pleasures. Much better ones. Please leave him alone.'

He made no answer, and she took off the bikini top, then the briefs. Even without music, he thought, she did it very well.

'For as long as you want,' she said. 'Whatever you want,' and took off her sandals, the movement letting her body flow from one pose to the next. 'Well?' she said.

Callan said, 'Pass me my drink will you, darling?'

She moved, slowly, gracefully, and brought his glass to him. Callan took it.

'If you knew,' Callan said, 'what a joy it is for you to bring me a drink when you are naked.'

For the first time she was aware of her nakedness as shame. Her face flushed red, her hands moved to cover herself. She was even clumsy.

'You should say: "I do know,"' said Callan. 'That's your next line.'

But she was scrambling into her bikini, zipping up her robe. Callan left the bed again, stood over her.

'It would have had to he the gun, darling,' he said. 'I should have warned you. I never could fancy another man's leavings.'

She swung at him, palm open, but he caught her wrist before she reached his face.

'Would you have shot me?' he said. 'Was that the idea?'

'Of course not,' she said. 'I intended to frighten you, that's all.'

'Oh you did, darling, you did,' said Callan. 'You frightened me last night as well. But I don't think you meant to frighten me. You meant to kill me.'

'I do not understand you,' she said. 'And please let go of my wrist.'

He continued to hold her.

126

'You used a rifle on me,' said Callan. 'It could only be you or Gunther, and last night Gunther was past it. Hitting a moving target by moonlight's a bit tricky—but you didn't do too badly, darling. A little more practice and you'll be good.'

'I think,' she said, 'that you are mad.'

'And I think,' said Callan, 'that you are right.'

He gathered up the cigarettes, matches, lipstick and towel; dropped them in the beach-bag, and added the unloaded Armi Galesi.

'Go and pour Gunther a drink,' he said.

'I shall be glad to,' she said. 'I have never yet achieved satisfaction with a drunk.'

Callan watched her go, and went back to his drink. She had a better exit line than mine, he thought. Ah well.... Can't win them all. Then Lonely came in, took one look at Callan and was appalled. Poor old Lonely, thought Callan. Nothing ever goes right for you, does it, son? You even missed the floor-show.

Lunch then. He didn't want it, but he forced himself to eat it: soup and pasta and sattimbocca. At least he didn't have to watch Lonely knitting spaghetti: the little man had conned the maître d'hôtel into supplying him with chips. After lunch, black coffee: about a quart, and after the coffee a ride to the town in the Alfa. Neither he nor the garage man believed the story about the stone in the road, but Callan paid up in full, and that was all that mattered.... After the garage, Signora Lunari. It took a while, and he hadn't much time, but at last she was alone and he went in. As always she wore black, and as always she made it look elegant, even cool.

'I'm afraid I've brought this back,' he said, and handed over a cardboard box that contained a 357 Magnum, webbing harness, and eleven rounds. 'I find that I no longer need it.'

'Very well, sir,' she said. 'But I trust it was satisfactory?'

'Oh yes,' said Callan. 'It was that all right.'

He bought Lonely another couple of ties that would do for Christmas, and left. As he reached the door she said, 'Please give my regards to Mr Robinson of Pimlico.'

After that there was the funicular, and one last look at the incredible view of the bay. Hallo Taormina, goodbye. No chance to look at Palermo or Salerno: not even time to take a nice tourist bus to Mount Etna and look down from the crater to the heaving fire below. Not that he needed it. When you worked for Hunter you had all the eruptions you could handle.... Back to the hotel, where Lonely had done the packing, one more call to London, then out to the Mercedes, where Bulky was waiting, and Lonely made his disapproval of educated fatties all too clear. But Bulky

127

was benign, as always, and Callan too whacked to bother. Just let him get on the Caravelle at Catania, he thought, and then he could kip, and when they switched planes at Rome he could have a drink. A real drink.

[ii]

Brooklyn Heights was all she'd ever thought it would be, and then some. From where she stood they weren't heights so much as bastions, bastions of privilege. But privilege that wasn't yet quite sure of itself, she thought. It had a kind of impermanent look: a sort of resting place for millionaires before they became multi, and moved to upper Manhattan.... or Palm Springs.... Barry Johnson's apartment building looked commodious and clean, there were flower-tubs on the sidewalk and an unflawed awning, but the hall man wasn't on duty and the elevator was do-it-yourself. She pressed the button marked seven, and listened to the muzak: '*I like New York in June*', the violins throbbed. Speaking personally, she wasn't crazy about it.

Apartment 7D. Door freshly painted, brass door-knob gleaming—and imported from Europe. It all meant money: Barry Johnson, she thought, doesn't have any worries about his future any more than I have. She pressed the bell and waited. She'd expected to wait as soon as she'd seen the spy-hole set in the door. If you went visiting in New York you expected to be spied on, so she stood in full view to make it easier: to show whoever was on the other side of the door that she was just a hundred-and-eighteen-pound girl with no visible machine-guns. She counted two bolts and two locks unloosed, and the door swung open, just a little, then held. The chain was still on. That also, she told herself, is New York, and found herself looking at a tall, faded blonde, about the same age as her gorilla's mate, whose face was either bleak, or devastated.

'Mrs Johnson?' she said.

'Yes?'

'May I speak to Barry please?'

'I'm afraid,' the faded blonde said, 'I'm afraid that's not possible.'

'Oh dear,' said Elizabeth Manette. 'Maybe I should explain. I know I didn't phone him first—'

And no way would I phone him first, she thought. It took me all my nerve just to come and face the guy.

'—but I did happen to be in New York and Barry did say he'd let me have some information. You know? For my studies?'

The faded blonde looked more bleak, or devastated, than ever. Butter, Elizabeth told herself. What is needed here is butter, spread very thick.

128

'Well you know what your son's like, Mrs Johnson,' she said. 'I mean he's really an intellectual, if you'll excuse the word, and some of the stuff he told me—well, it would be such a big help to me if only—'

Mrs Johnson did three things: unhooked the door, said, 'Come in, please,' and began to cry.

Elizabeth went into the hall and waited politely for Mrs Johnson to stop crying. Busted, she thought. Her wunderkind's been busted. Just smoking, maybe, or was it possession? Surely to God a one-joint, two-drink man wouldn't be a pusher? ... Mrs Johnson cried neatly and quietly, as if she knew very well that her tears would cause embarrassment, or maybe even offence. But then that sort of went with her personality, Elizabeth thought. She was tall, but she was slim, almost skinny, so that if you took her either by volume or area she didn't occupy all that much space. And her hair, her eyes, her skin, were pretty but faded. I get by, was Mrs Johnson's motto, but I don't offer that much competition. The same principle applied to her clothes: she wore the little black dress that would be just great for cocktails and then theatre and then supper, if only she'd added a brooch, or pearls maybe. But brooch or pearls there were none. Even the gorilla's mate knew better than that. Come *on*, lady, Elizabeth thought. What is this? Shades of the prison house begin to close about the growing boy? Don't tell me you couldn't get bail. Not for one joint.

Mrs Johnson mopped at her eyes and said, 'I'm sorry, Miss—?'

'Manette. Elizabeth Manette.'

'A friend of Barry's?'

'I wouldn't say a friend,' Elizabeth said. 'We met at a party a friend of mine gave, and we got along pretty well.... You know, talking about the things we study. All that. You've got a very bright son, Mrs Johnson. I mean I know a bit about sociology too, but Barry can lose me. Every time.'

'Not any more,' Mrs Johnson said.

'I'm sorry. I'm afraid I don't understand.'

Mrs Johnson said, 'My son's dead, Miss Manette,' and once more, neatly, quietly began to cry.

Elizabeth thought, Daddy darling, what are you *doing* to me? How am I supposed to offer aid and comfort to the faded mother of a boy I only spoke to once?

'I'm terribly sorry,' she said. 'I didn't know. Was it a street accident?'

'A motor-bike,' Mrs Johnson said. 'We bought him this big motor-bike because he liked to move around. The policeman told us the speedometer showed over a hundred. There was some oil on the road....'

That doesn't sound like a guy who would ration his prick, Elizabeth thought.

'I better go,' she said.

But Mrs Johnson was too absorbed in grief to hear.

'You knew Barry?' she said.

'As I say, we met at a party and talked,' Elizabeth said.

'You look like a clever girl,' Mrs Johnson said. 'I hope that doesn't sound rude—'

'Of course not.'

'In my day girls didn't like being called clever,' Mrs Johnson said.

Elizabeth thought: Forty-three. You can't be a day over forty-three. Oh you poor, distraught dear, your day should hardly have begun.

'I know that's silly,' said Mrs Johnson. 'When Barry came along, he always liked clever people. They got on. I guess it was because he was clever too. It seemed so strange. He learned so quickly. Nothing was difficult for him. His father and I—we were neither of us like that.'

A cygnet reared by ducks, thought Elizabeth. A cygnet who only just made swan.

'Where did he go to college?' she asked.

'That's another thing' said Mrs Johnson. 'The grades he had— he could have gone anywhere. Harvard, Princeton, Cornell. But he wouldn't.... NYU. He chose NYU.'

In her voice horror and incredulity mingled: it was as if her son had opted for reform school.

'Barry,' Mrs Johnson said, 'had a strong sense of duty.'

'I expect that's why he chose sociology,' Elizabeth said.

'That's right,' said Mrs Johnson. 'That's exactly what he said.... If you're a sociologist you can help.'

And maybe you still can, Elizabeth thought, even though you're dead. She had enough to go on now, but Mrs Johnson still didn't want her to leave. She could risk one more question.

'Did he get on well with his teachers?'

'Oh yes,' the mother said. 'They all liked Barry.'

'Was there a special one?'

Mrs Johnson looked puzzled, and any minute she might look wary. Elizabeth hurried on: 'What I mean, in my case there's one teacher I think is just the greatest.' And it was true enough, but in deference to the fact that Mrs Johnson considered her day was done, Elizabeth changed Professor Martinez's sex. 'She's a Mexican lady, started out with nothing, and climbed right to the top. I mean academically she's a very, very big wheel. Only it hasn't changed her. She's not proud, and she's not sour. She's just—well—good, I guess. As a person I mean. I just wondered— I hope you don't think I'm being nosey—but I just wondered if Barry had ever met anybody like that. It's a very rewarding experience.'

And that also was true. And maybe Bill Yerkes is right, she thought, and maybe I do dig the more mature male, and so what?

'Professor Uhlmann,' Mrs Johnson said. 'Barry always liked his lectures. ... The notes he made. He never missed one, no matter what. He used to say, I dig the guy. I really do. Dick Uhlmann is socially aware.'

And he, thought Elizabeth, will be the one. Somehow I just know it.

'It really is rewarding,' Elizabeth said. 'Working with someone like that.'

'It should have been,' Mrs Johnson said. 'It should have been wonderful. Only I killed him.'

'Mrs Johnson, you mustn't say that,' said Elizabeth.

'But it's true,' Mrs Johnson said. 'His father never wanted him to have that bike. It was all my fault. I *made* him—'

Somehow Elizabeth found she was holding the tall, faded woman, and making the kind of soothing noises she would have made to a child who had grazed a knee: and somehow, at last, the contact and the noises worked; but she had a hell of a time getting away....

18

Her father had gone back to Washington, leaving mom back in their home in New England. Mom didn't get on with Washington in summer, or at any other time come to that, but for dad there were always committees.... But they weren't as important as this cloak and dagger routine he'd set his daughter on, she thought. They couldn't be. Not when he'd bought her a seat on the shuttle to Washington and given her the taxi-fare to take her to his office on Capitol Hill.... When she arrived his committee was still sitting, but you expected that. You even brought along a book to read. Genet. Gorillas don't like Genet, but if gorillas employ their daughters in prying into domestic grief, then they must lump Genet.... She was still reading it when he came in. My God he looks exhausted, she thought, but the sight of her seemed to bring him back to life. He didn't even look at her book.

'You've got something?' he said.

'I think so.'

He went over to the bar, mixed Scotch, water and ice.

'I'd like one too,' she said.

'You don't drink liquor.'

Elizabeth said, 'We both know that's not true.' He made no move to serve her. 'Daddy dear,' she said, 'I've had a rough day. I took the train to New York and the subway to Brooklyn, and New York is almost as stinking hot as Washington. Then I met Barry Johnson's mother, and she told me her son, her only child, is dead. And using sympathy for a cover, I milked her, daddy darling. I milked her dry. Then I flew to stinking Washington, and reported to Command HQ. Only General Manette wasn't quite ready to receive my report.... But I didn't have a drink on the plane because somebody might know who I was, and I didn't have one here till now because I don't steal liquor. But believe me, daddy darling, if you want Lieutenant Manette's report, you'll give me a goddam drink.'

He looked at her, passed her the highball he had made, and mixed another.

'Rough, huh?' he said.

She drank, and shuddered. 'The roughest.'

'You say the boy is dead?'

'Motor-bike crash,' she said. 'His mother told me all about it.'

He looked at her again. My daughter is twenty, he told himself, and the knocks you take at twenty are the ones that leave the scars. And I sent her in there to get knocked.

'Tell me about it,' he said.

'I hope to God it's important,' she said. 'After what you made me do—'

'Of course it's important,' he said.

'For who?'

'For our country,' he said, then added reluctantly, 'For me.'

Let us hope, dear gorilla, she thought, that you never consciously learn that, when it comes to manipulating your daughter, honesty is the best weapon you've got.

'He was at NYU,' she said. 'I think—I'm almost certain—that the guy we're after is a Professor Richard Uhlmann.'

'Why so sure?' he asked.

'When Barry talked about Uhlmann to other people, he called him Dick Uhlmann,' she said, 'just like when I refer to Professor Martinez I call him Paco. He's the one he loved, and he's the one he would quote.'

'Loved?'

She smiled, and sipped her whisky.

'A verb with a variety of definitions,' she said. 'In your day it even used to apply to God.'

'Don't try to talk sophisticated,' he said. 'It makes you look younger. Now we don't want that, do we?'

Damn him, she thought. Damn him. He hasn't acted smart in so long I'd forgotten he knew how. So why does he have to remind me now?

'Professor Uhlmann,' he said. 'NYU.'

'That's right,' she said, and finished her drink. 'You better find yourself another recruit, general. Because when it comes to professors of sociology, you don't send a jejune sophisticate.' She put down her glass, gathered up her purse and Genet, then kissed her father. 'See you around, general,' she said. 'Lieutenant Manette's just gone AWOL.'

[ii]

London Airport was just like it always was, over-crowded, none too clean, and with far too many long corridors. Lonely didn't mind the people, and a bit of dirt never harmed anybody, but the corridors was murder. Trouble was, Mr Callan was drunk. Soon as the plane took off he'd started. Scotch. Not rushing it, just steady. Two at a time, miniatures. Like doubles they were. And when the duty free came round he'd bought himself a bottle and started in on that. Chairman of the Board I don't think, thought Lonely. Not unless he gets hisself a distillery. Mind you let's be fair, he could walk. If you could call it walking. Like those monsters they show on the late night horror films so you can stay up till one in the morning and then not sleep for terror. Legs all stiff, and not much idea where they were going. Still he was moving.

Getting him off the plane had been the worst part. Up that gangway thing. He'd bounced off every seat and when the air-hostess said she hoped they'd enjoyed their flight he'd bounced off her an' all. Then he'd smiled at her and in the end she'd smiled back, and her bruised all over. Say what you like Mr Callan had got it, drunk or sober—only then he'd grabbed hold of Lonely and asked him what she'd said. Lonely still went hot at the memory of it: passengers piling up behind and him yelling:

'She hopes you enjoyed your flight.'

Callan had bowed to her then. If Lonely hadn't grabbed him he'd have gone head-first down the stairs.

'Every glass,' Mr Callan had said.

It was worse than embarrassing, it was demeaning. And steering him along these dirty great corridors was demeaning an' all. And that fat git had been no help at all. Straight out of the first class he'd gone, and scarpered. Never even looked back.... Lonely eased Callan into the queue for passport control, then on to the customs hall, propped him against a pillar, and waited by the carousel for the luggage. And that was another problem. How was he going to cope with two lots of luggage and Mr Callan? Get a porter, that was the answer; but it was Mr Callan who always did the la-di-da bit, like tips and that. The state he was in now he'd never even find his pocket, never mind his change.

But when he got back to Mr Callan he was standing nearly upright.

'Gave you a bit of a time, didn't I?' he said.

'That's all right, Mr Callan,' said Lonely.

'Problems, you see,' said Callan. 'Lots of problems.'

Lonely didn't see, but it was better to stay stum.

'I'm being met,' said Callan.

'I see,' said Lonely.

'No you don't,' said Callan. 'It's—in connection with the job. Feller that's meeting me—he's a real hard case. Better you shouldn't meet him.'

Lonely agreed at once. 'Much better, Mr Callan,' he said.

134

'Now you push off and I'll be with you in a couple of days.'

'Sure you'll be all right, Mr Callan?'

'I'll be fine,' said Callan. 'So long, old son.'

There was nothing wrong with the words, but for some reason Lonely found himself near tears.

Callan picked up his case, and walked with his monster's stride to the wash-room. The Sikh in charge gave him one look, and decided it was time for his tea-break. Callan bathed his face in cold water, over and over, dried off, then bought himself a squirt of cologne from a vending machine and used that. He was still drunk, but it was just about containable. He picked the case up, and headed out through the green, and nobody stopped him. Waiting outside in a dark grey suit, chauffeur's cap under his arm, was Spencer Perceval FitzMaurice. He moved at once to Callan, took his case, slipped a supporting hand under his arm.

'Well well,' he said, 'and to think I was going to ask if you'd had a good trip.'

He led him to where a Daimler was waiting and eased him inside: the way he handled him was impersonal, but not malicious, and he waited till Callan was settled before moving off....

From his place in the bus queue Lonely might have seen them, if he'd been looking, might even have remembered the darkie that night he'd gone down the Bird in Hand with Uncle Lennie and met Spanner. But Lonely wasn't looking: he was too busy being indignant. He'd just seen that fat git Berkeley drive off in a Rolls-Royce....

[iii]

'Well at least you have the book,' said Snell.

'Oh yes,' said Hunter. 'Our code people are working on it now. But I haven't got Callan. He's still sleeping it off.'

'You resent the fact that he's escaped you?'

'I should be obliged,' Hunter said, 'if you would refrain from analysing me. Callan is the one I'm interested in.'

'I beg your pardon,' said Snell. 'I've done it so often it's almost automatic these days. What a Pavlovian would call a conditioned reflex—if there are any Pavlovians left.'

Hunter stirred in his chair.

Snell said quickly, 'But you wish to know about Callan. Well, in a sense he has escaped you of course, and that particular escape-route is always accessible—'

'The bottle?'

'Precisely. But there is rather more to it than that.'

'You always say that,' said Hunter.

135

'It is almost invariably true. Callan is suffering from remorse.'

'Don't be absurd,' said Hunter.

'But he is,' said Snell. 'Consider. If his drunken meanderings are to be believed he has brow-beaten two men—Berkeley and Lonely, two men for whom he feels a high degree of friendship: he has cheated another, Kleist; and shot and tortured a fourth, Lord Hexham. He hates himself for it: he wishes not to remember it: he drinks. Q.E.D. The fact that he has escaped from you is a welcome bonus, no more. It is purely temporary.'

'So is his oblivion.'

'Manifestly. But he can always drink again. He will.'

'Can you cure it?'

'No.'

The flat negative irritated Hunter.

'I should be obliged if you would elaborate on that.'

Snell sighed. Why couldn't laymen just believe?

'He can only cure himself,' he said, 'and he could only do that by removing himself from an ambience that forces him to shoot, hurt and maim.'

'Meaning me.'

'Of course. So long as you're involved with him Callan will drink. It's been evolving for some time.'

'I'm aware of it,' said Hunter. 'I've read your dossier on him.' He brooded. 'Can you stop him drinking temporarily?'

'Over how long a period?'

'Two weeks—three.'

'Not with any certainty of success. I could try.'

Hunter reached a decision.

'Then do so,' he said.

[iv]

Meres liked Taormina, it was his sort of place: elegant, affluent, slightly camp. A bit like the assignment, he thought: keeping an eye on a gun-girl and a clerk with delusions about honour. They were an ill-assorted pair, he thought. Not beauty and the beast exactly: more the princess and the peasant. The poor bastard couldn't have been more hooked on heroin. Take her away and he'd go to pieces. Well, that could be arranged too.... He watched from the bar as they walked into town for lunch, and broke into their room. Really hotel locks were dreadful. Anybody could walk in, do what they liked, he thought, and carefully, methodically searched.

German paper-backs; Gunther Grass, Heinrich Böll, good, liberal reading. Nothing in French: Mlle Nivelle, it seemed, was

136

not a reader. She kept the little Armi Galesi in the bottom of a flower-pot on the balcony, under a spray of geraniums. The colour of blood, he thought. Wonder what Snell would make of that? and checked the magazine. She'd got more ammo from somewhere. He put the gun back and went through their possessions. She had far more clothes than he had, and much prettier ones.... West German passport, French passport, both in order, and under the woman's pants a book of travellers' cheques. French francs, rather a lot of them. Whatever money Kleist had he carried with him. Could it be, Meres wondered, that the princess was financing the peasant? He went to the telephone, and inserted the bug he'd picked up from Signora Lunari, and took one more look round. There was nothing more. No souvenirs, no gifts, not one letter or postcard. That was a mistake. Bad cover. Be as impersonal as that and maybe hotel servants will remember.... Still, he wasn't there to give lessons. Time for a quick lunch before they got back, then he could check if the receiver was working.

Fish and salad, and half a bottle of white wine, then back to his bedroom, switch on and wait. Door clicked open, door locked, shutters drawn, the rustling sound of clothes discarded, a drink poured, and no words spoken, until:

'Always I love it when you bring me a drink,' said Kleist.

'I am glad that I please you,' said Jeanne-Marie, but Meres caught the hint of boredom in her voice.

Who knows? he thought; this could turn out to be fun.

But it wasn't, not really. There was a Teutonic thoroughness about it, true, but all sadly orthodox. Nothing inventive at all. Sex by numbers, and only two of them. *Ein zwei, ein zwei.* Would he never get to *drei vier fünf?* Come on, Gunther old sport. How about some hard rock. No? Not even an old fashioned waltz? But ein zwei was all he knew, as regular as jack-boots marching, and just about as exciting, thought Meres. The bird hasn't even gasped. It seemed that Gunther was in charge of the gasp department. When the time came he did enough of it. Meres yawned, and listened as Kleist babbled endearments, the girl went off to the bidet. This one would have been boring even with pictures....

'I think,' Jeanne-Marie said, 'that we ought to leave this place.'

You and him both, darling, thought Meres.

'But you forget, darling,' said Kleist, 'we cannot leave until I have talked with Hexham.'

'I have talked to him,' she said.

'You?.... When?'

'The night we lost,' said Jeanne-Marie. 'After you took your

137

sleeping tablets I went back to the palazzo. He wishes us to go away. It is over, Gunther.'

'Such damnable luck,' said Kleist.

'Luck?' she said. 'Does it not occur to you that we were cheated?'

'Of course not,' he said. 'We cheated.'

'But not well enough, it seems. That is why we lost.'

'I don't believe it,' said Kleist. 'The old man was drunk. And in any case, *we* raised the stakes.'

She said sharply, 'Those two men should be investigated. I do not think there is any reason to pay them anything. Let us go back to Bonn.'

It would seem, Meres thought, that I have work to do after all.

'But I must talk to Hexham about the other matter,' said Kleist.

'Hexham has no wish to discuss the other matter,' she said. 'He told me so.' Then, her voice rising, she added: 'For God's sake, Gunther. Can't you understand? I want to go.'

No doubt about it, thought Meres. There's work crying out to be done.

[v]

He'd showered, and shaved, and even swallowed some breakfast, but he felt terrible, and, the mirror told him, he looked it. With a hangover like his he was in no state to face Hunter, but that was what he had to do. He knocked and went in, and Hunter took one look at him and poured out coffee. When Callan took the cup and saucer his hands were not quite steady.

'Well, at least you got the book,' said Hunter, 'and that's something.'

Callan sipped at his coffee: bitter, scalding, black.

'I hope it's what you wanted,' he said.

'The book is exactly what I wanted,' said Hunter, 'which is more than I can say for you. What happened?'

'I shot an earl,' said Callan. 'My first. Mind you I don't feel too badly about that, because he was going to shoot Lonely—or he said he was.'

'You told me all that,' said Hunter.

'Then I interrogated him,' said Callan. 'I used a few of those tricks Snell showed us—on a fine, brave, upstanding lad like that.'

'And what happened?' said Hunter.

'You know what happened,' said Callan. 'He went to pieces. Just like I would or you would. Told me things his mother would blush for. I told you that an' all.'

'You were less than coherent,' said Hunter. 'Tell me again.'

'He's skint,' said Callan. 'He's got a bloody great palazzo full of

138

art-treasures and he's skint. Only the way he sees it, he doesn't deserve to be. He's a gentleman of quality, Hunter, an aristo, and gentlemen of quality were born into this world to have money. He first realised that when he had to resign from the Guards on account of impecuniosity, and his first reaction was that he was no longer a gentleman. How could he be if he was broke? So he became a painter on account of it's O.K. for painters to be broke. Incidentally what our brave lad uses for logic I'll never know.'

'Get on,' said Hunter. 'Just get on.'

'He turned out to be a bloody awful painter,' said Callan, 'so he thought maybe he'd be better off being a gentleman after all and went into the antique trade. To make money, you see; to support himself in the manner. All that. Only would you believe it; the antique dealers he was in with turned out to be a bunch of crooks, and being a gentleman the idea that he would be swindled by persons in trade never crossed his mind.'

'He can't have said that,' said Hunter. For once he was almost pleading.

'I was there,' said Callan. 'He said it. He said he lost money he didn't even have. So he became an urban guerrilla.'

'I am not in the mood for jokes, Callan.'

'Nor me,' said Callan. 'They were his words. Urban guerrillas work for the overthrow of the society that is so they can replace it with the society they want. He wants aristocrats. So he met up with this Kleist geezer and started robbing the bourgeois over a friendly game of cards. He had another bright idea an' all.'

'Go on.'

'Antiques again. Not his own stuff. He's never going to part with that. What's yours is mine, what's mine's me own. That's his motto. That's how he got into the urban guerrilla lark. All he had to do was sell a few things and he'd be set for life, but that would be cowardly. That would be giving in. So he'd sooner live in that damn great barracks on his tod, weed the gardens himself and hire servants twice a year—and fleece Bulky and me. Or try to.'

'Tell me about the antiques.'

'There's a lot of good stuff about,' said Callan. 'Even behind the Iron Curtain—East Germany, Hungary, Czechoslovakia. Buyers' market—if you can get it out. And he could. His mate Kleist has a lot of contacts in East Germany. Am I telling you anything you don't know?'

'No,' said Hunter, 'but I like to have things confirmed.'

'Confirm anything, Hexham would,' said Callan. 'Once I got him to see that we were chums.'

'Did he know about the book?'

'Of course he does,' said Callan, 'but he'll stay quiet about it.'

'You're sure?'

'Certain,' said Callan. 'You don't think he got that furniture out legally do you? He even fakes the provenances—says the stuff's his own. I'm on to his racket and he knows it. He'll stay stum.'

'And the gambling debt?'

'Oh come on,' said Callan. 'He cheated. We cheated better. How can I claim on that?'

Hunter leaned forward, moved a file, and uncovered a leather-bound book. 'This was found in your luggage,' he said. 'The Essays of Montaigne—the Florio translation.'

'Oh that? Something to read on the plane,' said Callan.

Hunter said, 'You couldn't even see on the plane.'

'All right,' said Callan. 'But he lost it fair and square. Or unfair and crooked. So he owes it to Bulky and me. So I took the book.'

'We'll see,' said Hunter. 'Tell me about the girl.'

'This may shock you,' said Callan, 'but she tried to seduce me.'

'Dear me,' said Hunter.

'She also took a shot at me with a rifle.' He began to relate the attack, and Hunter listened.

'It has to be her?' he asked at last.

'I think so,' said Callan. 'Nobody else was in on it—My chum Hexham told me.'

'And where would she get a rifle?'

'From Hexham,' said Callan. 'She mightn't even have bothered to tell him she'd borrowed it.'

'I see,' said Hunter.

'D'you know, I rather think you do? That bird's a pro, Hunter, and I rather think you knew that, too.'

'Are we back with the SSD again?'

'You tell me,' said Callan.

'We may be,' Hunter said. 'It would answer a lot of questions. But if she should belong to them, you've been fortunate. After the amount of whisky you've consumed you should be dead.'

'She passes for French,' said Callan. 'Bulky doubts it unless she's from Alsace. Otherwise his guess is she's German.'

'You feel you can rely on his judgment?'

'I had to,' said Callan. 'He didn't let me down.'

Hunter changed course. 'The book you brought me was everything I'd hoped,' he said. 'Perhaps even more.'

'That should make everything worthwhile,' said Callan, 'but it doesn't.'

Hunter ignored him. 'People defect from East to West for one of two reasons: either sheer greed, or because of an accumulation of horror—seen, undergone, even initiated, it makes no matter which—that finally becomes insupportable, and so they run away.

140

To us. There is nowhere else to run. But people who defect from West to East go East by choice. Moscow, East Berlin, Prague, Budapest—to them these are the Promised Land.'

'If you don't mind,' said Callan, 'I've got a terrible headache.' Hunter handed him some aspirin and continued.

'There is something rather touching about the ones who are disappointed, and quite a few of them are. It is as if when General Booth died and went to heaven he found that God did not live up to his expectations and one of the angel-trombonists couldn't sight-read.'

'Military history's my field,' said Callan. 'I never could cope with Religious Instruction.'

'The poor creatures are in despair,' said Hunter. 'The heaven they have reached is inferior to the hell they have abandoned. They long, they yearn, to return to hell. But one cannot commute between ideologies, Callan: not unless one can pay for the return trip—and the price is high.'

Callan sipped more coffee: his head was booming like a Salvationist's drum, and Hunter knew it. Hunter was having a ball.

'Consider the case of Siegfried Lindt,' he said. 'Bonn civil servant, thirty-three years old. Pretty little wife, charming little daughter. Secretary to a cabinet minister. Well-placed, doing well. Just bought his first Mercedes. But Siegfried had friends in the Bader-Meinhoff gang. He told them things: he participated, from a distance and by proxy, in their murders and their robberies. One day he learned that West German security were getting close to him, and he fled: West Berlin—East Berlin—Dresden. He became a civil servant, got a divorce and acquired another pretty little wife and in the fullness of time an enchanting little son. By then, if there'd been an equivalent of the Bader-Meinhoff gang in East Germany he would have joined it, but of course there isn't.'

'Not with the SSD around there's not,' said Callan.

'Spare me your obsession for the moment,' said Hunter. 'Lindt's trouble was boredom. East or West, in time he became bored. One of our people approached him, and he wanted to move— could even pay for his ticket.'

'With a book,' said Callan.

'Marx's *Kapital*,' said Hunter, 'copiously annotated in his own hand—the most puerile code I've ever seen. He was to give us the book, and in return we would get him out. Unfortunately—'

'The SSD got him first,' said Callan.

'How very perceptive of you. They very nearly got our chap too. The book had disappeared, but our chap was fairly sure it was in a piece of furniture. Lindt, you see, was a friend of the man who

141

was smuggling the stuff out to Hexham. That was of course quite in character. Once in a Communist country Lindt would inevitably revert to private enterprise. It was then I decided to use you.'

'And my friend the minor genius.'

'You were clumsy but effective. I have the book. It contains—'

'I don't have to know what it contains,' said Callan.

'Who says so?'

Callan said, 'You, usually.'

'In this case I'll make an exception. The coded notes contain information about the present whereabouts of Ludwig Bauer's daughter. You know about him, I take it?'

'The most recent German I know about is Marshal Blücher,' said Callan, 'and I lost interest in him after Waterloo.'

'Bauer is West German minister to the Common Market, and a man of great influence—as well as having access to knowledge this country would dearly love to possess. There is also the fact that West Germany is rich, my dear David, and we, not to put too fine a point on it, are poor. It would be nice, even appropriate, if for once the rich would help the poor. There is, after all, good scriptural precedent for such a gesture.'

'You mean you've got something on him,' said Callan.

'Bauer is a widower,' said Hunter. 'He had one daughter, Ortrud, a brilliant if wayward girl. It was believed that she died in a car crash while under the influence of drugs: but it was in fact another girl who died. Ortrud Bauer was thrown free. She was also responsible for the other girl's death.'

'The other girl had no relatives?'

'Drop-outs never admit to any.'

'Where did Lindt get this stuff?'

'The Bader-Meinhoff gang,' said Hunter. 'I'm satisfied of its authenticity.'

'I see,' said Callan.

Hunter said, 'You usually do. Just think, David, how pleased the good Herr Bauer would be to learn that his daughter is alive and under treatment for her unfortunate craving. How pleased— and how grateful.'

Change the subject, thought Callan. Don't let him go on. You're in no shape to fight him now.

'But how does Kleist fit into all this?' he said.

'Kleist,' said Hunter, as if the word were a tantalising puzzle that he had finally solved. 'Kleist is a romantic. The family were *Gräfen*—counts—in what is now East Germany. He is in fact the Graf von Kleist, but neither the title nor the von is suitable for the profession of archivist. And yet Kleist remembers the days of family grandeur, and yearns for its restoration. What is he to do?'

142

'Join up with Hexham,' said Callan. 'Another urban guerrilla.'

'Exactly so. They met over their little involvement in antique furniture, and diversified into gambling. They'd actually done rather well—until they encountered Berkeley—and yourself.'

'He must have been there for months.'

'Six weeks,' said Hunter. 'Extended sick leave. Nervous breakdown, according to his medical certificate. After he'd encountered Berkeley and yourself, it wouldn't surprise me if it were true.' He paused, and Callan knew he was savouring something.

'Men of honour,' said Hunter.

'Why are you after him?' said Callan.

'Lindt left a copy of his book in Bonn archives,' said Hunter. 'A first attempt. Rather inept, I believe, but it exists, and Kleist knows where it is: but not what it is.'

'He knew Lindt?'

'He thought he did. I should think the Bader-Meinhoff connection would shock him deeply.'

'If you want that book from Kleist you'll have to get the girl out of the way.'

'Naturally.'

'You have somebody in mind?'

'It's being attended to.'

Callan was cautious not to show relief.

'That's all right then,' he said, and rose. 'Now if you'll just tell me when I can expect our money in Zurich—'

'All in good time,' Hunter said. 'Do sit down. I haven't finished.'

Callan sat: he needed all his strength for his hangover.

'I'm about to offer you a bonus—' Hunter began.

'Twenty-five thousand'll do me,' said Callan.

'Which you will of course accept.'

'Yeah. I know. Red file and all that. But be reasonable, Hunter. Why me? I drink too much and I get upset and I'm starting to like people again. What use am I to you?'

'You're likeable,' said Hunter. 'For once I need somebody likeable. You won't drink because Snell will treat you before you go—and FitzMaurice will go with you in any case, to make sure you don't. When you return I'll pay another five thousand.'

'Return from where?' said Callan.

'Las Vegas.'

'And what do I bring back from Las Vegas? Frank Sinatra?'

'Nothing so easy,' said Hunter. 'Ortrud Bauer. You'll be briefed before you go. Now cut along and see Snell. He's waiting for you.'

Slowly, Callan moved to the door.

'And, David,' Hunter said, 'I do hope your headache is better.'

143

19

Kleist went swimming: Jeanne-Marie Nivelle took a car-ride. Meres had hired an Alfa-Romeo, with touched up paintwork on the bonnet and a new passenger door-handle. He followed her. Soon he was sure of her destination. After that it was easy. He overtook and kept on going, and reached a point beyond the Hexham palazzo minutes ahead of her, moved across the parkland and waited. The palazzo was dead quiet: no sign of life at all: not even one impoverished earl, working in the gardens: not even cleaning the windows, although they could do with it. He stayed in cover behind a plane tree, and waited, till the VW chugged its way up the drive and turned into the raked gravel parkway. She took her time looking about her, and when she got out at last she didn't look too happy. It could be the absence of other cars that bothered her, thought Meres, but whatever it was she went up to the house at last, opened the side-door with a key and disappeared inside.

Meres ran softly across to the door and pushed. As he'd thought, she hadn't latched it. That's a good girl, he thought. Always leave your escape routes open. Soundlessly he moved among the palazzo's dusty grandeur, and listened. She called out almost at once, 'Ludo! Ludo!' Ludovic Maurice Anthony Staples, thought Meres, seventh Earl of Hexham, and known to his chums as Ludo. Really, how utterly sweet. I bet at school they called him Tiddly-Winks. He followed the sound of her voice, and she led him from the long gallery to a series of salons, then up a flight of stairs to a bachelor apartment. She spent time there going through a wardrobe full of clothes, and didn't much like what she discovered. Some of the clothes were missing, Meres thought. Naughty Jeanne-Marie, to carry drinks to Gunther and know where Ludo keeps his clothes....

She led him back down the stairs to the gallery, and stared at the dismembered cabinet, the shattered ruins of the glass panel. 'Dummkopf,' she said, and then, as she crunched across the glass, 'Schwein.' She sounds as if she really means it, thought

144

Meres, and then: What funny French she talks to be sure. She went towards the library and he followed. Ah well. Best get on with it. He stepped into the library and coughed in a manner he hoped was deferential. The girl swung round.

'Ludo,' she said, '*du bist*—' She stepped backwards, peered at him, and switched to English. 'Who are you?' she said. 'You're not Ludo.'

Her hand went to the pocket of her driving coat, and Meres brought his hand from behind his back. In it was the 357 Magnum revolver that Signora Lunari kept oiled, cleaned and available, for the friends of Mr Robinson of Pimlico. The Magnum was aimed at a point just below the girl's left breast. She had no doubt that the intruder knew exactly how to use it.

'Please keep still,' he said, and she obeyed him, and he moved behind her. His left hand flicked to her coat pocket, and came out holding the Armi Galesi 22. He dropped it in the side-pocket of his own coat, then moved round to face her again.

'It's quite true that I'm not Ludo,' he said, 'but then you're not Jeanne-Marie Nivelle, are you?'

'I don't know what you mean,' she said.

'But it's so *simple*,' he said. 'When you say that you are Jeanne-Marie Nivelle, a citizen of France, you lie.'

'Why do you say that?' she said.

'Because when you thought you were alone, you spoke German,' said Meres. 'When you thought I was Ludo Staples you spoke German. Surely that would imply—'

She gave him no warning at all: her face gave no signs of her intentions, but she kicked out at him in mid-sentence, neat and accurate; a dancer's kick, or a footballer's. The squared-off toe of her shoe caught Meres on the fore-arm, hard on the muscle above the ulna bone. The Magnum shot from his hand and she dived for it, but Meres was already moving into her, his clenched left hand thumping into her diaphragm in a fist strike that slammed her into the fireplace. She bounced off it, pitching sideways, and the hand became an axe-blade that bit into the nape of her neck, knocking her prone.

'Bitch,' said Meres. 'Stupid, stupid bitch. Cow. Whore.'

She neither moved nor answered. Meres cursed her steadily, and at the top of his voice, as he nursed his bruised arm. Two inches lower and she'd have broken it. Suddenly he broke off in mid-sentence, found the girl's handbag, and winced as he opened it, took out a pocket-mirror, and held it before her nose and mouth. There was no clouding: none at all. Jeanne-Marie Nivelle or whoever the hell she was would neither move nor answer ever again.

145

And that was bad. Very bad. Hunter had told him to get rid of the girl, true, but that didn't necessarily mean to kill her. He'd only been supposed to kill in an extreme emergency, and in any case not repeat *not* before he'd found out who she was; who she was *with*. Hunter would say that he'd lost his temper, and Hunter would be right, sod him. Meres had told Snell, over and over he'd told him, how he hated to be hurt by a woman: how it always, *always* made him mad. But that wouldn't worry Hunter. His orders had been to find out about the girl, and they hadn't been obeyed. And that was bad. When you worked for Hunter you bloody well did what he told you—or else.... Maybe she had something on her.... He went through her handbag. Women's junk and that was all. Change-purse, lipstick, mirror, comb, matches, cigarettes.... On her body? Deft and impersonal as a surgeon, Meres stripped her. Really she peeled off very prettily.... If only she hadn't kicked him.... He went through what there was of her clothes. Nothing. Not a bloody thing. For a moment he considered leaving her there, but he knew it wouldn't do. She had to be dressed again. He managed to do it at last, but it was a hell of a job.... He looked around and gathered up the things he'd thrown from her bag, ramming them back, and found that the lining of her handbag was slit at the bottom. He tore the silk lining wider, and found that something was lodged between the silk and the leather. Carefully he coaxed it out.... An address book. A rotten address book. Still, it was something to take back, to show Hunter that at least he'd tried. After that all he had to do was get rid of the body.

[ii]

'Be reasonable, dad,' Elizabeth said. 'How can I?'

They were having dinner in a French Creole place that was in at the time, staffed by people chosen apparently only for a close resemblance to Hattie Daniels or Step 'n' Fetchit, but the food was good, the clientele both numerous and influential. It would do Congressman Manette no harm at all to be seen there with that cute daughter of his, but he didn't fight fair, fussing to make sure her food was just right, ordering hock which he detested and she adored. Gorillas had no business being nice: not when you wanted to turn them down.

'Surely you must see that I can't do anything?' her father said.

'I don't see anything,' she said. 'I don't know what you're up to.'

'Up to?' he said. 'What kind of language is that? I'm trying to do something for our country.'

146

She remembered an earlier conversation.

'And for yourself,' she said.

'All right,' he said. 'And for myself. But in that order. Our country comes first, Elizabeth.'

'It would do you a lot of good, humh?'

It would really make me, he thought. I'd be so big....

'Yes,' he said. 'It would.'

He couldn't fool her: she could sense the urgency behind those wary monosyllables. But how could a polar bear play Pollyanna? It didn't make *sense*.

'Look, dad,' she said, 'it's one thing fooling a bereaved mother who's too much in shock to start wondering what the hell I'm playing at—'

He winced at that. Well O.K. So let him wince. *He* hadn't had to do it.

'But fooling a hip professor could be a hell of a lot more tricky. That could be heavy.'

'Stop saying hell,' said her father, 'and answer two questions. How do you know he's hip—and what do you mean by heavy?'

He pushed aside his jambalaya and reached for his salad.

'He's hip because Barry Johnson dug him,' Elizabeth said, 'and by heavy in this context I mean both complicated and difficult.'

'Then why not say so?'

'Dad,' she said, 'we didn't come here to argue semantics. Now. Do you want this information or don't you?'

'Of course I do,' he said.

'Then you're going to have to use some clout,' she said. 'And don't tell me you don't know what clout means. Not here. Not in Washington.'

*

The whole place was a temple of the young. Corridors and classrooms thronged with them: long hair and beards and acne and sandals, and every kind of garment from studded leather to kaftans. The only kind of clothing not in evidence was the kind of suit he was wearing, and when he did see one at last, it was on a woman.... And this is vacation-time, he thought. What brings them? Extra courses? Did they flunk out? Can they achieve happiness nowhere else? He pushed his way down a corridor, running a gauntlet of radios and books, beads and beards, and found the office at last: Professor Uhlmann, Department of Sociology. Manette knocked and went in, and did not like what he saw. One look and he knew his daughter was right: Professor Uhlmann was hip. Big and handsome, sure, but the jeans were

147

faded, the sweat shirt old, the hair long. A few years ago there'd have been a flower in it.

'Professor Uhlmann?' he said.

'Congressman Manette?'

And you don't like what you're seeing either, thought Manette. But you don't have to like me, professor. All you have to do is fear me a little.

And it wasn't so difficult at that. Uhlmann, it was obvious, had done a little checking, a little asking around, and although he would never, never vote Manette's party ticket, he knew that Manette was a wheel of more than modest dimensions, a wheel that might one day be big. And Assistant Professors of Sociology yearned for Washington, even lusted after it, had done so ever since the New Deal. Manette played a hand that held all the court cards. He'd chaired more than one investigating committee: he knew not only how to bully, but when.

'So to get right down to it, professor,' he said at last, 'I'm interested in the case of that girl you quoted.'

'I'm honoured that my poor lectures provoke such interest,' Uhlmann said.

'You should be,' said Manette. 'It shows people listen to what you say. I like to think that people do that for me too.'

'I'm sure they do, Congressman,' said Uhlmann.

And you can shove your polished irony, you bastard. I don't like you and I've had enough.

'Because when people listen, really listen, I can get things done,' Manette said. 'It's when they don't, when they have to be made to listen, that you have to start getting rough, and that way you make enemies. I don't need enemies any more than you do, professor.'

And there it was. Uhlmann made one last try.

'May I ask why you need to know this?' he asked.

'You may not. There is a possibility that it may concern some of the people I represent. That's all I can tell you. Except that it's confidential.'

'Yes of course,' said Uhlmann, and then, 'I'd have to make a phone call.'

'Go right ahead,' Manette said, and sat right where he was. The bastard looked as if the phone call might be embarrassing, and Manette didn't want to miss a word.

In a way it was nice to be paged in the Plaza: it made you feel important, in demand. On the other hand it wasn't so good when the call came and you were with a prospect and just about— maybe—you were going to get a nibble. Charlie Berman smiled his most deprecating smile at the prospect—the smile that said,

148

'We busy men of affairs have to take phone calls all the time, but isn't it a bore? Just when you and I were getting to know each other,' and hoped it would work, and knew it was an even money bet. He went into the booth and yelled, 'Hello?' The fact that he was yelling didn't surprise him. He was good and mad.

'Charlie?' Dick Uhlmann said. 'This is Dick. Hey, listen. I just called Sally.... She said you were there.'

Dick, he thought. My trusty brother-in-law. Who else?

'For Christ's sake,' he said. 'Didn't she tell you I'm buying for a client?'

'She said you were selling.'

Charlie used his vaudeville Jewish voice: 'Uhlmann hated his vaudeville Jewish voice. 'Automobile accessories I'm selling,' he said. 'Lunch I'm buying.' He waited for the outrage: it didn't come.

'Hey, that's great,' Dick Uhlmann said. 'I like it.'

Charlie Berman figured he'd got a crossed-line.

'I need your help, Charlie,' Uhlmann said. 'It's urgent.'

'For you or for me?'

'Now look, Charlie—'

'No,' Berman said. 'You look. I've loaned you enough money. If I don't get back to the prospect even I won't have money.'

'O.K.,' said Uhlmann, 'so I owe you sixty dollars.'

'Sixty-five,' said Berman.

'So there'll be a cheque in the mail. Today.... All right?'

Charlie Berman looked at the handset as if it were making up dialogue.

'Today?' he said.

'That's a promise. Now listen Charlie....'

Charlie Berman was so bewildered that he told him. In confidence, but he told him. Big, confident Dick Uhlmann begging for a favour from his consumer-orientated brother-in-law, and getting it. Because even when Dick begged for favours he managed to make you feel it was your fault he had to beg, and anyway it was time to get back to the prospect. But when he did get back the best he could do was go through the motions. His mind was still on his brother-in-law's pleadings. Funny thing was, the prospect got worried: figured the phone call was a better offer than the one he'd just made, and upped it by three and a half per cent. Charlie Berman considered the possibility of writing phone calls into his scenario.

'The man's name is Caulfield, Harry Caulfield,' said Uhlmann. 'He's an automobile distributor. Offices in Detroit and Manhattan. He's apparently very—successful.'

The word you want is 'rich', thought Manette. But you find it degrading.

149

'I'm obliged to you,' he said.

'My brother-in-law hopes that this will be kept confidential.'

'So do I,' said Manette.

'You can rely on me, Congressman,' Uhlmann said.

Manette found himself quoting his daughter. No way, he thought. No way.

He left the campus, and went back to his hotel, put in a call to his secretary in Washington. When she called him back she had quite a bit on Caulfield: womaniser, loud-mouth, heavy but cagey drinker. Worth around two million. And at present in Mexico, address unknown, which was bad. Expected back in a couple of days, which was better, but not much. A hell of a lot can happen in two days.

[iii]

Kleist was by the pool. He wore trunks, sunglasses, and a wrist-watch he looked at every five minutes. Meres sat nearby. He'd showered and changed—humping a body about in the Sicilian summer had made him glad to do both—but when he went to the pool he was fully-clad: safari-jacket, linen slacks, heavy yachting shoes. Kleist looked to be the nervous type, and with the nervous ones you never knew. They might turn violent, and if they did, it was better to have your clothes on, especially your shoes. He sat at a table near Kleist's, and ordered a Bloody Mary. Shouldn't be long, he thought, and hoped to God it would be over before dinner. All that exercise had made him hungry. He lay back in his chair, and watched the girls in the pool. Dreary, for the most part. Cows. Nothing to compare with Jeanne-Marie. Then he spotted the manager moving towards Kleist, and behind him an officer of carabiniere. They lined up in front of Kleist as if they were going to sing a duet by Puccini, Meres thought. Really, Italians were marvellous. They were about to relate disaster: their faces would portray nothing but sorrow and compassion—and they would enjoy every minute of it.

The manager was the linguist, and broke it to Kleist in German, with occasional promptings from the carabiniere. And really that was a pity, thought Meres. In Italian they'd have been much better. But even so they made the most of it. A mountain road, and a puncture of a front tyre, and the signorina had got out to attend to it. Only it would seem that the signorina had not applied the handbrake fully. The road was steep, and the car had rolled forward on her, and she had been crushed, utterly crushed. Terrible, terrible. Kleist fainted.

What scurryings, thought Meres, what summonings of waiters

with brandy, maids with water. Everything but the kiss of life. Then they took him up to his room and summoned the doctor. Meres finished his Bloody Mary and went inside and up to the desk, where the manager was telling the concierge all.

'Forgive me,' said Meres, diffidently British, 'but I was by the pool. I couldn't help seeing—I do hope the poor chap hasn't caught something infectious?'

The very word will trigger him off, thought Meres, and it did. Nothing like that, the manager assured him. Absolutely nothing like that. The poor gentleman's fiancée had suffered a car accident. Dead. Absolutely dead. Her face, her torso smashed. All smashed.

'I say,' said Meres. 'What rotten luck. I do hope you called a doctor for the poor chap?'

A doctor had been called. An excellent doctor. The unfortunate gentleman was now under sedation.

'Poor fellow,' said Meres. 'Poor fellow,' and went into dinner.

It was a bore of course, but obviously he couldn't go out that night. Pity really. He'd spotted some places that looked really rather interesting. But he'd put up one black already: he didn't dare risk another. He had coffee and brandy sent up to his room, switched on the bugging device, and flicked through a magazine. All Kleist did was groan in his sleep, and Meres considered the possibility of going to his room, having another look round. But where was the point? He'd been over the place already.... Then the groaning stopped, the bed creaked, and Kleist began to sob: dry, racking sobs so intense they must have hurt.... And where was the point in that? thought Meres. But they diminished at last, and Meres caught the sound of drawers pulled out, a suitcase being opened. That wouldn't do at all. He got up and went to Kleist's corridor, knocked at the door and went in.

'Forgive me for butting in, old boy,' he said, 'but I couldn't help feeling that something was wrong.'

Kleist looked at him: the poor fellow seemed literally dazed by grief.

'I don't know you, do I?' he said.

'No no. My name is Meres.... Toby Meres. I'm staying at the hotel.'

Kleist bowed. 'Gunther von Kleist,' he said.

'You sounded so upset,' said Meres, 'I just wondered if there was anything I could do.'

'There is nothing anybody can do,' said von Kleist. 'I have suffered what I think you call a bereavement.' He hesitated, then said, 'Perhaps I may offer you a drink?'

'I don't like to butt in,' said Meres.

151

'Please,' Kleist said. 'It would be a kindness. I have nobody to talk to, Mr Meres. Nobody at all.'

'Well perhaps a little brandy,' said Meres. 'Just a small one.'

What he got was the edited version, but then he'd expected that.... Once upon a time there had been a sad and lonely widower who had lived a mean and circumscribed life as an archivist in the civil service at Bonn. And then one day a beautiful princess had come along and taken one look, and seen that beneath the prim and self-effacing exterior was the soul of a knight who longed only to serve her, and she, so young, so beautiful, had responded: loved him, cherished him, encouraged him to use those knightly qualities which the world so lacked. (Though what they were, thought Meres, is a teeny bit vague. Smuggling antiques? Cheating at cards?) They had set forth on holiday, and reached this enchanted island, and there—oh tragedy! oh horror!—the knight had failed his princess, let her venture forth alone—and she had been trampled to death by her erstwhile faithful steed, one of millions of VW's produced since the war in the town of Würzburg in the Republic of West Germany.

'And do you not know anyone here?' Meres asked at last, his voice soft, low, oozing compassion.

'One person only,' said Kleist. 'An English lord. The Lord Hexham. But he has gone away.'

'Hexham?' said Meres. 'Good lord.... Not old Ludo?'

'You knew him?' Kleist said.

'He was in the Brigade,' said Meres, and then explained kindly: 'The Guards, you know. In the Coldstream. I was a Grenadier myself. You don't mean to say you *know* him? ... Oh, of course. He has a place here, hasn't he?'

'A palazzo,' said Kleist. 'It is quite near where my—where Jeanne-Marie died.'

'And you say he's away?'

'He left yesterday. Quite suddenly.'

'Then he probably heard I was—No. That's ridiculous.'

'I beg your pardon,' said Kleist. 'I do not understand.'

Meres went through the motions of a man struggling in the toils of embarrassment. He did it rather well.

'I'm sorry,' he said, 'but if this chap's a friend of yours—'

'I am by no means sure that he is my friend,' said Kleist.

'Then perhaps I had better tell you,' said Meres. 'You seem to have enough troubles already without my adding to them. Hexham owes me money, old chap. Rather a lot of money. In fact I rather misled you until now. The fact is I came here to ask him for it back.'

'I see,' said Kleist.

152

'You couldn't tell me where I could find him, by any chance?'

'I regret not,' said Kleist. He looked speculatively at Meres. Knowledge and ingenuousness mixed, and not one ounce of cunning.

'Do you have a card?' he said. 'A visiting card?'

Gravely Meres took out his wallet, extracted a strip of pasteboard from Harrod's: T. D. F. Meres, it read, and an address in Belgravia.

'It gives no indication of your army rank,' said Kleist.

'One doesn't, you know,' Meres said gently. 'Not after one has retired.'

And that was all that was needed to make Kleist aware that he had committed a social solecism. He even blushed.

'Permit me,' he said. 'Another drink?'

'Better not,' said Meres. 'I'm interrupting your packing.'

'That was foolishness,' Kleist said. 'There is nowhere for me to go, even if the police would permit it.... Please.'

Meres took another brandy. It was nice that dear Gunther had found a new chum: cheered him up a bit. It might even make him communicative.

20

Callan said, 'You'll be all right. I'll only be away a few days and then we'll be back in business.'

But Lonely didn't even look at him. He had eyes only for Spencer Perceval FitzMaurice. Lonely had always been one for collecting things: Mickey Mouse clocks, ladies with no clothes on holding up lamp bulbs, Edward VIII coronation mugs, flags of all nations, stuff like that. And while Mr Callan had been away he'd got some more indisposable junk. And all paid for out of his own pocket.... Ready money. The result was that there wasn't a lot of space going in his living-room, and whatever there was, the big darky filled: every inch.

Callan said again: 'You'll be all right.'

Eyes still on the darky, Lonely said: 'Course I will.' It came out a croak.

'Who'll you stay with?' said Callan.

'I'll wait here,' said Lonely. 'You can trust me, Mr Callan. I won't nick anything.'

'Course you won't,' said Callan. 'All the same, old son, it might be better if you had a bit of company.'

'I'm not much of a one for company,' Lonely said. 'Do better on me own.'

Callan, head still aching, desperate for a drink, forced himself to be reasonable. 'The thing is, old son,' he said, 'you're big-time now. I mean five thousand quid and expenses just for a night's light exercise, it's hardly what you'd call washers, is it?'

Lonely pondered, savoured the fact that he was big-time, and to do him justice, Spencer Perceval FitzMaurice didn't laugh: didn't even smile.

'You put it like that, Mr Callan,' said Lonely, 'I suppose I am. Big time I mean.'

'Well, when you're that big you got to take care of yourself—On account of reprisals.'

'Beg pardon, Mr Callan?'

154

Niff or no niff, it had to be said.

'The higher you climb, the harder you fall,' said Callan.

Lonely understood that all right, and inevitably reacted. Spencer Perceval FitzMaurice opened a window.

'I suppose I could go and see Uncle Lennie again,' said Lonely.

Callan looked at FitzMaurice. He nodded.

'You do that,' said Callan. 'Give him my regards.'

'You going far, Mr Callan?' said Lonely.

Callan forced himself to look relaxed.

'Business trip,' he said. 'If we're going public, old son, we've got to raise more capital.'

'Oh,' said Lonely. 'Oh…. Yeah. I suppose we do.' He looked at the darky. It took all his courage to ask the question, but it had to be asked—'Is your friend coming in with us?'

'Business consultant,' said Callan. 'Time and motion, diversification, tax avoidance. All that.'

Lonely hadn't a clue, but it sounded all right. Particularly tax avoidance. 'I see,' he said. 'Well, that's all right then.' But why should a business-consultant go to a pub like the Bird In Hand in a donkey jacket, even if he was a darky?

Callan rose. 'See you at your Uncle Lennie's then,' he said.

'Look forward to it, Mr Callan,' said Lonely. 'Have a good trip.'

Again FitzMaurice didn't laugh, didn't even smile.

They went out to the waiting Daimler, and FitzMaurice drove.

'Where now?' Callan asked.

'My place,' said FitzMaurice. 'I have to don my disguise.' To Callan they were only words: he needed a drink.

'You handled him well,' FitzMaurice said. 'The little stinker trusts you.' He sounded admiring, even envious.

'I've always tried to be honest with him,' said Callan. 'Ever since the nick. And he's always been honest with me.'

'You've tried and he's succeeded,' said FitzMaurice. 'Is that how you define trust?'

'I've never let anybody hurt him,' said Callan.

'Only you.'

'Yeah,' said Callan. 'That's right. Only me.'

'I could hurt him,' FitzMaurice said.

'And I could kill you.'

'Not unless you gave up drinking.'

'If you hurt him I'd do even that,' said Callan. 'Have you got any more messages from Hunter?'

FitzMaurice chuckled: a deep and lazy sound as of energy well throttled back, like a Ferrari before the flag goes down.

'I like you,' he said. 'I really do. With you I don't have to draw pictures.' He stopped at a red light and looked at Callan. 'But you

155

don't take a drink till we get back.'

He hadn't been fooling about the disguise: when they left for Heathrow he wore a gown of alternating stripes of blue, brown and cream that stretched from his neck to his feet, a neat, Nehru-like cap on his head, and carried a fly-whisk. Callan's disguise consisted of a brief-case crammed full with every fact available to Hunter about Nevada. There were a hell of a lot of facts. They travelled first on the Jumbo to Chicago, and FitzMaurice was very much the chief economic adviser of an emergent African republic to Callan's L.S.E. consultant. But in his way he was a compassionate man: like Callan he drank only coffee throughout the entire trip, and only once did he touch on Callan's past.

'You were in the Section a long time,' he said.

'Yeah,' said Callan. 'I was.'

'Only red file stuff?'

'Mostly.'

'The word is you did a lot.'

'The word doesn't go far enough,' said Callan. 'I did too much. Could I have another cup of coffee?'

FitzMaurice really was a compassionate man: he dropped the subject and ordered the coffee.

At O'Hare Field a limousine was waiting. Chief Shekwe and Mr Arthur Tucker, B.Sc. (Econ.), drove to the Sheraton where their suite was waiting, ordered dinner, showered, and relaxed. Or rather Chief Shekwe relaxed. Arthur Tucker stayed awake all night, trying, failing to persuade himself that he didn't need a drink.... Next morning there was a little shopping to be done in a complex off State Street. Chief Shekwe finished his third cup of coffee, and dressed: white on white shirt, pale-blue lightweight suit.

'You don't have to come,' said Callan.

'They tell me you can get a drink in this city any time, day or night,' said FitzMaurice.

They took a taxi to State Street, and after that they walked. When they reached the shop, FitzMaurice waited outside.... All Callan had to do was point, and hand over ten dollar bills. Two .357 Magnums, two sets of webbing harness, twenty-four rounds of ammo. He took it out wrapped in brown paper, and FitzMaurice looked more relaxed than ever.

'You got the lot?' he asked.

Callan nodded.

'Well, that is nice,' said FitzMaurice. 'Now that we's equipped, boss, let's you and me go to Sin City.'

Harry Caulfield caught a Pan Am flight to New York, and Manette was his first visitor. Caulfield's office was bigger than his, and far more modern. It featured a good deal of black glass and white leather, and it was glittering clean. It was also monumentally untidy, but Caulfield could head with utter certainty to whichever pile of papers contained the one he wanted, every time. He had not wanted to see Manette: he had said so when the receptionist had buzzed him to announce that the congressman was waiting, and said so in tones that were clearly audible to both of them, but Manette had persisted, and Caulfield's secretary came out for him at last. The receptionist had been pretty well what Manette had expected: a slim and elegant blonde with the remains of a Brooklyn accent that were like a dash of chilli in a too-bland sauce, but the secretary didn't fit the picture at all: a fifty-year-old workhorse who knew her job and did it thoroughly even when her feet hurt, and to judge by the way she walked her feet hurt all the time.

As she ushered Manette in, Caulfield thrust a sheet of figures at her.

'Check these, will you?' he said. 'Zimowski's mileages look way off. Hell, I know gas is dear, but—' He turned to Manette.

'Glad to know you, congressman,' he said. 'I gather you're in a hurry. I'm that way myself. Been on vacation. There's a lot to catch up on. Sure it won't keep till later?'

'Positive,' said Manette.

The workhorse had sat down at a black-glass desk that was a scaled-down version of Caulfield's own: a circumstance that was less than ideal.

'Take a seat,' said Caulfield, and Manette backed cautiously into what looked like an abstract sculpture of padded white leather and stainless steel, and which, once you got the trick of it, proved very comfortable.

'This is an extremely confidential matter,' said Manette.

'There's nothing we can't discuss in front of Mrs Grummon,' said Caulfield.

'It concerns your recent visit to Las Vegas.'

'On the other hand I can see you might find it difficult to discuss confidential government matters like Nellis Field with a third party present,' said Caulfield at once. 'Ida—go and take a coffee-break.'

Ida Grummon tired-footed out. Manette observed without surprise that she took the sheet of figures with her. What did surprise him was that Caulfield was blushing.

'What the hell you want to mention Las Vegas in front of her for?' he said. 'Ida's my sister.'

'I mentioned it because we're both in a hurry and that's what I've come about,' said Manette. 'I gather you never went near Nellis Field?'

'I don't do business with the government,' said Caulfield. 'Not that I don't want to. I just haven't been asked.' He let it hang.

'Maybe you will, one day,' said Manette, 'and if you do, maybe you and I will talk. Maybe.'

'Three maybes in one speech,' said Caulfield. 'That's three too many. What did you come here to talk about, congressman? Without any maybes.'

'A girl,' said Manette.

'A *girl*?' Caulfield's face darkened again, but this time he laughed. Coarse and brutal laughter, thought Manette. Jeering laughter. The laughter of a man whose only amusement is another's weakness.

'You've come here so I can fix you up with a piece of ass in Vegas?'

Manette said, 'Yes,' and the laughter died.

'You're kidding,' said Caulfield. 'You have to be kidding. I don't even know you.'

'You know a piece of ass in Vegas.'

'I know dozens. You're trying to tell me that it's a crime? Like I violated the Mann Act or something?'

'If you had,' said Manette, 'it would be a matter for the F.B.I. Not for me.'

'Now look,' said Caulfield. 'I don't know what you're trying to pull—'

'Mr Caulfield,' said Manette. 'For a man in a hurry you waste the devil of a lot of time. I don't want to pull anything. All I want is the address and preferably the telephone number of a girl who calls herself Trudi von Nichts.'

'You want *Trudi*?' His voice showed only disbelief: thank God no laughter.

'Her address and telephone number.'

'But—but—' disbelief became bewilderment. 'Honest, congressman, I don't think she'd appeal to you at all.'

Manette said, in a voice of New England primness, 'I don't want her for any sexual purpose. You may believe that or not. It is immaterial to me.'

Caulfield's first reaction was one of relief.

'Oh, I believe it all right,' he said, then shut his mouth and pondered. 'I don't think I can help you, congressman,' he said. 'I don't keep addresses of broads I boff.'

158

'Just the street would help. The general location.'
'Sorry.'
'Maybe your sister could help me,' said Manette.
'I doubt it.'
'The quickest way is to ask her,' said Manette, and rose.
'You'd do that,' said Caulfield. 'You'd fucking do that.'
'I fucking would.'
'Norn Street,' said Caulfield. 'Number 34 Norn Street. For some reason she thought Norn Street was funny. She thought everything was funny.'
'That time she was right,' said Manette. 'According to Scandinavian mythology a Norn is a virgin goddess—and she lived on their street. Telephone number?'
'I don't have it,' Caulfield said. 'A guy called Wino pimps for her. He fixed me up.'
'What's his real name?'
'I doubt if he's got one,' said Caulfield. 'Big guy. Big drinker. But he packs a lot of muscle. That's all I know.'
'That'll have to do then,' said Manette, and added formally: 'I'm obliged to you.'
'You wouldn't care to tell me why—'
Manette freed himself from the chair and moved to the door.
'I would not,' he said.
'There is just one thing,' said Caulfield, and Manette turned. 'I heard that maybe Trudi shoots a little acid now and again, but I want you to believe one thing, congressman. Never when I'm there. No drugs. Definitely no drugs.'
Manette left.

[iii]

Bulky sometimes wondered about Callan, but not too often and not too much. He'd been a nice enough feller to work with—after their first encounter: and Bulky bore him no malice for that. It was all part of the game after all—and he'd done a nice, smooth job, apart from his drinking. Moreover Bulky had been paid. A young chap in a crash helmet and goggles had handed over a neat little parcel that turned out to be ten-pound notes, and just the right number. Bulky had kept a couple of hundred for expenses and bunged the rest in his safe-deposit. Nothing wrong with *that*. Only he didn't want to work with Callan again, money or no money: didn't even want to know what Callan was up to. Rough stuff, he thought. The roughest. Secret stuff, too. You're too old for that kind of nonsense, Bulky old boy. Just take it easy and enjoy your declining years.... Stay in your flat, and read Lord

159

Chesterfield's *Letters To His Son,* and cook yourself the odd gourmet dinner and open a half-bottle of Lafite '66. You can afford it. Only it wasn't all that much fun being on your own all the time. Fred hadn't been an intellectual giant but at least he was company.... Bulky wondered if he should replace Fred with a dog: a dobermann say, or an alsatian. But the damn brutes needed exercise, and Bulky didn't. Join a club? he thought. It was an idea that occurred to him about twice a year, and always he dismissed it. He dismissed it now. A sensitive man, he dreaded the possibility of being asked to resign from a club that had been decent enough to elect him.

He went for a drink instead. Little pub he knew in Belgravia. Barmaid handsome, if mature, and a clientele of well-to-do, middle-aged men who, like Bulky, never seemed to have anything much to do. Really it was as good as a club any day, except you couldn't get a game of cards.... He arrived there at mid-day, and settled down in his favourite chair, the leather one by the window. Once he'd finished with *The Times* he could watch the world go by. It was a nice day, warm, the flowers on the bar were fresh, the barmaid trim in the kind of summer-dress, patterned cotton with a wide skirt, that young girls somehow didn't seem able to wear. And not a bore in the place. Bulky ordered a half bottle of Bollinger, and invited the barmaid to take a glass, but she opted for sherry instead. They exchanged pleasantries, Bulky initiating what he hoped would be a memorable, if fleeting, courtship, when Fred came in.

'Well well,' he said. 'Mr Berkeley.'

His surprise was spurious: he'd seen the old fatty come in minutes ago. Checked his favourite boozer a couple of times a week come to that. No sense trying to explain why, because he didn't know, except he was skint, and the old fatty usually had money coming in from somewhere. Well, look at him now. Just turned twelve o'clock and on the champagne already.

Bulky sighed and folded up *The Times.*

'Get yourself a glass, Fred,' he said, 'unless you'd prefer something else?'

'No no,' said Fred. 'Champagne's fine.'

And the barmaid's fine an' all, he thought, you disgusting old devil. Bulky filled his glass.

'Been away, Mr Berkeley?' Fred asked.

'I'm not at liberty to answer, any more than you're at liberty to ask,' said Bulky.

'No offence, Mr Berkeley. I just wondered,' said Fred.

Bulky looked at him with distaste. To think, he told himself, that I was wishing you were back. Maybe he *would* get a dog.

160

Even exercise was better than watching Fred swigging down Bollinger in the hope his old employer would tip the bottle again.

'Are you—working?' he said.

Fred shrugged. 'Bit of this, bit of that,' he said.

That means he's skint, Bulky thought.

Fred said, 'I was wondering, Mr Berkeley—I mean now you're back like—'

'No,' said Bulky. 'We were both told our association was at an end by a gentleman who meant what he said. I'm sorry, Fred.' He filled up the other man's glass.

'Yeah,' said Fred. 'Me an' all,' and this time he sipped because he knew that was all the fizz he'd get. It wasn't fair: it wasn't bleeding fair. Nobody else wanted a minder, and he wasn't no good at thieving. Too clumsy.... Bulky pulled out a wallet of ostrich skin, and extracted two of Hunter's tenners. Both Fred and the barmaid were aware that they were two of many.

'Buy yourself a little something,' Bulky said. 'I'm sorry that I can't take you back.'

Twenty quid, thought Fred. Twenty bleeding quid. True, the old fatty didn't owe him anything, but all the same.... Twenty quid. There had to be more in the thing than that.

'Thanks very much, Mr Berkeley,' he said, and went back to swigging. No sense in hanging about. He took the glass back to the bar for another look at the barmaid's knockers, and left. Bulky reached for his *Times*, and saw that the barmaid was looking at him, puzzled; and that wouldn't do. Puzzled people start asking questions, and then where are you?

'Old employee of mine,' he said. 'Fallen on rather hard times, I'm afraid.'

'Oh.' The look of puzzlement vanished. 'Oh, I see.'

Bulky reached for the bottle and poured. There was scarcely half a glass left.

'Poor Mr Berkeley. He didn't leave you much, did he?' said the barmaid.

'Poor chap,' said Bulky. 'I don't think he gets many opportunities to drink champagne.'

'He makes the most of the ones he does get,' said the barmaid.

Bulky chuckled. The barmaid found it a pleasant sound: even sexy in a refined sort of way.

'If I were to buy another one of these I wonder if you'd share it with me?'

'Not in the morning,' she said. 'I'd be quite woozy. I'll take another sherry if I may.'

'Please do—and Bollinger some evening perhaps.'

'Why not?' she said.

'Your evening off?'

'Thank you, Mr Berkeley,' she said, 'I'd like that.'

'In that case,' said Bulky, 'I also will drink sherry for now. The dry kind, please.'

*

Fred said, 'I seen him, Mr Higgins. Honest.'

'So you seen him?' said Higgins. 'So what?'

'Well I thought it might be useful,' said Fred.

'Shut up,' Higgins said. 'I'm thinking,' and Fred waited, respectfully silent, as was his custom when in contact with thinkers; even by telephone.

'Where are you?' Higgins said at last.

'Phone booth in Belgravia,' said Fred.

'Come to the garage sharpish,' said Higgins and hung up.

When he got there was only three of them: no sign of Loopy Nichols at all, and one look at their faces and he knew better than to start asking questions. He hadn't been sent for to ask questions: he'd been sent for to be told: stay away from us, and don't make no phone calls about Berkeley or his friends. And afterwards Boston Smith had belted him, just to help him remember what they'd said.... But there had to be money in the old fatty's return. Had to be. And anyway, it was the only thing he had to sell.

21

'He shows no desire to avoid your company?' Hunter asked.

'On the contrary, sir,' said Meres. 'He seeks it.'

'Extraordinary,' said Hunter. 'Really quite extraordinary.'

Meres scowled at the handset. He was being punished because Jeanne-Marie Nivelle was dead. The punishment so far was mild, because even Hunter couldn't decide by telephone how much Meres was responsible for her death. But when he got back, Meres thought, he'd better take something good back with him....

'He really likes you?' said Hunter.

'Yes, sir.'

'Then I think you'd better do your decent chap act,' said Hunter. 'Is he drinking at all?'

Meres grimaced. 'Italian brandy,' he said.

'He suffers from nerves you know,' Hunter said.

'Yes, sir. It's on his file.'

'If he has a breakdown you must restrain him, Toby.'

'Yes, sir.'

'Gently but firmly. But let the poor chap live. I may have further use for him—This is what I want you to do.'

Meres sat in the back-shop of Signora Lunari's establishment, surrounded by bales and boxes of ties, scarves, table-cloths, napkins, and saw nothing at all. He was too busy listening. The job was not one he would enjoy—being nice to people was always tiresome eventually, but if he got it right, dead right, he'd be off the hook for the Nivelle bitch. Hunter finished at last.

'You understand all that, Toby?'

'Yes, sir.'

'Get on with it then. And don't kill anybody—'

'Of course not, sir.'

'Particularly Kleist. Or did you say he is von Kleist now?'

'Von Kleist, sir. He says it's to make it clear where his allegiance lies—whatever that means.'

'I am quite aware of what it means,' said Hunter, 'and so would you be if you used your brains.' He hung up.

Meres left by the back entrance, and walked to the café where

163

he was due to meet von Kleist. Automatically he ordered two espressi and one brandy, and as it arrived, so did von Kleist. He looked terrible, but then that was to be expected. He'd been to see the police. He pushed the brandy over to the German.

'How was it, old chap?' he said.

'They were nice,' said von Kleist. 'Really very nice. Even sympathetic.'

Oh, the mighty power of the Deutschmark, thought Meres.

'They say I do not need to stay for the—enquiry?'

'Inquest,' said Meres. 'In England we would call it an inquest.'

'I am free to go,' said von Kleist, and finished his brandy, looked round at once to find a waiter who would fetch another. 'I would like very much to leave this place. But I cannot think of anywhere to go to.' He went on looking about him.

Meres waved a hand, and a waiter appeared at once. He ordered brandy.

'Thank you,' said von Kleist. 'The English have a vision of Germans, have they not, Toby? Stern, phlegmatic, unemotional. I am not that kind of German. In fact I very much want to cry, and I may do so.'

Hell, thought Meres. Bloody *hell*.

Aloud, he said, 'My dear chap.'

'They talked about her, you see,' said von Kleist. 'Talked so much....'

'Did you—see her?'

The question was a mistake: but the opportunity for malice irresistible.

'Oh no,' said von Kleist. 'She is not to be seen.... Her clothes. I identified her clothes.' Now the tears really were flowing.

Easy now, thought Meres. Take it very easy.

'You are quite sure,' said Meres, 'that it really was an accident?'

'But of course,' said von Kleist. 'What else could it possibly be?'

Meres looked around him. The café was filling up.

'We can't possibly talk here,' he said. 'Come for a ride in the car and I'll tell you.'

It took a while, but at last von Kleist finished his brandy and got to his feet. Once in the car it would be easier, Meres thought. He had a bottle of brandy in the glove-compartment.

Meres drove along the incredible coast-line—no mountain roads for Gunther: they might start him off again—pines and olive-trees, sun-warmed rock and the heaving, feminine sea, and pulled up at last on a headland by the ruins of a Norman castle.

'Thirty years ago my country and yours fought over this land,' said von Kleist. 'For you that would be something to read in books.'

164

I've had my wars, Gunther old chum. And mostly I've won them.

'I missed it by a few years only,' said von Kleist. 'It would have been better if I had come here and died here.' He put his hands to his face. Meres could not remember when he'd last met a man so incurably lachrymose. Ah well, better get on with it. He opened the glove-compartment, took out the brandy and plastic-cups, and poured. The one he kept for himself was about a third the size of von Kleist's, but where was the fun in drinking brandy out of plastic—and Italian brandy at that?

'I know you don't wish to talk about it, old chap,' he said diffidently, 'but I rather think we *ought* to talk about it.'

'I am afraid,' von Kleist said, 'afraid that you are going to tell me something horrible.'

'In a sense it is horrible,' said Meres, 'but it is a horror that we can do something about, you and I.'

Oh my God, I'm overdoing it, he thought, and risked a look at von Kleist. To judge by the German's reactions he was underplaying.

'Let me put you in the picture,' said Meres....

It seemed that when Captain Meres had left the Brigade he had joined a branch of British Intelligence that existed for one purpose and one purpose only: total opposition to the communist states of Eastern Europe: a patient, methodical determination to thwart their every purpose. With the West they had no truck at all: the West was clean. And he *believes* it, thought Meres. The silly sod actually believes it. But then his estates, like his title, were in the East German People's Republic....

To this end Meres' task had been to monitor illicit traffic between East and West, and quite early he had come across Lord Hexham, fellow-Guardee, Old Etonian, peer—and a smuggler. It was all very shocking.

'You must not say so,' said von Kleist. 'Ludovic would never, never work for the Reds.'

'You seem very sure,' said Meres.

'Of course I am sure,' said von Kleist, and added heroically, 'I helped him.'

'My dear fellow,' said Meres, 'don't you think I know that?'

'You *know*?'

'Of course. Hexham needed a contact in that region—and you were a friend of his: a fellow nobleman who had been robbed of his East German inheritance.'

That went down a treat: he could go on pouring that sort of syrup all day.

'But you were no threat to us. On the contrary, you were even

165

helping—finding money for people like ourselves who desperately needed money. To the East Germans it may have been the smuggling of antiques: to us it was pure altruism.'

'Thank you,' von Kleist said. 'That is exactly how I regarded it—though it was true I took a percentage—'

'My dear chap,' said Meres. 'We all must live. But I'm afraid Hexham took rather more than a percentage. He went double.'

And that meant more explanations. Von Kleist, when you got down to it, was *thick*, and not a bad thing either when you were looking for a dummy.

Gently, even tenderly, Meres explained that Hexham had been shipping information, to, as well as furniture, from Eastern Europe. And von Kleist was appalled. He really was. It was like convincing a mother-superior that the rest of the nuns were using the convent as a brothel. But not once did he ask for proof. There was a lot to be said for subjects with nervous breakdowns. Meres finished at last, and waited.

'But he has been using me,' said von Kleist, as if he hadn't been born to be used.

'I'm afraid so,' said Meres, in tones of manly regret.

'That I understand. I really do. But what has it to do with Jeanne-Marie?'

'She loved you,' said Meres, 'and she was as intelligent as she was beautiful—from what you have told me.'

'She was. Oh, my friend, she *was*.'

'And she died quite close to Hexham's palazzo,' Meres said. 'It occurred to me—forgive me, old chap—that she might have discovered what Hexham was up to—and gone to have it out with him.'

'No,' said von Kleist. 'She went to the palazzo the day before. She told me he had left it.'

'Forgive me,' said Meres, 'but might she not have lied to you?' then added quickly, 'To spare you pain?'

He offered the brandy bottle to the German, who poured, and drank.

'It would be like her,' he said. 'So very like her.'

Meres pondered the phenomenon of love. It was one he had never known, never wanted to know. If it made the impossible that easy to believe, what chance would you have?

'I have reason to believe that's what happened,' he said. 'She met with Hexham and he killed her.'

'Word of honour?' von Kleist asked.

Gravely Meres said, 'Word of honour,' and von Kleist wept yet again. Meres pondered the idea of offering his chum a handkerchief, and rejected it. The only handkerchiefs he'd brought

166

were Irish linen, and monogrammed. If von Kleist wept all over one, he'd have to throw it away.

Von Kleist said at last, 'You spoke of revenge.'

'I did.'

'How please? It must be obvious to you I want revenge. I need it.'

Meres noted that occasionally his tearful chum was at least capable of self-analysis.

'You can put your hands on a book that Hexham wants, and the SSD wants,' he said.

'The SSD? They are in this?'

'Up to their sweaty armpits,' said Meres.

It was a calculated risk, but von Kleist was beyond fear. His only need was revenge.

'A book? How can I hurt them with a book?' he said.

'I can't tell you,' said Meres. 'All I can say is that you *will* hurt them—very much. There will almost certainly be a risk—'

'Risk?' said von Kleist. 'What do I care about risks? I want to die.'

But you won't, thought Meres. Hunter has said you won't, and that's good enough for me.

'A risk,' he said again, 'but you'll be compensated for it.'

'How compensated?'

'We'll pay off your gaming debts.'

'Let me understand you,' said von Kleist. 'You'll pay off my gaming debts if I give you a book?'

Meres nodded.

'And where is this book?'

'In the Bonn archives,' said Meres. 'You can get it easily.'

'And what is the book?'

'Marx's *Kapital*. A paper-back.'

'What will you do with it?'

'Burn it,' said Meres. 'In front of you if you like.'

'And that's all?'

'That's all.'

Von Kleist poured more brandy.

'You remind me of a song,' he said. 'On the radio. Just after the war. AFN—Munich Stuttgart. Jimmy Dorsey, was it? Tommy? Glen Miller? I forget. But one phrase I always remember: "I'm content, the angels must have sent you And they meant you, Just for me." ... Let us go to Bonn, my friend.'

Oh God, thought Meres, is he going to be whimsical all the way to Bonn?

22

Callan put twenty-five cents in the bandit and pulled the lever. All around him the casino throbbed and crashed like a boiler-factory: men and women pouring quarters, half-dollars, dollar plaques into the machines with the intent, devoted stance of supplicants performing a ritual. His machine hiccupped, and he stuck out his paper-cup, watched the stream of quarters pour into it, then went to the cash-desk, turned the quarters into chips and walked over to the black-jack table. He hit the dealer three times, eighteen, nineteen, twenty-one, and they changed the dealer on him. Callan quit. Bulky would have been proud of him, he thought. A girl in a costume composed largely of ostrich feathers and fishnet offered him a drink, and he turned her down. Spencer Perceval FitzMaurice, regally robed, was being shown over the place by a man in a midnight blue dinner-suit who was talking with a kind of polite hysteria that seemed endemic to Vegas, and not once had he looked at Callan; but as soon as he took a drink, Callan knew, the bells would ring, a sign saying Tilt would light up.... Callan tried the roulette wheel and won on that, too: won, he knew, because it didn't matter whether he won or lost, because he was bored, because all he wanted was a drink.

He went back to the desk and cashed in. In Vegas chips were money, you could spend them anywhere, but he preferred money that felt like money: and anyway he didn't want to stay in this town any longer than he had to.... He walked out of the games room towards the coffee-shop, and realised that he was sick of coffee. Nine cups so far today, and he hadn't even had dinner. He went over to the water-cooler instead, and a bell-hop came up to him.

'Looking for some action, chief?' he said.

'I just cashed in,' said Callan.

'All kinds of action in Vegas, chief.'

I could give this man a five dollar bill and he would bring me whisky, thought Callan, and Spencer Perceval FitzMaurice would beat me unconscious.

'Broads,' said the bell-hop. 'You want broads? Or a little speed maybe? Grass?'

'How about both?' said Callan. 'A girl and grass?'

'Not many smoke while they're working, chief.'

'Let me know when you find one that does.'

'Cost you fifty.'

'As soon as your memory works,' said Callan.

He wandered over to the cocktail-lounge. A large and lovely black lady was singing songs he hadn't heard in years: 'Stardust', 'Someone to Watch over Me', 'I'll be Waiting where the Blue Begins'. But all around her people were drinking. He went back to the casino, and up to the black-jack dealer once more. The black-jack dealer didn't like him. That suited Callan: he didn't like anybody. He hit the dealer again, then walked around and watched. The large and lovely black lady had joined FitzMaurice, and the geezer in the midnight blue was smiling up at them as if he'd just married them. And maybe he had.... On a temporary basis. Callan watched him edge away at last, leave them alone. As soon as he'd gone the bell-hop appeared again.

'Message for you, sir,' he said, and handed over an envelope.

Callan looked at him as he handed over a fifty. Dope, girls, boys. You name it: he would sell it. A bloke doing that should look like the portrait of Dorian Gray, but this was a clean-cut young specimen, frank blue-eyes, good sun-tan, toothpaste grin, like an ad for a better business bureau. And maybe that's what he was.... Better business.... The dope business, the girl business, the boy business.

'Thank you, sir. Have a nice evening,' the fresh-faced kid said. Callan looked at the envelope. Maureen—ask for Howard—Noonan Avenue. Helga ask for Johnny—Valley Road. Trudi—ask for Wino—Norn Street. Three so far. It would do for a start. Three whores and three pimps. Only they probably called themselves personal managers, and why not? They were in the entertainment business.

He went back to his room, and settled down to wait. All three girls had phone numbers, but he didn't want to expose his English accent till he had to. He got on to the Smith and Wessons instead, cleaned them both, then put on the harness, practised a draw. At least his hands weren't shaking any more, but he'd slowed up, he thought. My God, he'd slowed up even since he'd shot Hexham. Helga or Trudi first, he thought. German names. The city-map showed him that Helga was nearest.... On the other hand, Norn Street bothered him. Norn had a meaning, but he'd need a dictionary to find out what, and the only book in the room was a Gideon Bible. He looked into the telephone directory, dialled

169

the *Clark County Star* and asked for the literary editor.

'The who?' said a disbelieving voice.

Callan's attempt at an American accent was terrible, but he'd spread a handkerchief over the mouth-piece and pitched his voice high. Maybe they'd think he was queer.

'The guy who writes about books,' he said, and got him.

'Settle a bet for me will you, pal?' said Callan.

'In Vegas? That's what we citizens are here for.'

'What would a Norn be?' he asked, listened, and said thank you, and hung up. Norn, in Scandinavian mythology, a personification of Fate, usually in the form of a virgin goddess.... And Bauer's daughter had a devious, and rather literary sense of humour, according to Hunter's file: had, also, a compassion for those who suffered as she had suffered. Her suffering was drugs, and her pimp was called Wino.

When FitzMaurice came to him he used the agreed knock, but even so Callan kept the door on the chain till he was sure the big man was alone. In this town you didn't take chances. FitzMaurice looked at the gun-harness.

'So we're dressing formally,' he said.

'Just as well to get used to it,' said Callan.

'You know your instructions,' FitzMaurice said. 'You don't go for that thing unless you have to.'

'I know,' said Callan, 'but I used up all my good luck at the tables. All I won was money. You get anything?'

'Miss Louella Knight,' said FitzMaurice, 'a charming and gracious lady, not a bit overawed by royalty, and full of good works. I do indeed have something.'

'What?'

'A date for later this evening,' said FitzMaurice, 'and a name I can work on during the date. The name is Trudi.'

'34 Norn Street,' said Callan. 'Ask for Wino.'

'You see,' said FitzMaurice. 'All you need is a lack of alcohol. How'd you do it?'

'We commoners have our methods,' said Callan, and told him.

'Nice,' FitzMaurice said. 'Very nice. Norn Street and Trudi. I like it. What do you think we should do?'

'Go there,' said Callan. 'Suss it out.'

'Well yes, of course,' said FitzMaurice, 'only Miss Knight awaits me.'

'And you await Miss Knight.'

FitzMaurice moved in on him, and Callan's hand described the short, abrupt arc. Slow or not, he was faster than FitzMaurice, who looked at the Smith and Wesson in Callan's hand and froze.

Callan said, 'The simple thing would be to apologise, but you

170

didn't need an apology. She expects a date and you've got to keep it. Whether she enjoys it or not—whether you do—isn't any of my business. But you've got to keep it, and that's all I meant.'

'No, it's not,' said FitzMaurice.

'All right,' said Callan. 'It's not. I talked nasty and I'm sorry. I apologise. But you know why I talked like that.'

'Apology accepted,' said FitzMaurice. 'If you're trying to say you're jealous—'

'Of course I'm jealous,' said Callan. 'Who wouldn't be? You get Louella Knight, and I get a seat in a car in Norn Street.'

'Now wait a minute,' FitzMaurice said.

'What I don't get,' said Callan, 'is a drink.'

FitzMaurice looked at him: a long appraising look, a gambler's look. But then they were in a gambler's town.

'All right,' he said at last. 'Go and suss her out.'

Callan put on his coat. 'Can you do a good Boston accent?' he said.

'Son,' said FitzMaurice, 'I can make the Kennedys sound like Ma and Pa Kettle. Why?'

'Ring her up,' said Callan. 'Make a date. If she's free we can do the job tonight.'

FitzMaurice reached for the phone, and dialled; in his voice Groton, Harvard and Wall Street blended and spelt out their message: money. It talked. FitzMaurice put down the phone. 'That was Wino,' he said. 'Trudi's busy just at present, but she'd love to see me tomorrow.'

Carefully Callan adjusted his coat before the mirror: all you could see of the Smith and Wesson was a thickening waistline.

'The sooner the better,' he said. 'I don't like it here.'

'Me too,' said FitzMaurice.

'Except for Miss Louella Knight, of course.'

'That's right,' FitzMaurice said. 'Except for Miss Knight. And Massa Callan, if Ah smells liquor on you' breath Ah's gwine to hurt you. Nothin' personal, Massa Callan. Jest doing what the Big Boss says.'

Callan went down to the car-park, paid a car-hop money for permission to drive his own car. Idiot, he told himself. Berk. What did you want to do that for—just when you and FitzMaurice were making sense together? He doesn't have to like you, but he was trying and now you have to go and screw up the whole relationship.... In the way of business FitzMaurice had once given him a beating, but that was all it was. Business. If Callan had to shoot the big man, it would have been with the same lack of animus. But not now. Not any more. Now Callan was slipping the needle into FitzMaurice even when he was trying not to, and

171

he knew why. The big man was his keeper, standing as long as the job lasted between Callan and a drink.

Fremont Street, thought Callan, was a failed version of the Strip, and as the Strip itself was a failed version of everything that Callan thought appalling he didn't think much of Fremont Street. Neon everywhere, soaring into the sky.... Brighter than a thousand suns.... He pushed the thought away, and concentrated on the car. They'd hired a Jaguar, the 4·2: the car he knew best. Room, comfort, and a hell of a lot of speed they might well be glad of. Air-conditioned too. They'd be glad of air-conditioning. A few minutes ago the temperature clock on the Strip had told him it was eight-seventeen: it had also told him it was 109° Fahrenheit. Callan waited at an interchange, turned right and right again. Norn Street. Little boxes. But they all had fresh paint and at least one car in the car port, and gardens with fountains that might even have worked, if you switched the electricity on, but why waste electricity at this time of night?

He parked on the opposite side of the street to Number 34, and looked around him. Nobody about: not even many lights. Maybe they all worked in the casinos, he thought. Maybe his mate the black-jack dealer lived here, and was so cheerful and friendly because he had only fifty more years to pay before he could call his home his own. Callan locked the car and crossed the street to Number 34. It had a eucalyptus tree that cast a shadow which was ideal for prowlers. He reached it and used the shadow, and listened to the sounds that came from the lighted ground-floor window.

'For myself I've always preferred Regency furniture,' the girl's voice said. 'What I believe the British call brown furniture when it's provincial. It is true that the French were more imaginative at the time, and certainly more ornate—I think I may safely say that I'm being period French at the moment, darling, wouldn't you? Imaginative and ornate, I mean. Shall we try just the teensiest bit harder?' A man groaned. 'There.... You see.... Now. Where was I? Oh yes ... Hepplewhite, of course, although we must categorise him as Georgian rather than Regency.... But Chippendale had both masculinity and a sense of style.... Just like you, darling. Masculinity you have, and style you're learning.' The man groaned once more. 'Yes yes, I know, poor pet, but all love is suffering, whereas a Sheraton sofa-table is pure delight.'

Furniture, thought Callan. Why do I have to get mixed up with fucking furniture?

The girl's voice chattered on, and the house-door opened, a man came out. A man: not the size of FitzMaurice, but big enough. Callan moved behind the eucalyptus tree and the big man left

172

the house and kept on walking. Callan gave him twenty yards start, and followed. The man with the girl was groaning again, and the girl's machine-gun prattle never stopped. Callan knew he had to leave that place: if he stayed where he was he would vomit.... After fifty yards he was sweating: after a hundred, his shirt was pasted to his back, but the feller he was following walked like it was spring in Hyde Park. Mind you the feller he was following didn't wear a coat, or, as far as he could see, a Smith and Wesson. They were going, it seemed, to a bar, and that really made Callan's evening. A dump labelled the 'Oasis' in red neon, and a green neon palm tree to prove it. The rest of it looked as if it was waiting to be condemned. Callan counted to a hundred before he followed the big man in. Scarred tables, uncertain chairs, and a clientele that looked as if it was waiting to be condemned too. Las Vegas, the playground of the world.

Callan sat at the bar and ordered root beer. The bar-tender was incredulous. 'Root beer?' he said. 'No shit?'

'Just root beer,' said Callan.

That made him a wit, and the bar-tender stuck with him, regaled him with homespun Western philosophy. It didn't stop Callan from watching the big man in the bar mirror. Wino. It had to be Wino—except he wasn't drinking. All he did was sit and chew the fat with a twitchy-looking geezer in cowboy costume and a tired little girl who should have been at home doing her geography prep.

'Where else you going to get a city of 300,000 people and 16,000 slot machines?'

'Where indeed?' said Callan.

'What d'you talk like a fruit for?' said the bar-tender. 'You ain't no fruit.'

'I don't like root beer,' said Callan.

'Who would? Say, listen, we even got a suicide rate that's twice the national average,' the bar-tender said.

'That's a good thing?' said Callan.

'Well, it keeps the losers down,' said the barman.

And so the long night wore on. The barman switched on the TV to watch a local chat show—Nice to see you, Henry: Very nice to *be* here, Fred. Peace and love, folks, peace and love—and the twitchy looking geezer in the cowboy costume made a big investment and bought three beers. Wino didn't touch his, but when a new customer came in and headed straight for the men's room Wino went too. So did the twitchy geezer. Nervous bladders? Or had they just made their connexion? Callan left his root beer and nodded to the barman. 'Peace and love, brother,' he said. 'Peace and love.'

173

'Over 25,000 hotel rooms,' said the barman. 'A thousand gaming rooms' ... Callan fled.

Wino didn't keep him waiting, but they didn't go straight back to Norn Street. Wino made a detour to a liquor store and came out with a bottle of Muscatel, the large economy size. Callan approved. Work first, and then booze. It was the only way. Ask his friend FitzMaurice. He dawdled back behind Wino, who went straight into Number 34, then took up his post by the eucalyptus tree. It was still hot, and she was still talking. Callan doubted if she'd stopped since he left her. 'Wagner I never did learn to appreciate,' she said, 'which when you consider my origins is odd. All those gods and that interminable twilight. Weight watchers with good lungs. Mozart now. Mozart makes *sense*. Form, you know? Construction? Design? Are you ready to go again, darling? ... Oh my goodness, you *are*.'

It was her, all right. It had to be. No point in hanging around. That was one way of putting it, but the truth was he couldn't stand any more. From the cover of the tree he looked over to his car. Two men were fiddling with the offside door. And wasn't that great? Wasn't that absolutely super? Two men trying to steal his car, and all he had to defend himself with was a 357 Magnum, and if he started blasting with that they'd never get near little chatterbox Trudi. Ah well, Callan, he thought, you're as fit as you're ever going to be. You haven't had a drink in three days.

He left the garden and crouched by its containing wall. The two men were dividing the job: one acting as look-out, the other trying keys on the car door. Callan waited until the lookout turned away to watch the end of the block. Make it good, he told himself, but don't kill anybody—then hurdled the wall and raced across the street. The look-out swivelled, and something gleamed in his hand. Callan aimed a kick at his stomach and connected as the gleaming thing slashed at his pants' leg. The man he'd kicked slammed into his partner, who dropped the keys and produced what looked like a tyre lever, tried to break loose from his mate, and face up to Callan, all at the same time. That made too many priorities. Far too many. Callan's left hand stabbed at the man's neck and he fell, taking his partner down with him. The loudest sound made had been the keys falling. Callan picked up their equipment, keys, tyre-lever, flick-knife—what they would call a switch blade—and looked at the casualties.... What a hero he was to be sure.... Two men he'd taken, with one kick and one hand-strike. All action Callan.... The elder of the two men couldn't have been more than sixteen. Callan felt sick, and noticed that his hands were trembling: noticed, too, that his pants' leg was ripped, and that he was bleeding. The trembling got worse. That

174

wouldn't do. There was work to be done. He opened the car door, and bundled the kids inside....

*

'You've been busy I see,' FitzMaurice said.

Callan swabbed more iodine on the cut, winced and applied an adhesive bandage.

'Yeah,' he said. 'Busy.'

He looked at FitzMaurice. The big man wore a short rope of ivory coloured silk. He looked like the Emperor of Africa.

'I trust you had a pleasant evening,' he said.

'Hey,' said FitzMaurice. 'You said that without ironic overtones. What happened?'

'I was keeping stoppo on Norn Street,' said Callan. 'Two geezers tried to steal the car.'

'And you prevented them?'

'I clobbered them,' said Callan. 'Did a real job. The way I was taught. They turned out to be a couple of kids. I'm a lovely feller, FitzMaurice. First I play Peeping Tom on a drug-crazy whore, then I hurt a couple of kids....'

'What did you do with them?'

'You dislike sentimentality. I used to he like that.'

'What did you do with them?'

'I took them out into the desert, about a couple of miles, lifted their money and left them.'

'Why the money?'

'So they'll think I was a crook,' said Callan, 'and stay away from Norn Street.'

'You hurt them much?'

'They were still unconscious when I left them.... But they'll live.'

FitzMaurice said, 'Miss Knight is really interested in good works. And I don't want any jokes about it.'

'My sense of humour's not what it was,' said Callan, and limped over to a chair.

'Drugs,' said FitzMaurice. 'She hates drugs.'

'No more than I do.'

'It took a while,' FitzMaurice said, 'because I had to play it carefully. But in the end I got it. The biggest pusher in the Norn Street area uses a bar.'

'The Oasis,' said Callan. 'I had a root beer there.' He eased the weight of the bandaged leg. 'It's her all right.'

'You saw her?'

'I heard her,' said Callan. 'It has to be her.'

175

'I take it you didn't like what you heard?'

'You take it correctly.... I saw Wino. He picked up some drugs for her then bought himself a bottle of wine. He looks tough.'

'Did he have a gun?'

'Not on him,' Callan said. 'But if he has one he'll use it.'

'Take her tomorrow?'

'Early,' said Callan. 'They're the kind who are never at their best first thing.'

FitzMaurice looked at him, considering.

'Hunter said I could give you a drink if there was an emergency,' he said. 'Is there an emergency?'

'Not unless you give me a drink,' said Callan.

'You're all right, Callan,' said FitzMaurice.

'Oh sure,' said Callan. 'I'm a lovely feller.'

23

Spanner was interested, and that surprised Fred. If the firm didn't fancy it, it stood to reason Spanner wouldn't. Any one of the firm was about nine times as hard as George and Spanner put together. But Fred didn't know about Spanner's humiliation: the way he'd been shown up in front of those two little darlings: didn't know either, about Spanner's capacities for fantasy, which were prodigious. Taken off guard, that's what he'd been. Couple of tearaways, that's all they were: a darky and a toffee-nosed twit. If he and George had been set for them—hell, if he'd been set he wouldn't even have needed George. Lovely stuff, the movie in his mind: the big scene was when he belted the twit with a chair and threw the darky out of the window. Then reality returned like a choc-ice interval. Those two weren't the problem now: they were after Bulky Berkeley.

George was the one to handle it. Spanner had the Flamingo to run and Fred couldn't do it on account of Bulky knew him so well, so George was the obvious one to cope. Funny thing, George didn't fancy it, but then George's fantasy-life was in no way comparable to Spanner's: mundane if anything. All the same Spanner wasn't taking any back-talk from a paid employee. Reluctantly, George went to the pub in Belgravia, and eavesdropped while Bulky made his tryst.

He took her to a little French restaurant he knew of in Kensington. The champagne came with the oysters: with the chateaubriand there was burgundy, and afterwards the sweet trolley: gâteaux, chocolate pudding, profiteroles: it had been obvious from the start that Rosie had a sweet tooth, and an appetite. Going back to her place was her idea. 'I don't ask men back often,' she said, 'and when I do it's because I like them. You should feel flattered, Mr Berkeley.'

'I do,' he said.

She had a place in Hammersmith; small, cluttered and extremely feminine: very much an extension of her personality. Dimly Bulky could remember a philosopher who'd said that being freed from the pangs of desire was like being freed from the attacks of a ferocious beast. Probably a Greek; he hadn't read much of that sort of stuff since he'd been sent down from Cambridge. And what nonsense it was anyway. If that was freedom give him this small, cluttered, feminine prison. All in all, considering his age and the amount of food and drink he'd consumed, Bulky felt that he'd acquitted himself well. He left her at two in the morning. They were both very sleepy.

Getting a taxi could be a problem at that time, but Bulky found he didn't need one. As he walked up the street towards a Mercedes 600 its rear door swung open, a man moved up from a shop-doorway and hustled him inside, jumped in after him and the Mercedes moved off.

'About bloody time,' said Spanner. 'A man of your age. It's disgusting.'

Bulky said nothing. The creature who'd hustled him was obviously incapable of intellectual argument. Better, far better, to straighten his tie, smooth his coat and relax on the seat. Really it was extremely comfortable. Spanner fished in his pocket and took out a short length of steel. It was in fact a six-inch spanner, and a taste for its use in his early career had given him his name.

'You dirty old goat,' he said, 'you're going to tell me things.' I made love to a charming and agreeable woman, thought Bulky. That makes me neither unclean nor a satyr, and I am not old.

'Very well,' he said. 'What do you want to know?'

The answer displeased Spanner. He had expected, even hoped for, resistance. Co-operation rendered the spanner unnecessary, and he'd rather wanted to use it, if only because George had been against its use. Come to that, George had been against the whole bloody exercise, and he kept sneaking a look back in the driving mirror.

'I want the lot,' he said, and tapped the steel spanner against his palm. 'The lot.'

'That is certainly comprehensive,' said Bulky.

'What I don't want,' Spanner said, 'is lip.'

Bulky sat in silence as they drove back into Kensington, found a quiet mews, and stopped. Spanner pulled out a small, battery tape-recorder and switched it on.

'Now,' he said, 'tell us about your little trip abroad.'

'I suppose Fred put you on to this?' Bulky said.

'Never mind who put me on to it,' said Spanner. 'Just tell it or I'll belt you.'

Bulky saw no reason to doubt him. Mildly psychopathic

178

personality, by the look of him. The kind that thrives on opposition he knows he can overcome. Bulky settled himself more comfortably, and told the lot: Callan, Hexham, Jeanne-Marie Nivelle, Kleist and Lonely; card games, cheating; the lot. And when Spanner asked questions, he answered them fully.

'You took an earl?' said Spanner, and there was awe in his voice.

'He tried to take me,' said Bulky.

Spanner gave Bulky a look that was almost pleading.

'I don't get it,' he said. 'I just don't get it.'

You mean you can't see what's in it for you, thought Bulky, glad that his fee was in his safe-deposit box.

'There's got to be a catch in it,' Spanner said. 'There's got to be.' He raised the spanner. 'What is it?'

'I've told you all I know,' said Bulky, and waited for his belting.

'He's telling the truth,' said George. 'Let him go.' Spanner hesitated. 'I'm warning you, I've had enough,' George said.

Spanner jerked his head, and Bulky opened the door, and had to walk all the way to the High Street before he found a taxi. Really he felt quite exhausted. The large young man wasn't watching his house at night now, either, which added to his exhaustion. He would have to be up betimes to catch him next morning when he made his daily check. When he did, Bulky was up, dressed and ready for him. Suppressing a yawn he walked to the large young man and said, 'I think you should know that last night, for a brief while, I was kidnapped.'

[ii]

They flew from Rome to Bonn airport, where Meres hired a Mercedes, and took the autobahn route into Bonn. The town was wet from recent rain, cold, and had nothing to replace Taormina's beauty except wealth: sleek cars for sleek citizens, bulging shops, busy restaurants and bars. Meres followed Kleist's directions and drove to the complex of old streets behind the market square: big, stone-built houses with narrow windows, and linden trees in every garden. Number 74, Schiller Strasse was much like the others, except that its grass needed cutting; its woodwork painting.

'You like it?' Kleist asked.

'It has a great deal of charm,' said Meres, and it was true enough. The house was solid and masculine in design, but its proportions were pleasing.

'It was my mother's father's house,' said Kleist, 'and it is all there is left.'

179

Here we go again, thought Meres. The disinherited aristocrat bit. All the same, it made a change from the lament for Jeanne-Marie. Still talking, apologising for the house's state of repair, Kleist took him inside, through a hallway that smelled of damp, and into a drawing-room that was full, even over-full of European eighteenth-century furniture. Meres looked around him. 'Your business enterprise with Hexham?' he asked.

'My share,' said Kleist. 'It was by no means the largest share. I had intended to sell it with the house, but now, thanks to you, dear friend, that will not be necessary.'

He opened a cupboard, rummaged furiously, and came up with a bottle one-third full. More brandy, German this time. Really, thought Meres, if he goes on at this rate he'll finish up worse than Callan. It's only twelve o'clock, for God's sake. He took a small one.

'It is wrong to be rootless,' Kleist said. 'A man should have a house—a house in good repair: full of elegant things.'

We're on the upswing again, thought Meres. Second brandy of the day always does that. Work, position in the community, status. Love now dead but marry a nice, respectable girl. The name von Kleist must not be allowed to die. He got it all, and answered at random, but it was all Kleist needed. The whole act was a monologue anyway. Meres picked up a photograph album and flicked through its pages, as Kleist gradually ran down. Mostly the dead wife. Really she hadn't been at all bad—even rather good. What with her and Jeanne-Marie Nivelle old Gunther's life hadn't actually been all anguish. He turned another page. Two men and a woman sitting in an open-air café in springtime. One of the men was Gunther: the girl was a dish.

'Who's this?' Meres asked. Kleist came over.

'That is Lindt,' he said. 'My contact in Dresden. I believe he is dead now, poor fellow.'

I know he is, thought Meres: then aloud, 'And the girl?'

'That was Ortrud Bauer,' said Kleist. 'She also died. A motor accident. It was once a big scandal here.'

Meres knew it all, but he let Gunther tell it. It was time Gunther became accustomed to telling him things.

When he'd done, they went out to lunch; and Gunther swallowed beer on top of brandy. Then, it seemed, he had to see his doctor; something about a certificate to be signed before Gunther could go back to the archives. It was the first time Meres had heard that nervous breakdowns were infectious, but Kleist meant what he said, and Meres let him go.

'And what will you do?' asked Kleist.

'I,' said Meres, 'will look around your charming city.'

He began with Kleist's house. Gunther, old chum that he was, had given him a spare set of keys. Apart from the drawing-room the house was sparsely furnished, and much of what there was turned out to be junk. But there were treasures, even so. A cedar-wood chest, for instance, and inside it, sealed in plastic, a uniform of what Meres guessed to be a captain of Uhlans that looked even earlier than World War One. Callan would know, thought Meres, if he was sober enough. He might even know what the medal ribbon on its tunic was. Pour le mérite, could it be? There was a helmet too, and a sabre, both plastic-wrapped, and an ancient revolver even bigger than the cannon FitzMaurice used to show off with. He replaced them carefully, and tried the attic. More treasures; a little library of genteel pornography, most of it mildly homosexual in character, to judge by the illustrations.... There were no more treasures. So that was Gunther, he thought. Needing women, enamoured of men (if only Hunter had told me: it would all have been so much *easier*)—and in love with his past. Meres locked up carefully, drove to the British Embassy, and asked for Mr Evers.

They were not pleased to see him: but then no embassy staff was ever pleased to see Section Operatives who appeared out of nowhere and asked for Mr Evers. He was on leave, or out, or unavailable: maybe all three. But Meres persisted, and was shown at last into a small room crammed with electronic equipment of unbelievable complexity. Bonn's particular Mr Evers was there too, a small, plump man with a row of screwdrivers clipped like fountain-pens to his work-coat pocket. He moved around his equipment, hands gently touching. To Meres it was as if he was soothing the damn stuff.

'They give you a cup of tea?' he asked.

'No,' said Meres.

'They never do,' said Bonn's Mr Evers. 'Where'll it be then?'

'Hunter's Section.'

The little, plump man got busy, and at last handed Meres a handset—the only thing in the room he could recognise—and left.

'Yes?' Liz's voice said.

'Let me speak to Charlie please,' said Meres.

There was a pause, then, 'Charlie speaking.'

'Meres, sir. I'm in Bonn. At the embassy.'

'All well?'

'Yes, sir. He'll have the book by this evening.'

'Good. Anything further on the Nivelle woman?'

'I'm afraid not, sir.'

There was a pause. The communications room was air-conditioned, but Meres found that he was sweating.

'A pity.... I may have to pop over for the day myself, Meres. If I do I'll let you know.'

The phone clicked, and Meres continued to sweat.

Hunter examined his balance-sheet. No word from or of Callan and FitzMaurice, and that was good. No word meant the operation was proceeding satisfactorily. Meres too was at least satisfactory. Kleist was ruined, greedy, and co-operative about the work. Perfect. Even text-book stuff. Only Jeanne-Marie Nivelle's death gave him cause for disquiet. On the other hand this Bulky Berkeley business really had gone awry. The fat man had been interrogated, naturally, and had made no attempt to deny his betrayal. Hunter had accepted it. There was no point in punishing a man one might need again. On the other hand he hadn't been able to pick up this Spanner person, and not even his chauffeur knew where he was. George had been interrogated carefully: he couldn't be lying. And that left Hexham—another loose end. Signora Lunari had checked in Taormina: others had checked in Reggio and Rome. The fact remained that Hexham was missing. How careless, Hunter thought, to mislay a belted earl. Two loose ends, that might or might not be tied up later. In the meantime, if Callan and FitzMaurice came through, he must certainly go to Bonn.

[iii]

After Bulky left the car, George and Spanner quarrelled. It was inevitable, and both men knew it. Chucking his weight about, thought George: insubordination, thought Spanner. In the end George was told to get lost, which suited him fine, and Spanner drove out to Uncle Lenny's place. Over and over Bulky had mentioned that Lonely geezer: it would do no harm to take a look. All the same, he didn't drive up to the front door. Romantic Spanner might be, but he drew the line at fool-hardiness. And just as well he'd parked the Merc, and walked down the street towards Uncle Lenny's house, and thank God he saw it in time. It was Uncle Lenny's dog. Sometimes he kept it in the vicarage stables, and sometimes it was in kennels, and sometimes—like when he had something valuable in the house—he let it loose in the gardens. It was in the gardens now. Nasty, he called it, and Nasty was what it was. A big amalgam of a dog: great dane, dobermann, alsatian and bull-terrier all figured obviously in its ancestry, and it had inherited the worst characteristics of all four; besides the ones Uncle Lenny had taught it. Uncle Lenny had worked in a circus: there was nothing he didn't know about training dogs. Spanner went back to the Merc and headed for his

182

club. Nasty was something he could do without: all the same he'd learned something. Uncle Lenny only turned the dog out when he had something valuable: the odds were that this time it would be his stinking nephew.

Spanner drove back to the club and went inside. Two in the morning and it was still going strong. Not bad, that. Not bad at all and it all meant money. Soothing, that was. Encouraging. The only thing was this Bulky business. He'd got a whole tape full of information, and he didn't know what to do with it. Lonely was inaccessible, and how could he find an earl? The ultimate, the gut-feeling, told him not to bother, but that was George's solution an' all, and who cared what George thought? A minder, a hired hand. There had to be another way, if only he could figure it. A way that would steer him clear of the posh feller and the big darky, and still leave him in the money. Had to be. Otherwise he was no better than George. Luck, he told himself. Luck. Just one lucky edge. Come on. Come *on*.

He was in his office when the Chimp knocked at the door. Five foot six the Chimp was, in every direction. The perfect doorman.

'There's this geezer,' said the Chimp.

'We're closed,' said Spanner.

'I told him that,' said the Chimp. 'He says its important.'

'What's he look like?'

The Chimp pondered. Get it right and I'll give you a banana, thought Spanner. 'Money,' said the Chimp at last.

'All right,' Spanner said. 'Show him in here. And don't let him gamble.'

What he got was a tall, elegant geezer with a stiff right shoulder: public-school elegant, all that. Could be loaded, could be skint.

'Sorry to harass you like this,' said the tall elegant one. 'My name is Hexham. The Earl of Hexham actually.'

'You need me, Spanner?' the Chimp asked.

'Not any more,' said Spanner, and the Chimp left. Tomorrow he would buy him a whole fruit salad.

'It's an awkward time to call,' said Hexham.

'Not at all,' said Spanner. 'You're very welcome.'

'Thank you,' said Hexham. 'I was wondering if you could put me in touch with a chap called Berkeley.'

Spanner heaved a sigh that was all content.

'I thought you might be,' he said. 'Took you to the cleaners, didn't he? Him and a chap called Callan.'

That was the sort of punch that was bound to hurt, but Hexham covered up fast. 'Dear me,' he said. 'You seem to know a great deal about my affairs.'

'Like you've no idea,' said Spanner. 'I've got it all on tape.'

183

Unhurriedly, Hexham selected a chair, sat, crossed one elegant leg over the other. 'I think you'd better tell me about it,' he said, 'or play the tape if you'd prefer it.'

'Why should I?' said Spanner.

Hexham looked at him and reached a decision.

'Money,' he said. 'Rather a lot of money.'

Spanner told him *and* played the tape, then said, 'You better have a good offer.' He patted the tape-recorder. 'This could ruin you.'

Unperturbed, still unhurried, Hexham made his offer. Spanner was delighted, and said so.

'The only thing is I don't think we should hang about here,' said the earl, in the diffident voice of one who hates to disarrange the domestic arrangements of his friends.

'Why not?' said Spanner.

'It's possible that this Berkeley person may have friends. Tough friends. It wouldn't do for them to find either of us here.'

'Hey,' said Spanner. 'That's right. We better scarper.... I'll just get some money.'

'You won't need it,' said Hexham. 'I've got plenty.'

Say what you like about the aristocracy, Spanner thought, they spoke beautiful words. Beautiful.

24

[i]

She hadn't wanted to go to Las Vegas, in fact she was sick of the whole scene, had been ever since she'd talked to Barry Johnson's mother in Brooklyn Heights. But General Manette was persuasive, you had to give him that. Hell—he had to be, all the years he'd been in politics—and she'd finally given in. Bill Yerkes would have called it the older man syndrome, but it wasn't that—or not all of it. He'd told her about the girl, too, and that had really got to her. 'There but for the grace of God' stuff—and curiosity too, good, old-fashioned, female curiosity. She'd heard so much about this freak. She'd be crazy to pass up the chance to see her. And darling Daddy knew all about that. Darling Daddy could read her like a book: a book not, but definitely not, by Genet. A sweet and wholesome book: Louisa M. Alcott maybe? Alfred, Lord Tennyson?

All the same darling Daddy wasn't just being altruistic. Once he found his freak, the chances were she'd be on a trip, or recovering from one, and darling Daddy didn't know how to cope with that, and darling Daddy was pretty sure that his sweet and wholesome daughter did. Not that he'd asked: not that he'd even wanted to know. He'd just put on that pleading look.... Gorillas shouldn't even know how to plead. All the same, she wasn't exactly doing this for nothing. Once the gorilla had found his freak and turned her over to the statutory authorities—oh, Daddy dear, what big words you've got—and the press and TV had done their worst, Daddy dear was going to take her on a vacation to Mexico, and a long, long visit to Professor Martinez, another older man. It was time the gorilla had some competition.

She turned off the shower, put on her robe, and went into the living-room of their suite. As she did so he switched off the television—what looked like a local newscast—and went back to his chair, made notes.

'Something about our secret mission?' she said.

'No,' he said. 'A couple of kids. Nevada State Police just picked them up. They'd been mugged and dumped in the desert.'

'Nevada?' she said. 'You're concerned about Nevada?' and wished at once she hadn't said it. He got the hurt look.

'I'm concerned about our country,' he said, then, 'I mean that, Elizabeth. It's not just my job—it's my life.'

And how could you fight that?

He looked at his watch. 'You'd better phone your mother,' he said. 'She'll be expecting to hear from you. Then we'd better get to bed. It'll be an early start in the morning.'

'And what do I tell mother?'

The gorilla blushed. He actually blushed.

'You know what to say,' he said.

And she did too. They'd planned it all. Daddy was working hard on a commission at Nellis Field, and she was having a perfectly lovely time exploring Vegas and keeping Daddy company when he wasn't busy. And no, mother, she wasn't gambling except when Daddy was with her, and certainly not, mother. Of course she wouldn't take a drink. Elizabeth reached for the phone, and wondered what the hell a teetotal non-gambler could find to do in Las Vegas.

[ii]

They had breakfast in the suite. Orange juice, dollar cakes, ham, eggs, coffee. There might be a long time to go before their next meal. That day Chief Shekwe wore a grey lightweight suit, white shirt, dark blue tie: all very elegant and restrained, but if he added the right type of hat he'd become a very superior chauffeur. Callan wore dark slacks, a white shirt, lightweight double-breasted blazer. He looked at himself in the mirror.

'Jesus,' he said. 'I look like Meres trying to be sociable.'

'You look like money,' said FitzMaurice. 'You'll do.'

Callan worked at drawing the Magnum, over and over. At the seventh try he found his speed and rhythm improving. FitzMaurice waited; as black as basalt, and just about as impressionable, thought Callan—and drew his own gun.

'I'll never be as fast as you,' he said. 'If anybody gets shot to death it'll be you who does the shooting. I just hope nobody gets shot. You better hope so too, Callan. They can still execute for murder in this state. Cyanide gas. They reckon it's painless, but nobody ever came back to confirm it.'

Callan picked up their suitcases.

'Let's go,' he said.

Early morning or not, the fruit machines were still going; you could still get a bet on black-jack, craps, roulette.... They went from the casino to the car-port, backed up and left. It would have

186

been good to leave, thought Callan, if he hadn't known what his destination was. He eased the car out and on to the Strip. A block behind him two men in a dark green Porsche followed with the sedate care of those who have nowhere to go but work.... Callan sneaked a look at the temperature clock. Eight-seventeen. Ninety-one degrees.

'She'll be out cold,' he said.

'Let's hope she is,' said FitzMaurice, and yawned. 'Then she won't start yelling.'

'This Wino geezer,' said Callan.

'I've got instructions,' FitzMaurice said. 'Just you leave him to me.'

Callan sighed.

Norn Street was still quiet. No milk trucks, no kids with morning papers, no postman. Just the way we want it, thought Callan. Let's hope it's vulnerable, too. He parked the car outside Number 34.

'Let's hope it doesn't get nicked,' he said, and they went down the path. It was ten yards, and by the time they reached the front door they were sweating. Callan put his thumb on the bell-push and kept it there; FitzMaurice kept on going to the back of the house. A minute, ninety seconds. Callan could hear the bell drilling holes in the silence. At last there were footsteps, the door swung open to the length of its chain, and Callan looked at Wino. He looked terrible: he also looked immensely strong.

'Jesus,' he said. 'Don't you Johns ever get tired? It's eight-thirty in the morning.'

'This is urgent,' said Callan.

'Urgent?' said Wino. 'Now I've heard everything. Go stick it in the ice-bucket. Come back after lunch.'

He moved to close the door and Callan said quickly, 'There's to be a narcotics investigation.'

Wino hesitated, and behind him a voice said, 'The man is right. Now why don't you be friendly and take the chain off the hook?'

Wino looked behind him, and his headache got worse. Behind him was FitzMaurice, a Magnum embedded in his massive fist. Wino unhooked the door, and Callan moved in. FitzMaurice stared at Wino.

'You look awful,' he said.

'I'm hung-over,' said Wino.

'Excesses have to be paid for, brother,' said FitzMaurice, and gestured to the living-room.

With the three men in it looked very small indeed, small and very nasty. Half-empty cups of coffee, overflowing ash-trays, empty bottles of wine littered the tables and floor. The furniture was

187

ugly, the room hadn't been cleaned in weeks. Wino picked up one of the coffee cups. The coffee was cold but he drank it anyway.

'You said something about a narcotics investigation,' he said.

FitzMaurice said, 'That's right.'

'Who's making it?'

'We are,' said Callan. 'Put that cup down. Move over to the wall.'

'I got a right to see your credentials,' said Wino, and FitzMaurice raised the Magnum.

'Brother,' he said. 'You're looking at them. Now you do what the man said.'

Wino moved, body bent forward, hands against the wall, and Callan went over him, a process as familiar to Wino as shaving.

'He's clean,' he said, and FitzMaurice put up the Magnum.

'That's nice,' he said. 'Now let's call on Miss von Nichts.'

Wino turned. 'You're not fuzz,' he said. They made no answer. 'Look—we don't make much. I could raise maybe a hundred dollars....'

FitzMaurice sighed and said to Callan, 'Show him your trick.'

Callan's hand moved and Wino looked down the Magnum's barrel.

'Miss von Nichts,' Callan said. 'This is my calling card.'

'She's tripping,' Wino said. 'She won't know from nothing.'

'Poor deluded soul,' said FitzMaurice. 'We come to bring her aid and comfort. Lead us to her, brother.'

The room was small, the air stale, the heat intense. They entered, Wino leading, Callan behind him, FitzMaurice last. It was her workroom all right, as well as her place of rest. Whips and boots, and porn for every taste. Trudi lay on the bed, naked, smiling, eyes wide open and seeing nothing. Nothing at all.

'The poor deluded soul,' FitzMaurice said again, and beneath the irony Callan heard compassion. Wino's hand moved slowly towards the whip on the bedside table, and Callan waited till he was almost there, then pressed the Magnum's barrel into his neck.

'I think I should tell you,' he said diffidently, 'that I've used one of these things before.'

Wino froze.

'Now, now,' FitzMaurice said. 'He's a tryer. We all like a man who tries.' Then to Wino: 'How long's she been out?'

'Hours,' Wino said. 'She should be round soon.'

'You got anything that helps?'

'Ice-cubes,' said Wino. FitzMaurice left, and Wino and Callan waited in silence until he returned. The girl on the bed lay motionless: an appalling, a heart-rending sight. FitzMaurice came back with an ice-bag, and Callan said, 'I thought you wanted her out.'

188

'Dazed,' said FitzMaurice. 'But not this unconscious. We forgot to bring an ambulance.' He went to the bed.

'Take it easy, will you?' said Wino. 'That stuff's torture to her.'

FitzMaurice looked at him. 'Well well,' he said. 'Well well well.'

He wrapped the ice-bag in a grubby towel, and placed it gently on the girl's forehead....

The desert this time had been biblical, with elegant ruins of marble surrounded by sand and rock.... Palmyra maybe.... Soaring shafts of marble; the remains of something that had once been geometrically beautiful, pure and cool even in the desert's consuming heat. Satisfying, fulfilling, even to be among its shattered ruins. And then, just like the Bible, the desert blossomed. There was a river that was cool but never cold, and grass and lark-song and the city was restored, and geometrically beautiful as she had known it would be.... And there was rain, and flowers that cupped it, welcoming and open; never furling, never shrinking away.... And the rain was on her body too, reminding her again that she existed, that the dream was about to fade. White marble, scarlet flowers, blue water, fading, fading: shadows racing across them like storm clouds till there was only blackness, but that too was good. Her eyes focused, she looked into the face of Spencer Perceval FitzMaurice, and her smile remained.

'Der Panther,' she said.

FitzMaurice said, 'Welcome back, *Fräulein.*'

The smile faded, but with three men looking down at her she showed neither embarrassment nor fear.

'But you're always there,' she said. 'At the end of the trip. When I get back there's nothing. Only my good friend,' she looked at Wino, 'and the stupid Johns.'

'From now on,' FitzMaurice said, 'things are going to be different.'

She looked once more at Wino. The gun in Callan's hand bothered her not at all.

'Am I still tripping?' she said.

Wino said gently, 'Who knows, baby?'

'But I can't be,' she said. 'You're never *there.* You're here.'

'What happens now?' FitzMaurice asked.

'I clean her up,' Wino said. 'Get her dressed.'

Wino got to work, and FitzMaurice moved over to Callan. The girl's eyes were fully focused now, and she could move her body enough to help Wino clean her, get her into her clothes, but she still showed no awareness of reality.

Softly Callan asked, 'What's this panther stuff?'

FitzMaurice shrugged. 'Whatever it is,' he said, 'it's real to her.'

189

They waited as Wino dressed her in T-shirt, panties and jeans, put a pair of sandals on her feet, then FitzMaurice gestured towards the living-room and Wino picked her up and carried her without apparent trouble. It was as he put her down on the sofa that the door-bell rang. FitzMaurice at once went for his gun.

'*Nein, Panther. Nein,*' said the girl.

FitzMaurice ignored her. To Wino he said, 'You expecting company?' Wino shook his head. 'Brother, I beg you. Don't try to fool me.'

'No Johns in the morning,' Wino said. 'House rule.'

FitzMaurice moved to the window, eased back the curtain, and peered. A grey-haired man with a briefcase, who'd brought his own girl.... Kinky.... As he watched, the grey-haired man began to pound on the door with his fist. He called Wino over. 'Know them?' he asked. Wino peered and shook his head. 'Look like social workers,' he said.

'You better take it,' FitzMaurice said to Callan. He nodded at Wino. 'And try to act like you've got a hangover.'

'If only I had,' said Callan, and went to the door....

So here they were, she thought, nearing the end of the mission, about to storm the enemy's fortress, if this Trudi was the enemy. And if she were, Elizabeth thought, who but her very own gorilla would come armed only with a briefcase? The door swung open the length of its chain, and a man stood there, a man neither big nor small, in a fancy blazer with one button undone, hair mussed, and the emptiest eyes she'd ever seen. They told her nothing at all. His left hand rested on the doorjamb: she couldn't see his right.

Her father spoke. 'Are you—er—Wino?'

'That's right.' His voice sounded hoarse, she thought. The hoarseness of excitement, or maybe it was only booze.

Her father hesitated.

'Something bothering you?' the hoarse voice said.

'Oh, excuse me,' said her father. 'It's just from what I'd been told I thought you'd have been bigger.'

'Sometimes I'm bigger than I look,' said the empty-eyed man, and suddenly Elizabeth believed him, and felt an urgent need to forget the whole thing: just leave it and go.

But her father said: 'I want to see Trudi von Nichts please.'

'A lot of men do.'

Manette flushed.

'My name's Manette,' he said. 'Edward Philip Manette. I'm a United States Congressman and I want to see Miss von Nichts.'

For a split second she thought she could detect an expression in the other man's eyes. Amazement first, then for whatever crazy reason maybe even laughter, and then it was gone.

'You better come in,' he said, and his left hand moved, she heard the scrape of a chain released, and he pulled the door towards him.

'Come in,' he said again, and Elizabeth went in: Manette followed.

'We never had a congressman before,' the man said, and pushed the door closed. 'Come to that we never had a man who brought his own girl.' Manette whirled, and looked at the Magnum revolver in the other's right hand.

'I'm warning you,' Manette said. 'I really am a congressman. And this is my daughter. I want no more cheap cracks. So put that gun away.'

'I'm awfully sorry,' the man said, 'but I'm afraid it isn't going to be that easy. In the living-room please.'

'Why,' Elizabeth said. 'You're British!' She instantly felt a fool. Of all the stupid, stupid things to say.

'Quite right, Miss Manette.' The hoarseness had gone from his voice. 'If you'll just lead the way, Congressman.'

Manette hesitated, and Elizabeth said, 'I think we should do as he says.'

Manette kept looking at the gun: it had never wavered, but now it flicked, just once, to point at his daughter before coming back to him.

Manette moved towards the living-room.

*

With six people in it the place was crowded. Wino was on his knees by Trudi, wiping her face with a grubby handkerchief, and FitzMaurice leaned against the wall. Trudi's eyes never left him as he looked from Manette to Elizabeth. Callan stood behind them, his gun-hand rock-steady. We are going to do it, thought FitzMaurice.

'You brought company,' he said aloud.

'Oh excuse me,' said Callan. 'Miss Manette, Congressman Manette. This is Chief Shekwe of Obutu. My name is Tucker.'

'I don't believe it,' said Manette.

'Why should you?' said FitzMaurice. 'We're lying. Take a seat, Congressman, Miss....'

'I demand to know—' Manette said.

'No no,' said Callan. 'What you do is sit. *We* do the demanding.'

His left hand ran swiftly over Manette's body, then he pushed him into a chair. Elizabeth sat before he could touch her, but he took her purse from her, spilled its contents out on to the floor,

191

examined them and handed it back empty. Mechanically she began to retrieve her property.

'You sure he's a congressman?' FitzMaurice said.

'Well,' said Callan, 'he's got a briefcase.' Still using his left hand he scooped it up and flung it to FitzMaurice, who fielded it neatly, sat down at a table, opened it and began to go methodically through its contents.

'Don't read, Panther,' Trudi said. 'Please don't read.'

'I'll see you go to gaol for this,' said Manette. 'Both of you.'

Placidly FitzMaurice went on reading.

Daddy, please, Elizabeth begged in her mind, come out from behind the 1940's. These men are real, their guns are real, and if you're not careful, my darling, their violence will be your last reality. She put her hand out to his, and he patted it gently. Oh dear God, she thought. He's trying to reassure me.

'It would seem that these are honest people,' said FitzMaurice at last. 'Their passports say he's a member of the House of Representatives, and she's his daughter. We're going up in the world, Tucker, my friend.'

'You're going down,' said Manette. 'To the bottom.'

FitzMaurice again ignored him. 'Big committee man, Mr Manette.' He gestured at piles of papers neatly stacked. 'Ecology, leisure activities, economic affairs—and just a teeny bit of espionage.'

From beside Trudi, Wino said: 'I need a drink.'

'Where d'you keep it?'

'That cupboard,' Wino pointed. 'Right there.' He started to rise.

'You stay with your lady,' said FitzMaurice. 'I'll get it.' He reached out, opened the cupboard, took from it a jelly glass and a bottle of wine, and gave them to Wino.

'You go right ahead, my friend,' said FitzMaurice. 'It's a little early for the rest of us.'

Wino poured out a glass of wine, gulped it noisily down and refilled the glass. Gently Trudi patted his shoulder, and he drank more slowly. FitzMaurice shuffled the papers together and restored them to the briefcase. He did not restore the briefcase to Manette.

'So you brought a congressman and his charming daughter,' he said to Callan. 'Have you any suggestions what we should do with them, Mr Tucker?'

'Well, chief,' said Callan, 'it's a little difficult just at the moment. They might prove an embarrassment, on the other hand they could turn out to be a positive bonus. Without more data it's hard to offer a suggestion. If they would tell us why they are here—'

'I am here,' said Manette, 'to talk to Miss von Nichts. If the two of you go now, and leave us alone together, I will take no further action against you. I give you my word on it. If not, I—' He broke off. The black man was looking at him: his face showed neither hostility nor the threat of violence: only profound, impersonal appraisal; yet for the first time Manette felt fear.

'I regret, Congressman,' FitzMaurice said, 'that what you ask is not possible. Tell us why you are here.'

'On business of the United States Government,' said Manette. 'Why are you here?'

'Please,' said FitzMaurice. 'After all, I did ask first.' He transferred his gaze to Elizabeth. 'And your position is very vulnerable.'

'You wouldn't dare,' said Manette.

'Congressman,' said FitzMaurice. 'We both know that's not true.' He rose.

'Panther,' Trudi von Nichts said. 'Please don't.'

Manette said, 'It has come to my knowledge that Miss von Nichts is addicted to certain drugs. As it happens I am at present collecting evidence on—'

'Manette,' said FitzMaurice, 'do you love your daughter?'

'Of course,' said Manette. There could be no doubt that what he said was true.

'Then stop lying.' FitzMaurice paused. 'Now tell me why you are here.' His hands reached out and plucked Elizabeth from her chair, turned her round to face her father. Over his shoulder she could see the man who called himself Tucker, and still his eyes told nothing. He could have been standing in line for a bus. FitzMaurice's left hand came up round Elizabeth's chin, thumb and first finger splayed, touching the vulnerable places of the jaw-bone just below the ears.

'Tell me,' said FitzMaurice.

Manette said at once, 'I serve on a Security Committee. You've seen the papers in my briefcase—you know it's true. I have reason to believe that girl—' he gestured at Trudi. 'That she—I have reason to believe she—' He hesitated. 'How *can* I tell you? This is top secret.'

FitzMaurice's fingers pressed a very little, and Elizabeth gasped.

'How can you not tell me?' said FitzMaurice. 'This is your daughter.'

Manette said, 'We think—we're almost certain—Trudi von Nichts is Franz Bauer's daughter.'

'Thank you, Congressman,' said FitzMaurice, and turned Elizabeth round, waited while she sat.

'Did I hurt you much?'

193

'You hurt me,' she said.

'I've been taught how to hurt,' said FitzMaurice, 'by people who know what they're doing. You remember that, Congressman.'

Oh Jesus, Manette thought. Oh sweet suffering Jesus.

Callan was looking at Trudi von Nichts. Her eyes were closed, her breathing even and perceptible.

'Wino,' he said. 'Is she all right?'

Wino took the glass from his mouth and looked at the girl.

'Oh sure,' he said. 'She always takes a nap like that after she gets back.'

'What happens when she wakes up?'

'She's O.K.' said Wino. 'You know. Normal. Only she's so goddam tired she can hardly move.'

'And how long before she wakes?'

Wino shrugged. 'Ten minutes, maybe. Fifteen. It's never long.'

Callan turned to FitzMaurice.

'It doesn't look as if we have all that much time,' he said.

'What did you plan to do with her?' FitzMaurice asked Manette.

'Give her back.'

'Back to who?'

Manette looked at his daughter.

'Back to her father,' he said.

'You sure about that, Congressman?'

'Of course I'm sure,' Manette said. 'It's where she belongs.'

Wino said, 'It's not where she belongs. She hates her father.'

'Then she has the capacity to learn to love him,' Manette said.

Well, hurrah for the gorilla, thought Elizabeth. He's started to act smart again. But he's left it just a teensy bit late.

'You'd kill her,' said Wino.

'She's killing herself,' said Manette.

'Maybe so,' Wino said, 'but it's the way she wants to go.'

FitzMaurice said, 'I'll say this for you, Congressman. You certainly believe in altruism. From what I read in your files you went to the hell of a lot of trouble just to find a man's daughter and give her back.'

'It was to be a goodwill gesture from our security services,' Manette said. 'The CIA doesn't have that good a reputation. This would help their image.'

'And yours?'

'All right. And mine. What's wrong with that. But believe me, my country comes first.'

'And now,' said Callan, 'we begin to approach the truth.'

Manette turned round to peer at him.

'And just what does that mean?'

Callan moved forward to stand where Manette could see him,

194

opened his coat, stuck the Magnum in his pants' waistband.

'Your country wants that mess,' he said, and nodded towards Trudi. 'She's valuable. But she won't be valuable if you give her back for nothing. Were you going to give her back for nothing?'

'Naturally,' said Manette, 'we would have expected something in the nature of a quid pro quo from Bauer.'

'Like inside information on Common Market negotiations? Revaluation of the Deutschmark? West Germany's defence allocation? Stuff like that?'

'Yes,' said Manette. 'Stuff like that.'

'And Bauer was going to give you all this *after* he got his daughter back? Come off it.'

Manette was silent, and Callan let the silence drag. They still had a few minutes. Like FitzMaurice he watched Manette as he waited. Behind him, Wino moved from a kneeling position to a crouch, his hand reached out for the almost empty wine bottle.

At last, Manette said, 'As you say, she's valuable. I—'

Wino flung the bottle at Manette, and yelled, 'You were going to sell her,' and launched himself after it. Once more the Magnum was in Callan's hand, but he made no move. The bottle missed, smashed against the wall, splattered his daughter with the sticky-sweet dregs of the muscatel it contained as Wino's flailing dive was blocked by a kick from FitzMaurice that sent the white man crashing into a table, stumbling, but even so he swirled round, came in at Manette again, but this time FitzMaurice was in the way. Manette tried to rise, and Callan laid the Magnum's barrel on the side of his head.

'Stay in your seat,' he said. 'The show's just started.'

Wino's one ambition was to get at Manette, and to do that he had to eliminate FitzMaurice. The negro waited warily, frowning in concentration. Drunk or not, Wino was hard all through, and somebody had taught him how to move and taught him well. Wino threw a fist, a looping right, and FitzMaurice caught it just in time on the shoulder and grunted with the pain, swerved away as Wino aimed a kick, and countered with a fist strike of his own, aimed too high so that it went over Wino's shoulder, and Wino moved in again, getting up close, fists moving like pistons against FitzMaurice's ribs. Still frowning, still grunting, the negro took it, and countered with a chop to Wino's neck. At once the battering fists stopped, and FitzMaurice chopped again and again. It was like felling a tree. Wino's massive strength kept him upright longer than Callan would have believed possible, but at last he went down on his knees before FitzMaurice, but never in supplication. FitzMaurice reached for him.

'It looks to me like you're getting rusty,' said Callan.

195

FitzMaurice hauled Wino to his feet.

'If he didn't drink he would have taken me,' he said, and drew back his fist.

Callan moved forward. 'His death isn't in my script,' he said.

FitzMaurice looked at the battered man he held.

'I don't think it's in mine,' he said, 'not any more,' and opened his hands. This time Wino fell prone.

From the sofa, Trudi von Nichts dragged herself over to Wino, crouched weeping over him.

'Oh my God,' she said, 'that was real. I saw it. It's real.'

'Yes,' FitzMaurice said, 'it's real.' He turned to Manette and his daughter. 'It's all real. So how about telling the truth, Congressman?'

Manette looked at Trudi, on her knees, weeping over Wino's destruction.

'She was a good card to be dealt,' he said. 'We would have played her.'

Almost imperceptibly his daughter moved away from him.

'You mean,' said Callan, 'that you were going to blackmail Bauer.'

'Yes,' said Manette.

'Don't let it get you down, Congressman,' said FitzMaurice. 'That's just what we're going to do.'

'We?' said Manette. 'Who's we? The British?'

'A couple of freelances,' said Callan. 'All we want is money.'

Manette said, 'I'll give you money. I'll buy her from you now.'

'Dad,' Elizabeth Manette said. 'For God's sake.'

'I'll give you a million dollars for her.'

Callan whistled. 'Chief Shekwe,' he said 'we've made the big time at last.'

'Mr Tucker,' said FitzMaurice, 'I rather think we have.'

'The trouble is,' said Callan, 'we've already got a contract. And the bloke we made it with likes his contracts honoured. Otherwise he tends to kill you.'

'I can give you protection,' Manette said, 'I can even guarantee it.'

For the first time that day FitzMaurice was worried. He had no doubt that Manette could be made to pay if Callan handled it right, and Callan would know exactly how to handle it: and CIA protection was good: it had to be. It was one of the best incentives for Russians and East Europeans to defect. The CIA could pass something between a conjuring trick and a miracle: they could make you disappear off the face of the earth then reappear in some place nobody would ever dream of looking, with a new background, new passport, even a new face if they thought it necessary. And Callan knew that too—and he had a gun in his hand. All FitzMaurice could do was sweat it out.

Callan said at last, 'I'm sorry, Congressman, but we really do have a contract.'

FitzMaurice let out his breath in a long, silent sigh. To wipe his forehead would be a dead giveaway, and Callan had too much edge as it was.

'You're being foolish,' said Manette. 'You can't possibly get away with this.'

'We are getting away with it,' said Callan.

'No,' said Manette. 'That's self-delusion. You haven't thought it through.'

'Think for us then,' said Callan.

'My daughter and myself,' said Manette, 'we've seen you. We can identify you—And even if you lock us in here we'll get out sometime. We'll put the CIA on you—and, sooner or later, I promise you, the CIA will track you down.'

'Lock you in here?' said FitzMaurice, as if testing a new and not very practical idea. 'Mr Tucker, were you considering locking them in here?'

'Certainly not,' said Callan. 'You're the one who hasn't thought it through, Congressman. What we're considering is killing you.'

Manette's first reaction was not one of shock, but outrage that they should even consider an assault on a member of the United States Congress, and that should have been comic, but it didn't last. The shock followed too swiftly, and with it the realisation that his daughter was in jeopardy.

'You couldn't do that,' he said.

'Oh, but we could,' said Callan, and looked at the Magnum, then returned it to its webbing holster. 'We have the means—and you're amateurs after all. You're very easy people to kill. Let's consider it.'

Elizabeth thought: This can't be happening, but it *is* happening.

'If we kill you,' said Callan, 'we get away clean. We and the girl disappear, and nobody's any the wiser.'

'The shots,' said Manette. 'Somebody's bound to hear—'

'No shots,' said Callan.

He even sounds reasonable, thought Elizabeth, as if this were some practical exercise in logic. Her father was ashen now; the quiet, reasonable, empty-eyed man was really getting to him. Then she remembered the other words the quiet man had used: His death isn't in my script.

'Does that consideration appeal to you, Chief Shekwe?' Callan asked.

'It certainly makes more sense than the Congressman's, Mr Tucker,' said FitzMaurice.

197

Stiffly Trudi von Nichts rose, touched Callan's arm.

'It would be better,' she said, 'if you were to kill me.'

'I'm afraid not,' said Callan. 'And anyway you don't want to die.'

'But I do,' she said. 'I'm going to die. If you try to take me back to my father, I will. So why not do it now? These people can't hurt you, any more than Wino could. And you said you wouldn't kill him.'

'Your friend has no influence,' said FitzMaurice. 'No clout. Drunks seldom have. But these two—'

Trudi began to shake: gently FitzMaurice led her back to the sofa.

'There's another possibility,' said Callan. 'We could take you with us.'

'I don't follow that, Mr Tucker,' said FitzMaurice.

'Think it through, chief,' said Callan. 'If we kill them Trudi will be upset, and we'd rather not upset her. If we take them with us, look how respectable we'll be: a congressman and his daughter conducting a foreign potentate and his staff on a tour of the great American West.'

'You'd never get out of the country,' said Manette.

'But we would,' said Callan. 'You brought your passports.'

FitzMaurice chuckled. 'Think it through, Congressman,' he said. 'Isn't a guided tour better than dying?' The chuckling stopped. 'We're giving you your life, Manette,' he continued, 'but of course we expect a little something in return.'

'Like what?' said Manette.

'Like co-operation,' said FitzMaurice. 'Otherwise we go back to Mr Tucker's first consideration. What's it to be, Congressman?'

'We'll co-operate,' said Manette.

'Good man,' said FitzMaurice.

A nightmare in courteous irony, thought Elizabeth. Polite forms of address, a gentle deference of manner, but all the same the knowledge that they might, just might, do what they said. The white man had said: His death isn't in my script, but she could remember, too, the black man's answer: I don't think it's in mine. Not any more. The black man still had doubts about letting people live.

FitzMaurice went back to the sofa, and Trudi. She was still shaking: an incessant trembling that seemed to attack her entire body. Shock, he thought: hearing talk of death, seeing her friend demolished: and drugs, pulling out of a trip, dreaming of panthers. He touched her arm: she was cold. In that sweating, steaming room she was cold. He went into the bedroom, came back with a blanket and wrapped it round her, but the trembling didn't stop, didn't even diminish. But Snell had thought of that one too, and

198

provided for it. His hand went to his pocket, came out with a syrette and a tiny bottle of alcohol. He poured a little on to his handkerchief, rubbed the girl's arm, prepared to inject her, but she flinched away.

'I don't use the needle,' she said. 'I never have.'

'This is medicinal,' said FitzMaurice. 'It's going to help you.'

But she wouldn't submit, and FitzMaurice's massive arm came round her, he handled her as easily as if she were a puppet, and the needle went in, he pressed the syrette's contents gently home, then held her still.

'You poor thing,' he said. 'You poor thing.'

Slowly the trembling eased and ceased, and at last she looked up at FitzMaurice and sighed.

'That's better,' he said. 'Isn't that better?' She nodded like a child.

FitzMaurice turned to Manette. 'Congressman,' he said, 'we await your co-operation.'

She went to the car almost briskly. Whatever the stuff was that Snell had mixed, so long as it lasted it worked well. FitzMaurice put her in the front seat next to Callan, and waited while Callan fastened her seat-belt in a way that practically immobilised her, then sent Manette out, to open up the back. Manette went without a word. His daughter was still with FitzMaurice, now looking down at Wino. He was just beginning to come round. FitzMaurice fetched water, dribbled a little on his face, handed him the glass to drink from as he sat up groaning.

'Man, you can hit,' said Wino.

'My one talent,' said FitzMaurice. 'That and giving advice. You got money?'

'Fifty-sixty bucks.'

FitzMaurice took out his wallet, handed over five hundred.

'I gave you a beating,' he said. 'You may as well take the advice as well. Go away, my friend. Be missing. You stay here and make a fuss and your friend Trudi will be hurt. I hope you believe that.'

'Yeah,' said Wino. 'I believe it.... O.K. I'll get lost. Hey—you won't let that grey-haired guy do anything to her?'

Elizabeth winced.

'So long as she's with us, nobody's going to do anything to her.'

'O.K.,' said Wino, 'O.K.,' and climbed wearily to his feet. 'You sure can hit.' He stuffed the money in his pants pocket, and headed for the back door.

'Hold on,' FitzMaurice said. 'What about your clothes?'

Wino looked bewildered.

'I'm wearing them,' he said....

Manette in the off-side rear seat behind Trudi, Elizabeth next to him, FitzMaurice next to her.

'When you're ready, Mr Tucker,' said FitzMaurice.

The big car moved smoothly out, and a dark green Porsche dawdled along after it, waited while the Jaguar turned on to Fremont Street, then followed on at two cars' distance. The Jaguar took the turn-off for the highway headed south, and the man in the Porsche's passenger seat picked up a radio-telephone, read off the Jaguar's licence number. Above them a helicopter soared towards the highway. Its pilot was an East German who knew all about helicopters, but could never begin to understand a country that made them so readily available. He used a pair of field glasses made by Zeiss. In the clear desert air the Jaguar was easily seen: by dropping low he could even read the number-plate, but once he'd got it he soared away again. No point in letting them know they were a target. Below him the Jaguar sailed sedately on at a steady sixty-five miles an hour, and the helicopter pilot used his radio telephone to give its position. The Porsche sprinted for a while, then its driver eased off: they were close enough, and he didn't want to risk being pinched for speeding. A Porsche is a small car built for tremendous speed. It can never hope to be sedate, but on occasion it can be discreet.

25

Hunter disliked Bonn quite as much as Meres did: it was stuffy, provincial, hideously expensive—and it was still raining. Moreover the air-conditioning in his suite had jammed: it was quite impossible to turn it off. He rang room service for a liverwurst sandwich and a Dortmunder beer. They were the cheapest things on the menu, and as an Englishman he'd be expected to order them. He didn't like either of them, but they'd been paid for on expenses, and so he ate and drank, and studied the notes he'd made from Kleist's file. When Meres brought Kleist up to see him the notes were already burned: Hunter was up to date. He looked at the two men facing him. They didn't look as if they were going to give him any cause for celebration.

'Herr von Kleist, isn't it?' said Hunter.

Kleist was delighted by the 'von' as Hunter had been sure he would be.

'I wish to say that this is an honour,' said Kleist. 'A very great honour. I am only sorry that—'

Hunter held up his hand.

'One moment,' he said, and turned to Meres. 'Your report, please.'

'I'm happy to say that Herr von Kleist has been very co-operative,' said Meres. 'He's done all he possibly could to help us, sir. I can recommend that he be paid the sum we discussed.'

'Thank you,' said Kleist. 'I am most grateful. Also happy to have been of service.'

'It's always a pleasure to recruit a good man,' said Hunter. 'I take it you'll be willing to help us again, Herr von Kleist?'

'At any time,' Kleist said. 'Whatever I can do.'

Hunter's hand moved to the briefcase beside him, hesitated, then came out again, empty.

'The book, please,' he said.

'I regret to report,' said Meres, 'that the book wasn't there.'

Hunter turned to Kleist.

'Is that the reason for your being sorry?'

'It is,' said Kleist. 'That I should fail you on my first assignment—no, not fail. The book truly was not there. But that I should disappoint you....'

Hunter began to ask questions, and Kleist, had he known it, underwent an object lesson in interrogation, as unalarming as it was thorough. Meres did know it, and marvelled. When he'd finished, Hunter was satisfied that Kleist was telling the truth: he'd searched with professional skill for a paper-back copy of *Das Kapital,* and had failed to find it only because it wasn't there.

'Thank you, Herr von Kleist,' he said at last. 'You are right not to condemn yourself. My information must have been at fault for once. The book wasn't there.'

'I am absolutely certain that is so,' said Kleist.

'I too.... I wonder if you would mind stepping into my bedroom for a moment. I have to consult with young Toby on another matter, and it's rather confidential.'

'Of course,' said Kleist.

Courteously Hunter escorted him to the bedroom, and with equal courtesy locked him in.

'Who got the book, Toby?'

'It can only be the SSD, sir.'

'I believe you're right. Via that Nivelle woman no doubt.'

'It would seem so, sir. One gathered that Kleist would tell her anything she asked.'

'He didn't know about the book,' said Hunter.

'I agree, sir,' said Meres, 'but the SSD may have done—and Kleist would be able to tell her where to look.'

'Sometimes,' said Hunter, 'not always, but sometimes, you are rather more than a pretty face.'

He sighed.

'I take it there's no word from FitzMaurice and Callan, sir?'

'Not a word,' said Hunter. 'Until now I'd taken that as a good sign.'

'It still may be, sir,' said Meres. 'After all it's most likely that we got there first.'

'Not by very much,' said Hunter, 'and we've still got to get the girl out. The SSD are an ingenious lot you know. They'll probably let our chaps do all the hard work, then lift the girl at the last possible moment.'

'But that means they'll have to find FitzMaurice and Callan,' said Meres. 'And in a town of that size.'

'Oh, I agree,' said Hunter. 'And I took it further than that—dressing up FitzMaurice like something out of Sanders of the River. Who could possibly think of him as working for British

202

Intelligence? I gambled because I had to, Toby. And I may have lost.'

'FitzMaurice was perfect, sir.'

'Of course he was. But I'm not referring to FitzMaurice.... It's Callan.'

'Callan, sir? You think he'll defect?'

'No,' said Hunter. 'He won't do that. He was the ideal man for the job, except for one thing. The Russians once had him for a week. It was when you were in Washington. I swopped him for one of theirs—a chap who called himself Richmond. But they had time to interrogate him first: to photograph, evaluate, examine. They'll have a file on him inches thick. And you can be pretty certain the SSD have that file too.'

Hunter looked at the bedroom door. Even so enthusiastic a recruit as Kleist could hardly be locked up indefinitely.

'Tell me about the Nivelle woman,' he said.

Meres reached a decision: he could give the police findings, and risk the kind of grilling that Kleist had just undergone, or he could tell the truth. Hunter was in a hurry.

'I killed her, sir,' he said.

'Indeed?'

'She damn nearly killed me.'

Out it all came: the visit to Hexham's palazzo, the missing clothes, the missing books, the Armi Galesi automatic, and there, and for the first time, Meres lied. In his version she'd held on to the gun, and Meres had no option but to kill her.

'But didn't Signora Lunari issue you with a gun?' asked Hunter.

'I had no chance to draw it, sir.'

'How odd,' said Hunter. 'You're lying of course. But there's no time to go into that now. My guess is that she was SSD second rank. And German.'

'German, sir? But—' Meres looked at the door.

'You're thinking of Kleist? But Kleist was bound to be suspicious of Germans, and if Nivelle were bilingual there'd be nothing to suspect.'

'Even so, sir—'

'I've taken expert opinion on this, Toby,' said Hunter. 'I'm satisfied.' Hunter paused, and assessed Bulky Berkeley's competence. He really was satisfied. 'She did a very useful job: tracing Bauer's daughter, liaising with Hexham.'

'You really think he went double, sir?'

'Oh, undoubtedly,' said Hunter. 'Otherwise his antique smuggling operation would have been shut down months ago.... You have no idea where he is?'

'None, sir, I'm sure that Kleist hasn't either.'

'We'd better find him,' said Hunter, and thought. 'An SSD man defected here years ago, in Gehlen's time. Quite a small fish, really, but he had a list of safe-houses the SSD used in the U.K.—a list we never got. We'd better get it now.'

'You've got something to trade, sir?'

'No,' said Hunter. 'I've got Kleist.'

'But he won't do it,' said Meres. 'That would be acting against his own people. We're supposed to be an anti-Communist organisation.'

'Oh, I know all that,' said Hunter. He even sounded testy. 'Didn't you find anything useful in his house?'

Meres spoke of a Uhlan's uniform, and mild, homosexual porn.

'A bit thin,' said Hunter, 'but we can stretch it. Better have him in.'

'There's just one thing, sir,' said Meres. 'After I killed Nivelle I searched her. The only thing I found on her was this.'

He handed over the address book. Hunter flicked through it, put it in his pocket.

'This may be your salvation, Toby,' he said. 'On the other hand it may not. Show Kleist in please.'

When Kleist arrived Hunter was once more fidgeting in his briefcase. He took from it a long manila envelope and a sheet of paper, handed the envelope to Kleist.

'Perhaps you'd better count that,' he said.

Kleist opened the envelope. It was stuffed with banknotes. When he had done, he said: 'But this is too much. There is almost fifteen thousand pounds here. I lost only eleven thousand.'

'We are always glad to pay for value received,' said Hunter, and passed over the sheet of paper. 'Now if you will kindly sign this receipt, Herr von Kleist.'

Kleist hesitated.

'My country is living through rather difficult times,' said Hunter. 'Every penny has to be accounted for.' For once Hunter sounded embarrassed.

Kleist read the document. Whitehall address, then a simple statement: the money paid was for certain services rendered by Gunther von Kleist in Taormina, services which, it was hoped, would promote co-operation between West Germany and Britain.

'Will it really do that?' said Kleist.

'It is my dearest wish,' said Hunter.

Oh you bastard, thought Meres. You unbelievable bastard, and took the paper which Kleist had signed, gave it back to Hunter.

'I should perhaps explain,' said Kleist, 'that I do not know where to reach either Callan or Berkeley at the moment, but no doubt they will come to see me.'

204

'No doubt,' said Hunter. 'But that is purely a matter for your own arrangement. In the meantime I wonder if you'd care to undertake another little job for us?'

'If I possibly can,' said Kleist.

'Oh you can,' said Hunter. 'I wonder whether you will, that's all. Of course you'll be paid.'

Kleist hastened to assure Hunter that he was proud and happy to serve. Only his impoverished circumstances made it necessary for him to expect remuneration....

Hunter told him what he must do, and Kleist was appalled. Real text book stuff, thought Meres. You never believe a mug could possibly be so stupid, and they invariably are. It's pathetic.

'But this is against my own country,' Kleist said.

'Agreed,' said Hunter. 'In a very minor way. But in a very major way it is against East Germany.'

'How?' said Kleist. 'Show me how.'

'I can't do that,' said Hunter. 'The information is most secret.'

'I don't believe you,' said Kleist, and looked from Hunter to Meres. 'I don't believe anything that either of you has told me.' He pushed the manila envelope at Hunter. 'Here. Take it back, I'm going.'

He moved to the door of the suite. According to the text book, thought Meres, he's reached the point where the mug believes he's touched bottom. The mug is always wrong.

Hunter said, 'If you please, Toby.'

Meres moved and Kleist's progress back to Hunter was a painful and humiliating business, as Hunter had intended it to be.

Kleist opened his mouth to yell.

'If you shout,' said Hunter, 'Toby will hurt you even more. He's good at hurting people. He enjoys it.' He settled back in his chair. 'You're foolish, but I suppose you know that. What on earth is the point of giving me back my money if I still have your receipt?'

'For co-operation between our two countries,' said Kleist. 'Co-operation.'

'Well, not really,' said Hunter. 'If the scheme I have going at the moment works, it will mean that a certain member of your government will co-operate with me, but not that I shall necessarily co-operate with him. And much of that will be your doing.'

Kleist lunged at Hunter, and Meres grabbed him again. Kleist gasped.

'Try not to be foolish,' said Hunter. 'I know it's your nature but do try. Surely you realise one thing by now? Resist us and you feel pain: help us and there is only pleasure. It was pleasant, wasn't it, to receive fifteen thousand pounds you had no intention of parting with?'

'Honour,' said Kleist. 'It was a debt of honour.'

'Not at all,' said Hunter. 'You and Hexham cheated, but your opponents cheated better. There's no honour in that.'

'You know about that?' said Kleist.

'There isn't much I don't know about you,' said Hunter. 'That little—er—specialised library in your attic for instance. Not perhaps the ideal reading for a man in your position, particularly now that you have embarked on a romantic friendship with a young and handsome Englishman.'

'You would betray me?' said Kleist.

His English has a dreadful tendency towards the melodramatic, Hunter thought, but perhaps this time it's justified.

'I hope that won't be necessary,' he said, reached for his briefcase again and took out a small tape-recorder, disconnected the tiny microphone which was hidden by the empty bottle of Dortmunder beer, ran back the tape and switched on.

Kleist's voice said, 'I wish to say that this is an honour. A very great honour. I am only sorry that—'

Then Hunter's voice. 'One moment.... Your report please.'

Meres' voice, 'I'm happy to say that Herr von Kleist has been very co-operative. He's done all he possibly could to help us, sir. I can recommend that he be paid the sum we discussed.'

Then Kleist's voice, 'Thank you. I am most grateful. Also happy to have been of service.'

Hunter switched off. 'There's more,' he said, 'if you really want to hear it.'

Kleist made no answer: he was weeping. Oh lord, thought Meres. That's all I needed.

'You really have no choice,' said Hunter.

Kleist dabbed at his eyes with his hands, then managed to find a handkerchief.

'You are a very evil man,' he said—Melodrama again. Hunter waited.

'I really have no choice,' said Kleist.

'None whatsoever.'

'But how can I possibly gain access to such a document?'

'Quite simply,' said Hunter. 'This document is classified as Secret rather than Top Secret. An archivist of your grade could have any number of reasons for going into the Secret section. We'll help you with that.'

'But it will be on microfilm,' said Kleist. 'How can I copy that?'

'No need,' said Hunter. 'I want you to get us the film.'

Kleist said, 'You mean steal it.'

'Precisely,' said Hunter.

Kleist mopped his eyes once more, then asked: 'How much will you pay me?'

Hunter knew he'd got him.

[ii]

They had two hundred and fifty miles to go, but the freeway was fast and arrow-straight. Even keeping the law as meticulously as they were doing, it wouldn't take more than four hours: across the state line at Goodsprings, then out to Palm Springs, skirt the Salton Sea, and then the border, go into Mexico at Calexita: law-abiding, polite, discreet, with the air-conditioning in the car going, it was even a pleasure to drive. The helicopter swept over them again, climbing, headed towards Los Angeles. FitzMaurice peered up from his window.

'Must be the movies,' he said. 'There aren't any crops to dust round here.'

He looked out at the limitless desert and yawned, and Callan glanced again into the rear view mirror. A long way back was a little, dark green dot. Callan put his foot down: seventy, seventy-five; eighty, and looked again. The dot was still there.

'Mr Tucker,' said FitzMaurice. 'I fear we are breaking the law.'

Callan eased off: the dot grew no larger.

'Sorry, Chief Shekwe,' he said. 'I never could resist the lure of speed.'

Trudi said, 'I have to go to the john.'

'Soon,' said FitzMaurice.

'Very soon,' Trudi said, 'or else I'll wet myself.' She looked brightly at Callan, as one imparting little-known information. 'Sometimes acid gets you like that.'

'Make a note, Congressman,' said FitzMaurice. 'It might come in handy for your commission.'

She managed to hold out till Palm Springs, and Callan pulled into a petrol station. The drill was simple. Elizabeth took Trudi to the powder-room, and Callan went to the men's room, leaving Manette with FitzMaurice. When he came back there was a dark green Porsche in the court, having its tyres checked. Callan ignored it, and held the doors for Trudi and Elizabeth when they came back.

'You want to go, Congressman?' said FitzMaurice. Manette nodded. 'Then I trust you're not too prejudiced, because I'm coming with you.'

They left, and Callan paid for the petrol, fastened Trudi's seat-belt, and got in beside Elizabeth.

'I should scream,' she said. 'Or struggle or something.'

'It might work,' he said, 'but the chief's with your father. If he heard you he might do something impulsive.'

She sank back against the cushions. Trudi turned to look at her.

'You should keep away from your father,' she said. 'Really you should.'

Manette and FitzMaurice came back, and FitzMaurice said, 'Mr Tucker, are you affording me the opportunity of driving this magnificent example of British craftsmanship and technology?'

'I thought you might like it, chief,' said Callan. 'It's quite easy. That pedal's the brake and that one's the accelerator and the round thing's the wheel. You steer with it.'

'I thank you, Mr Tucker,' said FitzMaurice. 'We leaders of emergent nations must learn to be proficient.' He eased the car out of the gas-station, then looked in the mirror.

'British racing green,' he said.

'It's possible,' said Callan. 'Also intrepid birdman.'

'Boy, you two are a real scream, aren't you?' said Elizabeth. 'Only now you've got so subtle I bet you don't even understand each other.'

'You're wrong,' said Callan. 'I hope we are too.'

FitzMaurice put on his peaked cap for Palm Springs. In a way he felt the place deserved it. All that money.... Some of the places looked as if they used dollar bills instead of grass on their lawns. Even fifty dollar bills. They drove through the town and out, still heading south, and FitzMaurice took his cap off and looked again in the mirror. The Porsche was a long way back, but it was there.

'Still the same colour,' he said.

Callan peered up from the window.

'No birds sing,' he said.

'So now it's culture,' said Elizabeth. 'Keats. My God.'

'Mr Tucker,' said FitzMaurice, 'I think you'd better put these good people in the picture.'

'Just as you say, chief.' Callan turned to them. 'We're being followed,' he said. It was the best news Manette had that day. 'But it isn't the CIA.'

'So you say,' said Manette.

'The SSD are looking for us,' said Callan, 'and it looks like they've found us.'

'What's the SSD?' said Elizabeth.

'East German security.'

'But that's ridiculous.'

'Is it?' said Callan. 'Ask your father.' She looked at him.

Manette said, 'It's no more impossible than these two men.'

208

'If they get us,' said Callan, 'they'll kill us. The only one they want alive is Trudi.'

The German girl reached out, and very gently touched FitzMaurice.

'Not alive, Panther,' she said. 'Not them.'

'Relax,' said FitzMaurice. 'You're with friends.'

He looked in the mirror. The Porsche still kept its distance.

'Shall we take them, Mr Tucker?' he said.

'I think we'll have to, chief,' said Callan.

They moved past a sign that said, 'Warpaint. Ten Miles. The Ghost Town That Refuses to Die.'

'Warpaint,' said FitzMaurice. 'How appropriate. I forgot to bring mine, dammit.'

The Jaguar approached a right-turn cut-off.

'Hold tight,' said FitzMaurice. 'When you're ready, Mr Tucker.'

Callan took out the Magnum.

'Just don't mix up your pedals, chief,' he said.

The big car swerved off to the right without apparent loss of speed, and in no time at all they were on a dirt road that began to twist and turn. Suddenly FitzMaurice's foot stabbed at the brake, the car slowed, slowed, and Callan opened the door and leaped out, rolled over the bank into a ditch, but FitzMaurice kept on going to the next bend before he stopped, and Elizabeth could lean over and shut the door. When she sat up, FitzMaurice was holding his Magnum, but he made no move to get out.

'Aren't you going to help him?' said Elizabeth.

'My dear,' said FitzMaurice, 'the day he needs my help we're all dead. Besides, I promised Miss von Nichts here.'

Trudi reached out; touched the Magnum.

'Panther,' she said. 'So beautiful, so terrible.'

'But you can't,' said Elizabeth.

'One day you must ask your father about that,' said FitzMaurice. 'But not now. Now you stay quiet.'

He'd fallen all right, the way he'd been taught, head tucked in, body loose, rolling over and over at once to lessen the impact, slow himself down. But the ground was hard, even the ditch was hard. His coat was ripped, and he'd be bruised for days. But he could move, and the Magnum was O.K. He wriggled along the ditch to where a boulder gave him cover, just before a bend in the road. In the distance he could hear the snarl of a Porsche driven hard. It grew louder.

They'd be worried, he thought. Bound to be. They thought all they had to do was follow Trudi all the way to Mexico: maybe wait till they got there before they kidnapped her, then first they'd seen FitzMaurice with two extra passengers they couldn't explain, and now they were heading for a ghost town, and who knew what would be there? Another car, maybe? Helicopter? Light aircraft? Callan eased off the safety catch and waited. The Porsche's snarl grew louder still, then stopped. They were good all right. Even a small car is far too big a target, and they knew it. But then the SSD always had been good, and to lift Trudi von Nichts they'd send only the best. He was sweating like a turned-on tap, his shoulder, ribs and knee ached from the dive he'd taken, and the cut that he'd had given him had opened up again and started to bleed. Otherwise, he thought, I'm fine—or I would be if those two geezers in the Porsche weren't after me.

They would come up the ditch, he thought, just as he had done—they'd have to, it was the only cover there was, and the ground was so dry it was impossible to move in silence. One feller leading, and probably not the better one, not even the faster one: leading because the better one would be in charge: the back-up man.... Callan crouched, motionless, and the sweat dripped off him in a steady stream, dried as soon as it hit the ground. For a boozer it was better than a Turkish bath.... From the ditch opposite there came a tiny sound, like a lump of soil crunching under the pressure of a hand or knee. Callan checked the road on either side. Nothing. Just that one tiny sound. Otherwise the desert was as silent as it was limitless. Come on, Callan. Time to get on with it. And oh God—let it be quick.

He moved up in silence, still shielded by the boulder. Crouching, he could see a flash of dark grey cloth, that disappeared as the ditch dipped. There was only one way—out in the open. He moved forwards and he was sure he made no noise, but even so the man in the ditch heard him, or maybe he just sensed him, and swung round to meet him, only just too late. Callan loosed off two shots, head and heart, and at that range it was impossible to miss, and his target stiffened, fired the Colt 38 he held by reflex. Poor old Callan, he thought, now even the dead are firing at you, and kept on going, hurled himself into the ditch beside the dead man. And just as well. A shot from behind him split the air he'd just been standing in and Callan kept on rolling, saw a second figure take cover behind his boulder, loosed off a shot and knew he'd missed. Nice. Very nice. If he hadn't heard that piece of soil go they'd have had him. No question. All he'd had to do was move and he'd be in a cross-fire. He wriggled up to the edge of the ditch to peer, and a bullet slammed into the ground an inch in front of him, a sliver of stone split the skin of his forehead. Callan eased back; careful, boy. That shot could have blinded you.... Time to think of his position. You could call it a stand-off maybe. Him in his ditch and Fritz in the one across the road. A sort of miniaturised version of World War One—except nobody was going to charge. Only it wasn't a stand-off, not really, because before Fritz and his mate came up the road they'd have phoned that damn chopper for reinforcements. Time was something he didn't have, and Fritz did. All the same there wasn't going to be any charge.

World War One, he thought. What he needed was a machine gun: or a couple of grenades. He had neither. All he had was a 357 Magnum and a corpse for company.... The corpse had a Colt 38. Not exactly a machine gun, but it was extra fire-power. Slowly, with infinite care, he crawled towards the dead man. This time no soil must be crushed.... Callan reached the dead man's leg then eased over on his side, hauled himself alongside the supine body, up and up till he reached the outstretched hand. Careful, son. Careful. The hand hadn't stiffened yet, but that finger on the trigger is tricky: and worse than tricky when you have to work in silence. The finger came free, and Callan eased the Colt away by the barrel.... Further up, the ditch was a hard tangle of tumbleweed. Callan eased back the hammer of the Colt, hoped to God the trigger action was easy, and lobbed it underarm at the tumbleweed. The Colt went off like a cannon and almost at once there came two answering shots, and as they sounded Callan rose up from the ditch, saw the man across the road sideways on to him and began firing. The first one went high, so that Fritz almost had time to swivel round and fire back, but that only made him a bigger target. The next two were spot on....

They could hear the shots all right. In the clear air of the desert they were like a cannonade. Three shots and a pause. Then one shot, two more; three in quick succession. FitzMaurice sat frowning, trying to work it out. Manette and Elizabeth sat huddled together, only Trudi sat easy, even relaxed. After all, the worst that could happen was she would die....

'Do you know what's happening?' Elizabeth whispered.

'No,' said FitzMaurice.

'And yet you can sit here?'

'I've got my instructions,' said FitzMaurice. 'So has he.'

From round the bend in the road came the crunch of footsteps. FitzMaurice laid the barrel of his Magnum on the open window of the car.

Trudi whispered, 'You promised.'

'I'll keep my promise,' FitzMaurice said. His words were no louder than a sigh.

Callan's voice shouted from the bend in the road: 'Chief Shekwe, I come in peace.'

211

'Come right ahead, Mr Tucker,' said FitzMaurice, and Callan appeared, tattered, forehead bleeding, walking with a limp; in his hands two Colt 38's.

'Two gun Callan,' he said. 'The Terror of Warpaint.'

'You get them both?' said FitzMaurice.

'Yeah,' said Callan, 'they're dead,' and opened the car's boot, sought and found a fresh coat.

'Why did you bring their guns?' said Manette.

'Congressman,' said Callan, 'you should never leave loaded guns lying about. They might fall into the wrong hands.'

He got in the back of the car, and at once Elizabeth moved away from him.

'Let's go,' he said.

Down the dirt road, with a body on each side of the ditch, to squeeze past the Porsche and get back on the freeway so that FitzMaurice could open her up, race for Westmorland, park in an uncompleted development on the outside of town, then walk. Callan and the rest sat in silence, looking at the empty, half-completed street.

At last Elizabeth said, 'I can't believe it. You just killed two men.' He gave no answer: there was no answer to give.

'Don't you feel anything?' said the girl.

Carefully Callan wiped off the places in the car that he and FitzMaurice had touched.

'Yes, I feel something,' he said.

'What?'

'I feel glad they didn't kill me.' She winced, and he added, 'If they had they'd have killed you.'

'That's what your partner said.'

'It's true,' said Callan. 'The SSD wouldn't leave witnesses on this job. Not even a Congressman and his daughter.'

Then FitzMaurice came back. He was driving a Lincoln Convertible, two years old at most: metallic blue body, pale blue seats.

'I got this from a place called Mad Maxy's,' he said. 'Our prices are insane, it said. I must have been insane to pay them.'

He and Callan transferred first baggage, then passengers, and moved off, skirting the town, rejoining once more the main highway south. Beyond Brawley a helicopter chattered down, its pilot looking for a black Jaguar 4·2. It didn't find one.

212

26

They crossed the border at Calexita. Once again Callan was driving, and Elizabeth was squeezed between her father and FitzMaurice. FitzMaurice's right hand was in his coat pocket, and Manette was well aware that the pocket also contained a gun. FitzMaurice didn't elaborate on the fact: he didn't have to, and knew it. As they went through the two frontier posts, all Manette had to do was yell. But Manette was well briefed on hi-jackers and terrorists, and knew, far better than the average newspaper reader, that in that kind of situation the hostages had no chance at all, not if the hi-jackers meant it. And these two had to mean it: he'd seen the two dead bodies. Manette thought of his daughter, and exerted himself to get VIP treatment. It wasn't difficult. A U.S. Congressman and an African potentate were the two most important people to come through that day. They didn't even have their baggage checked. The car moved into Mexico and through the town: cantinas, souvenir shops, brothels, the chance of grass—then they turned and headed east, mile after mile, and thank God the Lincoln had air-conditioning too.

At last Elizabeth said, 'I'm hungry,' and they pulled into a drive-in that was Mexican as hell: tortillas and tacos, eight kinds of chilli, and cold dark beer. Callan drank coke.

Manette said, 'What's the matter, Tucker? Are you another Wino?'

'I don't drink when I'm driving,' said Callan.

'Or killing?'

Callan looked at FitzMaurice and quoted: 'If I drank they would have taken me.'

FitzMaurice chuckled.

'Where are you taking *us*?' Manette asked.

'All in good time, Congressman,' FitzMaurice said.

'I warn you,' said Manette. 'I'll be missed.'

FitzMaurice considered. 'Oh, I don't think so,' he said at last. 'Didn't you tell me you and your charming daughter were coming to Mexico? You're *in* Mexico.' He leaned forward to Trudi. 'My dear,' he said, 'won't you eat just a little?'

'I don't need food,' she said.

'You mean you don't want it.' He broke off a piece of tortilla, dipped it in sauce, and held it to her mouth. 'Come on,' he said. 'Oblige your panther.' She managed three mouthfuls without gagging, and they drove on through country that was hardly different from that which they'd left behind in the States: Baja California, Sonora, Sierra Madre: desert and more desert. Only in Mexico the poor people they saw really knew they were poor.

When they reached Gallego it was dark. The town, for some reason, displeased FitzMaurice: perhaps it was too dusty, or too hot, or even too ill-lit, or perhaps it was that corrugated iron played too prominent a part in its architecture. For whatever reason he waited till they were through the town, then said, 'I think this will do, Mr Tucker.'

Callan eased the car to a halt, and FitzMaurice turned to Manette.

'This is where you leave us, Congressman,' he said.

Manette looked bewildered.

'I don't understand you,' he said.

'It's quite easy,' said FitzMaurice. 'You open the door, you get out, and you walk back to Gallego. After that you're on your own.'

Manette said, 'My briefcase please.'

'You don't have a briefcase,' said FitzMaurice, 'just a passport.' He handed it over.

Manette took it and put it in his pocket, then reached for the door-knob.

'Come on, Elizabeth,' he said.

His daughter was more perceptive: she made no attempt to move.

FitzMaurice said, 'She stays.'

'I won't leave her,' said Manette. 'I can't.'

'You think I'll hurt her?'

'You already have,' said Manette.

'No,' said FitzMaurice. 'Not *hurt*, Congressman. If you want to know what happens when I hurt people, ask Mr Tucker here.'

Manette said, 'I can't just leave her.'

'You must,' said FitzMaurice. 'You keep your mouth shut and she'll be fine.'

'How do I know that?'

'She'll call you,' said FitzMaurice. 'You go back to Washington and she'll call you in a couple of days.'

'Couldn't I go home?' said Manette.

'Your wife's at home,' said FitzMaurice. 'Do you think you could

214

hide it from her? Now, you kiss your daughter and go.'

Manette turned to his daughter, who embraced him very quickly. FitzMaurice opened the door and Manette climbed out.

'I'll be all right,' said Elizabeth. 'Honestly, dad. You'll see.'

'Of course you will,' said FitzMaurice, 'unless your daddy does something foolish.' He turned to Manette, 'Oh, Congressman, I almost forgot. Do you have enough money?' He reached for his wallet.

'Yes, damn you,' said Manette. 'I have.' The Lincoln moved off.

They had a place ready near Chihuahua: the tatty ruins of a hacienda with two habitable rooms and a landing strip that ran almost up to the front door. Waiting there for them, too, were a suitcase filled with women's clothes and a supply of canned food, but no sign of another human being. Save for themselves, the hacienda, the entire landscape, was empty. Callan lit wood in the stove, added charcoal, put water on to boil, while FitzMaurice looked at Trudi.

'You did well, my dear,' he said, and reached out to touch her arm.

'It doesn't last,' she said. 'It never lasts.'

'I can give you something for that,' he said.

'Acid?' she said. 'You brought some?'

'Tomorrow,' he said. 'I promise you. Tomorrow. Today I—'

'Tomorrow's too late,' she said.

'Today I can help you to survive,' he said. 'Come with me. I'll show you.'

He moved away, and she followed like a child.

Elizabeth looked at Callan. He was opening a can of stew, his hands deft and easy as always: craftsman's hands, killer's hands.

'Are you by any chance hoping to cure Trudi?' she said. 'Because if so acid is the last—'

'I'm not going to cure her,' he said. 'All I have to do is deliver her.'

'But why, Tucker? Why?'

'I've been told to,' he said. 'In this business you do what you're told. Ask—'

'—My father. I know. Isn't that kind of a cheap way to argue?'

'He knows,' Callan said, 'and I know. You don't.'

'Like chess, isn't it?' she said. 'To you that poor girl's no more than a pawn.'

He smiled then. He became a different person when he smiled: relaxed, even civilised.

'Oh no,' he said. 'We're the pawns. Chief Shekwe, your father, you and me. Trudi's a queen.'

'A red queen?'

He emptied the stew into a pot, set it on the stove to heat.

'Honestly,' he said, 'if I were you I wouldn't get involved.'

Dear God, she thought, he means it. He's killed two men and he means it.

'You said you were a freelance,' she said.

He stirred the pot. 'So I did,' he said, 'but freedom is a relative term, Miss Manette.'

'But who could possibly force you to do this?'

'Do you think,' said Callan, 'do you really think your father's the only one who's held by a hostage?'

'Your wife?' she said.

'A mate,' said Callan.

'Mate? Oh.... Like a friend.'

'Yeah,' said Callan. 'Like a friend.'

FitzMaurice came in, and sniffed at the pot. 'Smells good,' he said.

'Just like mother used to make,' said Callan.

'Jesus, I hope not,' FitzMaurice turned to Elizabeth. 'I beg your pardon,' he said, 'but you never tasted my mother's cooking.... Trudi's asleep. She should be out till early morning. There's a plane due at dawn.'

'Can I ask where we're going?' Elizabeth asked.

'Not yet.' The words were gently spoken. 'It won't be long.' He turned to Callan. 'Could I have some of that stew? I've got to go into Chihuahua.'

'To speak to Charlie?'

'He'll be avid to hear,' said FitzMaurice.

When he'd gone Callan went to take a look at Trudi: Elizabeth followed. The German girl wore a shirt of FitzMaurice's in place of a nightdress, her hair was combed, her face clean. She looked young and vulnerable and ill. Despite the heat, a sheet and blanket covered her. Gently Callan touched her forearm: it was cool to the touch. He pulled the bedclothes up to her chin, and she sighed in her sleep.

'The poor kid,' said Elizabeth.

'Kid?' said Callan. 'She's older than you.'

'After what she's been through,' said Elizabeth, 'she's older than God.'

They went back to the other habitable room, and shared out the stew. Outside, the moon shone on an arid landscape: hard-baked earth, cactus and scrub. No sight, no sound of any living thing. Elizabeth looked out and shuddered.

'Dear God,' she said, 'it looks like the Bomb already fell.'

Callan went on eating stew: it wasn't much good, but it was fuel.

'Maybe now's when I should run,' she said. He didn't even put down his spoon.

'Run?' he said. 'Run where? The chief has the car. You want to go out in that on foot?'

'You really had it all figured out,' she said.

'We didn't figure on you and your father.'

'But you handled us well,' she said. 'You really know your job, Mr Tucker.'

'Thank you.'

Jesus, she thought, have you got an armour-plated hide. Somehow it wasn't just important, it was essential to make a dent in it.

'You must feel pretty good,' she said, 'using that wretched girl as a weapon against her own father.'

'Oh, I won't do that,' he said. 'I'm not nearly important enough. All I do is deliver her.'

'And me.'

'That's right.'

'You saw that place in Norn Street,' she said. 'Don't you realise what a mess she is? If you hand her over you'll make her worse.' He went on eating. 'Do you know what a Norn is? Do you?'

'Yeah,' he said. 'A virgin goddess.'

'I bet you and your tribal friend had a good laugh at that.'

He finished eating, took his bowl and cutlery into the kitchen, came back with two cups of coffee.

'You have the makings of an ironist,' he said, 'but you still lack polish. That's because you're still young, of course.'

'You disgust me.'

'Do I? I've done no more than your father would have done. Does he disgust you too?'

She found she couldn't answer.

'I killed two men today. But you didn't have to watch. And if you'll forgive the cliché, Miss Manette, if I hadn't killed them they'd have killed you. I saved your life.'

'And what do you expect in return? My beautiful body?'

He went on as if she hadn't spoken.

'Your father talked about his country—and himself. In that order. I could talk about my country too. And I could certainly put that unfortunate cliché to good use. I could pretend I'm Saint George, Miss Manette, but it wouldn't be true. I told you. I have a mate they can put the squeeze on, just as we can put the squeeze on you to manipulate your father.'

'Who's they?' she asked.

'I hope a nice girl like you never has to know,' he said.

She looked again out of the window: at the dead moonlit land.

217

'In the midst of death you are in death,' she said. 'You really belong here.'

'Culture,' he said. 'Elegant misquotation. I'm glad to see your expensive education wasn't wasted, Miss Manette.'

He was as impassive as ever, but she'd got through, and she knew it. The dent in the armour had been made.

'I'm sorry,' she said. 'I shouldn't have said that.'

'That's all right.'

He'd taken off his jacket: the gun in its harness was still in place.

'Do you have to wear that thing?' she asked.

'You might forget I'm not Saint George and start being Joan of Arc,' he said.

'What would happen if I did?'

'You'd get hurt,' he said. He spoke without emotion, as one stating an obvious fact, and she couldn't bear it. She began to cry.

Callan reached for the Magnum, broke it open. He'd cleaned it and reloaded the first chance he'd got, and he took out all six shells, slipped them into his trouser pocket, put down the gun and shrugged off the webbing harness.

'Is that any better?' he asked.

She nodded. 'Now you look like a man,' she said. 'Just a man,' and went on sobbing, looked for, failed to find her purse. Callan gave her his handkerchief, and she took it, then grabbed his hand, turned her body into his. Gently, paternally, his arms came round her, and her sobbing eased at last, but she made no move to be free. His body felt hard all through, with a hardness that seemed burned in, the way steel is forged.

'I'm afraid of you,' she said. 'You know that, don't you?' Then she kissed him. Her lips tasted innocent and sweet.

'Miss Manette,' he said, 'this is no way to buy me off.'

'I'm not doing that,' she said. 'You know I'm not.'

His arms tightened round her: he was gentle and very patient, until at last her body found its release, and with it, courage. She slept.

Callan covered her with a sheet, poured water from a jug into a basin, and splashed water on his face. It was well-water, and bitterly cold. He soaked the end of a towel, rubbed his sweating body, dried off and began to dress. A car's tyres crunched on the hard-packed earth, and he grabbed for the Magnum, punched the shells home, and took up a position behind the door. FitzMaurice came in, and Callan put the Magnum's muzzle to the nape of his neck. FitzMaurice froze, then said, 'I see you found yourself a Norn.'

218

Callan moved round to face him.

'I wish you wouldn't fool around with that thing,' said FitzMaurice.

Callan said, 'You told me not to take chances.'

'I did indeed,' said FitzMaurice, 'but I don't think you did as you were told.' He looked towards the sleeping girl. 'Young love isn't good for middle-aged men, Mr Tucker. It makes them vulnerable.'

27

It was not difficult: merely dreadful. All he had to do was carry out the appalling Toby Meres' instructions, and that perhaps was the most dreadful thing of all: the knowledge that if one did precisely as this Englishman said there would be no trouble: virtually no risk.... He had gone to work and been made welcome, and had undergone a certain amount of good-humoured leg-pull because he'd gone back to work the day before he need have done. Good old Gunther, they teased him. No sooner had he seen the doctor than he comes back to us. Can't keep away. The fools. The poor, blind fools. They didn't know that the *hochgeboren* Graf von Kleist had come back to steal a copy of Marx's *Kapital*: an East German paper-back. They didn't know that he'd failed. These pedestrian, pension-orientated helots didn't know anything that mattered. The knowledge of this fact had cheered him briefly, but when the time came for him to go to the closed archives he'd felt no cheer at all.

Even so, Meres had been right about one thing: it was not difficult. The mechanics of the exercise were easy, if anything. What was difficult was the fear of discovery, and even if Meres had assured him that that risk was minimal, how could one believe such a liar? He went into the secret archives, and waited, patiently, as the guard inspected his pass, made the inevitable telephone call. Just do it as you always do it, Meres had said. So long as you've got a good reason for being there you're all right. Just look bored or patient or fed-up. Whatever it is you usually look. And being himself he looked patient; not because he'd worked it out, he thought later, but because that was his nature. He looked patient because he *was* patient. He endured.... The secret archives had once been a wine merchant's cellars. The wine merchant had been bankrupted long since, but the cellars remained: vast, bone-dry, grey-stoned. A place of unrelieved gloom, even though the neon lighting was overwhelming. To be patient here wasn't just a help, it was a necessity.

The guard he got was Traub: slow, cautious, middle-aged. He walked with a slight limp, but his big hands were competent: the Walther automatic he carried was there for use. There were rumours among the archivists that he'd been in the SS. Traub had known Kleist for years, but even so he took his pass from him and read it through word by word before he gave it back.

'Herr Kleist,' he said. 'I haven't seen you for a long time.'

'I've been ill,' said Kleist.

'Nothing serious, I hope?'

Do not talk about nervous breakdowns, Meres had said.

'Rheumatism,' said Kleist.

'Ach, what I could tell you about rheumatism,' said Traub, and did so. Mostly it was the Ukraine, and the impossibility of finding shelter from the snow.

'You saw a lot of action,' Kleist said.

'I did,' said Traub. 'Believe me, Herr Kleist, we are better off in the cellars, even if they have taken the wine way.'

They walked down the corridors that echoed to the sound of their footsteps, and even though he limped Kleist could hear in Traub's tread the sound of jackboots: the rigid discipline, the assured sense of purpose, the days of Germany's greatness. The days of Graf von Kleist.... As they walked they passed on either side deep recesses, carved into rock and faced with stone. Each recess was covered by steel mesh, and set into the mesh was a solid steel gate. The mesh, Kleist knew, was resistant to anything short of high explosive: the gates had been supplied with a few tricks to combat even that. Every recess had the very latest anti-burglar devices, and every recess had a guard armed with a machine pistol and a Walther automatic. The archives were proof against everything, thought Kleist, except perhaps treachery.

At last they arrived at Bin Gamma 17. It had amused some senior civil servant long retired to go on calling the recesses bins, to keep the memory of the wine trade alive. Meres had discussed the method of his approach in great detail. Gamma 17, Kleist knew, was a depository for 'soft' secret stuff in espionage, stuff that didn't warrant the ferocious expense needed to guard the hard stuff in the alpha and beta bins. It was also the repository for industrial secrets, electronics, atomic experiments, the republic's so far abortive experiments in space-rocketry. Kleist had long since been briefed to collate information on all three. 'After all, Kleist,' his head of section had told him, 'Germany may be a creditor nation, but there is a recession. We must cut down. I want a full report. A very full report. See to it please.' They were hardly the words to use to a graf who could trace his ancestry back in an unbroken line for three and a half centuries, but Kleist endured them. He pressed the buzzer on the door of Bin Gamma 17.

The inside guard was young and bored. When Traub said, 'This is Herr Kleist,' he accepted Kleist's pass through the mesh and hardly bothered to look before he opened up. Traub was outraged.

'These young people,' he said to Kleist. 'Half asleep all the time. Just because I said you were Herr Kleist, does he have to believe it? You might have been anybody. An enemy even.'

The door swung open and Kleist went through. As he moved over to the clerk in charge the steel door shut with a controlled thud.

The clerk in charge of Gamma 17 was Neumann, and he was on duty: the one bit of luck that they needed, Meres had said, but then Meres hadn't had to go into Gamma 17. Even so, Kleist had to admit that having Neumann there helped. He and Kleist were of an age and, in a tepid way, friends, their friendship based on common interests, and a scholar's nostalgia for the kind of things that had no relevance to their workaday lives. Books, calf-bound, manuscripts, holograph. These were the things they yearned for: not these electronic toys.

Neumann was as always pleased to see him, and totally unconcerned about his state of health. The British Council had recently mounted an exhibition of books and manuscripts from Oxford's Bodleian Library. Had Herr Kleist seen it? Too bad, too bad. Sick leave, even in Taormina, was no compensation for having missed such esoteric delights. There had been some fifteenth-century Italian stuff. As he spoke he checked the list that Kleist had given him.

'Non-ferrous metals,' he said. 'That isn't classified, Herr Kleist. These will be in Delta Five.'

'Yes,' said Kleist. 'I know. It would seem that I am in for a very busy day.'

He turned to Neumann, who saw how ill he looked, even after Taormina. Neumann was a compassionate man, and this also had been allowed for.

'I'll get them for you,' he said. 'You can do them here. Just help yourself to the other stuff. It's all in the index.'

He went to the guard, murmured something, and the door opened and closed. Help yourself, thought Kleist. Is this what the discipline of our country has come to? Then, be charitable, he thought. Neumann is your friend. With friendship goes trust, and you repay it with betrayal. And then: How Meres would despise me for such thoughts. He went to the index, noted the numbers of three items: a government committee on electronics, a Ph.D. thesis, and a survey of copper futures, then he memorised the number for the espionage spool. Neumann would take at least ten minutes to get to Delta 5 and back, so don't take the espionage stuff first, said Meres. He might just change his mind. Kleist pulled open the tray on raw-materials, took the copper-futures survey from its slot, and laid it on the copying-table. Behind him the guard yawned: there was no sign of Neumann. It was now. It had to be now, otherwise Meres and the man called Hunter would destroy him: there would be no more money. He slid open the espionage tray and, glanced, unhurriedly, at the guard. The guard was peering out through the mesh. Kleist heard the click-click of a woman's footsteps and hoped she was pretty. He took out the spool Hunter needed, and replaced it with the blank he'd been given, using his handkerchief to hold it. There must be no fingerprints, Hunter had told him. They didn't want him discovered.... Kleist pushed the tray closed and went in search of the doctoral thesis. By the time Neumann came back Kleist was already busy at the photo-copier, and Neumann, the friend who trusted him, fussed round and gave assistance.

Every sheet of photo-copying had to be checked by Neumann and signed for by Kleist, every item of micro-photography restored to its place, and both men performed their tasks meticulously. When they had done, Kleist locked the sheets in his briefcase, chained it to his wrist while Traub was summoned, then walked under escort to the ministry car with its uniformed chauffeur to be driven back to the office of his Head of Section, hand over the sheets, wait while his Head of Section counted them and signed a receipt. The instructions were, Kleist knew, that when the information required had been collated, the section head should burn the sheets, and Kleist knew that he would, and break up the charred remains, and flush them down the lavatory. And it was all no good. A total waste of time. All that thoroughness, all that security, and good old Gunther, harmless, trustworthy Archivist Kleist, had walked in and helped himself to one of his country's secrets, and as a result, rather a lot of deutschmarks. And nobody would have cause to suspect him, that was the beauty of it. By the index was a record of withdrawals book that was renewed every six months, in which the use of every spool was recorded. The page for the spool he had stolen was blank. Six months, and nobody had even looked at the thing, so who would suspect good old Gunther? When you came to think about it, Kleist considered, most people, even most Germans, were fools.

[ii]

'I don't think much of this place,' said Spanner.

Hexham yawned. 'I shouldn't think anybody would,' he said.

It was a bed and breakfast place in South London, the kind that catered for itinerant businessmen on the way up, or down: technical representatives, sales representatives, the chap from the Costs Department who doesn't rate a hotel up West because it might spoil him, but even so is indispensable. It was in a street where there were a dozen like it: two or three terrace houses knocked into one; adequately clean, adequately equipped, catering not bad if you liked eggs and bacon, but otherwise appalling, and fire traps all of them. Interchangeable as processed peas, except that the Balmoral Private Hotel, terms strictly cash, was owned and serviced by the SSD. Not that they didn't take in paying customers as well: their cover made that essential. The Balmoral was in fact the only SSD operation in the U.K. that showed a profit.

All the same, Hexham conceded, it had its drawbacks: it was as clean, antiseptic and dull as the people's republic itself, and if you weren't allowed to go out it was incredibly boring, particularly if you had only Spanner for company. The perfect place to grow a beard, in fact, which was precisely what he was doing.

'Hand of cards?' said Spanner, for perhaps the thousandth time.

'Old chap,' said Hexham reproachfully. 'I thought I'd made my position clear on that. Not with a professional. Never again.'

'Yeah,' said Spanner. 'Old Bulk knows his stuff all right.'

He got up and switched on the telly, glared at a picture of an old bird unwrapping a loaf of bread, and switched it off again.

'What are we going to do then?' he said, also for the thousandth time.

'We're going to wait for a word,' said Hexham, 'and when we get the word we're going to take care of Berkeley and Callan, and you're going to get paid.'

'I'm neglecting my business,' said Spanner.

Hexham said patiently, 'We're keeping an eye on it. I told you. It's all right.'

Abruptly as a switched off telly, Spanner went to sleep. It was a trick he'd learned in the nick, the time he'd done solitary. Even when he was asleep Hexham looked on him with patience. Spanner was live-bait, and live-bait's useless when it's nervous. Hexham went back to passing the time by growing a beard.

224

Callan yawned, almost went back to sleep, then opened his eyes. Elizabeth sat up in bed, looking at him. The one paraffin lamp showed her body half in shadow. It did nothing to obscure the Magnum she held.

'You're holding it wrong,' he said, and stood up to stretch.

'I could have killed you,' said Elizabeth.

'Not with the safety catch on,' he said.

She looked down at the gun and he was on her at once, the patient, gentle hands savage and quick. Callan broke the gun open, spun the six empty chambers.

'And anyway,' he said, 'if you weren't going to use ammunition you'd have had to clout me over the head with it.'

She nursed her bruised hand. 'You knew all the time,' she said, and he nodded. 'Then why—'

He tossed the empty Magnum on to a chair.

'Guns are only for experts,' he said, 'and not always for them.'

'You hurt me,' she said.

'You had a gun.'

'I could have done it,' she said. 'Hit you and run.'

'You think the chief would let you?'

'He's back then?'

'Yeah,' said Callan. 'He's back.'

She thought of the black man: cultured, civilised, perhaps even wise: but she shuddered.

'You're a great team, aren't you?' she said. 'Is his best friend a hostage too?'

'I don't know his motivation,' he said, 'and I don't want to know.' He looked out of the window. The moon had set, but in the darkness the first pale light of the false dawn would soon appear.

'We'll be moving soon,' he said.

'How long?'

He shrugged. 'An hour. Maybe a little longer.'

She pushed the sheet aside. 'We've time then.'

'You're a very greedy little girl,' he said.

'But, grandpapa,' said Elizabeth, 'you make such delicious candy.'

Later she thought that Bill Yerkes was right. She really did prefer older men. No, wait now. That was going too fast. She preferred this older man. He'd hurt her, terrified her, and she'd forgiven him for it almost without thinking, but he'd humiliated and frightened her father, too—most loved gorilla—and she'd forgiven him that. No, that was wrong too. How could she have forgiven him? Forgiveness meant being aware of a sin to be

225

pardoned. She hadn't even considered it: all she knew was that he was there and she wanted him, demanded that his body should entwine with hers. He'd been beautiful, and my God she was sleepy, and soon it would be time to go. She washed herself in the icy water, did what she could with lipstick and comb, and Callan came in with a jug of coffee and cups, the Chief came out of Trudi's room. Both men had shaved, both men were neatly dressed—the Chief even managed a certain elegance, and both were, incredibly, relaxed. They even looked rested. FitzMaurice looked at his watch.

'He'll be here in twenty minutes,' he said.

No coy little jokes, she thought. No cute cracks about lovebirds. Chief Shekwe, you really do know about tact.

'How's the patient?' said Callan.

'Not good,' said FitzMaurice. 'She'll need a little more happiness powder before we get her aboard.'

'Would you like me to stay with her a while?' said Elizabeth.

FitzMaurice said, 'No, Miss Manette, I would not. But I thank you.'

'Honestly I'd be glad—' she began.

'You would not,' said FitzMaurice. 'Believe me. The things she does, the things she says. You would not be glad, Miss Manette.'

He poured a cup of coffee, and went back to Trudi. As he opened the door they could hear a rhythmic thumping, and a voice that was quite mad repeating the same phrase in German, over and over.

'I understand German,' she said.

'Me too,' said Callan. 'At least I know enough to understand that.' He smiled. There was neither mirth nor pleasure in the smile. 'The head of our little group thought I would be the one to handle her,' he said.

'You handled me instead.'

'Even he couldn't reckon on you turning up,' he said.

'I'm going to miss you, Mr Tucker,' she said.

'And I you, Miss Manette. But not quite yet. You're coming with us.'

'You're going to use me?' she said. 'Like Trudi?'

'No,' said Callan. 'You know better than that. You phone your father, you take a little trip with us, just for insurance, then you're free to go.'

'If you promise me, I'll believe you,' she said.

'Then I promise you.'

She looked out of the window. The dawn was real now, a delicate, slow-deepening pink that warmed even this nightmare land. But it wouldn't last. Nothing so beautiful could last.

226

'Will Trudi ever get better?' she asked.

'She'll see a man who can do it—if it can be done at all,' he said.

'Then go back to her father?'

'For me the operation's over when we get back,' he said. 'What happens after that—' he shrugged.

'Is none of your business?'

'That's right.'

'You shouldn't say that,' she said. 'Not you.' He made no answer. 'What will you do when you get back?'

'Get drunk,' he said.

'You don't have to.'

'Oh but I do,' he said. 'You'll be going back too.'

She took it because she was learning how to. In this business you learned how to absorb all the punishment thrown at you, and keep on going.

'You told me last night that you weren't a mercenary,' she said. 'You're not one, are you?'

He thought, for some reason not being a mercenary will make me look better. Then he thought of Meres.

'No,' he said. 'I'm not a mercenary.'

From outside there sounded the drone of a light aircraft.

'Drink your coffee,' he said. 'We'll be leaving soon.'

28

They had told him that under no circumstances was he to visit Hunter's hotel on his own. Always he must check with Meres first, and this to him was incomprehensible. He was perfectly competent—hadn't he just proved it?—and anyway he was at home now. This was Bonn, not Sicily. Here he could take care of himself. When he got back to Schiller Strasse at the end of the day and Meres was out, he was furious. He'd stolen the damn thing for them; the least they could do was take it from him. And pay him…. There was a café nearby where he and Meres had eaten: Meres seemed to like the place. Maybe he was there….

Meres sipped at his lager and tried to remember when he'd last been so worried. It must have been a long time ago. Killing that stupid bitch could ruin him. Hunter hadn't said so: Hunter rarely used emotive words like 'ruin', 'blackmail', 'destroy'. You had to work it out from his mannerisms; the sarcasm, the silences. Well, he *had* worked it out, and he was worried. If that *bloody* address book didn't have something…. He looked at his watch. Time to be getting back to Gunther. More than time. And suddenly there Gunther was, looking down at him and far from pleased.

'We told you,' said Meres. 'Don't go out alone.'

'You weren't there,' Kleist said. 'I want to get rid of it.'

Meres finished his lager.

'And I want to be paid,' said Kleist. 'Now.'

Meres looked at him. Our Gunther was feeling his oats: he'd done a big job and he wasn't going to be messed about.

'We'll go outside and you can give it to me,' he said. 'You'll be paid.'

'Now,' said Kleist.

Decision time, Meres thought. There's bound to be a tail on him, but Hunter really needs that list. He'd have to chance it.

The café was in a busy square, but somehow Meres had managed to find parking space for the Mercedes. Nobody tried anything on the way to the car: there were too many people about,

228

too many cars. Far too many. One of them, or more probably two, was tailing Gunther. There was no point in going for a drive: they could follow him all the way, not even bother to hide what they were doing. Sooner or later he'd have to go to Hunter's hotel, and that would be that.... He eased into the traffic and drove carefully away. This was no time to have a traffic accident, not with what master-spy Gunther was carrying. The two cars assigned to follow Kleist did a neat, smooth job, just the way they'd been taught. They used an Opel and a Volkswagen: in Bonn traffic they were about as identifiable as blades of grass in a field. When Meres spotted the lead car, the Opel, and turned right, away from the Square, the Opel headed straight on, and the VW took over. Meres didn't even know: there was no way he could.

He parked away from the hotel and walked back as the VW slowed for traffic lights. By the time the lights turned green he and Kleist were entering the hotel, but he looked back from its doors. The VW drove away. He'd got the address he needed.... Meres phoned Hunter's room from the desk, and Hunter was down in three minutes, suitcase packed, briefcase firmly held. Neither he nor Meres had time for Kleist. They hustled him out by a side-door, took a bus, then a taxi, and on to a café, where they phoned for a car that took them to a house in Bad Godesberg. During the car journey Kleist was blindfolded. The event displeased him, but it occurred.... It was a quiet house in a quiet neighbourhood, but nobody was unduly worried when three men arrived rather late, and one of them looked rather disturbed. Homes for wealthy alcoholics quite often do attract disturbed-looking gentlemen at all kinds of hours.... A male nurse built on the general lines of a heavyweight wrestler brought them coffee.

'You'll get rid of the Mercedes tomorrow,' said Hunter.

'Of course, sir. Will I need another car?'

'Not hired,' said Hunter. 'They're too easily traced. If necessary you must buy one, Toby.' He sighed. 'This operation is costing a fortune. Cars. Hotels.'

Then why didn't you come here in the first place? Meres wondered. It's the safest house we've got. Hunter looked at him.

'You're wondering why I didn't come here,' he said.

'Not my business, sir.'

'Agreed,' said Hunter. 'But you were wondering. I'm known here, Toby. The house is not. If I'd been spotted at the airport—'

'Quite so, sir,' said Meres, and wondered yet again how anybody could hope to hide anything from Hunter.

'I think it is time,' said Kleist, 'that someone gave me an explanation.' His tone was pleasant, but firm. He would stand no nonsense. 'After all I did procure the microfilm for you....'

'Ah yes,' said Hunter. 'The microfilm. May I have it please?'
Kleist handed it over.

'There is the matter of my payment,' he said.

At once Hunter opened his briefcase and handed over a manila envelope. 'I think we'd better have the film checked before you open that,' he said.

'Of course,' said Kleist. That was reasonable, even fair.

Hunter handed the microfilm to Meres, who went out, and returned almost at once. Hunter poured coffee.

'And now,' said Kleist, 'I should like to know why we play this ridiculous game of cops and robbers.'

Hunter looked at Meres.

'Because you're being followed,' said Meres.

'Followed?'

'By the SSD. Don't worry, old chap. There's nothing to worry about.'

Neither he nor Hunter believed it.

'But why should they follow me? How could they know—'

'You've been seen with an Englishman,' said Meres. 'Me. Naturally they are interested.'

'But—'

'My dear fellow,' said Hunter, 'Bonn is a hot-bed of espionage.' The cliché pleased him. 'A positive hot-bed. I sometimes wonder if there's one adult in the place who isn't spying for somebody. Consider yourself for instance.'

But the implied threat didn't work: not at once.

'Then they'll investigate me?'

'They'll discover,' said Hunter, 'that you met an Englishman on holiday: that he drove back to Bonn with you, and then went home.'

'But they know I went to Taormina. And he—'

'Thousands of Englishmen go to Taormina,' said Hunter. 'There really is nothing to worry about. Toby won't be your controller ever again.' Kleist relaxed. 'Next time we'll use somebody else— and change him after every operation.'

'Next time?' said Kleist. 'Every operation?'

'My dear chap,' Hunter said, 'you're far too valuable a tool to be allowed to go rusty....'

They missed Hunter, Meres and Kleist by minutes, but they heard all about the two cool Englishmen, the bewildered German. One of the hotel desk-clerks was sympathetic, and showed them the older Englishman's registration. His passport had been impeccable, but the clerk hadn't checked him in. They didn't get a description, and all the chambermaid could remember was that he was tall, and looked like the kind of English film-actor who plays lords. They took their crumbs to their controller, who was displeased, and said so, dismissed them and pondered.... The controller had seen photographs of Hunter when he'd attended the Munich Olympics to do a little quiet recruiting. Hunter could well play a lord. Maybe he was one. And Kleist had been to the archives that day. There was no sense in taking chances. Either their people in Las Vegas would pick up Ortrud Bauer, or this would degenerate into a revenge operation. He wasn't going to risk good operatives for anything as useless as vengeance. The controller booked a call to London, and worked on a coded message as he waited. A bewildered East German helicopter pilot had just reported from California. It looked as though it would be revenge after all.... He was still looking at his watch when the call to London came through....

The wrestling nurse came in, and handed Hunter a sheet of photo-copy. Hunter examined it and was pleased. He rose.

'I'd better talk to London,' he said. 'You may open your envelope now, Herr von Kleist.' Then to Meres, 'See our friend home safely.'

That meant more indignity, but Kleist endured it. They had told him there was nothing to worry about, and he'd made rather a lot of money. Meres handed him over to another wrestling nurse, who blindfolded him and drove him back to Bonn. He was obliged to lie on the floor of a car, which was unpleasant, but the feel of the deutschmarks in his pocket was not. The nurse released him at a taxi-rank. Kleist didn't even know he'd been to Bad Godesberg.

Meres bodyguarded Hunter to see Bonn's Mr Evers. The duty officer at the embassy was of course displeased, but Hunter outranked him. There was nothing he could do. Hunter talked to his headquarters and read off a list of addresses from the photo-copy sheet.

'That's all, Liz,' he said. 'See it's attended to.'

Liz said quickly, 'There's one urgent signal, sir. In clear.'

'Very well,' said Hunter. Liz knew well what was urgent, and what merely seemed so.

'From F.C.,' she said. 'En route. Two m. Two f.'

'Thank you, Liz,' said Hunter, and hung up, turned to Meres. For once, Meres noted, he looked bewildered.

'Mexico City,' he said. 'FitzMaurice and Callan are on the plane.'

'That's excellent, sir.'

'Indeed it is. It would appear they have the young lady we require.... They also have another young lady, and I do not require two. Just what the devil are those two playing at?' He looked at his watch. 'Can you arrange for somebody to take your hire car back?'

'They'll squawk, sir.'

'Inevitably. See to it, will you, Toby? We have a plane to catch. Thank God we won't have to buy a car after all.'

[ii]

They'd flown by Piper Cherokee from Chihuahua to Mexico City, a cramped, uncomfortable journey of eight hundred miles. Three hours, and one refuelling stop, and a bored and competent pilot who couldn't have cared less if they were spies or Mafiosi or the Salvation Army, so long as he'd been paid. Elizabeth looked down at the land beneath her: it was vast, as America was vast, but she'd been used to the orderly neatness of New England: the hard-baked browns and reds, the occasional cool flash of green, were new to her, and beautiful; but she knew it would be a hard, even a cruel place in which to survive.... Beside FitzMaurice Trudi sat, drugged and tranquil. She was happy to be near him, to touch his arm sometimes and watch him smile. Somewhere beneath her consciousness there were thoughts that could worry, even hurt, but her Panther had given her something that kept them buried. Her panther was kind.

As they neared Mexico City airport, FitzMaurice produced bandages, began to wind them over Trudi's face, his big hands gentle and skilled. Trudi submitted because it was good, even inevitable, to submit. The panther was dangerous only when you did not allow him to be kind. When he had done, FitzMaurice injected her again, his hands as gentle and competent as ever. Trudi turned drowsy at once: in a minute she was asleep, and his massive arm came round her, supporting her.

Elizabeth said, 'She's been drugged so much.'

'She's a strong girl,' said Callan. 'She must be.'

'It's crazy,' she said. 'He could destroy her, and he's so gentle.'

'You've got it all wrong,' said Callan. 'We don't want to destroy her. Just use her.'

'Like my father?'

'Like your father.'

The plane began a long, shallow descent to the airport. Beyond it Elizabeth could see the dark mass of the volcano and the ordered sprawl of the city, but she looked only once, and then her eyes went back to Callan. He was accepting a series of documents that FitzMaurice pulled out of his briefcase, stowing them into his pockets. Before her eyes he seemed to acquire an air of fussy efficiency that reminded her very much of her father.

'Thank you, chief,' he said.

'You're welcome, doctor,' said FitzMaurice.

232

The plane touched down among a gaggle of light aircraft, and at once an ambulance appeared, proceeded by an Oldsmobile driven by a policeman. The Oldsmobile's passengers were a police captain who seemed to have a certain amount of authority, and a civilian who seemed to have a great deal. Callan left the plane at once and went up to them: FitzMaurice followed more slowly. He walked, Elizabeth thought, with the unhurried certainty of a man who knows beyond doubt that wherever he goes he will be listened to and deferred to, and so it was. The police captain and the civilian left Callan at once, hurried over to FitzMaurice, and waited respectfully as he handed over four passports. The civilian inserted a typewritten form in each, the police captain snapped his fingers at the ambulance, and two attendants raced out with a stretcher, entered the Cherokee to collect Trudi. Now, she thought, was the time to yell, to stop the whole thing, and as she thought it Callan came back aboard the small plane, waited till Trudi was carried out.

'Shall we go?' he said. She made no move.

'You're thinking you can yell,' said Callan. 'But it wouldn't be fair to Trudi. Look.'

From the window she could see FitzMaurice hovering solicitously by the stretcher, hands tucking up a blanket so close to the thin, vulnerable throat.

'You'd do that?' she said.

'If you made us,' said Callan.

Hi-jackers' logic, terrorists' logic, that wasn't really logic at all. The only trouble was you couldn't refute it. She got up and left the plane, went into the Oldsmobile. Callan took over by the stretcher, and the black man joined her in the car. As they drove, the civilian asked in broken if deferential English how soon his country would join O.P.E.C. She didn't have to talk at all....

Mavis Smith thought it didn't make sense. All the way from Venezuela Roddy had been fine, honestly, and yet as soon as they touched down at Mexico City he said he had the trots and BA just *happened* to have another first pilot to take his place, all ready and waiting. Roddy couldn't possibly have Montezuma's Revenge. After the night they'd had together, she should know. And of all people to replace him they had to have that bastard Gittins. Not that she'd ever flown with him, but she'd talked with those who had. A VIP's pilot, Gittins was. All stiff upper lip politeness to the first-class show-offs, but never a kind word for the hired help. I suppose Roddy isn't good enough for them, she thought, and looked out of the window to where a car and an ambulance pulled up. A black man, big as a gorilla and good-looking with it, walking like the king of Wolverhampton, and with him an American girl, the classy kind. Luggage, too, not a lot, but expensive, and taken straight into the first class. Roddy would never have stood for that.... Then out of the ambulance a fussy sort of feller, watching while two attendants carried out a woman with her head bandaged. Oh how super, she thought. That really makes my day. I'm the only trained nurse on the flight, and I bet Gittins knows.

She walked through the empty first class to the flight deck, knocked and went in. The co-pilot and engineer smiled at her, but Gittins took his time even to look up.

'Yes?' he said.

'I'm sorry to bother you, sir,' she said, 'but I see we have an injured passenger. I wondered if you'd need me.'

'No, love,' he said, 'you just stay in the cattle-pen. They've brought their own doctor.'

She went back at once, and almost collided with the big blackman as he came aboard.

'I'm sorry, sir,' she said.

'That's perfectly all right.'

Even better accent than Roddy's she thought. What was the world coming to?

She tried to delay as the injured girl was brought up, but the chief steward appeared and gave her one of his looks and she went back to tourist class. Cattle-pen indeed. Gittins' take-off was perfect: real text-book stuff. Poor darling Roddy could never hope to do a take-off like that. But there was more to life than take-offs. At least Roddy was a gentleman.

[iii]

The Special Branch were too late at the Balmoral. The fact disappointed Hunter, but failed to surprise him. Procuring warrants, overcoming the inertia of policemen, these things take time. There would be a few pickings in the place he was sure: the SSD operatives there hadn't had time to do a thorough clean-up—but even so he had lost a battle. On the other hand it was possible that he had won a war. Battles and wars alike involved casualties. That had to be considered.... It was certain that Hexham and that petty crook Spanner had been at the Balmoral. They were still at large, and Hexham at least would be armed. Hunter considered their targets. Trudi Bauer of course would be their ideal objective, but Trudi would be invulnerable. Hunter would see to that and the SSD would know it. That left them with much smaller fry—a matter of retribution, no more. Still, the SSD was quite keen on retribution. Even the KGB accepted their losses more philosophically.... The smaller fry were FitzMaurice, Callan, Berkeley, and Lonely. FitzMaurice too was invulnerable: he'd be guarding Trudi Bauer. Hunter considered the other three. Useful, all of them: with Callan in charge, extremely useful. And they could, perhaps, be preserved, but it would be a long and costly operation with no certainty of success. Reluctantly he decided that the other three must take their chance. After all, the war was as good as won. He'd warn Callan of course, but even so he must take his chance. After all, twenty thousand pounds was a lot of money. To earn it was inevitably to take risks. Besides, there was always the chance that Callan might settle the business himself.... Liz buzzed him from the outer office.

'I have Jamaica on the line, sir,' she said. 'In clear.'

Hunter picked up the phone, not pouncing exactly, but moving with unusual speed.

'Charlie here,' he said.

FitzMaurice's voice was calm, even relaxed, and gratifyingly clear.

'Our little friend's not quite as well as she could be,' he said. 'If you could arrange an ambulance at your end—'

'Of course. I understand she's brought a friend with her?'

'Under the circumstances we thought it best,' said FitzMaurice.

Hunter let it go: FitzMaurice always had his reasons.

'Her name,' said FitzMaurice, 'is Elizabeth Manette. Her father is a member of the United States Congress.' Then he hung up. There was nothing they could say to each other across such a distance.... Hunter blinked at the handset and put it down. A US congressman could only be bad news.... Or could it? Surely somewhere he had a file on a man called Manette? He rang for Liz....

FitzMaurice turned to his escort, a very light Jamaican in a suit by Mr Fish. FitzMaurice once more wore his tribal robes.

'I am obliged to you, sir,' he said.

'Not at all,' said the Jamaican. 'It's a pleasure to help an emergent nation.'

FitzMaurice looked at the scribbled paper in his hand: Callan's message to Lonely at his Uncle Lenny's to let him know they were on their way home. Callan hadn't touched a drop, and they had the American girl to thank for that, but even so he deserved one telegram.

'If I might send a cable, sir? My doctor would like his family to know that all is well.'

'Of course,' the Jamaican said.

He didn't even want to let FitzMaurice pay for it, but FitzMaurice insisted. As they drove back to the plane FitzMaurice started to talk about his aide's accident. The Jamaican was far more concerned with O.P.E.C. negotiations....

She was tired, but she couldn't sleep. Trudi was sleeping the sleep of the drugged, but she couldn't, wouldn't relax. They'd offered her pills and she wouldn't touch them. Oblivion was all very well in its way, but what happened when you woke up? She looked across at Callan: he was still neat, still clean, but his eyes, his whole face showed his exhaustion. Even so, she knew, he would stay awake, stay deadly, till it was over. 'It,' she thought, and wondered what 'it' was. Maybe terror for her, humiliation for her father, and she could concentrate on neither fact. All she knew was that she wanted him: wanted him *now*. As randy as a bitch in heat.... FitzMaurice came back aboard, the mobile stairway was driven clear.

FitzMaurice said, 'I spoke to Charlie. So far as I know he's happy.'

'Happy?' said Callan. 'You've just had a unique experience. Did you send my telegram?'

FitzMaurice fastened his seat belt. 'I did,' he said.

'How much?' said Callan.

'On the house,' said FitzMaurice.

But Callan said again, 'How much?' and FitzMaurice told him and Callan paid.

29

To go to Brussels so soon after leaving Berlin was a bore, of course, but the circumstances palliated the boredom. It was pleasant, too, to have one's own aircraft, and with Toby for a bodyguard really one didn't have to worry, not even when one was going to break bad news.... Hunter settled himself in the seat of the executive jet—really it was as big as an armchair at his club, and even more comfortable—and contemplated Toby. The dear lad seemed quite on edge. Hunter forced his mind away from the contemplation of the rich pickings that would be his once he'd had his chat with Bauer, and thought about Toby as the Lear taxied into position for take-off. Of course. That wretched girl and her address book....

He waited till they were airborne. Hunter hated flying, and preferred to suffer it in silence. And this, of all times, they must not crash. Even inside his own mind, Hunter would not contemplate the word 'die'. The plane levelled off at last.

'That address book,' said Hunter. 'I've had it checked.'

'Yes, sir,' said Meres, and thought the old sod's so happy he should be singing the Hallelujah Chorus, yet his voice tells me nothing. Not a damned thing.

'Miss Nivelle's list of addresses was simply that,' said Hunter. 'A list of addresses. They are real enough, but I doubt if their occupants were acquainted with Miss Nivelle. Cover, Toby. No more than cover. They are not the slightest use to us.'

'I'm very sorry, sir,' said Meres. 'I—'

But the old bastard held up his hand and smiled. He actually smiled.

'Her list of telephone numbers, however,' he said, 'was a different matter.'

'Indeed, sir?'

'Indeed. One of the numbers was that of the Balmoral Private Hotel—doubtless there for Hexham's benefit. It was a pity that you couldn't have let us have it sooner. We might have got him.'

'But, sir—'

'Yes, I know,' said Hunter. 'Other circumstances obtruded. Don't let them obtrude again, Toby.'

And that was all there was to it: let off with a caution. Make the most of it, Meres told himself. It's never going to happen again.

They had a Bentley waiting to drive them to the party, and still Hunter was genial. ('They offered me a Rolls, Toby, but I insisted on a Bentley. So much more dashing.') It took them to a château that over-looked the Bois de Cambrai: a château of heavy opulence that was, thought Meres, just the place for a German trade delegation: balanced, ornate, successful; deutschmarks wrapped round it like armour. Now let's see what happens when a wasp gets in between the chinks.... There was champagne, and a lesser-fry of O.E.C. delegates talking about restaurants in the Old Town. Meres attached himself to a pretty Dutch girl, and watched discreetly as Hunter circled his prey. And that was about the only way to describe it. Hunter tracked Bauer like a falcon after a pigeon with a damaged wing.

The German was big-boned, heavy-set but not fat: heavy-jawed, grey-haired, with grey eyes that regarded the world with a sort of shrewd amusement. He was the guest of honour, and getting to him was not easy. Hunter made it at last by using a legation secretary to introduce him. The secretary had no idea what Hunter was doing, but nonetheless would never forgive him for using a member of the Foreign Office to do it. They were alone at last: it wouldn't take long.

'Are you an economist, Mr Hunter?' said Bauer.

Hunter sipped his champagne.

'No,' said Hunter. 'I'm a sort of Autolycus.'

Bauer was proud of his Shakespearian scholarship, and Hunter knew it.

'A snapper up of unconsidered trifles?' he said.

'Precisely that.'

Bauer chuckled, then looked at Hunter. The Englishman was not making a joke.

'You are thinking perhaps that you have such a trifle that might interest me?'

'I know I have,' said Hunter.

'Really, you know, a party is no place for such discussions. Come and see me—'

'Your daughter,' said Hunter. 'We will discuss her now. You're a difficult man to reach, you know.'

Bauer took it well, he thought. There was no denying that he took it very well indeed. For a moment he froze, then the mask was once more in place, the same blend of politeness and irony.

238

One hand made a slight pushing gesture to a hovering aide, and they were left alone.

'I have no daughter,' he said.

'But you have,' said Hunter. 'She was in America, poor child. Rather a mess, I'm afraid. Now she is with me.'

'A mess?'

'Drugs,' said Hunter. 'Promiscuity. The penalties of modern living? A classic case of father-rejection? Who can say?'

'I believe my daughter to be dead.'

'Then what a delightful surprise if you should see her again.'

'You will permit me to see her?'

'Of course,' said Hunter. 'Do what we ask and she'll be restored to you—If that's what you want.'

Bauer accepted that, too; even though Hunter had no doubt the German had understood his last five words. If Bauer didn't want his daughter back, that could be taken care of too.

'Suppose I cannot do what you want?'

'Then we'll do a smear job on you.'

'I am not familiar with that expression,' said Bauer.

'Smear job? It's a kind of inverted PR in the sense that we use the media: *all* the media. We'll destroy you, Herr Bauer. Socially and politically.'

'I shall need rather more than your assurance that this is possible,' said Bauer, 'and we cannot talk here.'

'Of course,' said Hunter. 'Do you read the London *Times*?'

'I take it.'

'Read it,' said Hunter. 'The personal advertisements. One day soon there will be a message—Daddy please ring, Autolycus; and a telephone number. Go to a booth—any time, day or night, and dial the number backwards. Repeat that please.'

'The London *Times*,' said Bauer. 'Daddy please ring. Signed Autolycus. I do so from a booth, but I dial the number in reverse order.'

He's not even surprised, Hunter thought. He's been expecting it: if I play this right he'll even welcome it. Expiation, that was the word. He'd never quite understood it, but it made a damn useful tool.

'I think,' said Bauer, 'that you are a very evil man.'

'A realist,' said Hunter. 'That's why we got on so quickly and so well. You politicians know how to come to terms with reality.'

Bauer said nothing: he was looking about the room.

'I trust you're not contemplating the possibility of recounting our little chat to your security people?' said Hunter. 'That would make the smear job inevitable.'

'I should like to do so,' said Bauer. 'I know I cannot.'

239

He gave a stiff little jerk of the head and walked away. An aide intercepted him at once, and led him towards a group of vehement Italians. Hunter looked round for Meres, and reluctantly he left the pretty Dutch girl, who was saddened, but not surprised. One's chief always wanted one at the most impossible moments.

'I think we had best leave, Toby,' said Hunter. 'Bauer really has taken it rather well, but he does have a tendency to rashness. Do you know of a decent restaurant in this city?'

The lesser-fry had talked of little else: unhesitatingly Meres recommended Rumbeke's, where they dined on mussels, steak and wild strawberries, and Hunter ordered the Haut Brion '66. And he was the one who preached economy, thought Meres, then found that Hunter was looking at him.

'I think we're entitled to celebrate,' said Hunter. 'If that damn plane from Mexico doesn't crash.'

'Jumping the gun a bit, weren't you, sir?'

It was a rash question, and he knew it, but he'd had rather a lot of champagne and a fair whack of the claret, and anyway the old boy was going on as if it were Christmas at Dingley Dell. He got away with it. This *was* a night to remember.

'A bit,' said Hunter, and called for coffee and Hennessy XO. When it came, he sipped, and smiled. 'This may turn into a rush-job, Toby,' he said. 'I want you on permanent stand-by.'

The Bentley took them back to the airport, and the waiting Lear, and they flew once more in armchair comfort to the RAF station, where another Bentley waited to take them to Heathrow. Meres quite liked the VIP lounge. Its chairs weren't as comfortable as the Lear's but the hostess assigned to them seemed to have been chosen for the length and shapeliness of her legs.... FitzMaurice's plane had left Bermuda on time. The weather was good, and there was a following wind. Nothing to do now but drink black coffee, and wait, and try to look alert, even when Hunter fell asleep in his chair, as neat and contained as a cat. He awoke as soon as the phone rang. The ground hostess took it, then handed it to Meres.

'They're coming in to land now, sir,' said Meres.

'Excellent. The ambulance?'

'Standing by, sir.'

'And the clearances?'

'All arranged. Gittins radioed ahead after Bermuda, sir.'

Hunter yawned, stood up, and was ready. He was still standing when Callan came in with Elizabeth.

'My dear David,' Hunter said. 'How tired you look. And no wonder, poor chap. And this must be—'

'Miss Manette,' said Callan. 'How are you, Hunter?'

'Never better, dear boy. Never better. Let's go to the car. Toby—
look after Miss Manette, will you? David and I have so much to
talk about.'

So his name is David, she thought, and walked out with the
younger Englishman. With Callan she'd known fear and love: with
this one she knew only fear.

They went to the country place: FitzMaurice and Trudi in the
ambulance, Callan and Elizabeth with Hunter in the Bentley.
Meres rode with the chauffeur, and a carload of the goon-squad
shadowed them unobtrusively. Hunter had pulled off his biggest
coup yet: he wasn't leaving anything to chance. And despite his
declared longing for a chat with me he isn't going into any details,
thought Callan. All he wants to do is hear how awful Las Vegas
is—at least so long as Elizabeth's listening.... And Elizabeth was
listening hard. The bug had bitten her all right: whatever they
said would go back to her father.... Not that there was any
nourishment in the crumbs Hunter let fall.

Hunter liked the country place. It was old, elegant, well run,
and staffed with enough servants to allow him to preserve the
illusion that all he did there was live graciously, in the manner
of his grandfather. But the dogs that roamed the grounds were
rather more than decorative adjuncts to the country-life existence:
there was a shooting gallery in the cellars and a permanent suite
for Snell that was a cross between a laboratory and a Harley
Street consulting room. Hunter never forgot that his country-
squire rôle was an illusion: the country house was as much a
place of business as the abandoned school. When they arrived
he waited only to see Trudi taken care of before he disappeared
with FitzMaurice. Elizabeth looked around the drawing-room. The
furniture was old and shabby and obviously expensive, one of
the pictures on its walls almost certainly a Romney: the view
from its long windows was of lawn and flowers. She looked at
Meres.

'Does he have to be here?' she asked.

'I don't know,' said Callan, and turned to Meres. 'Do you?'

Meres grinned. 'Aren't you pleased to see me?' he asked.

'Come off it,' said Callan. 'I'm never pleased to see you.'

'You haven't changed a bit, have you?' said Meres, and lounged
to the door. 'The whisky's over there in the cabinet.'

When he'd gone Elizabeth said, 'That line about the whisky,
that was some sort of a crack?' Callan nodded. 'You drink a lot?'

'Sometimes,' said Callan.

'Like an alcoholic?' she said.

'That's right.'

'I don't like that man,' she said. 'I don't like him at all.'

241

Callan pondered the obliquity of women's thought processes. It was a weird substitute for logic, but quite often an effective one.

'Shall I get you a drink?' she said.

'No thanks.'

'You mean you don't need one?'

'Not just now.' She had made no move to sit down: her whole body was tense and strained. 'Why don't you have one yourself?'

'No.' The word was almost wrenched out of her. 'That man you called Hunter—I guess that's not his real name?' Gravely, Callan admitted that it wasn't. 'He'll want to talk to me. Interrogate me.'

Callan said. 'Just a chat. Congressmen's daughters are never interrogated.'

'When do I call my father?' she asked.

'Soon.'

'I want you to be with me when I call him. Could you fix that?'

'I could try,' he said. 'But why?'

'If you tell my father I'm O.K., he'll believe you. He's afraid of you, David, but he trusts you.... David. I didn't even know that was your name till Hunter said it. Is it your real name?'

'Yes,' he said.

'But not Tucker.'

'Not Tucker.'

'Any more than your partner's an African chief. I'm glad your name isn't Tucker. It doesn't fit—like you'd bought a pair of shoes the wrong size.... I love you.'

'I don't think so,' he said.

'Oh but I do. A clever bastard back in New England had it all worked out before I even met you. An older man, he said. I was looking for my father.'

'You think I'm like him?'

'Like he wants to be,' she said. 'Oh yes. You're like he wants to be but he's not. And I'm glad for him. But all the same I love you. Will I ever see you again?'

She deserved the truth: whenever it was possible he would give it to her.

'I doubt it very much,' he said.

She nodded, accepting it. She was shrewd and realistic enough to keep her longings buried. 'I better stack up a few more memories,' she said, and moved into his arms.

He kissed her, comforted her. Shrewd, realistic, innocent. She had a long way to go before she'd accept automatically that every room in a house like this would be bugged....

*

242

'Honestly, dad, I'm fine,' she said.

Manette said, 'Put Tucker on,' and Callan took the phone.

'You assure me that what my daughter says is true?' said Manette.

'I do, Congressman.'

'I'm afraid of you, Tucker. I guess you know that.' Callan made no answer. 'But I don't believe you'd lie to me about my daughter.'

'I wouldn't,' said Callan.

'I hope you're telling the truth, because if you're not I'd find the means to destroy you. Do you believe that?'

'Yes,' said Callan. 'I do.'

'When's she coming back to me?'

'Soon,' said Callan. 'If you behave.'

'Let me speak to my daughter again.'

Callan handed over the telephone, and listened as she talked to her father, wondered if, three thousand miles away, the happiness in her voice would be as obvious as it was in her room, where she sat and talked to him. In that room happiness was an alien emotion. When she'd done he left her to bathe and change, and went to speak to Charlie.

Hunter was already changed for dinner: dark suit, discreet tie, shirt cuffs gleaming like icing sugar. As Callan had expected, he was playing over the tapes of Elizabeth's talk with her father—and with Callan.

'What a lovable chap you are,' he said at last, and Callan waited. There had to be more than that. 'Almost adorable, in fact. Drink?' He gestured to the decanter on a cabinet.

'Not sherry,' said Callan.

'My dear fellow, of course not. Forgive me,' said Hunter, and opened the cabinet. There was a full bottle of Chivas Regal, Waterford tumblers, ice and water. Callan poured himself a drink, and Hunter watched.

'I rather think her father suspects,' he said at last. 'They're obviously close, but he is closer to her than she is to him—or is that Irish?'

Jokes, thought Callan. Chivas Regal and jokes. We really are celebrating.

'He'll hate you for it, you know,' said Hunter. 'You bedded his daughter.'

'He'd hate anybody for doing that,' said Callan.

'But you more than most. You defeated him.' He looked at the tape of the drawing-room conversation. 'And—how did she put it? You're like he wants to be. But he's not.... He'll hate you more than most, David. If I were you I should keep out of his way.'

243

'I intend to,' said Callan.

'You're not drinking your whisky,' said Hunter.

'That's right.'

'Reformed by true love?' said Hunter. 'No matter. Not to me at any rate. You're leaving us, David, no doubt without regrets. But I must say you and FitzMaurice make a remarkable team. You did very well indeed.'

Callan allowed himself one cautious sip.

'The Manette girl is a complication of course—but under the circumstances quite unavoidable.'

'What will happen to her?'

'Happen?' Hunter spoke the word as if it bewildered him. 'What you said of course. We'll send her back quite soon.'

'You think she'll stay quiet?'

'Of course,' said Hunter. 'Her father is implicated too, you know. She won't hurt him—or allow him to be hurt. And this could ruin him. Don't worry Callan. She'll be as quiet as her father.'

'What about the other girl?'

'The delectable Trudi? Snell's looking after her.'

'Getting her off that stuff?'

Hunter shrugged. 'That may not be possible.'

'I hope she's worth it, Hunter.'

'Of course she is,' said Hunter. 'You and Lonely have been paid by the way. It's in your Swiss bank now.'

'You must be happy,' said Callan.

'Call no man happy till he dies; he is at best fortunate,' said Hunter. 'Solon said that, and with good reason. You may say that I am fortunate.'

'Me too,' said Callan.

'Well—yes and no,' said Hunter, and told him about Hexham and Spanner. Callan listened, and learned that he was not so fortunate after all.

'Lonely and me,' he said at last. 'A revenge list.'

'I fear so.'

'And Bulky too.'

'Berkeley?' said Hunter. 'Yes I suppose that's possible.' Berkeley, it seemed, was the least of his worries. 'Hexham might even have a bit of help,' said Callan. 'The geezers you flushed out of the safe-house.'

'Small-fry,' said Hunter. 'Nothing of any interest.'

'Except to me.'

'Except, as you say, to you. And you have been paid.'

'So that's it then? You're not going to help me?'

'We had a contract,' said Hunter. 'You fulfilled your side: I fulfilled mine.'

244

'A favour then,' said Callan. 'One small favour.'

'Why should I, David?'

For old time's sake, thought Callan. Because I nearly got my head shot off for you and it could still happen because of you.

'Because it is possible that you might need me again,' he said. 'Me and Lonely.'

'Tell me the favour.' Callan did so, and Hunter said, 'I can arrange the rendezvous for you, but the man you ask for must be a volunteer, David. I can't order anybody to do this—and I doubt if Toby would oblige you.'

'I know he wouldn't,' said Callan. 'Anyway Toby's blown. I'll try FitzMaurice.'

'Very well,' said Hunter, 'but only as a volunteer.' Callan rose. 'You haven't finished your drink.'

'Can you blame me?' said Callan.

30

'She asks for you almost continually,' said Snell. 'I really think it would be a good idea if you were to talk to her for a little while.'

FitzMaurice said, 'Is that an order?'

'If necessary, yes,' said Snell, and FitzMaurice shrugged. If he had to, he had to.

'She keeps referring to you as the Panther,' said Snell. 'Does that have any significance for you?'

'She has dreams,' said FitzMaurice, 'when she's bombed.'

'I beg your pardon?'

'Tripping,' said FitzMaurice, and allowed himself a flash of anger; imitated Snell's precise tones. 'When she's under the influence of hallicinogen.'

'And the panther figures in these?' Snell asked, as impervious to irony as he was to anger.

'Frequently,' said FitzMaurice. 'The panther is black—and loved and feared. There are dogs, too. But the dogs are merely despised.'

Snell made a note. 'We'll go in,' he said.

She was in a bed with an iron frame: the kind they used in hospitals, the kind they could tie you down on, but she wasn't tied. She wore a pretty nightdress, her hair had been combed and her face was clean, and Snell was having her fed through a glucose drip. From that, if it worked, he would move on to solid food, and in a week or two, when she'd got some meat on her bones, she could turn into a very pretty girl, FitzMaurice thought, but she'd never be the chick from Saint Lucia. She turned to look at him, and smiled. Until she smiled there had been no life in her eyes: she had seemed beyond hope, beyond even despair.

'The black man,' she said.

'That's right.'

'You hurt my poor Wino,' she said. 'I didn't dream it, did I? You hurt him.'

'I had to,' said FitzMaurice. 'I'm sorry, baby. He was hurting me.'

'There was a fair girl,' she said, 'and a pompous man. And another man who was very terrible—and very sad. I dreamed we went to Mexico—then we went on a plane. Flying and flying. Only it stopped being the desert and became the sea. When I trip it's never the sea.'

'This was real,' said FitzMaurice.

'You held me in your arms?' she said. FitzMaurice nodded. 'Was I afraid?'

'Not once,' he said.

'When I tripped I was afraid of you. But I wanted you. They say I don't need to trip any more. They've got other things—even more fun—'

FitzMaurice looked over at Snell: the white man's face told him nothing at all.

'—and it's true I don't need it. I mean I don't scream or anything,' she said, and her voice expressed her amazement of the fact that she didn't scream or anything. 'But I like to trip,' she said. 'When I tripped I had a name for you.'

'The Panther,' he said.

'That's right. The Panther. Cruel and wonderful and always alone. You care for nobody, Panther.... There were dogs when I tripped, too. The dogs were obscene.' She turned to look, briefly, at Snell, and said dispassionately, 'He is a dog.'

'Why are the dogs obscene?' said FitzMaurice.

'They want to give me back to my father,' she said.

Snell's really dragged her back, FitzMaurice thought. Any second now she's going to cry....

When he went down to dinner he found Callan alone in the drawing-room.

'How's your girl?' he asked.

'All right,' said Callan. '—Or as all right as you can be when you're talking to Charlie. How's yours?'

The negro rushed him, and Callan barely had time to duck: a massive black fist smashed over his head. Callan grabbed it, twisted and pulled. FitzMaurice was in a rage so total that it both slowed him up and made him impervious to pain until Callan threw all his weight against the arm he held, and at last FitzMaurice groaned.

'All right,' he said, 'all right.' But Callan held on.

'I asked you a polite question,' said Callan. 'If I didn't ask you nicely, I meant to. No irony intended.'

'All *right*,' said FitzMaurice. 'I believe you. I apologise.'

Callan let him go.

'You meant that, didn't you?' said FitzMaurice.

'Of course I bloody meant it,' said Callan. 'She *was* your girl, wasn't she? I mean you looked after her, all that. I was the one who was supposed to, but the way it worked out—you were the one who did. So I thought maybe you'd seen her. So I asked how she was.... And you damn near killed me.'

Cautiously FitzMaurice tested his right arm and shoulder.

'You damn nearly killed me,' he said.

'You lost your temper,' said Callan. 'I didn't know you could.'

'Snell took me to see her,' said FitzMaurice. 'Just before I came down here.' He hesitated. 'That's all I can tell you, David.'

Callan looked at him. 'It's enough,' he said.

'She said you were very sad, and very terrible,' said FitzMaurice. 'She said I was—' he flung up a hand. 'No,' he said, 'I don't want you to know what she said about me.... How do you get out of this business, David?'

'You don't,' said Callan. 'You know you don't.'

'You did,' said FitzMaurice.

'Only they keep dragging me back,' said Callan. 'Stay in your nice prison, old son. That way you'll never miss the outside.'

'I hate my job,' said FitzMaurice. 'I think I hate it the way you did. I hope so.'

'Admirable sentiments,' said Callan, 'but do you think you should put them on tape?'

'I tell Hunter that once a year,' said FitzMaurice, 'and the twelve months is just about up. Even so, I thank you for your advice.'

'You're very welcome, Chief Shekwe. As a matter of fact I wanted to ask you a favour.'

'Anything within my humble power, Mr Tucker.'

*

The dinner had been simple, but delicious: mushroom soup, cold salmon, strawberries and cream, and with it hock of a quality her father rarely served. Callan had drunk nothing before dinner, and did little more than sip at his wine, though that *swine* whom Hunter called Toby kept passing him the bottle. Four men and one girl should have made things awkward for her, but the table was a circular one, Hunter had placed her between Callan and FitzMaurice, and Callan had treated her with affection, the black man with respect. As dinner parties went, it could have been worse, and Hunter had kept up a flow of small talk that was at once erudite and witty, and, under the circumstances, bizarre. Like a computer that told jokes, she thought. But nothing, not a damn thing that was worth remembering. She looked at the men around her. For all his affection, Callan had something on his mind and she knew it at once. FitzMaurice too, was bothered

248

about something. Only the awful Toby seemed pleased with himself, pleased and relieved, too, but about what she had no idea, no way of finding out. She had nothing to take back to her father; not a damned thing.

She'd talked to Hunter, and she knew she'd been interrogated by an expert, an expert's expert even, but she could recall no pattern to his questions, no technique for her to analyse. All the same, he knew all about her—and her father, she was sure of that: sure, too, that she had nothing to worry about. She'd be going home soon. She'd tried to ask about Trudi, but he'd shut up like a clam. Trudi was receiving care, he said, and something else he'd said made her think there was a doctor looking after her. But Hunter would use the German girl, Elizabeth knew. Without pity and without remorse, no matter how much he hurt her.

Hunter rose and fetched a decanter of port from the sideboard, set it on the table. 'I wonder, my dear,' he said, 'if you include anthropology in your really formidable list of studies? The dining habits of the English perhaps?'

She rose.

'I know enough to realise that I must ask you to excuse me.'

'Good girl,' said Hunter: 'You'll find coffee is served in the drawing-room. But if I were you I shouldn't go out into the gardens. The dogs are enjoying a run, and they are inclined to be rather boisterous.'

She sat in the drawing-room and yawned her way through a magazine. From time to time she heard laughter in the next room, but it was usually the repellent Toby's. When the men came to her, Hunter and the horror swallowed their coffee and left almost at once, then FitzMaurice came up to Callan and said: 'That little job you wanted. Charlie says O.K. Tomorrow morning?'

'Fine,' said Callan. 'Thank you, Chief.'

'Any time, Mr Tucker,' FitzMaurice said, and left them alone.

'Are you staying on for a while?' she asked.

'No,' he said. 'I go tomorrow, too.'

'Then we'd better go to bed now,' she said.

Her body pleased him, and she used what skill she had to intensify his pleasure, but even so it was she who found delight.

'What a gentleman you are,' she said.

He thought of the bug in the room, of Hunter playing back the tape next morning. It didn't matter: she had earned the right to be herself, and to warn her of what was being done would be only to teach her shame.

'I'm a gentleman because I've found a lady,' he said.

She reached out to stroke his face.

'A nice man,' she said. 'My mother's always saying: If only you could meet a nice man. And now I've met one—and she'll never know.... You're worried, aren't you?'

'About you?' he said. 'Of course I—'

'No,' she said. 'Not me. You'll forget me very quickly. I know that. There's something else—Is it that awful man?'

'Which awful man?'

'The one called Toby.'

'No,' he asked, 'Toby doesn't worry me.'

'Hunter then?'

'My only worry is that I have to leave you and I don't want to,' he said.

She didn't believe him, but he'd told a nice man's lie. It was all he had to offer, and she took it and was grateful.

[ii]

Lonely opened Uncle Lennie's front door, stared at Spencer Perceval FitzMaurice, and felt first annoyance, then dismay.

'Oh my Gawd,' he said.

'Gas Board,' said FitzMaurice. 'I've come to see your Uncle Lennie.'

Lonely looked at the donkey-jacket FitzMaurice wore, the dungarees, the beret. Looks right, he thought. What they call a disguise. All the same the darky meant trouble. Bound to. 'I'm not sure,' he said. 'I'll have to see.'

Behind him Uncle Lennie said, 'For Gawd's sake stop messing about and let him in.'

So once more FitzMaurice found himself in the big kitchen, accepted a quarter pint of cowslip wine.

'I bring greetings from a mate of yours,' he said.

'Mr Callan?' said Lonely. 'He's back?'

FitzMaurice nodded, and Lonely knocked back his glass in one relieved gulp.

'That's all right then,' he said.

FitzMaurice found it touching. What it must be, he thought, to have such faith in a human being: any human being. Callan's back, so everything's all right. Uncle Lennie was more perceptive.

'Couple of questions,' he said, and refilled their glasses. 'What you dressed like that for, and why didn't Callan come hisself?'

'Now the bad news,' said FitzMaurice.

Uncle Lennie said 'Ah!' and Lonely looked bewildered as he so often did.

'There's a bloke out to get you—and David.'

'What bloke?' said Lonely.

250

'Hexham,' said FitzMaurice.

To FitzMaurice's amazement, there was no smell.

'Him?' said Lonely, in accents of scorn. 'Mr Callan could break him in two.'

Gently FitzMaurice said, 'Hexham will have a little help.'

But even that didn't perturb Lonely.

'Mr Callan'll manage,' he said.

'He's a little worried about you and your uncle,' said FitzMaurice.

'Wants us to run, does he?' said Lonely. 'That's all right then. I got a bit put by—'

'I'm afraid you can't run,' said FitzMaurice. 'You're being watched.'

'No we're not,' said Lonely. 'Believe me that's one thing I know all about. If we was being watched, I'd know.'

FitzMaurice moved to the kitchen window, leaving the net curtain in place. From where he stood he could see the hill's smooth, gentle rise, the ruin of the windmill on top.

'Up there,' he said. 'A man with binoculars. Maybe in the windmill: maybe he just uses a hollow in the ground. It's nice weather for it. All he has to do is make himself comfortable and watch.'

Lonely came over to join him and peered cautiously.

'The country,' he said disgustedly. 'The bleeding country.'

Uncle Lennie hadn't even bothered moving.

'The one thing wrong with this place,' he said. 'Never really bothered me before though. Mostly I work nights.' He sipped at his wine. 'Whoever it is'll be waiting for us to lead him to Callan.'

'That's right.'

'We're in a box then.'

'Not really,' said FitzMaurice. 'Callan's idea is that you lead them to him anyway.'

'You're joking,' said Lonely.

'No,' said FitzMaurice. 'I'm quite serious. He reckons it's the only way. You lead them to Callan and he can get rid of them. If he doesn't he'll never have any peace. They might even get him.'

'So we're decoys,' said Uncle Lennie.

'Strictly speaking *you* don't come into it at all,' FitzMaurice said. 'They're not interested in you, just your nephew.'

'Callan tell you that?'

'He did.'

'Well you can take it from me I don't let my nephew get into any trouble without his uncle's with him.'

FitzMaurice said, 'He told me that, too.'

'He takes a bloody sight too much for granted,' said Uncle Lennie,

251

then added, 'What's he want us to do?'

FitzMaurice told him, and Uncle Lennie listened and considered, then turned to Lonely. 'There's some Ordnance Survey maps in me bedroom,' he said. 'Slip up and get them.'

Lonely left at once. When Uncle Lennie talked like that he didn't want no back talk.

'This could work, no question,' Uncle Lennie said to FitzMaurice, 'but it'll be like the war.'

'I don't think I follow you,' said FitzMaurice.

Uncle Lennie said affably, 'You're ahead of me, son. If this thing works we'll have to kill a few.'

'I'm aware of that.'

'And it doesn't bother you?'

'I'm only the messenger boy,' said FitzMaurice.

'Ah,' said Uncle Lennie. 'Pity. But let me put it another way. You don't get topped for murder, not any more, but you go down for years and years.'

'If you're caught,' said FitzMaurice.

Uncle Lennie chuckled.

'I like you, son,' he said. 'I can't remember when I liked a bloke as much. All the same you're asking a hell of a lot just because I'm fond of my nephew.'

'There could be some cash in it as well,' said FitzMaurice.

'How much?'

FitzMaurice told him, and Uncle Lennie whistled.

'I'm not asking you who sent you,' he said. 'You wouldn't tell me—and anyway I don't want to know. But all the same I want you to tell me this. Would it be like patriotic?'

FitzMaurice considered the pieces of the jigsaw: the cheating of Hexham, the blackmailing of Kleist, Trudi's abduction, the possible ruin of her father: they were the means. Until now there hadn't been time to consider the end.

'Yes,' he said at last. 'I think you could call it patriotism.'

'I'm glad I haven't got a phone,' said Uncle Lennie. 'If I had I mightn't have met you again.'

'You'd have met me,' said FitzMaurice. 'If you'd had a phone it would have been tapped.'

When Lonely came back with the maps, FitzMaurice had gone. Suited him. He had nothing against darkies, but that one always seemed to bring bad news. Uncle Lennie sifted through the maps, set aside the ones he wanted.

'Early lunch,' he said. 'Bit of a kip, then cut a few sandwiches, brew up and fill the flasks. We could be in for a late night.'

'Uncle Lennie,' said Lonely. 'These geezers that's helping Lord Hexham, will they be like gangsters?'

What Lonely didn't know couldn't hurt him.

'That's right,' Uncle Lennie said. 'Like gangsters.'

'I knew it,' said Lonely, and his voice was bitter. 'I knew all the time it was the Mafia.'

From a hollow in the hill Hexham watched FitzMaurice stick a tool bag in the back seat of a mini, then ease himself cautiously behind the wheel and drive away. Hexham lowered his field-glasses, but Spanner, the fool, went on staring.

'Gas Board,' said Hexham. 'Nothing in that for us.'

'Oh isn't there?' said Spanner, and for once he sounded superior. 'Well let me tell you that one of the geezers who took George and me was a big darky.' He pointed to the mini, now a tiny dot on the road. '*That* big darky.'

'Indeed?' said Hexham. 'How *very* interesting. Do you know, old chap, I think we may have work to do.'

31

Bulky was the least of his worries, but he was a worry, and it was up to him to get rid of it. Meres would regard it as indulgent, Hunter as naive, but Bulky belonged now: whether he knew it or not he'd signed on, and it was up to Callan to see he didn't suffer for it. Gently, cautious not to disturb Elizabeth, Callan climbed out of bed, dressed and went down to the duty room. The man on guard poured him coffee, and said, 'There's a Jaguar ready for you, sir.'

'That's nice,' said Callan. 'Anything else?'

The man on guard handed over a 357 Magnum, webbing harness, and twenty rounds.

'Compliments of Mr Hunter, sir,' he said. 'You don't have to sign.'

'Just as well,' said Callan. 'I wasn't going to.'

Callan smiled as he said it, but the man on guard didn't. The way he looked at it he was a civil servant: flippancy was something he could do without.

The Jag was every bit as good as he'd expected it would be, and he made the journey to London with no pain at all. At that hour of the morning even getting to Chelsea wasn't all that difficult, but even so he was too late. He knew that as soon as he saw the ambulance outside Bulky's mansion block. That was one thing he hadn't allowed for: that they'd take care of Bulky before they tried for Lonely and himself—take care of him because he was there. He parked the car and walked over to the ambulance. There were people about—given an ambulance there always would be—but at that hour of the morning not enough to stop him walking through. As he arrived two men had just finished loading a fat and blanket-shrouded figure into the ambulance.

'Good God,' said Callan, 'that's not Mr Berkeley, is it?'

'Flat 15,' said one of the attendants.

'But I'm his broker,' said Callan. 'Hunter and Meres—you know?

254

I was supposed to have breakfast with him. What happened?'
'Letter bomb, sir,' said the attendant.
'Not—dead, is he?'
'No,' the attendant said. 'Very spry he was—considering. He threw it down the well of the building. But it didn't half make a mess of his hands. Now if you'll excuse me, guv—'
The attendant joined his mate in the ambulance and it moved off, and Callan didn't waste any time either. Already there were rozzers about, talking to eye-witnesses, and soon there would be scores of them.... The bastards. Oh, the sadistic bastards. Bulky was far too small a fish to waste a man on, so they'd posted a bomb instead.... A mess of his hands, the ambulance man had said. If you used that kind of letter bomb, the hands always copped it, always were a mess.... The punishment to fit the crime, he thought. And then he thought of Lonely. No doubt they had something appropriate lined up for him, too. He went back to the Jaguar; it was time to go to the coast.

[ii]

'Nice of you to drop in,' said Bishop.
And that, thought Hunter, was typical. Bishop had always had a soft answer, even at school, even when Hunter had been his fag, and Bishop had reached for the squash racket. And now here he was in this dreary office in Whitehall. Information secretary to the Cabinet, or whatever the current euphemism was ... and still with a squash racket within reach.
'Not at all,' said Hunter. 'It isn't all that much out of my way.'
'Too good,' said Bishop, and poured out a cup of the Ministry's appalling coffee. 'One always knew one could depend on you, old man.'
Now what, thought Hunter, is this all about?
'This Bauer business for instance,' said Bishop. 'I got your memo on that. Exemplary, old chap. Positively exemplary.'
'I'm glad that my poor efforts please,' said Hunter.
'Oh they do,' said Bishop. 'Believe me, my dear chap, they *do*. And the operation itself—positively masterly. Though perhaps just a teensy bit expensive.'
Hunter said stiffly, 'I should have thought the ends justified the money.'
'Oh but they did. Believe me, my dear chap, they *did*.—I suppose there is absolutely no doubt that it *is* the right girl?'
'None,' said Hunter. 'We had access to her medical history. Snell verified it.'
He thought: 'we had access to'—'Snell verified'. I'm talking like

255

a pompous ass to this man, and I have done since I was twelve years old. It's high time I stopped.

'Splendid,' Bishop said. 'Absolutely splendid. Though one can't help feeling you put up just a teensy black with that American— or rather your cohorts did?'

'My cohorts as you call them acted with my full authority,' said Hunter, 'and they put up no blacks. If you read my memo again you'll find that my department is fully covered. Manette can— and will—do nothing.'

'You know one admires you,' said Bishop. 'One really does. So *thorough*. The only thing is—' He hesitated, and Hunter thought he detected reluctance in his voice. In anybody else's it might even be called shame.

'Tell me the only thing,' he said.

'I'm afraid,' said Bishop, 'that it just isn't on.'

'Come off it,' said Hunter. 'My Section's done the thing.'

'Oh, agreed,' said Bishop, 'and done it superbly, if one may say so. But our masters—' he leaned back in his chair and looked whimsically at the ceiling, as if their masters brooded, malevolent, on the floor above: 'our masters are not happy. Far from happy.'

'For God's sake,' said Hunter, 'I've just given them the best lever into West Germany they've ever had.'

'Agreed again,' said Bishop, 'but one fears, old boy, that in the process you've managed to alienate the United States.'

'One congressman,' said Hunter.

'One congressman. But unfortunately one must use the definite as well as the indefinite article. In fact—*the* congressman. Excuse the pedantry, won't you?'

Hunter shifted in his chair: already the squash racket was beginning to smart.

'After I got your memo I talked to our chaps in Washington,' said Bishop. 'They think Manette could go a long way. With a bit of help, a *very* long way. They also think he's not the type who would forget his old chums.... Now a German minister in the bag is one thing—and if I may say so, a very good thing too—' he bowed sitting down; a trick Hunter had never quite learned to master: 'but a future Secretary of State, perhaps even a President—how should one put it? one can hardly regret losing the grouse provided one has secured the pheasant.'

'I should prefer plainer speech,' said Hunter.

'Then you shall have it.' This time Hunter could almost see the squash racket. 'My masters have instructed me to instruct you to hand over Trudi what's her name to Manette.'

'I don't believe you,' said Hunter.

'Then you're naive,' Bishop said, 'and I know that to be untrue.

256

Consider'—he ticked the points off on his fingers: 'One, they will pay the price Manette offered your cohorts for her—one million dollars; enough to keep your Section functioning for some considerable time. Two, she will be handed over in such a way that Manette will never be able to forget his obligations to us, even if he should wish to do so.'

'But why Manette?' said Hunter. 'Why not the CIA?'

Bishop said reproachfully, 'You haven't been listening, old boy. Manette is our investment for the 1980s.... If only we could get the equivalent Russian as well.' He sighed, and then dismissed a roseate dream.

'I set this up,' said Hunter. 'I worked on it for nearly a year. I risked five men's lives—three of them are still at risk. And now you're telling me it's over?'

'Precisely that,' said Bishop. He shuffled his papers together and rose. 'See to it, will you? My secretary has written instructions for you. You can pick them up on the way out. Oh—and by the way, give me a ring sometime, we must arrange a game of squash; it's about time I gave you another hiding.'

[iii]

The stretch of coastline could have been designed for the purpose. An estuary, mud flats on either side, a rotten jetty and the sea beyond, and nothing in sight for miles except more mud flats and bents grass: Suffolk at its most welcoming, he thought, and looked at the power-cruiser Hunter had moored for him: paint chipped and brass unpolished, but twin-screwed and heavy enough to take the open sea.... Just the thing for running in Pakistanis on a moonless night. Well, it hadn't come to that yet, and with Lonely for a crew it never would. He went aboard the power-boat and ran the engines.... Sweet as nuts. He could take off now, hop over to Dieppe, be in Switzerland by morning, grab his money and disappear....

Except for Lonely.... And Uncle Lennie, he thought. And Bulky with his hands all burnt. The thought of Bulky made it vengeance after all. He moved carefully back on to the jetty's crumbling woodwork, and looked about him. The O.K. Corral-on-Sea. Mud, mud, glorious mud. Well, one thing about the stuff: it was easy enough to work if you didn't mind getting dirty. And that made him think of Elizabeth for some reason. Maybe it was because he'd stopped minding about getting dirty years ago.... He pulled on a pair of wellington boots, levered a couple of planks from the jetty and got to work.

257

'Fancy a sandwich before we start?' Uncle Lennie said.

Lonely shook his head. 'No thanks.'

Uncle Lennie spread mustard on top of corned beef, added sliced tomatoes and more bread, then pressed down heavily until the sandwich was suitably squashed, trimmed off the crusts.

'My teeth,' he explained, and poured tea, added milk and four sugars.

'Drink that,' he said.

Lonely sipped and grimaced. 'It's too sweet,' he said.

'Energy, that is,' said Uncle Lennie. 'It could be you'll need it. Drink up.'

So Lonely drank, and Uncle Lennie, still chewing, went from the kitchen to the garage, and loaded up the ancient Rolls: a hamper with flasks of sweetened tea and coffee, corned beef sandwiches, tinned salmon sandwiches, chocolate and boiled sweets, half bottle of brandy, half bottle of Scotch, bandages and iodine—just in case: then the Mannlicher on the back seat loaded and with the safety on, then the two Purdeys, also loaded. Uncle Lennie laid them out in neat alignment, then added the sawn-off Spanish shotgun. Lonely couldn't hit a barn door if the whole nation prayed—not when he got niffy, and that was a certainty—but at least he could help make a noise. Uncle Lennie covered the guns with a tartan rug, then checked the glove compartment. One Luger: Wehrmacht issue, 1943, clean, bright, slightly-oiled, and loaded. Liberated that in Crete, he had, thirty-two years ago. That time he'd killed a colonel. What the Germans called an Oberst. He looked at the car, polished, gleaming, and hoped to Christ the paintwork wouldn't get scratched. The old girl would do them a lovely job, he thought. Built them to last them days—and as much fire-power as a tank. He opened the side door of the garage and went back into the kitchen.

'Ready?' he said.

Lonely put down his cup and Uncle Lennie noted with relief that he hadn't started niffing yet. On the other hand he was shaking all over, and he was the colour of dough.

'Uncle Lennie,' he said. 'I can't do it. I'm too scared.'

'I seem to remember you telling me that you was big time,' Uncle Lennie said. 'Thousands and thousands of pounds you was making.'

'Well, so I did,' said Lonely, 'only that was my own line. Thieving. Opening up drums and that.'

'With your mate for a minder.'

'Mr Callan always does the physicals. I'm no good at it.' His voice rose to a wail. 'You know I'm not.'

'I know you fancied yourself with a shot-gun so much I taught you to use it.'

'But that was like pretend,' said Lonely.

'Well, so is this like pretend,' said Uncle Lennie. 'Your mate's still doing the minding.'

Lonely made no answer.

'Your mate,' said Uncle Lennie. 'The geezer that made you big time—all those thousands of pounds. The geezer that's relying on you.'

Lonely said, 'I can't do it, Uncle Lennie. I just can't.'

Uncle Lennie loosened his belt.

'Oh yes, you can,' he said. 'You can do it all right. Unless you fancy a lick of this.'

[v]

He should have known that it wouldn't last. Good things never lasted. Jeanne-Marie had died, Hexham had deserted him, the beautiful young Englishman had betrayed him without a qualm. To keep the people you love, it was apparent, you must have money: and he had tried. Money from foolish gamblers; money from smuggled antiques.... All gone, all spent on Jeanne-Marie. And then the beautiful young Englishman had shown him how to make more money; lots of money, and so simply. All that was needed was to deceive the kind of fools he despised anyway: the kind of fools who had no inkling that he was the Graf von Kleist: who would have laughed if he had tried to tell them. And now that money too was unavailable, and without money he could not buy a loved one....

Methodically Kleist ripped the pages from his collection of genteel pornography, put them in the fireplace, arranged the bindings and colour plates on top. They were spoiled, anyway. The beautiful young Englishman knew they existed; he could not take pleasure from them ever again. He struck a match and watched the flames take hold, the pages writhe. With him it was always the same; pleasure always ended, died in pain.... He remembered what his Head of Section had said. 'Disturbing rumours, Kleist. Very disturbing. Of course I don't believe them, and they are from a source I cannot reveal, which makes it even more distasteful. But even so I feel that you should take leave of absence pending immediate investigation. Not that there's any doubt of your being cleared, of course.' But there was already doubt and Kleist knew it. He could see it in his Head of Section's

259

eyes.... He wished he could wear his grandfather's uniform, but he'd tried that once before, and it was much too big for him. In the cavalry boots he looked grotesque, and there was no time to order new ones, or have the uniform altered. There was no time at all. He reached for the last of the brandy, found he didn't want it, and poured it into the fire. The pictures, the bindings, roared and turned to ash, and his life had ended. No friends, no pleasures, no money. He went up to his bedroom, changed into his best suit, a clean shirt, and the tie of Italian silk that Jeanne-Marie had given him, then came down again to stare into the fire, watch till the last flame flickered and died, then broke up the ashes with the poker. Nothing left. Nothing at all. He picked up his grandfather's revolver, leaned back in his chair, and blew out his brains.

[vi]

'They still following us?' said Lonely.

Uncle Lennie glanced into the driving mirror.

'Course they are,' he said. 'That's what they're here for. Mind you,' he added fair-mindedly, 'they're doing it very well.'

They were too, no question. None of that amateur lark of jamming themselves up against the Rolls's backside. Always two or three cars behind. Of course his old girl was built for comfort rather than speed, and there weren't all that many like her on the roads. All the same their tail knew how to do the job properly. They were easy, as you might say. Tactful. And they'd chosen the right car for it an' all. Big, dark green Ford with a lot of power—and thousands like it.

'How many in it?' said Lonely.

'Same as last time,' Uncle Lennie said. 'Four. They haven't stopped to take on no reinforcements.'

'They'll be good,' said Lonely.

'Three of 'em maybe,' Uncle Lennie said. 'The fourth one's Spanner. And he's a dead loss.'

He signalled and edged over left to leave the motorway, taking his time, giving the gits in the Ford plenty of warning. It wouldn't do to lose them now....

'I wouldn't have believed it,' said Spanner.

Beside him on the back seat Hexham smothered a yawn, but even so Spanner's words amused him. It had seemed to him that Spanner would believe almost anything.

'What wouldn't you believe?' he asked.

'That bastard Lennie getting into this,' said Spanner. 'He was supposed to be getting me pheasants and steaks.'

260

'Maybe he's just the chauffeur,' said Hexham.

'Blimey I hope so,' said Spanner. 'It's them other two I want a go at. Specially that Lonely.' He hesitated, then added, 'You sure he can't use that shotgun?'

'Positive,' said Hexham. 'He's an utter coward. Believe me, I know.'

Spanner relaxed. 'I won't half give him a belting when we catch up with him,' he said, then looked out of the window. 'Where d'you suppose we're off to?'

The sign said Ipswich and Woodford.

'It would seem to me,' said Hexham, 'that we're off to the seaside.'

32

'You will no doubt be pleased to learn that you're going home,' said Hunter.

Elizabeth shrugged.

'I'm not yet hypocritical enough to say thank you,' she said. 'When's my flight?'

'Whenever you wish,' he said.

'Boy, you really do want to get rid of me, don't you?'

'You? Yes.... Of course I do. It's always a little disconcerting to be obliged to entertain a congressman's daughter.'

'You're not afraid I'll raise a stink when I get back?'

Hunter winced. It bothered him when young, well-educated women used words like 'stink'.

'Not in the least,' he said. 'You won't be going alone.'

'Won't I?' she said. 'You think an escort will keep my mouth shut?' Then more gently—'You're not sending Mr Tucker with me, are you?'

'There is no Mr Tucker,' said Hunter, 'just as there is no Chief Shekwe, no man called Toby, no man called Hunter.'

'Oh come *on*,' she said.

'You're going back with a girl called Trudi von Nichts,' said Hunter. 'We've just sold her to our American—er—counterparts.'

'I don't believe you,' she said. 'You're trying to fool me.' He made no answer. 'All right then,' she said. 'How much are you getting for her?'

'A million dollars in cash,' said Hunter. 'There will also be—er—fringe benefits.'

She remembered that small, sticky-hot room in Vegas, her father's voice saying: 'I'll give you a million dollars for her.'

'You'll be going home very privately,' said Hunter. 'An airline called Air America has chartered a plane just for the two of you.'

'Air America?' she said. 'But that's the CIA.'

Hunter said bitterly, 'Is it, Miss Manette? I feel sure you would know.'

'You don't like this deal, do you?'
'I do not.'
'Then why—'
'Because I was ordered to,' said Hunter. 'For the good of my country. Are those words familiar to you at all, Miss Manette?'
'You're saying my father's involved in this?'
Really, she was a very bright child.
'He's conducting the American end of the negotiations,' said Hunter.
The advertisement would still appear in the London *Times*, he thought. Daddy please ring.... Autolycus. And a telephone number. But when Bauer rang, an American voice would answer.
Elizabeth said, 'Are you saying that my father will be one of your—er—fringe benefits?'
Really an extraordinarily bright child.
'I'm saying that under the circumstances you will remain silent,' said Hunter. 'You have no choice.'
For the second time in a week, and the third time in the last seven years, Elizabeth Manette wept.

[ii]

From motorway to A road to B road, Uncle Lennie sailed sedately on, and the big Ford discreetly followed, but when he turned off at a sign marked Harl Ness, Hexham had a problem. The road was narrow and not much used, by the look of it, but he didn't dare risk losing the Rolls now. He told the driver to turn off and follow the Rolls, and had a bit of luck. A Jensen was parked on the headland, its owner looking out to sea through binoculars, and there was no doubt he had a view worth looking at: planing seagulls, a scattering of rocks, and waves battering against them in bursts of spume that flashed like jewels as the light faded. Hexham ordered the Ford to be parked nearby and got out with his binoculars to follow the Rolls as it waddled down a shingled track that led to what looked like an estuary, and mud flats. Then Hexham had another bit of luck; the Jensen's owner, apparently a man who valued his solitude, glowered, got back in his car, did an angry three-point turn and drove off, scattering pebbles. They had the place to themselves.... The Rolls stopped, and it seemed that driver and passenger were having an altercation....
'You *got* to do it,' said Uncle Lennie.
'It's just—me knees won't work,' said Lonely.
'They will if you make them,' Uncle Lennie said, and glanced in the rear-view mirror.

263

At once Hexham swung round, stared through his glasses at the wheeling gulls. Uncle Lennie reached out behind him, grabbed the sawn-off shotgun and thrust it at Lonely.

'All you got to do is carry that under your coat, get aboard the cruiser and keep your head down.'

'They'll kill me,' said Lonely.

'You think I'm going to sit here and let them?' Uncle Lennie's voice grew gentle. 'You got to get on with it, Mr Big. Your mate's waiting.'

Lonely shuddered, but even so he stowed the shotgun under his coat and left the car.

'Good lad,' said Uncle Lennie.

'I'm barmy,' Lonely muttered. 'I must be. Why did nobody ever tell me I was barmy?'

He left the track and slogged across the shingle towards the mud-flats, and at once Uncle Lennie drove off, following the pebbled road round a corner that took him out of sight....

'How very gratifying,' said Hexham. 'We really have got the place to ourselves.'

He got back in the car and it took off at once down the track, following the shingle to the very edge of the mud. Hexham turned to Spanner.

'Get him,' he said. 'Good boy.'

Like I was a bloody dog, thought Spanner, but even so he took off at once, spanner in hand. He'd waited a long time to give Lonely a belting.... Hexham and the two Germans took cover behind the car, and watched.

From his hide in the mud Callan watched, too. The geezer from the car had a nice easy stride, and he was gaining on Lonely, even though the little man's legs were churning like egg-beaters. And he'd lost a couple of seconds looking back over his shoulder when the car arrived. Foolish, that was. Very foolish. He'd have to speak to him about that.... Slowly, with an ageing man's caution, Uncle Lennie climbed on to the bonnet of his Rolls and from there to its roof, taking the Mannlicher with him, and looked down on the mud flats. This was one race Lonely was going to lose, he thought, and the other bastard looked like he was carrying a spanner. No sign of Lonely's mate, either. Or maybe that was a good sign. It better be. Uncle Lennie lifted the Mannlicher to his shoulder, squinted down the sights....

Spanner was getting very close now and still had enough breath left to yell at Lonely what he was about to do to him. By any reckoning that was a mistake, giving aural proof to Lonely how close Spanner was, how far away the jetty and the boat. He skidded round in the mud, and produced the shotgun from under his coat. Spanner looked at the snarling, grimacing face and knew at once that Hexham had lied. This was a killer, he thought, just as he'd always known, and tried to stop, to raise his hands. But the mud made him slip forwards, he needed his hands for balance, and Lonely, grimacing more than ever, pulled both triggers. Spanner went down flat. From his hide, Callan lowered the Magnum, then eased round to cover the Ford.

'Jesus,' he said.

Lonely swung round again and carried on running. This time his speed was Olympic: he seemed scarcely to touch the surface of the mud, hurdled the jetty and shot straight down the cruiser's companionway.

'Well I'll go to France,' said Uncle Lennie.

Callan looked at the Ford. Three men behind it were waiting to kill him, and if they drove off now, they'd be back another day with something worse, he thought. Maybe what Bulky got. Better, far better, to get it over with, even if he was scared out of his socks. He lay prone, held the Magnum two-handed, and put a bullet through the Ford's front offside tyre.

So his mate hasn't nodded off, Uncle Lennie thought, and knocked out the Ford's back nearside tyre, then loosed off a second one that landed inches away from where Hexham crouched. No sense in killing unless he had to: it was that Callan's fight after all.

The two Germans knew at once that they were in a crossfire, but Hexham knew only that the car had been hit from in front, and from a point not far from the cruiser. And that could only mean that Callan had tricked him. All that time spent watching from the hill, the discreet shadowing of the ancient Rolls, the tossing of his live-bait to a demented coward who had turned out to possess—most unfairly—a sawn-off shotgun: all this had been foreseen, even provided for. There was only one thing left to be done. He drew his Walther automatic and turned to the two Germans.

'Come on,' he said, and set off, running in a crouch, across the shingle and into the mud. The brighter of the two Germans watched him go.

'An optimist,' he said.

The duller one said, 'Must we follow?'

'Certainly not,' said the brighter one.

Uncle Lennie squeezed off another shot that ricocheted from a pebble near his foot. At once the brighter German threw away his gun, then stepped out into the open, hands above his head. After a second the duller one did the same.

Callan watched Hexham plough on through the mud. Like

Flanders, he thought. Like bloody Flanders. 1916, or whenever it was, and the gallant subaltern leads the charge, and never once looks back, because if one looks back at one's men one implies that one isn't really sure of their courage.... Stupid, he thought. Oh my God, how stupid. And yet beautiful, too, because Hexham hadn't hesitated, not once; any more than the subalterns had hesitated in 1916 or whenever it was. And Hexham didn't even know for sure where he, Callan, was dug in: he just kept on coming. 'Golden lads,' thought Callan vaguely. But that was the wrong quotation. In Flanders fields—that was it.

> In Flanders fields the poppies blow
> Between the crosses, row on row
> That mark our place, and in the sky
> The larks, still bravely singing, fly....'

Hexham had tried to cheat him, and been cheated: was trying to kill him, and could so easily be killed, and yet he came on. He didn't deserve a subaltern's death in the mud, with seagulls planing instead of larks, and not even a poppy.... Callan loosed off a shot at Hexham's feet, and Hexham swerved and kept on coming.

'Stop now,' Callan yelled, 'or I'll kill you.'

It was debatable whether Hexham even heard him.... Callan rose up in a crouch, and at once Hexham loosed off a shot that splintered into the timber of his hide. Callan fired once, and then again, and Hexham shuddered to a halt at last, dropped to his knees and kept on falling until the handsome, ruined face sank into the mud.

Callan left the hide and raced past Hexham, kept on going till he faced the two Germans.

'No trouble,' the brighter German said. 'Believe me, no trouble.'

Callan backed off, picked up their Walther automatics, then gestured with the Magnum and they squelched off ahead of him through the mud, their hands on their heads. More 1916 stuff. He took them aboard the cruiser and into the tiny saloon. Hunter had thought of everything: there were three sets of handcuffs on the table. Callan handcuffed them to the table that was bolted to the floor, and left them there.... No sign of Lonely, but the air niffed a bit, even with the porthole open. He went back into the mud, and over to Hexham, turned him over. One through the heart, one through the head, the way he had been trained. He stooped to wipe the mud from the face, then straightened up again. Hexham wouldn't care ever again. Dead was dead. All the same he couldn't leave him there. He picked up the body, and

266

struggled to get it over his shoulder. When he walked the mud sucked at his boots, dragging him down inches deep.

So Hunter's won again, he thought: set up another killing, and six-gun Callan rides again. All I got rid of was an enemy: but for Hunter it was far worse than that. Hexham could never be an enemy to Hunter; he would never know how to reach him, but he was an embarrassment. A belted bloody earl going against the establishment—that would never do. For all Callan knew Hunter might even be related to Hexham: only one thing for it. Hunter had set him up and Callan had knocked him off. All included in the price. He tipped Hexham's body into the cockpit, and went back for Spanner. As he did so, an elderly Rolls waddled up to the Ford and Uncle Lennie got out. Callan slogged on and thought of the two Germans. They'd speak to Charlie all right, sooner or later people always spoke when Charlie asked them, but they wouldn't have much to say. Small-fry never did. But at least they were alive, and if they got lucky they might even be exchanged for other small-fry: swopped like inferior properties on a monopoly board. Callan reached Spanner as Uncle Lennie squelched up, and Callan noticed without surprise that Uncle Lennie too wore wellies. Uncle Lennie, he thought, was ready for every emergency. They looked down at Spanner.

'Gawd help us,' Uncle Lennie said. 'Whoever would have thought it?'

His voice sounded awed, yet there was regret in it too. An era had ended. Callan stooped and turned Spanner over. There was nothing on his face but mud.

'Missed,' said Uncle Lennie disgustedly. 'Ten feet range and the bugger missed.' Even so, he sounded relieved. Between them they carried the unconscious Spanner to the cruiser and laid him on the foredeck, then set about looking for Lonely, ran him to earth at last beneath a tarpaulin.

'Wotcher, killer,' said Callan.

Lonely shrank into the tarpaulin.

'It was him or me, Mr Callan,' he said. 'He was carrying an offensive weapon. If I get nicked I'll plead self-defence.'

'If you get nicked you'll plead Act of God,' said Uncle Lennie. 'You great ham-fisted berk, you bloody missed him. At that range.'

This time it was Lonely who fainted....

Callan accepted a couple of sandwiches, a corned beef and a salmon, and the whisky, then watched Uncle Lennie help his wilting nephew over to the Rolls and drive off before he used the R/T. Charlie was pleased that Hexham was dead, but not exactly effusive. Ungrateful bastard, thought Callan, and noted his instructions. Toby would be along with a goon-squad team. Once he arrived all he had to do was hand over the living and the dead, and drive back in the Jaguar.... And make sure he returned it as soon as possible. Callan bit into the salmon sandwich and yawned. Something had really upset Hunter this time. Ah well.... Not his business. Nice to have a bath, he thought. To wash off all this mud, then swigged at the whisky. He didn't want it, but he was thirsty, and it was the only drink there was. He tried not to think of Elizabeth....

Next morning he rose late, took his second bath in nine hours, made coffee, and phoned the hospital. Bulky was due for an operation on his hands that afternoon, but they didn't sound hopeful. He left the flat, and called in at a jobbing printer's, then went to the pub where Lonely was to meet him, and sure enough, there he was—11.32 in the morning and his pint half finished already. Still, be fair he thought. Riding shotgun's bound to give you a thirst.

'Scotch, Mr Callan?' said Lonely, and gestured to the barmaid.

'Half of bitter,' said Callan.

'But you don't like beer,' Lonely said.

'Then I won't get drunk, will I?' said Callan.

The barmaid brought him his half, and he sipped and grimaced. No chance he'd ever get drunk on that stuff. No chance at all.

'What happened to Spanner?' said Lonely.

'He's being taken care of,' said Callan. 'He won't bother you again.'

'And the others?'

'They won't bother you either.'

Especially Hexham, he thought. But Lonely didn't even know he was dead, and what was the point of making him niff on a bright summer morning?

'Ah well,' said Lonely. 'All's well that ends well.'

Callan thought: if I told him he'd just quoted Shakespeare he'd think I was kidding. Then he thought of Bulky, but what was true of Hexham was true of Bulky too. The sun was shining; best to keep it that way.

'Your money's through,' he said. 'Banque de Lausanne. Ten thousand nicker.'

'Mr Callan, that's smashing,' said Lonely. 'You sure you won't have a Scotch?' Callan shook his head. 'How about champagne then?'

'A bit early yet,' said Callan. 'Maybe when we go out to lunch.'

'Lunch,' Lonely said firmly, 'is on me. The Savoy. And no arguments.'

'All right,' said Callan. 'You're on. By the way I've got a present for you.'

He reached into his pocket and handed it over to Lonely. The little man took it in his hands and looked at it, his lips moving slowly as he read.

'Mr Callan,' he said, 'that's the most wonderful thing I ever got in my whole life.'

He looked utterly and completely happy. Almost he smelled of roses. What he held was a strip of pasteboard. It read:

> Callan's. Specialists in Security.
>
> Roger de Vere Bullivant.
>
> Technical Director.

Lightning Source UK Ltd.
Milton Keynes UK
UKHW022212171218
334172UK00011B/215/P